I REALLY AM W
THE MEMOIRS OF
BY JENN

~~It was our first gig together, and after an emergency dress rehearsal, we set off for the club.~~
~~We were four people with the same dream.~~
~~It was dark when we reached the club.~~
~~All my life I'd dreamt of being a rock star.~~
Insert riveting beginning that I will think of later here.

When we got to the Palace, there was a line around the block of punks, badasses, rockaholics, and murderers, all of them ready to rock, and all of them expecting to see a different warm-up band. I was terrified. Suddenly the fact that we'd practiced only once together wasn't a minor detail. It was a hippo-sized Achilles' heel.

This was a mostly male, mostly underage audience, which meant raging hormones and pent-up anger. Suddenly our pseudoglam white dress theme seemed glaringly wrong, about as cool as showing up in Western wear. We looked like a bunch of sissies. Dinner was about to be served, and we were the main course.

EMERGENCY NOTE TO SELF:
It is better to have rocked and lost than never to have rocked at all.

Don't Sleep with Your Drummer

/Jen Sincero

POCKET BOOKS
New York   London   Toronto   Sydney   Singapore

Written by Jen Sincero

An *Original* Publication of MTV Books/Pocket Books

POCKET BOOKS, a division of Simon & Schuster Inc.
1230 Avenue of the Americas, New York, NY 10020

Produced by 17th Street Productions,
an Alloy, Inc. company
151 West 26th Street
New York, NY 10001

Library of Congress Cataloging-in-Publication Data is available

ISBN: 0-7434-5391-3

First MTV Books/Pocket Books trade paperback printing August 2002

10 9 8 7 6 5 4 3 2 1

For my excellent mom

I, the undersigned, do hereby solemnly swear that at this very moment I am officially getting off my lazy, oversized, pretending-I-don't-want-to-be-a-rock-star ass and becoming the gigantic rock goddess I was born to be. If I do not try every single solitary thing in my power to accomplish this, I do hereby solemnly swear I will:

1) Do exactly what my mother wants me to for an entire year. This includes wearing what she wants, dating who she picks, and working where she says.
2) Give up cheese forever.
3) Attend every single baby and bridal shower I am invited to and act happy about it.
4) Hand over to my most hated ex-boyfriend ever, Jonny Dutcher, all the lyrics to the love songs I wrote about him before I wanted his head brought to me on a pointy stick.

Signed,

_____ Date: _____
Jenny Troanni, Rock Star

Witness:

_____ Date: _____
Marie Troanni, Mother

I'm about to drive out to Mom's house to have her sign my declaration of independence. Momentum is key. So is her baked ziti. She had that tone in her voice, though. The same one she had when I called to tell her I was shaving my head and moving to Brazil. Terror, disappointment, irritation, all squeezed out through a tiny, dusty hole in her windpipe. I call it The Croak.

But there must be something about The Croak that I get off on. I'm twenty-eight. What the hell does my starting a band have to do with my mommy? Why not just have the mailman sign this? Why does anyone have to sign it? I guess it's because our lifelong goal is to win our parents' approval, like it or not. Especially when getting their approval is like getting struck by lightning: shocking enough to kill and highly unlikely ever to happen.

Will I ever just accept the fact that I'm *that* damn child? They even provided me with the perfect sister to keep it all in perspective, should we ever doubt my extraordinary capacity to suck. From day one it's been crystal clear that although Carla's two years younger than I am, she's several rungs above me on the family food chain. This fact reared its head every Christmas, and it became sort of a holiday tradition to sit around and listen to Mom marvel at the differences between the two of us. I think it was the combination of free-flowing wine and Mom's desire to remind us that she, like Mary, is the mother of God.

"My Carla's always been a delight. The easiest child from the moment she arrived. Came out as effortlessly as a sneeze!" my loving mother would slur, waving her wineglass around like a sword. The eight thousand members of my extended Italian family sitting trapped behind a wall of pasta and veal scallopini helplessly prayed that this year she wouldn't go into details. "This one, on the other hand"—she'd glare in my direction, impaling a giant sausage with her fork—"this one put me through twenty hours of labor and a breech birth. It was like giving birth to a sofa. Believe me, she was plenty big even then."

This was another black mark against me: I had had the audacity to grow to a towering 6'1" by the tenth grade, making it impossible for me to fit into pants and making my tiny mother look like a hand puppet in my presence.

"Give it a rest, Marie. Can't we for once have a nice family meal without you pissing in the soup?" my Uncle Tony would beg, failing to confiscate the wine bottle before Mom snatched it up and emptied it into her glass. He wasn't on my side or anything (I taught his daughter how to spit): he just hated being out-complained by his sister. Dad was a great comfort too, having long since escaped into a private, happy place in his head. He barely even spoke, and when he did it was clear he wasn't listening to what was going on around him at all. But Mom was The Unstoppable Mouth, and the stories flowed forth while Carla shot me an all-too-familiar apologetic look.

It wasn't until six years ago, when I got my copywriting job at the McCauley & Doyle advertising agency, that the Christmas rantings came to an end. My mother replaced them with self-congratulatory tales of accomplishment, crediting herself with encouraging me to pursue (read: humiliating me into earning) a degree in communications and urging me (read: threatening to kill herself) to interview with her friend at McCauley & Doyle. When I got the job, she threw me a huge party packed to the rafters with all her friends and paraded me around as Exhibit A: Biggest Living Letdown Turned Proud Corporate Employee. She presented me with a smart blue business suit and made a big dramatic show of consoling all her friends whose children didn't have access to full benefits.

Dad, on the other hand, had no idea what I was talking about when I called to tell him my big career news. He'd faded off into Divorced Fatherland when I was sixteen and hadn't asked me a question about my life since. I knew all about his life in New York and the fascinating research his botany group was doing on self-pollinating plants. Meanwhile he could never remember the details of my life, and when I called him from my new office, he was most impressed by the fact that I wasn't calling him collect.

I figured my decision to quit would have a similar, earth-shattering effect, so I decided to not even bother telling him.

But Mom would be devastated. I was about to take away the only thing she had to talk about when the ladies at her real estate office asked about me. I figured the least I could do was do it in person.

BRILLIANT OBSERVATION #1:

You can hear something over and over and over and over and over and still not really hear it. It does not click. No lo comprendo. Until you're ready to hear it. And then it is deafening.

March 3

I swear I've been complaining about my job for years. I've also been whining about starting a band and pretending that my boyfriend, Jason, has good enough taste in music for him to really be my boyfriend. Poor, trusty Henry, winner of the Olympic gold medal for the Most Patient Friend competition, has spent years listening to me wail, with the patience of a social worker. In fact, he's gotten the gold every year since we met in drivers' ed twelve years ago. At sixteen he was already a brick wall of a person, cramming his massive 6'4" frame into the tiny clown car they gave us to drive around in. He had a huge blond 'fro that made him look as if he were wearing a baby sheep on his head, and I remember watching it flatten out on the roof of the car like a bunch of soap suds. Henry sealed our friendship when he calmly talked me through my fear of parallel parking, using much the same tone he was using to get me through my latest drama.

"Quit your job. Start a band. Dump the drip," he'd chant over and over, droning on in his nasal voice like a dying bee of wisdom.

Then yesterday I'm sitting there clipping my toenails on the kitchen counter when suddenly I nearly go flying to the floor. I can quit my job! I can be a rock star! My boyfriend loves Hootie and the Blowfish!

I wasn't really even thinking about anything. It was 8:24 A.M. A time that means nothing to me. Nothing. I think I just suddenly . . . ripened.

I immediately called Henry and told him of my breakthrough. He was as thrilled as an unconscious person could be and thanked me for the wake-up call before he drifted back to sleep.

Then I called in sick, wrote up my little manifesto, and drove out to Long Beach to have Mom sign it. I sped by row after row of cookie-cutter, SoCal suburban-white-person-type houses and refused to let that familiar feeling of claustrophobia creep its way into my chest.

DECLARATION #1:

I will never live in suburbia. Just because I drive a practical 1998 Volvo V70 station wagon with 4-wheel, power-assisted disc brakes does not mean I lack rock-and-roll cred.

I cranked up the stereo and rolled down the windows. I was on a mission.

When I pulled up to her house, Mom was bent over in the driveway, getting her newspaper, sporting that timeless, early morning casual look of nightgown and hiking boots. She jumped back, instinctively covering her pendulous bralessness with the rolled up paper, no doubt to prevent her boobs from swinging up and taking out an eye.

ME: Put on a bra or get some pants with deeper pockets, lady!

This was a favorite line she jokingly batted around with my sister (I was exempt from this game, tits being among the many things I lacked). I figured it might be just the thing to break the ice after nearly flattening her with the car, but apparently she was in no mood for games. She ordered me to turn off that racket and get in the house. I skipped in behind her, shoving my manifesto in her hands before she could launch into a tirade about my shameful lack of visits home.

She looked at it like I'd handed her a dead rat and asked me to explain exactly what doing "every single solitary thing in my power" meant. Since I had no fucking idea what it meant, I reminded her instead to focus on the fact that for her it's a win/win situation.

ME: If I succeed, I'll be buying you a house in Palm Beach, and
               if I fail, I'll be wearing Ann Taylor . . .

THE CROAK: Why aren't you at work?

ME: . . . and dating Mrs. Reilly's upwardly mobile son (whose
               breath smells like he's been chewing on the dead).

*An eyelock. We are the only two people in the universe. The moisture in
our eyes is just drying glue.*

THE CROAK: You can't come back and live at home, you know.

The eyelock is broken as mine uncontrollably roll toward my forehead.

THE CROAK: You're too old to be farting around with this band stuff.
               Don't you think it's time you grew up?

ME: I will regret it for the rest of my life if I don't at least try.

The Croak is silenced. As obnoxious as I am, she'll always lose, because way deep down in her bitter soul, she loves me. Unconditionally. Which really sucks for her, because I'm the queen of conditions.

DO OR DIE-A-BORING-PERSON LIST:

1) Quit Going-Somewhere job and get Going-to-Band-Practice job.
2) Break up with Hootie-and-the-Blowfish–lovin' Jason.
3) Do laundry.
4) Cash in 401(k) and go buy a guitar amp.
5) Give up meat, TV, trying to make Mom understand who I am, and everything else that sucks up my energy.
6) Find a practice space.

7) Practice.
8) Buy cat food.
9) Go to skanky bars. Meet musicians.
10) Do fifty sit-ups a day.
11) Remember I am gigantic and can do anything.

March 4

I'm in the supply closet at work, crouched on the floor in the dark with a glow-in-the-dark Super Ball in my mouth. One of the big ones. Not as good a flashlight as I'd thought. If anyone walked in right now, I'd have to pretend that someone horrible did this to me. But I can't think about that. I'd laugh. Drop my ball.

I'm supposed to be in the Nabisco meeting right now—actually, ten minutes ago—but I didn't have time to quit my stupid job this morning, and I just couldn't deal with it. What's the point? So I'm hiding in here, Land of Free Office Supplies, until they stop looking for me. Then I'm gonna steal stuff and quit. I feel insane! And free! And awake!

And my boss just walked in!

I have just suffered a serious humiliation. Thanks, brain, for really being there when I needed you. She jumped a mile when she flicked on the light. Then I went totally blank. Nothing at all. I just looked at her and spat the ball into my hand and told her I was looking for my pen.

Looking for my pen! That's all I could think of! I should have told her I was looking for a reason to stay at this soul-raping job. But I froze. She glared at me and said we'd discuss it after the meeting.

NOTE TO SELF:
Just because it's your brain does not mean it's on your side.

Now I'm in the meeting. But I refuse to be an active partic- ipant, even though the entire ad campaign was my idea. Why does it still amaze me, after six whole years, that nobody notices when I'm too disgusted to comment on my own stupid concepts? Everyone here loves to hear himself talk so much, I swear my sole purpose for being in this room is to provide body heat.

I really have to pee.

Maybe I'll just get up and walk out. Fuck it. I think I will.

Okay, I'm in my office now. I just walked out! I am huge! There's no turning back. Here she comes down the hall. Clickety-clack. Heels like daggers. Mad as hell. Right on time.

NOTE TO SELF:

It's better to burn out than fade away.

WHO ROCKS?

BRILLIANT OBSERVATION #2:

Today is March 4th. March forth. The only day of the year that's a command, and it just so happens to coincide with my own personal mobilization.

On my way home from my ex–stupid job, I stopped in at Rudy's Barbershop and had all my hair chopped off. It's on Sunset, a few blocks down from my house, and I drove right up to it as if I'd planned this last-minute decision weeks ago. I told the hairdresser to make it look like she'd gone at me with a lawn mower and had her dye huge clumps of it blond and red. Part of me feared walking out looking like a bad spin-art project, but I was on a roll and couldn't help myself.

Much to everyone's surprise, I looked awesome. Chaos suits me, and short hair makes me look taller and skinnier, something I never thought possible. I also learned that few things are more liberating than cutting all your hair off, especially when you've been hiding behind a frizzy brown wall of complacency and denial for six years. I felt like I could suddenly do anything, including finally stick a fork in my idiotic relationship with Hootie-and-the-Blowfish-lovin' Jason. I went straight to his house, stinking of chemicals and ignoring the millions of hairs down the back of my shirt that were torturing me.

It always amazes me how quickly these things go. You can spend every night with someone for six months, and then the actual Big Talk takes a tiny two minutes. Literally.

ME: Um, this isn't really working for me anymore.

HIM: What isn't?

ME: Us. I mean, I really care about you, but I just don't feel like
        it's going anywhere.

HIM: Where do you want it to go?

ME: Well, I guess I don't want it to go anywhere. I'm not in love with
        you.

HIM: Oh. And when did you discover this?

ME: I don't know. It's been building for a while.

*Five-hundred-hour pause. I panic. Am I really going to sit here and hurt
this dear sweet person? More importantly, am I really going to voluntarily
throw away my only source of regular sex?*

HIM: Well, if that's the way you feel, that's the way you feel. What can
        I say?

*I manage a weak smile and a few tears. I contemplate a hug, think it
inappropriate, and stumble out the door.*

THE END

I doubt I'll ever really think about him again. This marks
another proud achievement in a relationship career that can
pretty much be broken down into three categories:

1) Dating guys that I pretend to like more than I do just
because I feel like having a boyfriend. They're usually equally
as enthralled by me, and the whole thing ends with the same
massive yawn it began with (see example listed above).

2) Falling ass-over-teacup in love with morons who treat
me like crap. I'll suffer the rudest of humiliations to keep them,
and obsess over them long after they've given me the big
heave-ho.

3) Treating love-struck guys like shit until I'm finally strong enough to shake them off my leg. Due to the fact that they're obsessed with me, I have trouble cutting the cord and tend to drag these ones on until they really start to stink.

This is not to say the odd semihealthy relationship hasn't sneaked its way into my life from time to time, but luckily, contrary to popular expectation, finding a man isn't first on my list of things to do. So why is it first on everyone else's list of things for me to do? It makes me feel like a loser, even though I'm happy being single and would duck if someone ever tossed me a baby. I swear, if my mother asks me one more time when I'm going to find a nice boy like Carla's John, I'm going to hang her by her freakishly tiny thumbs.

I spent the rest of the day marching forth. I tore apart my entire house and separated the things that needed to go from the things that could stay from the things I could wrap up and give to people as presents.

I also called my friend Katie at Capitol Records for the first time in months. We used to work together at McCauley & Doyle until she got her dream job as a product manager at Capitol. Which she now hates. Which isn't surprising, because Katie hates everything. Which is surprising, because Katie's as blond and blue and pink and tiny and perky-looking as they come. Candy on the outside, piss and vinegar on the inside. I used to find this quality amusing, but after a while I just couldn't listen to her complain anymore (I had my mother for that), so I stopped returning her calls. Even though that meant I had no one left in town to go see live music with.

But now I wanted to celebrate breaking free from the Evil

Empire, and Katie was the perfect person to call. Plus, of course, I was going to need her. I had to pump some air into my only record label contact, regardless of how long and hard a bitch session I would have to endure. And I was in for a doozy. Her deceptively squeaky voice launched into a mudslide of complaints and obscenities that went on for over an hour.

"Oh my God, it's you, you fuck. Where the hell have you been? Wait, hold on a second." She put me on hold. Some terrible, overproduced rock song that I didn't recognize came blasting over the receiver until she picked up again.

"Sorry. Where was I?"

"You were calling me a stupid fuck."

"Oh my God, hold on again." I heard the muffled sounds of her talking to someone in her office.

"You wouldn't fucking believe this place!" she continued as she came back on. "Everyone walks around here like they're God's fucking gift. I can't believe I work for these shitbags."

"Sounds like you love it as much as you loved the advertising industry."

"I know, right? So what's up with you? How's everything at the Evil Empire?"

"Well, actually, I walked out today. Right in the middle of a meeting. It was awesome!"

"Hold on," I was now treated to the bridge of the same bad rock song. Right in the middle of my big news! Between her and the hold button I didn't know which was more obnoxious.

"Sorry. So, no way! You're lucky you got out while you could. So what are you going to do now, call your friends back every once in a fucking while or what?"

"I know, I suck, but I was being crushed by the Evil Empire. You know how it goes."

"Do I ever fucking know! Those whoremongers screwed me so hard, it's a wonder I can still walk."

And it went on and on, back and forth, until I was finally put on hold for so long, I just hung up.

BRILLIANT OBSERVATION #3:
Negative people are a B-O-R-E.

I was almost sure she'd gotten worse. Either that or I was getting more intolerant in my old age. Whatever the reason, I realized the only way I was going to get through it would be to take her in tiny doses, like going to the occasional free concert or hooking up for random lunches with powerful people at her company.

I fell into bed around three o'clock the next morning, giddy, exhausted, and still covered with my own hair. My head was now against the north wall of my bedroom (did I mention that I also found time to rearrange all my furniture?), ensuring that the polarity of the energy was flowing in a positive direction. Or some shit like that. I read it in a hippie magazine once. I've officially decided that from this moment on, every single thing in my life will be pointed in the right direction. No matter what.

UNEMPLOYED OBSERVATION #1:
Cats do not lead very interesting lives.

March 8

I swear Schmoo slept for ten solid hours the other day. It was an impressive display. He rose only to eat, of course, and to lick his butt. My other little overachiever, Neil, manned his usual post on the windowsill for five hours. Then he demanded I let him outside, where I later spotted him sleeping under a bush. This is what my cats did all day while I was hard at work? What the hell do they do that makes them so exhausted anyway? I guess maintaining their holier-than-thou cattitude requires more energy than I realized.

Henry came over and played cards with me while I had a little sidewalk sale. I needed to purge. He needed to kick my ass at gin rummy. I swear, he may be quiet, but he's deadly. I win about one in every fifteen games with him, and the only reason I don't flip the table over in his lap out of frustration is because I figure it's all part of the balance of life. I get to be the dumb one, he gets to be the dork. Still, it wouldn't kill him to let me win once in a while.

It feels great to have unloaded all my stuff. I made a hundred and seventy-eight bucks and found the bike-lock key that's been missing for over a year. I also uncovered this eerie picture of Carla and me stuck to the back of a shoebox. We're standing side by side with matching haircuts (abstract bowls with crooked bangs, compliments of Mom) and weirdly identical faces. It looks like there's one head slapped onto two different bodies. Genetic proof that my parents are totally uncreative people.

I'm making huge progress. Henry says he's never seen me so hell-bent. I got a few leads on some practice spaces that I'll look at next week. Since escaping my job, I've transformed my home, done my laundry, and practiced guitar every single day.

ROCK-AND-ROLL TRUTH #1:

Real jobs are for people who are too lazy to practice.

I also sat down and wrote a letter to my oldest and bestest friend ever, Ms. Lucy Stover Hanover II. I've got an address for her in Kenya, but writing to Lucy is a lot like writing to Santa Claus. I'm never sure if she actually gets my letters or if she even really exists.

FACT: Lucy's only capable of keeping in touch with you if you're standing right in front of her. (Her incarceration at Miss Thom's Boarding School for Girls doesn't count. I was her suicide hotline. It was either letters to me or a hunger strike.)

FACT: Lucy's one of the best guitarists on earth. She's also more fun than a barrel of monkeys.

FACT: Lucy's a flake and deathly allergic to commitment. The best way to get rid of her is to ask her to stick around.

FICTION: No matter how hard she begged, I'd never be foolish enough to count on her if she wanted to, say, start a band.

Lucy and I met at the supermarket the summer before our sophomore year of high school. Both of us were tall and cranky, slouching around behind our mothers as they pushed their carts and chatted up every boring housewife who came down the aisle. Lucy was home from boarding school for the summer and was just as bored stiff as I was. She went to the aforementioned Miss Thom's Boarding School for Girls, which she eventually got booted out of for driving butt-naked while standing up in a convertible. (She drove right through their homecoming ceremony steering with her foot, wearing nothing but ski goggles and a roach clip dangling from her nipple ring. Some cops have no team spirit. He even gave her a ticket for not wearing a seat belt.)

We ended up getting stuck in the same checkout line together, but she looked way too cool for me to ever talk to.

She was wearing tons of makeup and had boobs. She smelled like cigarettes and was talking to her mother in a tone I'd be blindfolded and shot in the woods for using. I almost capsized when she said she liked my guitar-pick earrings.

ME: Really? My mom hates them.
LUCY: That means they're even cooler. I'm Lucy. Want to sneak out and
          see The Cure tonight?

It was full speed ahead from then on. She had every U2 album and I had a T-shirt signed by Prince himself. Every inch of wall space in my room was covered with rock posters, and I had a stereo system that could blow a hole through a wall. And by the age of fifteen, we could both play every note of Zeppelin's Houses of the Holy with our eyes closed. It was a match made in heaven. We had the same blood rocking through our veins.

When she got kicked out of Miss Thom's, she came to live with my family and finish out high school with me. It was the greatest time of my life, even though both our worlds were taking serious nosedives. She witnessed my parents' marriage swirling down the toilet bowl while I watched her try and deal with the fact that her crazy mother had abandoned her. She's got major intimacy issues and tends to disappear before you can disappear on her, especially since her dad pulled the ultimate ditch-out and died when she was five.

So I cut her a lot more slack than I'd give most people, even though she flakes on me all the time. In fact, in our adult lives, she's only ever written to me once. And then it was only a postcard. And then it was only one sentence: *JENNY, HAVE YOU EVER NOTICED THAT AN ANGRY WOMAN ISN'T A POPULAR LADY?*

This touching and revealing note arrived about eight months after I dropped her off at the airport for her big trip to Guatemala. I checked it a hundred times for clues and/or secret codes that she'd been kidnapped and was crying out for help. Why else would she suddenly write? What kind of trouble had her big mouth gotten her into this time? Why did she cross all her *t*'s in the middle?

I didn't learn until she pulled into town four months later, after I'd pictured her bound and gagged in a white slavery camp somewhere, that that line was an idea for a song lyric. She'd started a one-woman, punk-guitar sidewalk act in her small, peaceful Guatemalan town. It wasn't a hit. Lucy was dubbed *La Furia Gringa*. The American Fury. Nobody got it.

I told her to either write or not write, but never to send a cryptic message once a decade unless she wanted me to put her head through a wall when she came home. She promised to never, ever write to me again.

NOTE TO SELF:

Learn better communication skills.

But as prone to spontaneous disappearance as she is, I want to play with her. We have that thing. She's the Keith to my Mick. The mayo to my tuna. When we were in high school, we started dorking around at open mic nights and stuff, and I swear we were getting huge. We had real people who didn't owe us favors showing up to watch, and some guy who knew some guy at some label was really interested. We started looking for apartments and agreed to put off going to college for a year and give it a go. There's no doubt in my mind that we could have really made it.

Then, the morning we were supposed to sign the lease on a two-bedroom shithole in Hollywood, Lucy disappeared. She called a few weeks later from New York, teary and apologetic, saying she just needed some space. I was crushed at first, but after a while my homicidal fantasies subsided and I missed having her around. That's when I realized: I'm obsessed with Lucy Hanover. Not in any psycho, sexual way, but I swear there's something about her that makes me feel like I can do anything. To this day, she's the most inspiring person I've ever met.

And now she's off flaking around Africa and I'm on a mission. If there's any chance in hell I could actually have a successful band, there's no one else I'd rather have it with. I had to give it one last chance. I wrote her a note on the lid of a donut box and sent it into the void:

> *Mama Africa!*
> *Behold the newest member of America's unemployment force! I finally puked up that hairball known as my job in the interest of handcuffing myself to my guitar. Don't yet know how the dough will flow, but I promise to take you out to eat at my favorite Dumpster when you get back.*
> *Enclosed please find a photo of me and my new power hairdo.*
> *Just wanted you to know what's up in case you suddenly noticed a shift in the Force and weren't sure*

why. Get your ass home so it can join mine on stage.
There's no one else I'd rather rule the world with.
Me love you long time,
Jenny

UNEMPLOYED OBSERVATION #2:
I'm everyone's airport shuttle. They know I'm home. I'm a sitting duck.

As dumb luck would have it, it turns out I have a pension *and* a 401(k). I thought they were the same thing. When you're an idiot, the world is full of happy surprises.

I cashed in the pension—a hefty $2,331, thank you very much, after major penalties that I won't describe—and then I went shopping.

A TINY TALE OF THUNDEROUS GLORY
BY JENNY TROANNI

I go into Black Market Music with my axe and my new stealth hairdo, looking the part, talking the talk— a big fat poser. I have no band. I'm shopping for an amp that could deafen people three states away, and I have no reason to turn the volume up past 2. Guys with bad hair and tight pants wank away on guitars at top volume, and I'm suddenly reminded of the six hundred dollars worth of camera equipment taking up space in my closet. I have a natural eye. I enjoy photography. Getting me to go out and take pictures is like sucking a horse through a straw.

BRILLIANT OBSERVATION #4:
Just because something is expensive doesn't mean you'll actually use it.

But then I see it. A 1969 Fender Twin Reverb with two twelve-inch speakers and a devil smoking a pipe hand-painted on its side. It stares straight at me. I freeze. Suddenly the sales guy has his arm around me. "Go ahead and crank it. That's the only way you'll know how she sounds." He leans over, flicks the power switch, and gives me a knowing grin.

Within five minutes I'm handing over the equivalent of two months' rent and rolling the new electronic love of my life down the aisle and out to my car.

The rest of my 401(k) is now safely locked away with the aforementioned pension, wearing a chastity belt until I'm ready to make a CD. For this reason, I need to get a job immediately.

I can't stop staring at my amp. It's the one I've always wanted but refused to get myself until I started a band. I just broke my own rule. I don't care.

I'd sleep with it if I could fit it in my bed.

THE END

QUIZ FOR PROSPECTIVE BANDMATES:
1) Were you born to rock, or do you just look good in super-tight pants?
2) Put the following in order of importance:
    Music
    Your job

> Renting videos with significant other
> Privacy
> Jane's Addiction
> Sleep
> Being on time
> Getting stoned and watching TV

3) Have you ever sported or would you ever sport a mullet?
4) Do you think Courtney killed Kurt? Please explain.
5) What would be your ultimate band experience?
6) Do you have a van?
7) On a scale of 1 to 10, how big is your ego?

Downtown storage spaces for use as artist studios and practice rooms. $250 per month. (213) 555-6323, ask for Brett.

NO WAY!
COLD AND SCARY.
FELT LIKE PRISON.
FELT LIKE RATS.

Practice space to share w/2 other bands. Available Tuesdays and Thursdays. $150 month. No pussies or narcs. Call Ajax. Pager: (323) 555-0564.

LEFT MESSAGE.
SOUNDS LIKE HE OWNS A BIG KNIFE.

562 COURT ST.
PARK IN ALLEY AND WALK UP FIRE ESCAPE.

WALLS COVERED IN PORN!
SMELLS LIKE A BARNYARD.
SHOWED ME HIS BIG KNIFE.
LISTEN TO YOUR
INSTINCTS, STUPID!

Killer practice space to share with one other band. Must
be responsible, clean, and respect other people's shit.
Come to practice, not to throw parties, please. Adam,
(323) 555-7634.

1367 S. GRAND ST. #3
TAKE ELEVATOR TO TOP FLOOR.
4 GUYS, ALL GORGEOUS, HUGE
TROUBLE. PLEASE, GOD, LET
THIS WORK OUT.

I cannot find a practice space. I can find every homicidal
freak in this city who has a smelly, scary room for rent, but I
can't find a decent place to practice. The only near miss was
with those four guys in that huge loft downtown. But it was
way too expensive, and they were way too sexy. I would have
slept with any and all of them in a heartbeat. I'd probably never
even get a band together. I'd just fill the place with candles,
mirrors, and a giant spiderweb and wait for one of them to
stumble into my lecherous trap.

March 18

SEX TRUTH #1:

If you don't have sex for a long time, it sucks, but you're calm about it. If you haven't had it for sixteen days, you're dangerous.

March 19

There's nothing more humiliating than getting turned down for a job you don't even want. I just got rejected by three—count 'em, three—temp agencies. What reasonably educated person knows half the shit on those tests anyway?

Apparently, not knowing Excel is worse than showing up drunk.

Time to move on to Plan B.

POSSIBLE JOBS I COULD GET SO I CAN PRACTICE, STAY OUT ALL NIGHT GIGGING, AND STILL AFFORD TO BUY SUPERGLAM STAGE CLOTHES:

1) Waitress
2) Dog walker
3) Babysitter
4) Bike messenger
5) Airport shuttle driver
6) Security guard
7) Seller of things at flea market
8) Clutter consultant
9) Clerk at record store
10) Camping equipment salesperson

Last night I went to Spaceland to hear this band called Treadmill play. My recently revived "friend" Katie recommended them but couldn't go because she was staying in and renting a video with her new boyfriend, Chris.

How does this happen to people? Few concepts sicken me more now that I'm single again (sleeping with Jason when I went to his place to pick up my stuff doesn't count). Especially when it's Katie. She loves going out to see music as much as she loves to hate everything else. When we worked at McCauley & Doyle, I'd get calls in the middle of the night because she just had to tell me about some new fucking awesome song she just heard on the radio. Or we'd stay out until 3 A.M. the night before a huge presentation because one of our favorite bands was playing.

Now some dopey guy had derailed her, making her just another body in the mass grave of once-fun friends who now say "we" all the time.

So sad. So much of life ahead of her.

Ennnneeeeway, Treadmill! Awesome. Huge. They rocked like pigs and totally inspired me. I somehow had the guts to go up and talk to the bass player ("somehow" = drank three shots of tequila). I said I was starting a band and would he be interested in a side project, and guess what? He asked me to drop off a tape.

His name's Jake Novicoff. He looks sort of like Bruce Springsteen, if Bruce had squinty blue eyes and some serious hat-head. He makes hilarious faces when he's deeply rocking, like he's going to suck his chin into his head. I noticed he had on a wedding ring, which was a relief since he's kind of cute and I'm trying to get a band off the ground here. I just hope his wife is cool.

I followed him to the bathroom and waited outside so I

could talk to him alone—an old stalking tactic I picked up from Lucy. Jake came out in all his tattooed, working-class glory and offered me a wet hand to shake.

NOTE TO SELF:
Stop waiting outside men's bathrooms.

March ?

Here's the scary thing: being unemployed sucks you into this weird world of being incredibly busy doing nothing. I'm amazed at the chaos having nothing to do can create. I don't know what day it is and I can never find my keys. Maybe not moving around as much makes me breathe less and brings less oxygen to my head.

Maybe I'm just turning into Dad.

I tore my house apart and finally found the demo tape Lucy and I made two years ago before she ran screaming off into the sunset. Thank God. I realize it's kind of cheating, but they're all my songs. And I'm not about to leave a giant, stinky turd (meaning a tape of me playing guitar into my answering machine) in the mailbox of someone as devastatingly talented as Jake Novicoff.

It's such a weird thing. Pouring your guts out onto a tape and mailing it off to a perfect stranger. I feel like I'm up for review in every part of my life. Handing out demos and résumés all at the same time. It's like getting a full body physical—being naked, spread-eagled, and rated by strangers who you blindly assume know what they're doing.

Then I sat down and wrote out a strict practice schedule for myself. I swear I've been trying to follow it, but my ability to focus ranks up there with my ability to give up meat.

2-HOUR PRACTICE SCHEDULE:

5 minutes of scales
5 minutes of chord changes
30 minutes: pick a song off any album and learn how to play it
10 minutes of theory
30-minute lunch break
5 minutes of finger exercises
5 minutes of picking practice
1 hour to work on original stuff

TODAY'S ACTUAL PRACTICE SCHEDULE:

5 minutes of scales
25-minute phone call from Henry
3 minutes of chord changes
35 minutes to check and read e-mail
10 minutes to learn song of choice; end up listening to whole album instead while making a lasagna.
0 minutes of theory, followed by entire evening of having friends over for lasagna and then going to a movie

I need a live-in nurse.

I still don't know what the hell day it is, and I'm far too lazy to go find out. It's like one giant Saturday around here. I swear, time goes by faster when you're standing still. Or lying down. I have got to get a job. I have got to get a job immediately. ASAP. FYI. PDQ. XYZ.

It's definitely harder than I thought. As if the temp agency

March marches on.

mockery weren't enough of a blow, I just loused up an opportunity to be employed by the world-renowned dining establishment, the Taste Castle.

DEGRADING JOB INTERVIEW #4:

22-YEAR-OLD
MANAGER: Why do you think you'd make a good member of the Taste Castle team?

ME: Because I really love the food. I really believe in it. I've been coming here for years.

MY BRAIN: Because I will degrade myself by answering the most idiotic of questions. In the most idiotic of ways.

22-Y.O.M.:   Have you ever waited tables before?

ME: Yes. When I was in college. It was fun.

MY BRAIN: I'm lying.

22-Y.O.M.:   What kind of establishment was that?

ME: Well, let's see, there were a couple. One was a burger place and one was more fancy.

MY BRAIN: Speaking of burgers, could I have a free one?

22-Y.O.M.:   What kind of system did they have? How was it set up?

ME: Well, one had the bar to the left as you walked in. . . .

22-Y.O.M.:   I mean what was the system for ordering and running the food?

MY BRAIN: I am leaving. You are on your own.

ME: Oh, that! People would order it and I'd give the cook

the slip and he'd ding the little bell when it was ready
and I'd go get it.

22-Y.O.M.:   Did you pool tips?

ME: No. Yes!

22-Y.O.M.:   How did that work?

ME: Oh, just the usual way. Actually, what does pooling tips
               mean again?

And that was pretty much it. I have to hand it to her though,
because she could have had some real fun playing with me.
Captured me, maimed me, and batted me around while she
went in for the slow kill, quizzing me on napkin folding and gar-
nish placement to keep herself entertained while the life slowly
drained out of me.

The part that really sucks is now I'm too humiliated to ever
be seen in that place again, and they do have the best burgers
in town. Luckily, I'm giving up meat.

NOTE TO SELF:

There is a Lying Gene. I do not have it.

Mom thinks I should get some freelance advertising work. I
think she should get some freelance Nazi work. That's like
telling a shark-attack victim to teach surfing.

Singer/guitarist looking for musicians to start a band with. Must have sense of humor, car, and be unable to focus on a conversation if a good song is playing in the background. If your will to play music is stronger than your will to live, please call Jenny @ (323) 555-1884.

THE FREAK PARADE:

1) *"Hi. I saw your ad for musicians and am calling to let you know my boyfriend Glen is a brilliant guitarist, but for some reason he just will not get out there and get in a band. Please page him at (213) 555-8944. You won't be sorry. And please don't tell him I called. He'll kill me. Thanks! Take care."*

2) *"My name is Rodney and I've been playing bass since I was eight. I'm only seventeen now, which seemed to be a problem with my last band since I couldn't hang out in clubs, but I don't really care. I just want to play. And I just wanted you to know that so you don't get mad or something. My number is (323) 555-4546. Thanks. Bye."*

3) *"Hey, yeah, this is Rob. I don't have any drums and I haven't played in a couple years, but we should hook up. I'm thinking of moving out of town, but if you're, like, cool or something, maybe I'll stick around. (213) 555-9998. That's my pager. Cool. Later."*

DO OR DIE-A-BORING-PERSON LIST, revised:

1) Quit Going-Somewhere job and get Going-to-Band-Practice job. *Do not ask Mom to call her friend about that job at the bank until you are fully, totally, completely desperate.*

2) Break up with Hootie-and-the-Blowfish-lovin' Jason. √

3) Do laundry. √

4) Cash in 401(k) and go buy a guitar amp. √!
5) Give up meat, TV, trying to make Mom understand who I am, and everything else that sucks up my energy. *Hello?*
6) Find a practice space. *Do not get sliced into tiny pieces in the process.*
7) Practice. *This is what you want to do with your life, right?*
8) Buy cat food. Again! *Teach cats to eat less or kill for their supper. I can't afford them.*
9) Go to skanky bars. Meet musicians. √
10) Do fifty sit-ups a day. *Ahem?*
11) Remember I am gigantic and can do anything. *Even find a practice space.*

My list is as pathetic as my answering machine messages. I'm attempting to think positive thoughts and visualize success, but I'm much better at taking naps.

I haven't showered in four days.

THE SOUND YOU HEAR IS MY WORLD SUCKING:

Rent is due soon. I'm dipping into the money put aside for my first CD. Again.

It has come to my attention via a strict practicing schedule that my skill level on guitar seriously plummeted during my long career as an advertising loser.

I haven't heard from Jake Novicoff. He said he'd call the second he got my tape, and I sent it weeks ago. What if the mailman put it in the wrong mailbox? What if I forgot to put

A dark day in April.

my phone number on it? Should I call him to make sure he got it? What if I call him and he did get it, and it's like a post-one-night-stand, why-are-you-calling-me kind of talk?

My sister, Carla, attempted to hook me up with a job. She has some friend with a catering company to whom she allegedly gave my number a couple weeks ago. She must have really talked me up, because the woman is clearly intimidated by the idea of meeting someone as fabulous as I am. I've heard not a peep from her, or anyone else for that matter. I swear, I've forgotten how to answer the phone, it's been so goddamn long since I've had to.

I haven't gotten any more calls—not even from the scariest of freaks—regarding my ad for band members.

I also didn't get that job answering phones at the doctor's office. And the Coffee Grind hired someone with more experience.

Henry's in the Bahamas. He sent me a postcard of a bunch of peoples' asses lying on the beach. It says, "Beach Bums." People get paid to write these things, and I can't get a job selling mocha lattes.

I saw Jason holding hands with some blond chick wearing a very scary tube top the other day. They were definitely together. Isn't that a little fast? I mean, he's still on my caller ID box.

I think I was in love with him.

I haven't heard from Lucy.

I have nowhere to practice and no one to do it with.

My cats lead more interesting lives than I do.

Okay, it's been a few weeks since I've written, but I was too depressed to lift a pen. Nothing was going right, and I was starting to seriously doubt my ability to do anything other than write a good toothbrush ad. I totally unraveled and hit rock bottom—hard. But then I did what I had to do to come back. Like a virus, I am now unstoppable.

April 26

HOW I CRASHED AND BURNED:

I checked out three more "practice spaces" located in various ghettos around L.A. and have since decided that it's way too dangerous a task to undertake without an armed escort. I sold my fancy new car and bought a 1987 Honda Civic with a leaky sunroof and a "Party Naked!" bumper sticker cemented to its hind end. I got a job at a snotty clothing boutique but was fired two days into it for falling asleep while folding. I also left my day planner at the DMV office and accidentally flushed my favorite earrings down the toilet.

In light of these events and countless others, I threw an impressive pity party for myself that lasted about two weeks. Festivities included:

1) Sitting on Mom's couch, eating mashed potatoes and watching Mary Tyler Moore reruns in my cat-hair-covered stretchy pants and sweatshirt.

2) Having a huge blowout fight with Mom when she accused me of trying to move back into her house.

3) Sitting on *my* couch, drinking cheap beer and staring at the wall in my cat-hair-covered bathrobe.

4) Napping. Ignoring the phone. Early to bed. Late to rise.

5) Playing with my growing stomach roll.

Then, somewhere between complaining to the cats and color-coordinating my bath beads, I figured out what would revive me. I needed to check into Mother Nature's rehab clinic.

The CD fund was raped and pillaged again. The car was loaded up and the cats were deposited at Henry's, and I went to the desert—the place where life cannot exist but does anyway. Rocks are blue and trees grow upside down off cliffs with no water. Wimpy little streams carve canyons the size of God's buttcrack through massive walls of stone. Huge boulders balance on top of anorexic pillars of rock like ten-ton lollipops.

The desert doesn't give a crap about the rules. The desert is punk. Period.

I returned a mighty superhero, with my cape and tights pressed and cleaned by the life-affirming, purple, blue, and red freakshow of in-your-face magnificence that is Utah.

I went through the looking glass and came out the other side ready to give the world a big fat spanking.

INSPIRATIONAL NOTE TO SELF:

Flowers grow in sand.
I can do anything.

It's weird how your house always looks a little different when you get back from a trip. Welcoming, but kind of alien. Just for a few hours. Like your stuff had all these experiences without you and is now somehow changed.

The cats are insulted and giving me their usual bratty silent treatment. Hell hath no fury like a cat scorned. Neil went outside immediately and will return at 4 A.M. to press himself against my bedroom window, screaming like he's on fire.

Schmoo repeatedly makes a dramatic show of walking up, turning his back on me, and sitting down just within petting distance, making sure to aim his gigantic ass in my direction like a cannon. If I dare touch him, he turns and glares.

I called Carla's friend at the catering company and told her to just hire me already, which she did. We were on the phone for an hour. She is hilarious and wants to start catering biker rallies and truck pulls along with her usual art shows and fancy parties.

I called Jake Novicoff when I figured he wouldn't be home and left him a message. Which I of course wrote out beforehand, because my brain is still on probation for betraying me at the Taste Castle.

"Hi, Jake, this is Jenny. I met you at one of your gigs and mailed you a tape about a month ago. I'm kind of glad you're not home because you may have gotten it and thought it sucked big fat ass or wasn't your style or something, but, because I think you're such an awesome player, I just had to double check that I had the right address and put my number on it and everything. I'm at (323) 555-1884. No need to call unless you're interested. Thanks. Bye."

I practiced for five hours and wrote a love song about driving.

I put my ad for musicians in the paper again and resolved to call every single person back, no matter how much of an axe murderer they sounded like.

I built a shrine on my dresser to bring good people my way. In the center I put the receipt for the first guitar I ever got (age twelve, $145 Fender Strat made in Mexico, bought with babysitting money and meager allowance). I surrounded it with guitar picks, my signed picture of Courtney Love, a mirror, candles, song lyrics, and glitter.

I unpacked, did laundry, went grocery shopping (no meat), and lint-rolled all the cat hair off my clothes, bedspread, oven, tongue, and every other goddamn surface in my apartment.

I got myself a guitar teacher.

And now I will sleep the sleep of champions.

May 8

All of a sudden I'm so busy I feel like I don't have time to do anything.

I've catered two weddings and an art opening already. The people working with me are funny as hell. It's such a huge relief to be around people again! This one chick taught me how to whistle through my teeth and (drum roll please), there's this food prep guy named Matt, who's a drummer looking for a band. He's this little bearded guy who can juggle knives and loves, loves, loves my demo tape. He was so enthused about it that I forgave him his mullet (permed-in-back version) and his annoying habit of sometimes looking me in the chest when he talks. I realize that he's a good six inches shorter than I am, but I suspect he could make the climb up to my eyes without getting too dizzy. He's going to sniff around his friend repertoire and see if he can find any guitarists or bass players or practice spaces.

Jake snoozes. Jake loses.

Tonight I got home and Schmoo had coughed up a hairball the size of Neil. He somehow managed to deposit it right in the middle of my recently erected shrine. Which definitely means something profound, but I don't know what.

NOTE TO SELF:

When you have a hairball in your shrine, prepare for the worst.

I had my first guitar lesson today, conveniently located five minutes away in Echo Park. My guitar teacher is a true genius named Jimmy Flowers. I found him on a bulletin board at the Laundromat, and I could tell I had scored the second he opened his door. He was wearing glitter, eyeliner, jeans, two heart-shaped nipple rings, and nothing else. I guessed he was in his late thirties and spent some quality time at the gym every day. He greeted me with the deepest, most baritone "Ms. Jenny, I presume?" I've ever heard.

"Nice to meet you, Jimmy."

"Call me Flowers. Welcome to my humble cubbyhole."

He'd transformed his gigantic, one-room studio into a glittering freak forest. Huge fabric trees grew up the walls with giant orange, red, and purple branches covering the ceiling. Human-sized plastic bunnies were nailed to the walls, and curtains of shimmery pink mylar hung from the rafters, making the place look like the inside of a drag queen car wash. I'm not describing it well, but suffice it to say that anyone who's ever tripped on acid has been there.

I learned that along with being a guitarist, he's also an artist.

". . . as well as a pianist, a feminist, a Buddhist, a costumist, an optimist, a colorist. I'm basically a fabulist," he said as he took my coffee and poured it down the drain. "Sorry, but you said you planned on being a singer too, and coffee is the best way to dry out your precious tubes. Apple juice?" he

May 9

asked. "It's either that or breast milk. My neighbor leaves her baby with me every morning. I'm not as weird as I appear."

"Your house is awesome."

"So's your hair."

He handed me some juice in a Bugs Bunny cup and steered me over to two chairs set up by a piano. A giant papier-mâché jelly donut loomed over our heads as he told me to unpack my things.

"Now, I'd love to chat, but we'll have to do it later because we have a lot to cover today."

No nonsense, all the way. Just what I need. He made me show him everything I know and coached me through a painful series of finger-strengthening exercises.

"Don't forget to breathe!" he'd scream like an army sergeant.

I left with four hours of homework, blisters, some teal nail polish, and a new spiritual leader.

ANSWERING MACHINE RESPONSES TO NEWSPAPER AD:

May 10

DEREK. BASS PLAYER. (310) 555-2109. WEIRD ACCENT. FRIENDLY. SOUNDS LIKE HE'S EITHER KIND OF SPACEY OR VERY DRUNK.

MIKE. GUITARIST. PAGER (213) 555-0433. HAS VAN AND SMOKE MACHINE! QUESTIONABLE PERSONALITY. TALKS LIKE CAPTAIN KIRK: "MUST ROCK. SEND ME A PAGE AND THE

FORCES WILL UNITE. THE TIME IS FIF-
TEEN PAST THE HOUR OF FIVE. ROCK
YOU. OVER. MIKE."

TED. BASS. VERY MELLOW. LISTED
ALL 6,832 BANDS HE'S INFLUENCED
BY. MACHINE CUT HIM OFF BEFORE HE
COULD LEAVE HIS NUMBER.

ALEXA. BASS. I THINK. COULD HARDLY
HEAR ANYTHING SHE SAID, SHE SPOKE
SO QUIETLY. (213) 555-6932 OR
555-6532 OR 999-6532.

PAUL. "NAME'S PAUL, BUT PEOPLE
CALL ME FLASH. BEEN PLAYING GUITAR
SINCE I COULD BREATHE. EARLY
PUMPKINS, STOOGES, NIRVANA, HENDRIX,
ANYTHING WITH HAIR ON ITS CHEST. DIAL
ME UP AT (310) 787-3900.
ESCALATOR."

Matt, a.k.a. Drum God Posing as Food Prep Guy, and I went over to his place after work. He lives in the Valley in an ugly, two-story apartment building overlooking the 101 Freeway. His place had that very specific frat-boy aesthetic to it: dying plants, velvet Elvis, mismatched furniture, swimsuit model calendar—all enhanced by the unmistakable smell of cheap lilac air-freshener. His faithfulness to form even led him to have nothing beyond

May 11

condiments and beer in his fridge, which I thought was pretty bizarre for a guy who works in the food industry.

He had his drums set up in his living room and told me to plug in by the life-sized cutout of Wilt Chamberlain propped up against the wall.

"Now you know how I feel when I stand next to you!" Matt laughed. Tall jokes. I just can't get enough of them. He ignored my obvious lack of enthusiasm and, still chuckling, went on: "I've got a twelve-pack that's been chilling all night, and my neighbors work until five. We can crank it as loud as we want." This was a truly beautiful thought. Since buying my amp, I've been unable to turn it up past a whisper for fear of my persnickety neighbor having me arrested. I love my little bungalow, but the acoustics suck—someone sneezes two doors down and it sounds like they're standing right behind me. Blowing my neighbor out of bed with an A chord would take little effort.

We started out with a couple of Nirvana songs and segued into a colossal jam that went on for about twenty minutes. My amp is delicious. Gigantic. A freight train full of honey. And for two people who'd never played together before, we really locked into a groove. Apparently Matt felt the same way, because when we were done, he jumped up from his drums, ran over to me, and gave me a huge hug. As sweet as the gesture was, the fact that he face-planted into what little cleavage I have made it less than appetizing. I peeled him away and patted him on the head.

"Jenny, we rock! This is already the best band I've ever been in."

He skipped into the kitchen and took out two glasses from the cabinet. "This calls for a celebration!"

We already had a can of Miller each, so I guess pouring the remainder into questionably clean glasses was the celebration part. Matt held up his drink and put his other hand over his heart.

"To rock and roll, pure and true," he said.

"I'll drink to that," I said. We both drained our glasses and burped. One of those sweet, bonding moments between two people with no manners.

"Hey, check this out." He ran over to what looked like a toolbox and pulled out a can of something and a lighter. He stood on his drum stool and took a bow. "Ladies and gentlemen, what you are about to witness is what happens when you don't brush your teeth in the morning. Do not try this at home."

He poured the contents of the can into his mouth and spat it out while he flicked the lighter. Flames came shooting out across the living room, stopping inches before Wilt Chamberlain's helpless cardboard head. Matt wiped his mouth with his arm and grinned. I applauded.

"I'm learning how to do that while playing the drums. It's gonna be killer!"

He was like a little kid. With a beard. I could see how he might get annoying, but he's a nice enough guy and an excellent drummer—overdoes it a bit but pretty damn good. Plus I was so happy to finally have someone to play with. So what if he had a few too many things in common with the apes?

I taught him a bunch of my songs and we jammed for another two hours. Then we hung out on his patio watching the freeway traffic and made a plan. He's been in a ton of bands. He says egos, drugs, and sex amongst bandmates are the leading causes of band failure. Makes sense to me.

Over his twelve-pack of Miller (the Champagne of Beers), we came up with a list to weed out unwanted prospective bandmates. We also decided we'll advertise ourselves as the Champagne of Bands.

FUTURE BANDMATE CHECKLIST

DO THEY HAVE:
1) Equipment?
2) An address?
3) Track marks?
4) A watch?
5) Talent?
6) A temper?
7) A police record?
8) A sense of humor?
9) Children?
10) Identification?

May 12

Carla just dropped the big fat white bomb on me. She got engaged. My itty-bitty baby sister! The slate was officially clean. I no longer felt guilty for convincing her she was adopted, locking her in the basement, or circling all her freckles with permanent marker.

But I did feel fully betrayed. All my cousins are safely married off, and Carla was my last buffer from the prying, concerned eyes of family members who fear I'll wind up The Spinster. Second only to The Lesbian. Trailed by The Inmate and The Unwed Mother.

And let us not forget the lemon juice on the open wound: I'm about to host a bridal shower.

The hairball in my shrine.

Mystery solved.

Carla invited Mom and me over for lunch, which should have tipped me off right away. Carla knows how much I hate driving out to Long Beach, and, unlike Mom, never asks me to do it. I'd figured she just wanted to test drive the new patio furniture she'd bought, but when I rounded the back of her perfectly darling house to her perfectly charming patio and saw the perfectly chilled bottle of champagne sitting by my perfectly hideous mother, I suddenly realized: I was officially about to be the only question mark left in the family.

"Jenny!" Carla squealed, running toward me with open arms, her engagement ring catching a sunbeam that burned a hole straight through my right eye. She gave me a huge, perfumed hug and whispered in my ear, "Thanks for coming. I know how much you hate it out here."

She is so sweet. I am such a witch.

"No problem. It's great to see you. Your house looks great." John, her supersweet, squeaky-clean boyfriend, came up and hugged me too.

"Good to see you. I love the new 'do," he said, winking at me.

"Thanks, John." I walked over to Mom, who didn't stand up, and gave her a weak hug.

"Hello, Jenny. Carla has a little surprise for you, don't you dear?" I had to pretend, for my sister's sake, that I had no idea what it could possibly be. This was one of the biggest announcements of her whole life, and as much as I'd have loved to squash my mother's smugness, I had to let her have it.

"Well," she rolled her eyes and put her arm around John.

"I'm sure you've figured it out by now, but John and I are tying the knot." She held out her hand and flashed the evil rock at me once more. I took her hand and did the obligatory ogle.

"It's beautiful, Carla. I'm really happy for you. You guys are awesome." I gave them both another hug, and Carla started to cry. She's so queer, but I love her anyway. And John is the perfect guy for the perfect girl. I really was happy for them, even if it meant I'd soon be ducking a flying bouquet.

THE RETURN OF LUCY STOVER HANOVER II

May 13

Well, it finally happened. Lucy Hanover, international superflake, finally reentered the United States of America. She just showed up on my doorstep this morning in her African WASP best—cornrowed and beaded hair growing halfway down her back, bright African robelike clothing, huge beaded jewelry swinging off her every limb. She was also sporting a totem-pole-type tattoo on her chest and some sort of rattle thingy with a bow on it.

"Hiya, homey!" she screamed, shoving the rattle into my hands. We hugged and she explained. "It's an African sistrum. They use them in magical ceremonies."

"Thanks. I'll let you know if it works." I pulled her inside and tossed my new rattle on the couch.

"You look awesome. I dig the hair," she said, looking me up and down.

"Thanks. You look . . . African," I said.

It was a bit awkward at first, the way it always is when we haven't seen each other in a while, but before long it was as if she'd never left. We gabbed and ate and screamed with laughter so loud my neighbor slammed his windows shut in huffy protest. It was great to see her, even though she was very affected and couldn't help but slip into some African language or other by "accident" whenever she started speaking. Because she was just so African. Every time Lucy comes back from another country this happens, even though she's never stayed anywhere for over a year. I always forget how annoying it is until she's standing in front of me rolling her *r*'s or giving her *e*'s a British slant or something. I knew it would wear off soon enough, but my irritation was heightened by the fact that she kept going on and on about some African dance troupe she was going to start performing with.

"Did you get my letter?" I asked, waiting for her to explode in excitement about the prospect of a band. She was wandering around my living room, checking out the many upgrades my ex-corporate lifestyle had afforded my bungalow.

"Yeah. Your place really looks great, Jenny! I like that you painted the living room red. Very *n'zuri*," she added in African, for my multicultural pleasure. "New stereo. Nice, very nice. You're still the tidiest, most anal retentive motherfucker I know!"

"I got a new guitar amp too. Sixty-nine Fender Twin. It's at my drummer's house." The bait was lowered into the water. If she didn't take it this time, I was going to have to open her mouth and cram it in. Luckily, she perked up.

"Really? You've gotten that far with the band thing already?"

"I told you I wasn't screwing around, Lucy. But it sounds like you've got other plans."

"Well, who says I can't do it all?" she exclaimed dramatically.

"My performance thing is an improvisational African dance, drum, and vocal ensemble. I'm going to need to get my rocks off too, you know. If you've got a band, I can't be here and not be in it with you. No way, baby."

Finally. Lucy was finally back. She even said it without her fake African accent. I was ecstatic. Not only is she my best friend, she's one of those people who plays the guitar like she was born with it in her hands.

ROCK-AND-ROLL TRUTH #2:

Lucy Stover Hanover was born September 18, 1970, which is the exact day the great Jimi Hendrix died. There is no doubt in my mind that his soul simply hopped on the Lucy Train and headed back to the planet.

"Can I crash at your place until I get settled in? All my shit's at Henry's because I wasn't sure if you'd be home," she said, flipping through my CDs.

"Of course," I said. She'd already seen Henry? (Remember Henry? My alleged friend whom I hadn't heard from in weeks?) I suddenly felt left out. Since when did she see him first?

"When did you get back, anyway?" I asked.

"Yesterday. Henry came and got me at the airport. I forgot you didn't have a job anymore or I would have made you do it." I decided that was a good enough excuse to put off my impending temper tantrum. Plus Lucy was staying with me, not Henry. I still felt kind of weird, though. Henry's always had a huge crush on her (like the rest of the goddamn world), and even though she couldn't be less interested in him, things always get a little tricky when she's in town.

"What the hell is Henry doing these days? I haven't talked to him since he took care of my cats," I asked.

"I don't know, Jenny. He seemed kind of sad to me. Maybe he's been too depressed to call."

Oh my God. For the first time I realized I'd been so wrapped up in my own stuff that I hadn't taken the time to think about Henry—aside from the fact that he hadn't called. There I was, getting all prickly because I wasn't the focus of his life, and meanwhile, he was quietly suffering away in some corner, not wanting to bother me.

BRILLIANT OBSERVATION #5:

I am a selfish boob.

I followed Lucy back to Henry's so she could give him his car back and pick up her stuff. He lives in one of those huge lofts downtown that's really cheap because it's in a totally scary neighborhood. Which describes most of downtown L.A.— they're trying to make it more residential, but at the moment, it consists of just a few brave pioneers, drug dealers, and throngs of homeless people. Very postapocalyptic. And I'm sorry to say the inside of Henry's place wasn't much more uplifting. He was sitting in the middle of his floor, surrounded by clothes, cereal boxes, and computer parts, doing something confusing to some piece of computer equipment. As usual. His place is always messy, but this was ridiculous. I wanted to go through his draw- ers and see if anything was actually left in any one of them.

His door was unlocked—open a crack, in fact—so we just walked in. He looked up blankly, taking several seconds to pull his brain out of the computer and put it back into his head. He looked beyond tired.

"Hey, guys. Hey, Jenny," he said. I sat down next to him and gave him a hug. Sitting there on the floor, he looked bizarrely tiny.

"What have you been up to? I feel like I haven't talked to you in months," I complained.

"I'm sorry, Jenny. I've been kind of . . . stuck. My investors sort of pulled out. It really threw me for a loop."

"What? Why didn't you tell me?"

Henry has been starting his own computer-type company thing (he's explained it to me a million times, and I haven't understood it a million times), and apparently it had all just fallen through. The poor guy's been working on it for years.

"I don't know. I'm sorry. I didn't want to screw up your momentum. I haven't been that much fun to be around anyway."

"Don't you be sorry. I'm the idiot who didn't even notice her best friend was losing his mind."

"I'm sorry. I should have told you."

"No, I'm sorry I just ate, because you two are going to make me puke!" Lucy burst in.

Ah, Lucy. So sentimental. Such a beautiful wordsmith. I shot her a dirty look. Henry laughed.

"So you guys are going to live together for a while? Just like old times?" Henry asked.

"Yeah, except this time around Lucy's African."

"Stop it. I have a real connection to the culture, that's all," Lucy said, annoyed.

"I think she looks great," Henry offered.

"Of course you do. You think everything Lucy does is great," I snapped, accidentally tossing my jealousy into the middle of the room with a loud thud. All three of us sat in silent embarrassment.

"I think you look great too," Henry finally said, getting to his feet and pulling me up with him. He was blushing. Lucy just stood there, silent. I think she was scared that anything she might say could and would be used against her.

"Thanks," I mumbled. These were my two best friends. Who better to fling my teething ring at? They'd forgive me no matter how much of an ass I was. "I think I'm done having my temper tantrum now. Lucy, you ready to go?"

"Sure." I'd successfully broken the ice. We said good-bye to Henry and had a nice, quiet ride home. We didn't talk about it or anything else, and by the end of the night the incident had pretty much blown over. Lucy would rather take a bullet than process how she's feeling, and in this case, I was glad of it. Because the only thing there'd be to talk about is what an insecure little sniveler I am.

But as poorly executed as it was, deep down I was still glad I'd said it. Henry's infatuation has been getting worse and worse, and it's time they both knew it.

TO DO LIST:
1) Buy clothes that make me feel like a sex goddess. Do this with the eight dollars left to my name.
2) Post signs around town for bass player.
3) Think of ways to get out of hosting bridal shower. Stop at nothing.

May 15

4) Buy black pants for work.
5) Come up with brilliant moneymaking scheme for Henry.
6) Stop saying "I swear" before every goddamn sentence.

Matt came over today so we could all hang out and he and Lucy could get to know each other. I was pretty nervous. I warned Lucy he was a little clueless, which she acknowledged by staring at me with raised eyebrows as Matt had a conversation with her breasts. I could tell she wasn't all that thrilled by him, but he made her laugh a few times. And I knew once she heard him play the drums, she'd feel a lot differently.

We sat around over pizza and beer and tried to come up with a name for the band. Here's a partial list:

1) Stump Fetish
2) Captain Banana
3) Rug Burn
4) Scarred for Life
5) Bad Witch
6) The Trotts
7) Dirty Little Secret
8) Raised by Wolves
9) Happypants
10) Eunice
11) Not for Nothin'
12) Earmites

It was much harder than I'd thought it would be. We decided they all sucked and switched from band naming to image creating.

We decided to wear all white and do as many idiotic stage antics as we could. Matt, God of Fire, was really pushing for this one. "He's not so bad. For a perverted elf," Lucy said after he left.

"Just wait until you hear him play," I lobbied. She had no idea how hard it was to find a decent drummer in this town. She *had* to like him.

"He seems hyper enough to last an eight-hour set. And if you say he's good, I'll take your word for it. Besides, I have a really good feeling about all this, Jenny. I'm pretty fucking excited."

"Does that mean you won't flake on me again?" I couldn't help it. I didn't want to have to hate her again.

She took my hand, looked me in the eye, and, in a very un-Lucy-like moment, said, "I'm over all that. I did some hard-core soul-searching in Africa, and I've come to terms with my be-or-flee instincts. You'll see."

We shall see.

NOTE TO SELF:

Start WASP Self-Realization Retreat in Africa. Make a ton of money.

Elaine, my new catering boss, walked into the kitchen at work today when Matt and I were bitching about having nowhere to practice. She said her father owns an office build-ing with some empty spaces he'd probably let us use at night. "He's very supportive of the arts. In fact, I'll phone him right now." Which she did, and then he did, and that was that. I now have a practice space in Koreatown for the low, low price of $150 a month.

I'm starting to notice a trend here. I kill myself trying to

May 20

make something happen, and just when I'm about to lose hope, something stumbles in the back door. From a direction I never even thought about looking in. Maybe we should call the band Dumb Luck. Maybe I should call my *life* Dumb Luck.

THEY CAME FROM THE CLASSIFIEDS
AN AWARD-WINNING FEATURE FILM BY JENNY TROANNI

FADE IN: INTERIOR PRACTICE SPACE—NIGHT

A large office filled with a drum kit, guitar amps, guitars, pedals, bubble machine, posters, and the rest of the usual rock-and-roll paraphernalia. JENNY and LUCY tune their guitars. MATT tweaks his drums and drinks a beer.

Enter CYNTHIA. Leopard-skin pants, biker boots, fully inked (lizards, snakes, daggers—more ink than skin), spiked blue hair, piercings all the way up both ears, killer body, T-shirt handed down from an infant, tits that could bash a man's head in half. You don't know where to look first.

CYNTHIA *(to Lucy and Jenny)*:

Sisters!

CYNTHIA *(to Matt)*:

Home slice!

High fives all around.

JENNY:　　　Thanks for coming.

CYNTHIA *(Nods in cocky surveillance of the room.)*:

All right, all right, this could work! This could totally work! Let's kick some fuckin' ass!

Cynthia plugs in and proceeds to turn her bass up so loud it alters Jenny's heartbeat. She has all the moves—leg up on amp, head banging, jumps, twirls, back-bends. She can even play the bass with her tongue.

She insists on screaming the backup vocals (even though she knows neither the words nor the tune) and tries to bond with the eye-contact/snarl-and-nod thing. She is fascinating, but Jenny is genuinely scared of her.

JENNY: Thanks for coming.

A knowing wink from Cynthia. More high fives all around.

CYNTHIA: All right then. Whew. I mean, I'm not crazy, right? You guys
                had to feel that too!

JENNY: We actually have a few more people to see. . . .

CYNTHIA: Oh, yeah. No problemo. I can wait. We're gonna RULE!

High fives again. Because one can never have too many. Cynthia slams the door and howls her way out of the building.

FADE TO BLACK.

FADE IN—INT. OFFICE SPACE—SAME BAT TIME, SAME BAT
                          CHANNEL. NEXT NIGHT:

Enter DEREK, deceptively WASPy looking, and in his early twenties. He is carrying a lawn chair, a martini shaker, and a glass.

LUCY: Can we help you?

DEREK: I sure hope so. I am so sick of playing alone to records!
                Mind if I smoke?

Derek starts setting up his lawn chair and making himself comfortable. The other three look at each other in bewilderment.

MATT: Um. Who the fuck are you?

DEREK: Why, I'm Derek! I made an appointment for five o'clock to
                be your bass player?

JENNY: Where's your bass? And yeah, we kind of do mind if you
                smoke actually.

Derek puts away his cigarette and pours himself a drink.

DEREK: I didn't bring my bass. I don't play for just anyone. I'm here to observe you tonight. See if I'm interested. Start whenever you're ready.

He leans back in his chair and waits expectantly.

FADE TO BLACK.

After that came James. Tight, acid-washed jeans, Van Halen tour shirt with the sleeves cut off, moderately inked (a chick, a panther, a sun with blood and tears dripping off it) black sneakers, and, of course, The Mullet (straight bangs, back section straight on top, curly on the bottom, perm-growing-out version). He brought a six-pack of Bud and his girlfriend, Cindi. Nice guy and a great bass player, but it was quietly understood: he wasn't for us. We weren't for him.

Next was Rodney, who needed me to go pick him up at his Mom's house because he didn't have a license. I almost didn't bother, but we were getting desperate. Unfortunately, he was even a young-looking seventeen—superscrawny, with a baby face and long, greasy brown hair. You could tell once he filled out and got rid of those braces he was going to be a real cutie, but at that moment I found it nearly impossible not to pat him on the head and feed him a cookie. He goes to the same high school I did, so we bonded on how nuts Mrs. Garza is and how crappy the burritos are at the cafeteria.

Not exactly the kind of conversation I'd expected to have with a prospective bandmate.

But the kid could play. He said we rocked pretty hard for old people! I thought that was hilarious, but he didn't laugh.

Then there was Whispering Alexa. Lanky, dyed black

stringy hair, looking for Goth in all the wrong places. Her bass was wilder than she was, and the five words she spoke— "What key is this in?"—were breathed as though they were her last. Her playing was okay, but I've never seen anyone so spooked in my life. Her ink consisted of a serpent peeking out from her cleavage. She smelled like wax. She gave me the creeps.

I just got back from seeing *The Blair Witch Project* with Katie and Lucy. We were sitting there waiting for it to start, and this guy sat two seats away from us. He was by himself, and I just knew he was gonna be a fucking perv. Which he was. Of course. Went right at it the second the lights went down, popcorn cleverly placed in his lap, looking right at us. So we got up and moved. Katie announced to the crowd "We're getting up and moving because this fucking creep is jerking off!" Thank you, Katie. It probably just made him get off harder.

Why does that happen so much? What is the thrill there? And I swear it happens to me more than anyone I know. I want to write a book called *Target of Perversion* and chronicle all my whacked-off-at episodes. I need to come up with a new term for that. Perved on? Jerkied? I don't know.

You never see women doing that. Can you imagine some chick with her hand down her pants, staring at some guy? She'd probably get beaten up. Or asked out.

NOTE TO SELF:
Write a song about the aforementioned phenomenon. Call it "Put That Thing Away."

May 28

Lucy found a place to live, and it's literally one street away! It's a small one-bedroom in a cheesy apartment building (questionably clean carpeting, smells like chicken soup), but then Lucy's never cared much about where she lives. It's on the second floor and has a porch with a pretty great view of Silver Lake.

It was actually really fun having her stay with me, which was surprising since having someone live with me usually makes me want to hang myself after about five days, no matter who it is. But we cooked and drank tons of beer and wrote music and laughed our asses off. We were listening to P.J. Harvey one night and decided to call the band Sixty-Foot Queenie. We're both amazons, and we figured P.J. wouldn't mind since we added ten feet to the name. Besides, if she sued, maybe we'd get to meet her.

I told Matt the next day at work. I don't think he liked it.

"That so blows! I mean, why not just call ourselves Sixty-Foot Weenie? At least that way people won't think we're serious."

"Well, do you have any better ideas?" I asked.

"Yeah, how about something that doesn't suck?" He was in a pissy mood because our boss had made him start wearing a hairnet.

BRILLIANT OBSERVATION #6:
It's impossible to take a guy in a hairnet seriously.

After work I helped Lucy get her stuff out of storage, and poor old Mark came over with his truck. Mark's her Sucker. We came up with that concept a few years ago. The Sucker is the one who has it so bad for you that you don't have the heart to sleep with him. You stay friends, he will cancel any plans at any moment to paint your living room, but you still never sleep with him. Ever. I had a Sucker named Steve for a while until he got married. When we worked at McCauley & Doyle, Katie was the Sucker of this guy named Evan. She's the first to admit it. She did his laundry once because he was going on a big date and didn't have time. Brutal. And very irresponsible behavior on the Suckee's part, if you ask me.

Out of utter desperation, we asked Alexa to play with us. I know that's the crappiest of reasons, but we need to get going already. Matt wanted Cynthia. He said she kicked ass. I said she *was* an ass. Lucy said, "Let's take a vote." Matt muttered something about us ganging up on him, but I let it go.

June 3

Now that Lucy has to pay rent, she's freaking out about the money thing too.

Lucy has a weird perception of money because
1) Lucy has a weird perception of everything, and
2) She grew up with plenty and now has none.

June 5

Her proud lineage is as follows: Her great-grandmother, Lucy Rivington Griggs, had truckloads of family money, which her daughter, Lucy Griggs Stover, squandered away on a very serious gambling habit, leaving Lucy Stover Hanover, the current Lucy's mother, with barely enough money to keep the kids in private school and the country club membership alive. What trickled down to our very own Lucy Stover Hanover II was just enough to afford her the occasional international plane ticket and a 1991 Mercedes.

I'm pretty sure that at this point my sissy little bank account could send Lucy's home bloodied and crying, but she somehow managed to scrounge together a tiny chunk to add to the sad little CD fund. Since it was only about two hundred dollars, I realized it was more a symbolic gesture of commitment than a helpful contribution, but I was thankful anyway. Then she picked up a job doing construction with some friend of hers. She's loving it. Says she's slept with two of the construction guys already. She's my hero. I wish I could be as free about sex, but I'm more of a one-dog gal. She likes an entire sled team.

We've been going on band field trips once a week to see live music. So far there are a couple of bands we want to gig with, and Lucy's seduced every bar owner she's met. But no screwing. We have agreed that only amateurs mix business with pleasure. Lucy was very serious about that, though she said stupid day jobs at construction sites don't count.

Catering is starting to drive me crazy. Working around food is gross—I feel like I can never get the smell off me. I hate waiting on people, and I spill more drinks than I serve.

And as much as I like Matt, I don't need to see him every waking moment. On top of being cranky, he has this annoying habit of repeating a joke over and over until you laugh. Or scream. He thinks that if you didn't laugh, it's because you didn't hear it, not because you didn't think it was funny.

I have to quit this job. I have no money and no new leads, but I officially can't take it anymore. Where, oh where will I get the strength to do the minimum-wage grovel again?

On a brighter note, I finished my latest masterpiece. It's got

three guitar solos and rocks like a pig. If I do say so myself.
Ahem:
PUT THAT THING AWAY ©1999
It was raining again
So I said to my friend
I said, girlfriend, let's go to the movies
We paid our nine bucks
Found some seats and sure enough
He sat right down with his popcorn in his lap
Our fun was over
Another unwanted boner
Had reared its ugly head so I said

(Chorus)
Put that thing away
You're just another dick in my day
Someone explain to me
The thrill of losing your dignity
Put that thing away
It's not my fault you never get laid
Instead of whacking off at me
Try getting off on therapy
Put that thing away
What the hell do you want me to say
That I'm sorry you turned out to be
The freak standing in front of me

It was a hundred and ten
So I said to my friend

I said, girlfriend, let's go to the river
We hiked a long way up, stripped it off and dipped in our
    stuff
And I swear I heard it sizzle
I saw him standing there
Pudgy hand tugging his underwear
For fuck's sake, here we go again
Our fun was over
Another unwanted boner
Had reared its ugly head

(Chorus)
Put that thing away. . . .

June 7

We all went out to see a band called Icky and the Yucks because Matt used to play in a band with the lead singer. They were hardcore punk, and the crowd was more disgusting than any I'd ever seen. Which is saying something.

It was the usual slam-dancing, beer-spitting, drunken, brawling free-for-all, with the added attraction of some asshole tossing firecrackers into the crowd. But I'd have to say the prize went to the guy who started puking and spun around to share it with everyone within a ten-foot radius. One guy in a red mohawk got a chunky face full and said, "Aw, man! I'm not that punk. I'm just not that fucking punk, man!"

Matt thinks we should book a show with them and got fully pissed when I asked if he was joking. He thinks I'm a snob. I think the honeymoon is officially over.

We had two uncomfortably shy and bizarre practices with Alexa before she evaporated into thin air. During the first one, she just kept completely to herself and stared at the floor. I felt like we'd found her in a cave and she'd never seen light or heard human voices before. I wouldn't have been surprised if she'd freaked out and bitten me.

I asked her afterward if the music seemed like stuff she'd be into and if she felt comfortable around all of us. She said yes and then complimented Lucy's playing. A full sentence! Then I asked her if she'd ever been in a band before, but I guess she'd used up her word quota for the year because she just nodded and took off.

The next practice she showed up all sweaty and panting, like she'd just been chased.

ME: Are you all right?
ALEXA: *Nods.*
LUCY: You sure?
ALEXA: *Nods again.*
MATT: Oh, come on! I've had enough of this deer-caught-in-the-headlights bullshit. I mean, are you for real? Because if you are, I'll tell you right now, I can't be in a band with a vegetable. I need to connect with you, you know? We're the rhythm section, man!

She glares at him. He looks at me and I just shrug.

MATT: What are you, on serious painkillers or something? I mean, look at you. You look like you just outran a ghost!

This made her burst out laughing. I swear I've never been so surprised in my entire life.

ALEXA: Ghosts can't run!

We actually had a decent practice after that, but she never showed up again. I question now whether she really existed at all.

Matt was right for thinking it wasn't such a good idea to call her in the first place. I know this to be true because he told me so five times.

June 12

I found my first gray hair today. It was surrounded by about eleven others. They are wiry and weird. This is a major turning point in a person's life. I'm no longer a youth. I'm not old, but I'm definitely not young and my hair is making sure I know it.

ROCK-AND-ROLL TRUTH #3:

In the music world, women are never too old to kick ass, while a lot of men just start to look weird.

Those Who Inspire: Chrissie, Patti, Debbie, Dolly, Madonna, Bonnie.

Those Who Frighten: Mick, Keith, Rod, Roger.

The opposite applies to movie stars, where men are never too old and women are never too young.

Another truth is that rock stars can be taken seriously as actors. Actors are never taken seriously as rock stars. So start with music if you want to do both.

June 17

As luck would have it, not one more person called about the bass-player ad so, out of complete desperation once again, we called little underage Rodney. I stopped by with a tape of all the songs so he'd have an idea what to play when he showed up for practice. Mrs. Nitzer, his mother, invited me in for cake. And a verbal cavity search. She must not have found anything too disturbing, because when I went back to pick him up for practice, there were no police waiting for me.

Rodney learned all the songs I gave him right away and was ready to go when I picked him up. A good little Boy Scout. Still, I can't shake the feeling that I'm doing something disgusting and/or illegal.

I went out for dinner with Katie and a bunch of our old friends from McCauley & Doyle last night. Katie sent her meal back twice. I'd forgotten just how rude she can be, and I suddenly wasn't sure I could hang in there long enough to make her of use. I still had to record a demo, go on tour, and get some sort of buzz going before I could hit her up for any favors. I haven't even told her I started a band yet.

June 19

ROCK-AND-ROLL TRUTH #4:
You're either famous or annoying. There's no gray area.

They all ordered appetizers, drinks, dessert, etc. and then wanted to split the bill. I had a bowl of pasta and water. They have real jobs. I threw in my fifteen bucks (a generous two dollars over my total with tip and tax). They were nice about it, but I definitely felt something shift. I was no longer one of them. I no longer ran with the wolves.

I was a drag.

Katie just put a down payment on her first house, and I'm hanging out with teenagers. I know I'm pursuing my biggest dream ever, but it's hard to not feel like a giant loser when you can't afford an appetizer.

BRILLIANT OBSERVATION #7:

No matter how big a loser you are, if you have money, you are socially acceptable. If you don't, you're a chore.

June 22

Lucy's new best friend at the Opium Den just called and offered us a gig. Some band backed out at the last minute, and he needs us to play tomorrow night.

It has happened so fast, I really don't have time to freak out, even though we're completely unprepared!

Everyone can make it, but Rodney said he could only play if he got all his work done. I guess he had some academic issues and was forced to go to summer school. I'm on my way to his house to help him with his math homework so he can get the night off. Disgusting. Illegal.

June 23

Oh my God, high school math is so fucking hard! I can't even add a fraction! And what the hell is the Pythagorean Theorem?

I was utterly useless. And as if that weren't humiliating enough, I spent the afternoon mowing Rodney's mother's lawn while he did his homework. Rodney apologized but said he absolutely had to get it all done or he wouldn't be allowed to play. I'm a desperate old person. I think I've hit a new low.

But we have our first gig! Who cares that we've only written five songs or that we've only practiced with Rodney twice? The songs rock, and Rodney's got a pretty good handle on everything because he clearly practices his ass off. And just in case I wasn't sure of this, his mother, the ever chummy Mrs. Nitzer, hammered it home as I was getting in my car to leave after a grueling day of yard work.

"If he cared half as much about his studies as he did about rock and roll, he'd be a straight-A student," she hissed, her arms wrapped around her chest like a tourniquet.

"Mom, can we talk about this later?" Rodney asked, mortified. He stared down at his feet like he'd never seen them before.

"She's just being a good mother," I whispered to him, loud enough for the entire neighborhood to hear.

Mrs. Nitzer wasn't impressed. "Did you ever stop to think that Rodney can't get into that concert of yours, or any of them for that matter, without a parent or legal guardian? Neither of which you are?"

"Mom, you promised you'd take me!"

"I know I did. I must be out of my gourd."

"Thank you so much, Mrs. Nitzer, I really appreciate it," I said, feeling completely nauseous. I'd just assumed we'd sneak him in and take him home the second we were done playing or something. I'd had no idea Mrs. Nitzer was going to be in the audience! How the hell was I ever going to let loose onstage in her horrified presence? I couldn't imagine her setting foot inside the Opium Den, especially since last time I was there, some drunk chick climbed on top of the bar and started stripping.

This, along with the fact that I hadn't performed in nearly a decade, was enough to make me suddenly too sick to eat dinner. Luckily, Flowers came by and dropped off his white feather headdress for me to wear onstage. He helped me put on my white go-go boots, white gloves (with the fingers cut off so I could play guitar), and a white towel that I swiped from a hotel.

"Girl, you've got to eat something. Collapsing on stage has been done soooo many times before." He made me a gigantic salad and sat there while I somehow crammed half of it down my throat.

"What if I forget the lyrics? What if Mrs. Nitzer gets hit in the head by a flying bra?" I wanted to cry.

"What if you remember the lyrics? What if Mrs. Nitzer climbs on the bar and flings her own bra across the room?" Flowers asked as he applied glitter to my face. I knew he was trying to make me feel better, but that last image was enough to make me sleep with the lights on for the rest of my life. "You have a choice: think yea or think nay. If you feel you must participate in the latter, I'm leaving." Flowers is very into the power of positive thought.

"You're right," I said, and let it go at that.

I managed to keep him around until Lucy and Matt showed up so they could all finally meet. Matt came to my door wearing nothing but a diaper. He was holding his kick drum. He wanted to show me he'd stenciled "Sixty-Foot Queenie" on it.

"I like the name much better written down," he explained. "Looks pretty awesome, does it not?" Matt was turning out to be very hard to stay mad at. Every time he did something annoying, he'd turn around and be excellent. He looked about as big as an actual baby standing next to Lucy, who'd taken out her cornrows and was sporting a 'fro that took up the majority of air space in my living room.

My band!

"My outfit's going to be a surprise. I'm Lucy," she announced, holding out her hand for Flowers to shake. He kissed it instead.

"I'm delighted," he said, marveling at the small hair planet circling her head.

"Matt, this is Flowers," I said. Matt held his hand up to high five him. Flowers bowed.

"Well, I'll see you all at the club. I've got to go prepare," Flowers said, giving me a huge hug and kissing Lucy's hand again on the way out.

"Are you guys ready?" she asked.

"Were us guys born ready?" Matt howled in my face, his breath making the unwelcome announcement that he'd already started drinking.

Well, this was it. We were going onstage as drunk, terrified, frizzy-haired, and underaged as we were. There was no turning back.

GOOD THINGS TO REMEMBER:
1) Pee before going onstage.
2) Always play in bands because it's the funnest thing you've ever done, hands down, period.
3) I love music.
4) I love my band.
5) I am drunk.

June 24

It's 4 A.M. and I just got back after unloading all our stuff at the practice space, and I just want to say that was so much god-damn fun, I can't believe it took me so long to get off my ass and do it. *We rocked like a gigantic fat huge rocking thing!* I was so proud of all of us, even though Matt was pretty drunk by the time we started playing and fucked up a lot. He needs to drink after we play, not before. But who can be mad at a guy in a diaper? And I couldn't even look at Lucy. Seeing someone tear through a killer guitar solo in a tutu was more than I could handle.

The Opium Den was its usual, skanky, low-lit self. It's got some couches tucked away in a small room (hence the Den), a couple thronelike chairs, and multicolored lights hanging down from the ceiling. The bar runs along the wall across from the stage, which is where we found Rodney sitting with his mother when we got there. He was in a toga, drinking a Coke and looking miserable while his mother sat speechlessly by his side like a protective gargoyle. She was clutching her purse so tightly her hand shook.

It was nine o'clock, so the place was pretty empty except for a group of tragically hip Asian kids playing poker in the Den. Rodney's face lit up the second he saw us, and he came bounding over like a puppy.

"My stuff's all set up. This place is rad!"

"I've seen some great shows here," offered big brother Matt. In his diaper. Rodney ran outside to help us unload, and after I got all my stuff onstage, I headed over for my obligatory grovel with The Parent. I made sure that Lucy was nowhere around for fear she'd join me. People love Lucy. Parents hate her.

"Mrs. Nitzer, it's nice to see you," I said as she clutched her purse tighter and gave me a thin little grin. She looked at my Indian headdress like it was going to leap off my body and eat her.

NOTE TO SELF:

Trying to convince someone that you're a good influence is impossible if you're wearing nothing but a towel and a bird on your head.

As I made my way to the stage, I saw all my friends start to pile in. Henry came with a video camera and Flowers came dressed like a banker. I barely recognized him.

"What the hell is this? Do you have a job interview after the gig or something?" I asked. I'd never seen him without eye makeup.

"Don't you worry about me, missy. You just get up there and rock the pants off these people." By this time the place was about half full with the typical Hollywood/Silver Lake bohemian-type rock fans (carefully sculpted bed head, thrift store apparel, not a job in sight). Lucy had finally changed into her tutu and chef's hat and was tuning her guitar. She looked like a giant pastry. I climbed onstage next to her and she turned to me and started laughing. Rodney was wearing dark sunglasses, and Matt was holding up his beer in a salute. We were ready to play.

The lights went down and the house music went off. Matt counted off the beginning to "Put That Thing Away," and from there on in it was a breeze. All my anxiety fled from my body with the first note, and I suddenly felt like I'd been standing onstage my whole life. I was more comfortable there than I was anywhere else, even though my go-go boots were half a size too small.

The crowd stopped talking while we played and clapped when we were done, which I'll take to mean they loved us. The one audience member I'd been most worried about was being pleasantly entertained by Flowers, in his suit. He had Mrs. Nitzer laughing and relaxed and thrilled, no doubt, that I had such nice, normal friends. How beautiful is that? Little did she know he was wearing leather panties and nipple clamps. I realized this was the point of the suit and I mentally dedicated every song we played to him.

I ran back and forth across the stage and Lucy danced her ass off, her bulbous hairdo rising and falling like a giant beach ball. Rodney did this shy little dance, sort of like the one you do when you have to pee, and stayed within the same two-inch radius the entire time. Then there was Matt. He was all hair and arms and twirling sticks, and he stood up after every song to roar at the crowd. The longer we played, the drunker he got, and by the end he was playing standing up. Which he doesn't know how to do. Luckily, the damage was minimal, and he was so excited, I couldn't really be mad at him.

When it was over I swear I felt like we'd only been up there for five minutes. Rodney's mother whisked him away the moment the last note was played. But she was friendlier than I'd ever seen her. She actually shook my hand and told me I had nice friends.

Guys were tripping over themselves to help us unload. Two chicks gave Lucy their phone numbers. Three guys asked for mine. We made our first hundred dollars. We are huge.

June 26

What the hell? Why did it take me until now to do this? Why didn't I go to music school or start a band or work in a recording studio or something? How did I end up in advertising hell?

I guess I was doing what I was supposed to do (i.e., becoming a giant mountain of chicken poo). I found a field that was allegedly creative, socially acceptable, and could make me a ton of money. But then writing ad copy morphed into writing jingles, and before I knew it, I was working nonstop and couldn't bring myself to pick up a guitar when I got home. Plus I got caught up in the Consumer Whirlpool: Make money so you can buy stuff that will make you feel better because you work so hard to make money to buy yourself stuff to make you feel better because you work so hard. . . .

Stuff's sole purpose on this earth is to make you believe you want it.

After the other night, all I want is to feel the all-fulfilling monster rush of making music.

Stuff can blow me.

BRILLIANT OBSERVATION #8:

I've never been broker or happier in my life.

Today is Mom's birthday. She demanded that Carla, John, and I come to her house for dinner to celebrate the fateful day. I dragged Henry along with me, figuring that if he was feeling crappy about his life, sitting around with my family would remind him how good he had it. Plus he's the only friend of mine Mom likes. According to her, Lucy's headed straight for the penitentiary and that Katie talks too much.

June 29

"Why don't you get together with Henry? He's such a nice boy. And he dresses so well," she'd gush. She saw him in a tie once and hasn't been the same since.

Henry and I did entertain the thought once back in high school, but after an embarrassing attempt at kissing, we let it go. It was like kissing my brother, and it literally made me puke. The fact that we'd downed an entire bottle of peppermint schnapps that we'd stolen from my mother had a lot to do with it too, and the next day we were both so sick, we could barely look at each other without getting nauseous. So now, aside from the fact that I'm not turned on by incest, we have a built-in Pavlovian reaction to anything beyond the platonic.

We sang along to the radio at the top of our lungs the whole way to Mom's house. Henry's the best. It's weird how when you don't hang out with someone for a while and then you do again, you miss them. It's like you forget to miss them until they show up to remind you.

When we arrived, Mom pulled a Mom and served enough food to fill a barn. Carla pulled a Carla and claimed to not be very hungry. Mom pulled a Mom and said, "I'd rather feed a thousand starving people than one person who says she isn't hungry." Carla pulled a Carla and ate more than all of us put together. As usual.

I knitted Mom a scarf. My first ever, and I must say I was pretty damn impressed with myself. Until I saw what Henry had made. He designed a screen saver for her computer. He took a picture of her face and made it change expressions and hairdos. Truly hilarious. And the sick thing is, he just figured out how to do it by screwing around on the computer. Sometimes I have no idea how someone so smart can hang out with a mental catastrophe like myself. I feel like I have lint for brains around him. We all gathered around Mom's computer to bask in its glory.

"Henry, this is *wonderful*!" Mom raved. Carla and I were laughing hysterically. For some reason, seeing her head morph around like that was more than we could handle.

"It's like a bad trip," I whispered to Carla, who nodded, even though she's only ever done hallucinogens vicariously through me.

"I don't think I'll ever be the same," Carla said through her tears. "I really don't." Everyone went back to the dining room while Carla and I continued to unravel in front of the computer. We cried and clung to each other and nearly pissed ourselves for I don't know how long until Henry finally came back in to get us.

"Jeez, you guys, pull it together. It's not that funny." He turned it off and waited while we decompressed.

"Henry, I mean it. Fuck your investors. You could be a billionaire making those things. I'm serious," I said, massaging my poor stomach muscles.

"Wow, I had no idea," he said, scratching his head. "You really think so?"

"Yes, Henry, I agree," Carla said. "You're going to be a very rich man."

I could see his wheels instantly start to spin. I knew he'd be mentally unavailable the rest of the evening, his brain already hard at work in the Virtual Henry Computer Lab.

BRILLIANT OBSERVATION #9:
Mom is even more screwed up than I thought she was.

When we finally sat back down at the table for dessert, Mom brought out a cherry pie, a pumpkin pie, a strawberry shortcake, and some cookies. On top of all this, Carla had brought a double-layer chocolate birthday cake. But because Mom and Carla are always on a diet, we got to hear them freak out about how they really shouldn't, while they totally did. As usual.

"Jenny, how come you didn't invite us to your gig? I would

have loved to see it!" Carla said, shoveling her second piece of pie into her mouth.

"Who are we anyway? Just her family," Mom whined. "If you're having a second piece, Carla, then so am I."

"It all happened so fast. I'll invite you to the next one," I lied.

I just couldn't imagine any of them in any of the bars we'd play in. Carla and John in their Gap best standing next to some guy crushing beer cans on his forehead? And I knew Mom was just complaining for appearance's sake. And because complaining is her favorite thing to do in general. You couldn't shoot and drag her to one of my shows if you tried.

Our practice schedule is as follows:

Whole band practice on Tuesday and Friday nights and Saturday afternoon.

Monday nights Lucy and I get together and write.

All goes well unless Matt and I have to work or Rodney has a test the next day. We've got a gig with Abiogenesis on July 11th and one with Abiogenesis, Bomb Squad, and Whizzy on the 15th. The guys in Abiogenesis asked us to play with them after they saw our first gig. We're their new favorite band. They're kind of nerdy and who knows what the hell their music sounds like, but if they like us, they have to have some sort of clue. Plus the lead singer works in a music supply store and said he could get us anything we want at the employee discount.

I'm reading Frank Zappa's autobiography. How is it that that guy never did any drugs?

TO DO LIST:

1) Get stickers made.
2) Get T-shirts made.
3) Find Rodney a math tutor.
4) Find me a math tutor.
5) Make fliers for upcoming gigs.

Lucy and I were supposed to work on a bunch of new songs so we'd actually have something to play at our upcoming gigs, but when I stopped by her place to pick her up, she was nowhere to be found. I taped a note to her door that said:

MEET ME AT THE PRACTICE SPACE.
I SURE DO HOPE I SEE YOUR FACE.
WE NEED NEW SONGS CUZ IN OUR CASE
WE HAVE A BUTTLOAD OF GIGS COMING
UP AND NOTHING TO FUCKING PLAY.

I somehow managed to write a new song from start to finish called "Gettin' High off the Lows" about people who love to be miserable. It's a thinly veiled song about my dear mother, Katie, and anyone else who puts the *y* in happy. Lucy ended up bursting through the door around nine o'clock, a good six hours late. She was in sweats and a T-shirt and looked like she'd run the entire way over.

"Oh my God, Jenny, I just got finished. Have you been here long?" she asked, ripping her guitar out of its case.

"Only about six hours," I said as I started packing my stuff up. I could've stayed and practiced longer, but the guilt trip would be much more effective if we didn't practice at all.

"I'm so sorry, but I was rehearsing with Afreaka! this morning and we just got caught up in this great groove, and before I knew it, it was dark out!" Her voice had an ethereal tone to it, like she'd just Afreaka!ed her way to enlightenment.

"Well, I worked all day without you. Wrote a new song."

"That's awesome! Let's hear it!" She was oblivious to my packing up. I'd have to help her out.

"Actually, I'm pretty spent. I've been here all day. I'm leaving." In reality, I was dying to play her my new song. It rocked! But I had to suffer for the good of the band.

"Oh, okay." She looked kind of hurt and started packing her guitar up too. "I'll get it together, Jenny. I swear. It's just with my job and all this practicing, it's getting kind of hectic."

"Maybe you're doing too much. Maybe you don't have time to be in a band." I knew it was safe to suggest this. The second we got onstage the other night she'd been totally hooked. I just wanted to fling my power around a little.

"No way. I can do this. It won't happen again. Scout's honor."

As usual, I felt like the schoolmarm to Lucy's juvenile delinquent. But they're roles we're both used to, and as long as neither one of us goes too far in either direction, everything will work out fine.

I hope.

Rodney, Matt, and I had a little band meeting before practice the other night. Lucy wasn't there because she had to get fitted for her Afreaka! costume. She's a good enough player to jump right in, but I'm definitely worried about her flaking capabilities. She swore up and down—again—that she could make it work, but she's getting harder and harder to pin down. Unfortunately, Matt offered to pick up the slack.

"I've got a million songs just waiting to bust out. They're all safely locked away right here," he said, tapping his head with his beef jerky. "When these babies are let loose, the world won't know what hit it!"

"I don't know, Matt, let's just see how it goes for a while. I think I can handle it by myself," I said. Was he high? Did he think I'd quit my cushy job so I could play songs about cheap beer and chasing tail? He got all pouty, so I ran out and spent ten bucks that I didn't have on a twelve-pack. It got him off my back. For a while anyway.

NOTE TO SELF:
Add "Childcare Professional" to my résumé.

NOTES FROM BAND MEETING:
1) Rodney's mother thinks we're a bad influence. She found my towel obscene and thought the Opium Den was full of ex-cons. Surprise, surprise. She's also concerned because he got a 72 on his last social studies test. He's getting straight A's on bass, however, which is nothing to sniff at.

2) BABYSITTING DUTIES: Bake Rodney's mom a pie. Pick him up early for practice on Tuesdays and quiz him on social studies. See how brown my nose can get.

3) Matt's having issues with "Put That Thing Away." It makes him uncomfortable. He thinks it's antimale, not antipervert.

4) BABYSITTING DUTIES: Spend a day walking around in a skirt with Matt trailing me. Make him write down all the lewd comments flung at me by various men.

July 10

I spent a particularly nauseating afternoon ramming vegetables up the wazoos of Rock Cornish game hens. Finally I snapped and told my boss that I needed to find a new job. I told her that the hours were just too zooey, with my band and all. I didn't tell her that her livelihood sickened me or that I would eventually julienne Matt's spleen if forced to spend that much time with him.

I said I'd help out if she had a huge party to do (and totally count me in if you ever do the biker rally) but I really had to find something else. She was great about it. Said that, like her dad, she was a great supporter of the arts. Then she told me that as a matter of fact, the biker rally gig had come through and would be on August 23rd. We decided that would be my last day.

Rodney brought his social studies test to practice—we got a 91! He didn't say anything about how the pie went over.

July 11

Lucy and I finally locked ourselves away the other day and managed to crank out two whole songs: "Sucker Punch" and "Juicy." Arguably two of the most important rock anthems of our time. It reminded me why I love working with her so damn much. It got us up to a hefty eight songs, just in time for our second gig.

THE SET LIST:

- Livin' with a Junkie
- Gone Johnny Gone
- Put That Thing Away
- Drivin'
- Born to Marry
- Gettin' High off the Lows
- Sucker Punch
- Juicy

We played at this place called the Joint. It was your average sticky-floored stink pit, but the stage was awesome—it loomed so high above the crowd, it was impossible to not have a bit of a God complex. Which all good rock stars should have anyway. The only setback was I felt like everyone could look up my skirt.

NOTE TO SELF:

Make panties with band logo on them.

Abiogenesis was good technically but a little on the sterile side. Too much time spent practicing and not enough time spent facedown in the gutter. I'd rather see a band that lays a few eggs but really tears up the stage than a bunch of persnickety technical geniuses. But again, nicest guys on the planet and they just love us. Maybe they want some of our grime to rub off on them.

We went first. We played even better this time, ditched the crazy costumes, and got all dressed up instead. Rodney went to town on the glitter. I sure as hell hope his mother loves glitter. I feel like I need to get a note from her every time he wants to do something so I don't get in trouble. We got eight people to sign the mailing list, and I only fucked up twice.

The only major setback was Matt's little mating-call drumming wankfest. I swear, every time a pretty girl walked through the door, his hormones would grab the drumsticks and he'd suddenly start playing like everybody was there just to see him. It was unbelievable. It sounded like we had eighty-five drummers. And the worst part was, the chicks dug it! He was swarmed.

We're never gonna get him to play like a normal drummer again.

Afterward, Rodney was immediately swept off by his mother. I made a disgusting show of reminding him to be on time for our tutoring sessions and thanked Mrs. Nitzer profusely for producing such a talented son. As usual, I was treated like a pedophile.

THINGS LIKE THIS DON'T HAPPEN
TO PEOPLE LIKE ME

A TRUE STORY BY JENNY TROANNI

July 13

Neil Young played last night and my best friend, Katie, hooked my whole band up with tickets. She even had extras, which she handed out when we got there. She was like Mother Teresa. She said that the big mucky-mucks at the record company get all these great tickets that they swear they're going to use, but by the end of the workday they're so tired that all you have to do is make the rounds and gather them all up.

Work in the music industry so you can be too tired to participate in the music. Pathetic.

Neil was life-changing. Completely religious. We had great seats, and he played like a monster for well over three hours. We were in the Neil Vortex. Breathing his air. Smelling his sweat. Wondering if he's ever brushed his hair. His guitar was like a third lung or a second heart. Part of him, keeping him alive. I wept.

Afterward, we were all in a deep contemplative silence. Me, Lucy, Matt, Katie, and Katie's boyfriend, Chris. Rodney didn't come. ("Is Neil Young the guy who sings that 'Night Moves' song?")

Katie said she could get us backstage. Which she did, but there were like four layers of backstage, and we only made it to the second. Katie called it the corporate-wanker holding pen and wanted to get the fuck out of there. I wanted to stay and suck up to anyone who might be able to get me a record deal someday, but no way was I telling her that. When Lucy realized she couldn't seduce the security guard into letting us through to the next level, we left.

Then a miracle happened.

We headed over to Chinatown to get something to eat. As we were walking up to the restaurant, a bunch of hairy guys walked out and crammed themselves into a minivan. It was all a blur, like it happened in slow motion. They piled in and the last guy in said, "Hey Neil, you got something stuck to your hoof." Then the guy in the passenger seat opened his door and peeled a Chinese menu off his foot.

It was Mr. Neil Young himself.

He winked at me.

And closed the door. They drove off.

I don't know how long I stood there with my mouth open, but all I know is that minivan could have plowed right over me and I would have died a happy girl.

When I'm driving, sometimes I'll be coming up to a green light and think, If that light turns yellow before I get to it, my band will be huge.

Or, If I download my e-mail before my cat climbs on my lap, I'll find the perfect new job.

And now, due to the fact that the phone rang before my toast popped up, Matt will quit the band before we have to kick him out.

Matt showed up to gig number three with a portable platform for his drum kit. Now he could loom high above the rest of the band like the God of Thunder. He also formed a ring of candles around his space and did five minutes of shirtless, pornographic stretches before straddling his drum stool. And once again it was Matt Mania, a Super Drum Spectacular to Drive the Ladies Wild! To add to his appeal, he got fully loaded and broke out his fire-breathing act, which, like driving, is a trick for the sober only. He swallowed by accident and nearly vomited all over his kit. Things got a little chilly after the gig.

ME: What was that?

DR. RHYTHM: What the hell is that supposed to mean?

ME: Matt! Come on! We talked about this.

DR. RHYTHM: What the hell are you talking about? You think I overdid it again? I think I was huge! The crowd loved it! You're just pissed I took away your spotlight.

LUCY: You were pretty heavy-handed, Matt. That's not the way we play the songs in practice.

DR. RHYTHM: Improvisation, hello?

ME: Forty-five-minute drum solo, hello?

DR. RHYTHM: Control freak, hello?

LUCY: How would you feel if I just wanked away on the guitar all night without even caring how the song is supposed to go?

DR. RHYTHM: I am so sick of you two ganging up on me. I really fucking am!

At my lesson the other day, Flowers reamed me for not practicing. He said I was a great player but that everyone had room to grow.

"Including you, buttnugget, but apparently you're just showing up for makeup tips and free food."

He'd just baked an awesome pan of cornbread and was cutting it up at his kitchen table. He was wearing a skirt and some flip-flops, which at this point in our friendship seemed perfectly normal.

"Any other student I would have dragged to the curb long ago for wasting my time like this. You're lucky I love you." He tossed some bread on my plate and plopped down in his chair.

"You do? You love me?" I threw my arms around him, attempting to avoid my verbal spanking. He wasn't fooled.

"You either take it seriously or take it somewhere else, girl. I mean it." He crossed his legs and raised his eyebrows, waiting expectantly for my lame excuse. I felt like it was 2 A.M. and Mom had just caught me climbing through my bedroom window, stoned out of my mind.

"I'm so busy making fliers and writing songs and babysitting my . . ."

July 19

"Tell it to the hand," he said, shoving his palm in my face.

"But Flow—"

"Tell it to the other hand," he said, shoving his other palm in my face. He did it over and over, turning it into a dance move. He was infuriating! But he was fucking right. I should practice. This is what I want to do with my life, so I should be as good as possible.

"Fine. You're totally right. Now knock it off." I bit into a piece of cornbread and pouted. "It's just that every time I sit down to practice, I start freaking out about booking gigs or dyeing my roots or something. I have so much on my mind, and I have the attention span of a grape," I complained.

He buttered some bread and stared at me. "What?" I asked. "I'm not kidding."

"I was looking at your roots, and they do need a touch-up," he said finally. "You should get Lucy to help you with promotion and stuff."

"Oh, right. I can barely get Lucy to remember she's in the damn band."

"Matt? Hmm, never mind. . . . How about Rodney? Couldn't he make band fliers in art class or something?" Flowers asked.

"I'll figure it out," I said, wanting to change the subject. The truth was, I wanted to do most of it. I loved the million different ways there were to be creative in a band. I just needed a crew of slaves to help me. But unfortunately I'd surrounded myself with the perfectly wrong people. I didn't want Matt's help, Rodney was child labor, and Lucy was physically incapable. I was doing my best to make peace with it all, but half the time I wanted to kill them. I realized it was either do it myself the

right way or toss it into the middle of the practice space and
see what everyone had to offer.

BRILLIANT OBSERVATION #10:
Being a control freak is exhausting.

Lucy said getting up at the crack of dawn to do construction is killing her. (I suspect the fact that there isn't anyone new
there for her to sleep with is killing her too.) She wasn't sure
how long she could hang in there.

"The other day I accidentally glued all the windows shut at this
new house we're doing," she said. We were sitting on her porch in
a rare moment of just hanging out. Me, Lucy, and pathetic,
crushed-out Henry, lounging around on dirty white plastic chairs
circling a flipped-over bucket. "I was supposed to be spackling
the cracks and I was so tired, I just spackled everything in my
path. It's amazing anyone there still has an ass crack left!" she
said, screaming with laughter and spilling her margarita all over
the porch. "Shit. I was really looking forward to drinking that too."

"I'd rather be glue-happy than staring at Matt all day while
fondling vegetables. I may never recover," I complained.

Lucy shook her head. "I don't know how you do it. That guy is
out of control. We should just lock him in a room made of mirrors
and throw away the key. Just think how happy everyone would be!"

"No kidding." We were both silent. We had an agreement
that today we weren't going to talk about anything band-related
because it was taking over our entire friendship. Even though I
was partly there on covert band business. I needed to endear

July 28

myself to her so she'd realize that her project with me was the most important out of all her eight million others. I figured some good hang sessions interspersed here and there would be just the thing. I didn't even object to having Henry there, drooling away in the corner. Besides, he'd been locked up designing screen savers since that fateful night at my mom's house, so I was kind of glad to see him. Even if he was acting like a baboon.

Lucy got up. "Okay, so who else wants another margarita?" she asked us.

"I can make them," Henry offered.

"I'm going inside anyway, it's no biggie," Lucy said.

"No, I don't mind," Henry said, fumbling for the door. "I make a paralyzing margarita. You have to try it."

"Since when?" I asked. Henry is a lot of things. Two things he is not are 1) cool and 2) a person who uses the word *paralyzing* to describe a guitar solo, a recently surfed wave, or a drink.

"I have a few tricks up my sleeve, little missy, just you wait," said The Alien, rolling up his sleeves and sauntering into the house. It was then that I noticed his tattoo for the first time. No doubt the main reason for the aforementioned rolling up of the sleeves.

"Hold on a second there, cowboy," I said. "Let me see that arm."

Henry stopped and strolled casually over to me. I grabbed his arm and studied the black-and-red inked depiction of Rodin's *Thinker* on his forearm. It was real!

"What the . . . these things don't wash off, you know," I said, practically speechless. He pulled his arm away.

"I didn't ask for your opinion, thank you very much," he said, annoyed.

"It's just that you've always said tattoos were for rednecks and prisoners. I'm just surprised, that's all."

"I think it kicks ass," Lucy said. "Now go paralyze me. I'm dying of thirst." She winked at Henry, plopping down in her chair.

When he was inside I asked her, "Did you know he was getting that?"

"Of course. How do you think he knew where to go? I took him to see my guy around the corner."

"You took him? Well, that explains it."

"Explains what?" she asked, defensively.

"He'd never get one of those things. No offense, but he thinks they're trashy and he's a germophobe. The whole process grosses him out completely."

"Well, our little germophobe ain't what he used to be," she purred, and the truth fell out of the sky like a giant birdshit right onto my head.

Henry was Lucy's latest boy-toy.

I felt sick.

"So how long has it been going on?" I asked, ever so casually.

"About a week," she answered, ever so casually.

"He's liked you for a long time."

"He's got good taste."

"Don't break his heart."

"Don't bust my balls," she whispered as Henry came back carrying three paralyzing margaritas. I suddenly noticed he'd gotten his ear pierced too. It was bad enough that Lucy was going to chew him up and spit him out, but I couldn't believe she was going to permanently scar his body while she was at it. A new Lucy Mantra, "I love my band," repeated itself over and over in my head, preventing me from flipping her over the porch railing.

"You guys are too fucking much," was all I could say, taking my margarita from the newly badass Henry and sucking it down.

She has no conscience. He has no brain. They are a match made in Stupidville.

July 31

Because the world is full of many miracles, I've picked up some tutoring gigs through Rodney's friends at school. How funny is that? I wonder if any of them need help mowing the lawn. None of them start until September, though, so I went to my favorite outdoor adventure supply place, The Great Outdoors, to fill out a job application. A minimum-wage job at a maximum-danger store (I could spend every single paycheck without ever leaving work). Plus it's close to my house, and since I never have time to go camping anymore, at least it'll put me in contact with people who do.

Afterward, I went to Kinko's to print up a bunch of fliers for our gig next week and made perhaps the most important connection of a musician's career: A devoted Kinko's employee. Tami, age twenty-one, size three, two eyebrow piercings, no hair, all business. Her shaved head and tiny, action-packed body got my job done in a blurred twenty seconds. She was like a bullet. She said she'd gone to our show at the Joint and claimed it was the best she'd seen in weeks. "Dude, you guys kicked so much fucking ass! You need anything, anything at all, you come right here to me." Then she charged me two cents for seven hundred fliers and told me she has a friend who makes killer T-shirts if I was interested, which I was, very. She said she was on the mailing list and would totally be at our next show. She gave me her phone number on a new pad of paper and told me to keep the whole thing because I rock.

Everything's moving so quickly, I barely have time to write, but I realize that I absolutely have to because we really are going to be huge. I can feel it. Plus Lucy read my tarot, which confirmed it as fact. She said I have incredibly strong psychic energy. I get that a lot. She also said I'm going to meet one of the big loves of my life soon and said it would be a good idea to get my eyebrows waxed. What the hell? Was that in my cards too? What is it with chicks and eyebrows? Does the fact that I don't give a shit what they look like mean I have low estrogen levels?

Now that the cat's out of the bag, Henry and Lucy hold hands and snuggle in front of me. It's truly revolting, but I've decided that Henry's on his own. He's known her as long as I have, and if he wants to toss his heart into the meat grinder, that's his business. I still think Lucy's totally irresponsible for toying with someone she knows is that crazy about her, but she can't be stopped. He even picked her up at practice the other day in leather pants and a freshly grown goatee. It's like watching your favorite stuffed animal trying to be cool. It makes no sense.

We've played five gigs in seven weeks. We have a real following! I finally let Carla and John come the other night when we played the Gig in Hollywood. It's the only place we've ever played that doesn't have gang graffiti all over the front door, backed up toilets, or toothless regulars nodding off to sleep at the bar. Carla and John hovered by the corner of the stage, completely incredulous and totally out of place. They, unlike the rest of the crowd, own and use an iron and were the original owners of the clothes they were wearing. They were "dressed down," in creased new jeans and cotton sweaters, surrounded by freaks in fake fur coats and ripped T-shirts. They were the J. Crew. Every time I looked down, Carla's mouth was open and John was clapping his hands.

"You guys are like, a real band!" Carla gushed, hugging me after I got offstage.

"What were you expecting?" I asked. "Magic tricks?"

"I mean, you really know what you're doing! It's like watching someone I don't even know, like a famous person or something!" Carla squealed.

"Yeah. You guys really groove," the ever-hip John added. They were so cute, but it made me kind of nervous having them there. Like I had to take care of them somehow. So I was pretty glad when John tapped his watch and said, "Time to make like a tree and leave!"

The Matt situation is sucking harder every day. We're just going through the motions at this point. I'm just hanging on because I can't bear to sound the Cattle Call for Crazies again and put in another musician-wanted ad. Plus Matt knows all the songs, and we want to go into the studio soon. I keep hoping he'll quit, but he doesn't. Probably solely because he knows I want him to.

He went out and bought a little strobe light that he points at himself while onstage. He got a tattoo of a thundercloud with two drumstick-shaped lightning bolts coming out of it. He's calmed down the stage antics but constantly shows up late for practice and disagrees with everything Lucy and I say. No matter what.

On the domestic front, I'm one PTA meeting away from officially being Rodney's mother. I picked him and his friends up from a movie the other day, gave him a haircut, and helped him with a paper on Paul Revere. His biological mother tried to get me to take him shoe shopping but I had to draw the line. I'm getting fully taken advantage of, and I know it. I just don't know if I can reverse the situation without losing my little boy.

I spent my entire birthday practicing my guitar. I did not pass go. I did not collect two hundred dollars. All I did was play.

August 7

I'm starting to get the songs ready for our CD even though the band is far from stable at this point. There is tons to do while waiting for the glue to dry or the bottom to drop out:

1) Find decent studio with 24-track analog setup that doesn't sound cheap but is.
2) Dissect songs and write harmonies, extra guitar parts, etc. Think about effects and cool instruments to stick in there.
3) Practice songs for CD. Practice until you can't practice anymore, and then go practice for another hour.

I went over to Katie's today to help her pack up her house. She bought a place up in the Hollywood Hills and asked me to

August 10

help her get ready for the big move. My brown little nose jumped at the chance.

"Can you fucking believe all this shit? Moving so sucks my ass!" she moaned, throwing thousand-dollar sweater after thousand-dollar sweater out of her closet and into a heap on the floor.

"Just remember that it'll all be over in, like, a week. And then you'll be living in your stylee new house," I attempted, knowing full well that tossing a positive comment at a negative person is nothing less than an out-and-out act of aggression. Like throwing water on a witch. But I'd been there all morning and couldn't take it anymore. Her new swimming pool was bigger than my apartment, and she expected me to feel sorry for her!

"That's easy for you to say. I have to live with this hell morning, noon, and night! You have *no* idea what it's like."

I just sat there, under a pile of sweaters and complaints, nodding and agreeing like the big fat phony that I am. During a rare break in her rant (she nearly choked to death while trying to talk and swallow a peanut at the same time), I casually mentioned that I'd started a band.

"Really?" She paused and was uncharacteristically silent. "Hmm."

"What?" She was actually kind of spooky when she was quiet.

"Well, I was just thinking, if you'd told me that a couple years ago, before I got this butt-ass job, I would've thought it was the greatest thing. But now that I work in the record industry, I think you're nuts. How fucking sad is that?"

"I don't really want to hear it, Katie," I begged. At the ripe old age of twenty-nine, it was slippery enough convincing myself I wasn't acting like a complete idiot. Hearing Katie confirm all my suspicions was way more than I could handle.

"I'll tell you right now you have a snowball's chance in fucking hell of ever making it. The system is so fucked. I spend all day watching musicians get reamed. That's my goddamn job. Nice fucking life, huh?"

"You should come check us out. Lucy's playing guitar. And that guy Matt that we took to Neil Young is our drummer," I said, ignoring her, determined to remain calm.

"Well, that explains that at least. I wondered what the hell you were hanging out with that butthose for. If he looked at my fucking tits one more time, I swear I was gonna punch him."

"I know. He's got kind of a problem." From there I managed to make the segue from Matt to men in general, a topic I knew she could chew on for the rest of the day, forgetting all talk of how hopeless my band was.

THE UGLY TRUTHS ABOUT KATIE:
1) She has not one fun bone left in her body.
2) She has terrible (though expensive) taste in clothes.
3) I don't like her.
4) I don't want to hang out with her anymore.
5) I really need her to help me get a record deal.

I stopped in at Kinko's today and picked up a huge box of posters (that little Tami helped me design), a thousand stickers (that Tami also helped me design), and a couple of notebooks (that Tami stole for me).

GIFT IDEAS FOR TAMI:

1) A case of Miller Genuine Draft
2) A gift certificate to Disco Bowling
3) A goldfish, complete with bowl and castle
4) A piñata full of wax lips
5) One of those plants that eats bugs

Then I headed over to Flowers' for my lesson. I asked him if he thought I needed to wax my eyebrows, and the look of relief on his face confirmed my suspicions: I've been an ape my entire postpubescent life without realizing it. He silently helped me into the bathroom and fired up some bubbling wax contraption that did not look like fun.

He went at it like a true artist. Very earnest and concentrated, while I sneezed a hole through the wall. The end result proved I had bigger eyes than I'd thought. He said he was going to stuff some pillows with all the hair. He was so funny I forgot to laugh.

Both Katie and Lucy noticed it the second I saw them. Girls are annoying.

We're officially part of the music scene around here. I'm blown away by how supportive other bands are. Everyone helps each other load and unload and tells you if your snarl looks real and stuff.

We've bonded with this band called The Meek. We've been gigging with them a lot and have sort of tried to wean ourselves away from Abiogenesis. Not an easy task, but somehow an eerily familiar one.

ME: Um, this isn't really working for us anymore.

THEM: What isn't?

ME: Us. I mean, we really like you, but we just don't feel like it's
        going anywhere.
THEM: Where do you want it to go?
ME: Well, we guess we don't want it to go anywhere. We don't feel
        like we're the right band for you.
THEM: Oh. And when did you discover this?
ME: We don't know. It's been building for a while.

*Five-hundred-hour pause. I panic. Am I really going to sit here and hurt
these dear sweet people? More importantly, am I really going to voluntarily
fuck up my only friendship with someone who works at a music supply store?*
THEM: Well, if that's the way you feel, that's the way you feel. What
        can we say?
*I manage a weak smile and give them an awkward hug before stum-
bling out the door.*

The Meek, on the other hand, are much more our speed.
Great songwriters, a gigantic sound, and severe drinking
problems. Three guys and one chick. We play together a lot
and act as each other's guitar techs and beer-runners and
stuff. I have a crush on all of them. Especially Pete, the lead
guitarist. Hellishly sexy and, God help me, he has a lisp. It's
the one I like to call the Chuh Lisp. The tongue becomes
rounded against the back of the front teeth in the presence of
an *s* or a *ch*, producing a slight shushing sound. Only a
refined few can execute it without showering their audience
with spit, but when it's done correctly, as Pete does it, it's my
personal favorite. The King of Lisps. I'm a goner. It's my
biggest turn-on ever. Aside from nice arms. Which he has too.
As well as a girlfriend. Oh well.

At their last gig, he mentioned that his cousin Scott just moved to town and is looking for a band.

"He'sh an aweshome drummer. You should kick out that little wanker guy you have," he said, making me feel like a giant loser for having him in the band in the first place.

"Believe me, we're seriously considering it," I said, genuinely interested in his cousin for reasons beyond the added contact with Pete. "Can you give him our demo?"

"No prob. He'sh living with me. I'll tell him how hot you guysh are too," he said winking.

How perfect! A great new drummer and a real live excuse to go to Pete's house on a regular basis. Now I just had to figure out how to get rid of the Evil Elf.

THE MATT BRODY TUTORIAL FOR HOW TO BE AN OBNOXIOUS DRUMMER:

August 14

The chip on Matt's shoulder is now the size of Texas, and his new M.O. is silence and moping. A major improvement, if you ask me, but wildly unpleasant all the same. He refuses to talk about it because he thinks I'm a control freak and Lucy is manipulative. I told Lucy about Pete's cousin, and we finally suggested to Matt that maybe he should find another band. But he said no way! He refuses to leave! He's convinced we're gonna hit it big, so he's not budging. But most importantly, he knows I want him out.

I swear he'd set himself on fire if he thought I didn't want him to.

In the meantime, he's going to martyr us to death, be an ass onstage, and glare at me every time I explain a new song to him. It got so tense, I thought Rodney was going to cry at practice the other day.

FIVE WAYS TO KICK YOUR DRUMMER OUT OF THE BAND WHEN HE REFUSES TO LEAVE:

1) Take his drums from the practice space and show up at his door early Sunday morning when you know he's home. Leave them on his doorstep, ring the bell, run away. Change locks at the practice space.

2) Get him a girlfriend. Suddenly nothing else will matter.

3) Find a new practice space and don't tell him where it is.

4) Write ten new songs about immature, dickhead drummers who never get laid and own the entire Ace of Base catalogue. Title each song "Fuck You, Matt."

5) Book gigs on Must-See TV nights. His priorities will take care of the rest.

NOTE TO SELF:

You do not need a new sleeping bag at the employee discount price. You need to make a CD.

August 18

I had my third day of work at The Great Outdoors today, and so far it's pretty great. I get to help all these studly guys try on hiking boots, and I don't leave work smelling like a chicken fajita anymore.

I think my manager, Brad, has a crush on me. He's actually kind of cute, but he's a vegan. I know it's supposed to be healthy, but I swear I have yet to meet a vegan who isn't yellow and doesn't smell like the elderly. He's taking me kayaking soon.

Lucy, Rodney, and I had a covert band meeting. Very high school and cliquey, I know, but Matt left us no choice. We've decided to go with option number one and leave his drums outside his door after we work the biker rally together.

Why is it that I always notice a person's strong points right when I'm about to do something mean to him? Suddenly I'm sad remembering the time Matt made me laugh so hard in the 7-Eleven that I wet my pants.

I should have known when I pulled up to my house and my car blew a radiator tube, spraying water and antifreeze all over the street, that I was in for a night of complete catastrophe. We had a gig at yet another loud and sticky place called the Garage with The Meek and this other band called Life in a Blender. I called Henry for a ride (Lucy had an Afreaka! performance and was barely going to make it on time as it was), and he coldly told me he wasn't going.

Uh-oh. Trouble in Stupidville.

"Why not?" I felt obliged to ask. Did Lucy sleep with five of your best friends right in front of you or something?

"I'm not allowed," he said sarcastically. I wasn't touching this one with a ten-foot pole.

"Okay, well, thanks anyway. I have to run, but are you okay and everything?" I asked while silently begging him to let me off the hook. A heavy sigh answered me. Followed by sobs. *FuckIhaveagigtoplayhere!*

"Henry, shit, I have to go. I'll call you when I get home, okay?"

I heard only sniffles. "Okay?" I said again.

Finally, a muffled "Mmmm hmmm" made it through and I hung up. I couldn't think about the drama that awaited me, because I realized I was kind of screwed. I had no ride. I couldn't call Matt because he hated me, nobody in The Meek had a phone, Flowers had a date, and I didn't want to invite Katie until we'd replaced Matt.

That left me only one choice. Under normal circumstances, if I'd had to choose between my one choice and sticking live bumblebees up my nose, I'd have picked the bees in a second. But, sadly, these circumstances weren't normal.

Mrs. Nitzer came to pick me up for the gig about half an hour early. When she got to my house, she refused to risk either her or Rodney's life by coming inside and opted for leaning on the horn instead. I wasn't even close to ready, so I tossed a bunch of makeup in a bag and threw on my white flared hip-huggers and brown fur vest. Finally out the door, I had my guitar and bag over my shoulder and was bending over, wheeling my amp out to her car, when I noticed a strange breeze blowing across my chest. I'd neglected to button my vest, much the same way I'd neglected to put on a bra. Of course, I was bending over, so whatever meager amount of tit I had was boldly swaying back and forth, waving happily at Mrs. Nitzer's blue Oldsmobile Cutlass. She leaned on the horn again in a Code Red, and I dropped my makeup all over the street in a panicked attempt to button myself up. I fumbled around like the idiot pervert I was, scooped my stuff back into the bag, and loaded my equipment into the car.

"They say it's supposed to rain," a tight-lipped Mrs. Nitzer offered. Rodney couldn't even look at me. I climbed in and she peeled out before I even had the door closed.

"Really? It looked so clear today," I said in my best I-didn't-just-wag-my-hooters-at-you voice. "How are you doing, Rodney? Psyched to play?"

"Yeah. Always am," he mumbled. He rarely spoke over a mumble when in the presence of The Mother. Or recently exposed breasts.

"So what sort of God-forsaken place are you dragging us to this time, Jenny? I was certain I would perish at your last concert!" said The Mother, pulling a cigarette out of her purse and firing it up with a lighter shaped like a Harley Davidson. I looked at Rodney in surprise. He rolled his eyes.

"I didn't know you smoked," I said cautiously.

"I don't," she grated. "But current circumstances have driven me to do many things I wouldn't normally be caught dead doing, now haven't they?"

What could I say to that?

"Cool lighter," was all I could think of.

"What, this?" she asked, holding up her Hog. "I'll have you know I earned this. I spent the worst night of my life sitting next to the drunkest, most revolting man at one of your concerts, and I grabbed it when he got up and left it on the bar. Ha! He didn't dare suspect the old lady sitting next to him. Makes me happy every time I light up."

I wouldn't have believed it if I hadn't seen it with my own eyes. Mrs. Nitzer was getting an edge!

The gig ended up being a total nightmare. Lucy never showed up, so I decided we'd just play without her. Matt rose to the occasion by being a larger asshole than usual and decided to set his drums up in the front middle section of the stage. Where I usually stand.

"What are you doing, Matt?" I asked, acting more surprised than I was.

"I'm trying out a new concept. The drums are what drive

the band. People should be able to experience them fully," he said flatly, staring at me with his signature "Go ahead, I dare you" look. I didn't have the energy to argue with him, so I just shook my head and walked away. Rodney quietly moved his amp to the back of the stage, where Matt usually is, and I set up next to Rodney. I figured if we were going to suck, it was actually pretty perfect that Matt should be front and center.

And boy, did we suck. I attempted to switch back and forth between Lucy's guitar parts and mine, and Rodney tried his best to sing backup. Matt played everything too loud and too fast, and I pulled the plug after about five songs.

"That was fun," I said to Rodney as we were taking our stuff out to his mother's car.

"I had fun," Rodney said. "I thought it sounded cool. How come you stopped us in the middle?"

"You thought it sounded cool?"

"Yeah, it was different. I mean, I think it's better when we're all together, but I thought it sounded cool. I don't know, kind of sparse or something."

"Really." I'd been so busy being pissed off, it had never even occurred to me we could do anything but suck. But maybe Rodney was right.

BRILLIANT OBSERVATION #11:
Being cranky is a waste of time.

When I got home, I was treated to the following answering machine message from Lucy:

"Oh my God, Jenny, you wouldn't believe what happened to

me tonight! Baobab Wanabi, only the most celebrated tamutamu player in all of Swahili-speaking Africa, showed up at our Afreaka! show, was blown away by our act, and now not only wants to join, but he's going to get his record label to sponsor a world tour! I figured missing one Sixty-Foot Queenie gig to wiggle my way into his heart wouldn't kill us. Especially since I'm going to convince him to use us as the warm-up band. I'll call you tomorrow and give you the details. Don't be mad at me. It'll be so excellent! I promise. A world tour! Hee-heeeeee!"

Mad? Me? What surer guarantee of success is there for a rock band than latching onto an African improvisational ensemble? I was seriously beginning to wonder why I found Lucy so indispensable. I was so annoyed with her, I was actually looking forward to calling Henry and helping him get rid of her. I felt like it was something that maybe we all needed to do at this point.

I imagined the poor guy all puffy-eyed and consumed by self-loathing, attempting to scrape *The Thinker* off his arm with a Brillo pad. But when I called, the phone was picked up after about five rings, and I listened to a woman giggling in the background while the answerer struggled with the receiver. It dropped to the floor, causing both Lucy and Henry to burst out in a chorus of uncontrollable laughter.

I hung up and went to bed.

I woke up this morning to a delivery guy holding a bouquet of daisies and a gigantic Italian salami with a bow on it. The card read:

I'm an imbecile. I was drunk. I am so sorry I missed the gig. Please forgive me. I promise to

> remove my head from my asss and to never, ever
> put it up there again. —Lucy

I was beyond annoyed. If she hadn't cowritten half our songs and wasn't allegedly one of my best friends, I would have booted her out of the band right then and there, salami or no salami. It was finally undeniably clear to me that her head and her ass had way too much in common and would be whooping it up again in no time. But at the moment, I had to keep her. Matt was on the way out, and I couldn't picture traveling the country with just me, Rodney, and Mrs. Nitzer, the lighter thief.

August 21

I've been driving all over the place checking out recording studios and have finally narrowed it down to two places. One is a 24-track fancy home studio with great mics, tons of effects, and pretty decent soundproofing. The guy who runs it is a great engineer. His stuff sounds pretty professional but it's digital, not analog. Which sucks. Plus the studio smells kind of like a hot dog.

Then there's this guy Eddie's studio. Two-inch analog, great old equipment with tons of effects. It's more expensive, but it's analog! And his studio is cooler. And he has all these cats running around.

Why are decisions never simple? Why isn't anything? Nothing's ever just right—friends, lovers, studios. Even my flawless purple coat is a tiny bit too small.

August 22

I bumped into Pete from The Meek, the lisping guitar god of my dreams, at the Guitar Center today when I went in to get some new strings.

"Hey Jenny. I've been meaning to call you," he said, giving

me a kiss on the cheek that I'll never, ever wash off. He smelled like men's musk aftershave.

"Really?" I cleverly said. Break up with your girlfriend? Need a neck massage?

"Yeah, my coushin Shcott totally loved your tape."

"Really!" I cleverly said. "Thanks, Pete!"

"No problem." Huge pause. In a daze, I heard myself asking him how everything was going.

"The band shtuff ish cool, but, uh, I kind of broke up with my girlfriend. Which I guesh ish pretty cool too, huh?" he asked, and I swear I detected a slight smile.

Suddenly my playful little crush on Pete grew a set of horns and big hairy arms and began stomping all over the store. I began sweating like a pig and couldn't talk anymore.

CRUSH FACT #1:
If you have a crush on someone and then they break up with their significant other, you suddenly become legally intellectually handicapped.

This has always puzzled me. If, in fact, sex was invented for the purpose of procreation, it would seem to be in the best interest of the species if we were all at our shimmery best when faced with a possible mate. Witty, charming, and sexy, as opposed to accidentally spilling soda on our left boob (he pretended not to notice).

Then there's always the chilling possibility that maybe it is all about survival of the fittest, and I just don't make the cut. Maybe the preferred procreators don't have this problem and the plan is for morons like me to die out.

I told Lucy about it while we were writing some new songs, and she said I was probably right.

"He's a babe. So are you. Makes sense to me," she said. "Just make sure he wears a condom. No doubt his herd has drunk from many a watering hole."

Lucy and I practiced our asses off today. There's nothing like a serious guilt complex to make people show up on time and do whatever you tell them to. Lucy was a machine—we finished my new song, "Rib Eye," and she wrote a guitar solo that made me do a handstand. But no matter how much fun we had or how well she played the guitar behind her back, I still acted annoyed.

"So did you get my salami or what?" she finally asked, wondering how I could possibly still be mad. I mean, she'd given me a salami!

"Yeah. But Lucy, just because you know how to order a salami doesn't mean you're suddenly no longer a giant flake."

"I know, I know. I was just worried you didn't get it, that's all," she said all huffy, handing me a bunch of dates scribbled on the back of an old phone bill. "These are the dates I can't practice or play or anything. Just so you know."

"Shit, Lucy, why not just write down the dates you can make it. It would have saved you a ton of paper."

"Oh, please, spare me the drama. I'm dedicating a significantly larger portion of time to this band than I am to everything else. I have no idea how I'm going to do it all," she said, nearly collapsing under the great weight of her life.

"Oh, please, spare me the drama! What if there are more conflicts? Like if we have a gig when you're supposed to be getting a plate put in your lip? And what about when we go on tour?"

"I don't know, Jenny. How about I'll worry about that when I have to, okay?"

"How about this isn't only about you, okay?"

"How about you have a giant pole up your ass, okay?"

It suddenly occurred to me that ever since we've been playing together, we haven't been getting along. I've been trying to get her to commit the whole time, which is like trying to herd mosquitoes or something. But what could I do?

"Fine," I said, "but if you fuck up again, I'm going to rip that pole out of my ass and beat you with it." She thought that was the funniest thing she'd ever heard.

I didn't laugh at all.

August 23

Oh my God, I cannot believe I've never been to a biker rally before!

It was exhausting and filthy but totally worth it. I made three hundred bucks and met a buttload of great people. My new favorite Kinko's employee, Tami, showed up with some friends. They rode in on Big Wheels, wearing swimming goggles. I didn't even know they made Big Wheels anymore.

Tami brought a stack of fliers for our upcoming gigs and shoved them in everyone's face. She hung posters of us on every tree until she got in trouble and ran around taking pictures and getting plowed. At some point she got thrown from the mechanical bull ride and twisted her ankle, so one of her friends tied a rope to one of the Big Wheels and pulled her around for the rest of the day.

The people were amazing. Everyone from Harley dudes to little old ladies on their Gold Wings. People retire and ride around on these bikes the size of Winnebagos. I had no idea. They have little walkie-talkies built into their helmets so grandpa can talk to his bitch on the back. I didn't have much time to talk to as many people as I wanted because I was so busy with the ribs and pulled pork.

Handling meat in slabs the size of a couch is the best way to launch a vegetarian lifestyle. And end a food service one.

And the pig roast. Disgusting. Humans are barbaric, primal, flesh-devouring grunt machines. Matt had to man that post. Because I am attempting to not say bad things about people anymore, I won't mention how smug that made me feel.

We were so busy, it was no big deal being around him for twelve straight hours. It felt weird knowing the axe was about to fall on him. I felt like a liar. Luckily, he wasn't fun or sweet or anything. I don't think I could have handled that.

I gave the Harley vendor a free turkey leg, and he gave me an excellent tank top.

When I finally got to take a break, I went over to the fiesta tent and watched Whiskey Blood southern-rock the crowd. They kicked ass. Dueling lead guitar solos and huge mustaches all around. People were fully hammered by the time I joined the party. Some big, bearded freak pointed at me and yelled, "The Meat Mistress!" and let out a huge burp. He then felt compelled to give me a big, stinky hug and smack me on the back with ten "only kiddings."

NOTE TO SELF:

Do not feed the animals.

Matt appeared beside me at some point, and we watched the band in silence. One of those hot, bloated silences. Brutal. Finally he turned to me and said, "I found another band. I have no idea why I thought you guys were so good. I'll have my shit out by tomorrow."

And that was that.

NOTE TO SELF:

Real artists don't have nice new tents. Also, I have perfectly good hiking boots.

August 27

Kayaking is so much fun! And even if you have weak-ass spindly little arms like me, you can be a monster. My manager, Brad, took me to Lake Arrowhead with two kayaks strapped to the top of his van. We made a huge picnic lunch and had a blast. He definitely has a crush on me, though. Feast or famine, man!

But there's no way. We work together, he's yellow, and he wears a Speedo! No can do. Yo no Speedo. It wins in my book for shock and obscenity value (with the tube top trailing behind at a very distant second). Also known as a nuthugger, banana hammock, or weenie wrapper. It roams wild, terrifying innocent women and children on beaches everywhere.

Poor Brad. Trying to woo me with his goods when I can barely look at him without running.

I learned he is only working this job while he's going to school to be a marine biologist. He thinks the underwater world is just like going through the looking glass. He stole my damn analogy! We agreed how ironic it was that the desert and the sea have so much in common. He said he'd take me scuba diving. I didn't say I'd take him to my sacred desert spots. I felt bad, but I just didn't want to. Then I realized something.

I have a new Sucker.

Lucy and I went to see the Meek play last night at Al's Bar. The giant wedge that's fallen between us is always temporarily lifted whenever we're playing or watching someone else play. Music calms the savage beast. So do five shots of tequila each.

I love Al's. It's a proud and true skankhole in the most terrifyingly shitty downtown neighborhood imaginable. The sound guy there is really nice too. He's from Canada and has one of those voices in perpetual puberty. Cracks and soars constantly. He's always reading some philosophy book and is a staunch advocate of earplugs. Reads me the riot act every time I show up plugless. "You can't get your hearing back. You absolutely cannot. Like piss down a drain." I know he's right. But earplugs are about as much fun as condoms.

The Meek were huge, as usual. Lucy and I went up to sing backup, and Pete did everything just short of humping me right there onstage. At one point he just put me in a liplock right in the middle of his guitar solo. Which inspired a drunken Lucy to do the same thing to Lynn, their lead singer, and Stuart, the drummer. She just hates to be left out.

It was a pretty wild night all around. By the time we all got offstage, it was obvious that Pete and I were going to hook up and that Lucy was on her way home with Lynn and Stuart.

"You two make me spin! How am I ever going to get to sleep tonight?" Lucy growled at them, putting a hand on each

August 29

of their chests. Stuart grinned, and Lynn stuck Lucy's fingers in her mouth. That was the last I saw of any of them. I was busy helping Pete load up the van and embarking on my own Meek adventure. Mine just took a little longer, but finally Pete shyly asked if he could stop by my place after they unloaded, which he could, and he did, and it was great!

NOTE TO SELF:
Friends make better lovers than strangers. Period.

He's an expert kisser and has a butt that should be polished and kept on a shelf like the trophy it is. We laughed our asses off and, as Bob Seger would say, worked on our Night Moves. Just rough enough to be exciting, and just soft enough to break a heart. And boy, did I need it. I said good-bye to him after a great breakfast at the Crest Diner. I love the way he wears his shirts inside out. And I swear his little lisp is devastating.

When I got back, Lucy called demanding the details. I told her everything, still riding the high even though my hangover was threatening to inform my greasy breakfast that it was no longer welcome in my stomach. In exchange, I heard all about her sordid evening.

"It was outrageous!" she concluded. "We didn't get even a second of sleep. Actually, I'm still at Lynn's house," she giggled. "I just took a time out to call you. We were all dying of curiosity."

"Well, now you know," I said, suddenly unamused now that the obvious had been confirmed in detail. "I know it's none of my business, Lucy, but what about Henry?"

"What about him? He knows how I am. Wait, what?" I heard

someone—Lynn, I guessed—saying something in the background. "Oh, okay. I've got to go. The delivery guy's here." Delivering what? A whip-o-gram? Another crate of condoms? "I'll talk to you later. Congratulations, stud!" she said, hanging up.

About two seconds later the phone rang again. I assumed it was her. "No, I can't swing by with some lube," I answered.

It was Henry. "Jenny?"

"Hold on. I'll go get her," I said, knowing full well he knew it was me. "Yes, hello?" I said in a high little voice, attempting to confuse my way out of an explanation.

"Hello? Freak? What's your deal?"

"My deal is that I'm so hung over, I feel like I have squirrels running around between my ears. Loud, crazy ones."

"It sure sounds that way. Hey, I was wondering if we could hang out soon. I feel like I haven't seen you in a million years," he said.

Perhaps because you haven't, Dumbo, I thought. You've been too busy starring in *The Lucy Show*. "Yeah, sure," I said, my compassion for him immediately replaced by irritation.

"How about tomorrow night?"

We made a plan to have dinner even though I was highly annoyed by the fact that I've been put in a really shitty spot. It was obvious from the tone in his voice that he has no idea Lucy just bedded half a band. I decided that if he asks, I won't lie. If he cries, I won't coddle. If he's totally clueless, I won't be at all surprised.

I spent an annoying evening learning all about the wonderful world of automotive fuel pumps. Apparently, if you can't park your 1987 Honda Civic facing uphill, chances are very good that your fuel pump is on the fritz. And if you're driving up

August 30

Laurel Canyon in rush hour traffic and your car jerks to a violent halt, causing some asshole in a black Bronco to lean on his horn for five minutes as if the mighty force of his honking will blow you to the top of the hill, your fuel pump is definitely dead.

I somehow managed to get the car over to the shoulder, backward, and coast it all the way down to the bottom of the hill. I borrowed the cell phone of some nice woman who stopped in her huge SUV when she saw me looking under the hood (for what, instructions?). Her four kids stared at me through the window, fascinated, like they were at the zoo, while I called Henry. We had plans, and he had Triple A.

"Hey, it's me. Are we still on for tonight?" I casually asked.

"Yeah, definitely. That'd be great. What do you feel like doing?"

"I feel like having you come get me and take me to a garage, okay? My car broke down on the valley side of Laurel Canyon. I'm at the bottom of the hill."

"Oh no. I'll call a tow truck. I'll be right there."

I handed the phone back to the woman, who then offered me a granola bar.

"I keep them in the car. In case of emergencies," she explained with a wink. I took it and thanked her and assured her she didn't need to wait with me.

BRILLIANT OBSERVATION #12:
Other people's mothers are the best.

Henry showed up about a half an hour later in brightly striped hipster pants, biker boots, and a Foo Fighters tour T-shirt. (I'd convinced him once that the Foo Fighters were the scrubbing bubbles in a bathroom-cleaning product. He'd believed me for months, and now he was wearing their T-shirt like they were *his* band, man.) He looked so out of character that it actually woke me from my auto-misery long enough to realize he was a lot farther gone than I'd feared.

"Hey, Coolio, what's up?" I asked, half expecting him to speak with a British accent.

"Nothing. You okay?" he asked, joining me in my search under the hood.

"Yeah . . . are you?" I asked, subtly trying to sense if he knew how very wide open his relationship with Lucy was. He looked at me sideways. Perhaps because my definition of subtle was to put my hand on his shoulder and ask as if I'd just found out he had terminal cancer.

NOTE TO SELF:
There is a Subtlety Gene. I do not have it.

"Why?" he asked, suspiciously.

"I was just wondering how everything's going, that's all."

"All of a sudden, so am I. What exactly are you trying to tell me, Jenny?"

Just then, the tow truck pulled up, getting my car and my big fat mouth out of their respective jams. For a little while, anyway. I was soon to learn that I needed a $450 fuel pump and that Henry was just waiting until I'd downed a few beers before continuing his interrogation.

We were at the Coach and Horses in Hollywood, having free popcorn and cheap beer for dinner. "So what is it that you don't want to tell me?" he asked. He was still working on his first beer. I was on my third.

"No way, buddy. I don't have to tell you anything," I said, lunging for the popcorn bowl as he snatched it away and held it out of my reach.

"Tell me."

"Screw you!"

"Is it about Lucy?" he asked.

I said nothing. My face screamed, *Of course it is, you moron!*

"Is she seeing someone else?"

"Define 'seeing'. Henry, give me the popcorn."

He slowly put the bowl down on the bar and looked like he was going to cry.

"How could I have been such an idiot?" he said, shaking his head. "Jenny, I know it's not fair to involve you, but you have to tell me who it is."

"More like who *they* are," I said, unable to resist the urge to kick him when he was down. Part of me felt truly bad. Part of me felt like he needed to wake the hell up.

"I've got to go," he said suddenly, getting up and putting some money on the bar.

"Jeez Louise, calm down. Let me finish my beer," I said through a mouthful of popcorn. He just stood there and stared at me.

"Please, Jenny," he begged, audibly upset.

"Okay, okay," I said, downing the rest of my beer and following him out the door. We barely spoke the entire way home, and as badly as I felt for him, I was glad the stupid charade was finally over. He dropped me off at home and no doubt went straight to Lucy's. Lord only knows what he walked in on when he got there.

It finally happened. I was at work at my dopey, minimum-wage job in my stupid uniform and nametag, and one of my old clients came in to buy a sleeping bag. Lydia Strauss, senior VP of Hilba's Home Furnishings. Where comfort and style sit side by side. Hilba's Home Furnishings. Making your dollar go the extra mile. Whatever the room, whatever the size, your dreams will come true right before your eyes! Hilba's Home Furnishings (cheesy keyboard solo, music swells to the song's exciting climax). Comfort-comfort! Fashion-fashion! Sit side by (cheesy piano walk down to finale) siiiiiiiiiide!

I swear, that fucking jingle sticks in my head like a meat cleaver.

If I'd had to pick one person I wouldn't want to bump into at this particular junction in my life, she would have been it. Lydia is one of those tight-assed executives who hates everything and treats you like the hired help you are. I worked on her account for years, rewrote a thousand notes in her honor, missed many weekends and parties sitting in her overlit showroom from hell pretending to have a deep, profound understanding of dinette sets.

I'll never forget when she unexpectedly appeared in my office and saw the dartboard I'd made with her face on it. From then on in it was war, which sucked because she had all the power.

We locked eyes immediately and I pulled the lame, way-too-late, look-away-and-pretend-I-didn't-see-her maneuver. I thought about running into the back room, but I would have literally had to run, because she moved right in for the kill. She hates me as much as I hate her. She wasn't going to miss this prime humiliation opportunity.

LYDIA: Jenny Troanni!?

ME: Hello, Lydia.

MY BRAIN: I have sex with lead guitarists while you clean out your cat box on Saturday nights.

LYDIA: I thought that was you! What on earth are you doing here?!

For the first time in my life I pause, giving my body time to sprout its first-ever Quick Comeback Gene.

ME: Well, you know, it suddenly occurred to me that I'd like to do more with my life than write irritating jingles about tacky furniture for people like you.

MY BRAIN: I'm here for you, baby. I am right here.

LYDIA: So you left your job to realize your dream of working at a sporting goods store?

ME: It's an outdoor adventure supply company. Have you visited your Mother Nature lately? I have a band now. We're making a CD and going on tour.

I hand her a flier to our next gig.

LYDIA: I hope your songs are better than your jingles.

MY BRAIN: Concentrate. Keep your eye on the ball.

ME: You wouldn't know a good song if it crawled up your ass and died.

LYDIA: I'd like to speak to your manager, and then I'd like you to show me some sleeping bags.

ME: Actually, I'm about to go on break. I'll get the manager for
               you, Lydia.

Then me and my brain skipped off hand in hand to get my Sucker
and let him know that the woman who'd forced me to write love
songs to patio furniture for four years would like a word with him.

I'm blown away by the fact that seeing that C.U. Next
Tuesday made me feel great about my life. Reminded me how
hideous it once was and how free I feel now. In the old days, I
never would have been able to stick up to her like that. But I
suddenly realized I'd grown. I'd changed from a doormat into a
brick wall. It was one of the most exciting feelings I've ever had.

BRILLIANT OBSERVATION #13:
You're never more invincible than when you're doing the thing you love.

Rodney and I were tuning up in the practice space when
Lucy came bursting through the door like a herd of buffalo.

"Thanks for ratting me out, Jenny. Henry won't talk to me
anymore," she said, not wasting any time on pleasantries. She
was enormously pissed. He must have just confronted her.

"You told me he knew!" I answered in disbelief. Was she
actually trying to blame me?

"I said he knew how I was! I never said he knew!"

"Oh, please!" I looked at Rodney incredulously. He was bright
green and looked like he'd much rather be elsewhere. Anywhere.
Bleeding to death. "Besides, he asked me, Lucy. No way was I
going to lie to one of my best friends to cover your ass."

"It was going fine until you fucked it up."

"I fucked it up?" I stood there and stared at her until the

September 1

absurdity of her own words had time to sink into her thick skull. "If someone's in love with you, you can't just have a fling with them, Lucy! It always ends in disaster! That's *your* rule! It's as stupid as fucking someone in your band, remember?"

As this eloquent sentence was leaving my mouth, a figure appeared in the doorway—a tall, dark, devastatingly shaggy figure with a six-pack in one hand and a pair of drumsticks in the other. He had several undecipherable tattoos crawling up his sculpted arms and an irresistible head of moppish brown hair that looked like it had been styled by a tornado. His huge dark eyes locked with mine and he smiled, revealing a space between his front teeth that I could crawl into and live happily ever after.

WARNING! DANGER!

I tried to speak and suddenly realized that my mouth was hanging wide open. I closed it and swallowed.

"You must be Pete's cousin, Scott," I croaked. "The drummer."

He held up his sticks and nodded. "Is this a bad time?" he shyly asked, delivering the knockout punch with one of the deepest, sexiest voices I've ever heard.

"No!" Lucy and I said at the same time, in the same stupor, our argument suddenly dispersing into weightless, glimmering, heart-shaped little particles.

"Cool. My cuz gave me your tape, and I was totally blown away!"

He loaded his drums in—one of those small kits with only one tom and a couple cymbals that he made sound huge. He knew all the songs, and he and Rodney locked in instantly. I've never been jealous of Lucy's playing, but tonight I wanted to slightly break just one or two of her fingers to slow her down a bit. She kept bending over a lot, and I swear she must have licked her lips eighty-five times. I felt hopeless. I was no match for The Master. Lucy could make a bowling pin fall in love with her if she felt like it.

Scott stood up and stretched at the end of our set. He looked around the room and said, "Wow." He shook Rodney's hand and said to Lucy, "You can really tear it up, sister." Rodney high-fived him and turned to me with a big, wide, grin.

"That was insane! I've never ever locked in with anyone like that, ever!" he said, searching my face hopefully with that "Can I keep him, Mom, huh, can I keep him?" puppy-dog look.

Since I was now the undisputed leader of the band, I stretched out my hand to Scott and sealed the deal.

"Welcome to Sixty-Foot Queenie. That is, if you'll have us," I said.

He shook my hand and replied, "Yeah, baby, I'll have you."

THIS VERY MOMENT MARKS THE FIRST TIME SCOTT AND I EVER TOUCHED, AND I'D JUST LIKE TO NOTE IT SO THE HISTORY BOOKS CAN REFER TO IT FOR THEIR SECTION ON THE MOST INFLUENTIAL ROCK-AND-ROLL COUPLES TO EVER WALK THIS EARTH.

Band lineup number three. Ladies and gentlemen, fasten your seat belts.

Dear old Dad flew into town for some sort of botanist convention. We of course recognized this as a front—his alien leaders needed to update his mission and find out what he's been talking to the plants about. Dad showed up late in his usual bumbling style, tripping up to the bar at El Coyote, where Carla, John, and I waited with horrible margaritas in our hands. I got his height but was luckily spared his equilibrium issues. "Faulty inner ear," he claimed, even though I knew it was his general obliviousness to the world around him. I mean, can we blame the fact that he's forgotten my birthday every single year on his faulty inner ear too?

Every time he came in from New York, he wanted to eat at El Coyote. Which meant that every time he left, I felt riddled with heartburn.

"Do you want to know the only thing I miss about California?" he'd ask excitedly, as if he were about to tell a group of children the secret ingredients to fairy dust. We went through this every single time he came to visit. Sometimes Carla and I would answer along with him. Sometimes we'd ignore him. Every time I'd be annoyed that his answer wasn't "You!"

"The chili con queso at El Coyote!" he'd announce with a satisfied grin. "Let's get two orders, what do you say? Yummy!"

He called me Carla for the first hour, eventually switching to CarJen. As concerned as he is that I have not yet wed, I'm sure he's relieved that he has one less name to remember.

"I'm thinking of using "Who Are You" as the song at my wedding for my big dance with Dad," Carla announced. "What do you guys think?"

John and I cracked up. Dad smiled and nodded, the joke flying over his head like a hockey puck.

The evening continued to revolve completely around Carla's impending wedding. Not because he's so enamored of his youngest daughter, but because he has to pay for it. As far as my big life change, all I got was a warning about money and my weight. (Too fat this time. Last time I saw him I was too thin, and I've dropped at least five since then.) Mr. Congeniality asked no questions about my music, my dopey job, my state of mind, my fancy new hairdo. I realize I should know by now not to expect a damn thing from him, but it makes me want to throttle him anyway. We were also treated to endless stories about exciting new discoveries in plant genetics.

NOTE TO SELF:

Dad is about Dad. You cannot change him. Focus on the few good points of the relationship and stare at them. Hard.

Okay, Katie just called in a panic and said that the warm-up band for Bullet Hole canceled because the lead singer fell out a window.

"He was trying to piss on some guy's head down in the parking lot," she informed me. "Goddamn fucking animals."

"Is he okay?" I asked.

"Okay? Does he sound like he's okay? He's a fucking moron! Listen, the show's in three hours. I don't have time to dick around here. Hold on." Ah, the relaxing world of hold music. This time it was some horrible woman screaming about integrity with way too many cheesed-out effects and a few scary horns thrown in. Who the hell are these people? How come they have record deals and I don't? Katie burst back on again.

"So do you guys want to play the show or what? It could be your big break, rock star. Time to dip your toe in the fucking shark tank for real," she said, talking a mile a minute. "We've been promoting the shit out of this show on all the hard rock and heavy metal stations. My boss is so fucking freaked that the warm-up band crapped out, he wouldn't care if I put a

September 3

goddamn tap dancer on first. You think you can handle it?"

"Of course," I said. "Let me get ahold of everyone and I'll call you back."

"Okay, but hurry the hell up. My fucking boss is crawling up my ass on this one."

Did I think we could handle it? Did she think I was working at The Great Outdoors because it was all I'd ever wanted out of life?

When I called her back to confirm, I did not mention that Lucy's been on an all-day vodka binge or that we've only practiced with Scott once. Bullet Hole is huge. Their fans make the biker rally look like a quilting convention.

NOTE TO SELF:
Be careful what you ask for.

Okay, I just called Tami and told her to sound the battle cry. We're gonna need as much human padding in front of the stage as we can possibly get.

Rodney sounded like he was going to wet his pants. Turns out he's a huge Bullet Hole fan. I forbade him to tell his mother what was going on for fear she'd find some reason to stop it. He said it was no problem, he'd tell her he was going to an SAT study group and to pick him up at the end of his street.

Illegal. Disgusting.

He also said his mom was going out of town the next day and he wanted to invite the Bullet Hole guys to his party. I told him to keep his pants on. The last thing we need is some hero-giddy teenager groveling to the band backstage. He certainly is getting ballsy in his old age. I'm sure that'll be blamed on me somehow.

This could be huge. This could be a disaster. There is no middle-ground outcome in this situation.

I REALLY AM WITH THE BAND:
THE MEMOIRS OF A ROCK GODDESS
BY JENNY TROANNI

~~It was our first gig together, and after an emergency dress rehearsal, we set off for the club.~~
~~We were four people with the same dream.~~
~~It was dark when we reached the club.~~
~~All my life I'd dreamt of being a rock star.~~
Insert riveting beginning that I will think of later here.

When we got to the Palace, there was a line around the block of punks, badasses, rockaholics, and murderers, all of them ready to rock, and all of them expecting to see a different warm-up band. I was terrified. Suddenly the fact that we'd practiced only once together wasn't a minor detail. It was a hippo-sized Achilles' heel.

This was a mostly male, mostly underage audience, which meant raging hormones and pent-up anger. Suddenly our pseudoglam white dress theme seemed glaringly wrong, about as cool as showing up in Western wear. We looked like a bunch of sissies. Dinner was about to be served, and we were the main course.

EMERGENCY NOTE TO SELF:
It is better to have rocked and lost than never to have rocked at all.

We had to fight to get backstage. No one believed we were the warm-up band until some high-strung wanker on a cell phone nodded to the gorilla at the door to let us in. Then he screamed at us to hurry the hell up and get out there. Keep it short and don't touch any of the equipment that's already on the stage or he'll sue our asses. Scott was cool as a cucumber. Rodney was desperately looking around for band members. Lucy was doing drunken imitations of the wanker. He glared at her and she glared back. He looked at me and said that we had a half an hour. Lucy said, "I know you are but what am I?"

We set up, and I could feel the crowd on the other side of the curtain heaving like a caged ape. We all strapped on our instruments, held hands, and agreed that no matter how much we sucked, no matter how hard they threw their bottles at us, we would just rock harder. The best defense is a good offense. Then we started playing. We didn't even wait for the damn curtain to come up.

The wanker appeared off to the side of the stage and motioned for us to stop. "What the fuck are you doing?" he mouthed. I screamed that we only had a half an hour and turned up my amp. Then the curtain yanked up and the crowd stared in collective surprise. Confusion. Horror.

I wonder if this is what soldiers feel like when they're forced to charge the enemy. All-out reckless fearlessness, panic so intense it's completely calming. I felt like I was on painkillers. Every time I looked at Lucy she was laughing hysterically. Rodney sprouted an I Can Do a Split in the Air Gene. These were his people. This was his show.

Scott fucked up left and right but did it with such conviction, it sounded great. On one song, he didn't realize it had ended, so he covered up the fact that he was still playing by unleashing a massive drum solo. He silenced the boys in the front row. They stopped throwing stuff and screaming obscenities. "Take it off" was replaced by "Fuck yeah!" At some point there was a shift in the crowd, and all the girls who'd been lining the wall in the back took over the front row. Tami and a slew of her friends were suddenly there, red-faced and raised-fisted. When the wanker motioned that it was time to stop, we'd won over the majority of the crowd.

The curtain came down and it was over. We had a much-needed group hug, dragged our shit off the stage, and went backstage for some free beer with Bullet Hole. They were as nice in person as they are scary onstage. Rodney strutted in as if he owned the place. I swear the kid transformed from pie-eyed toddler to swaggering stud in one half of an hour. He acted like he'd known these guys his whole life and those finger sandwiches were put out there for him.

Scott had attached his DVD camera to his drum set and filmed the audience while we played. He built this contraption so he could pan it with his foot. While he's playing. He's a genius. He brings his camera everywhere. When he tried to get some footage backstage, the wanker had a hissy fit and tried to confiscate the camera. The Bullet Hole guys told him to chill the fuck out and let Scott interview them. He got some great shots of the lead guitarist juggling his effects pedals.

When Bullet Hole played we went out onto the floor to watch, and Rodney had to peel the chicks off him. I was stunned and somehow hurt. My little boy was all grown up.

Jeffrey Todd, Rosebud Management Company, approached

me and gave me his card. He was a little guy with a big nose and friendly eyes who seemed to be in a hurry. He looked like a beagle with glasses on. He stuck out his hand and said he was very interested, very interested indeed. He said he wanted to set up a meeting for next week!

BRILLIANT OBSERVATION #14:

If you truly dread something, it almost always turns out amazing. But if you try to dread something so it will turn out amazing, it won't work. The universe knows when you're trying to pull a fast one on it, so don't even bother trying.

September 8

The Pete thing is in its second week. We've had the Just Fuckbuddies talk, which precedes the Don't Flirt in Front of Me talk, and in another two months we'll be having the inevitable, one-sided, I Have Real Feelings for You talk.

All casual sex relationships have a three-month shelf life. To the day. Someone always falls. I just hope it's not me.

If I were wise, I'd end it at month two so we could keep our flawless band relationship. Of course, he'd have to spend some major time in speech therapy for me to access that kind of willpower. I'd also have to find someone new immediately, or else I'd be in serious danger of raping Scott and fucking up my already fucked-up band. The number one no-no on the Thou Shalt Not list.

In fact, I felt the need to reinforce the importance of this rule to Lucy. She and Scott have become fast buddies, and due to the fact that he's a homo sapien with a pulse, it's only a matter of time before her name is his next tattoo. Luckily,

Lucy's already in a doghouse the size of the Taj Mahal for playing soccer with Henry's heart—I could use this as leverage in
my quest to keep the two of them apart. Because this was
obviously not just about Thou Shalt Not Bed Thy Band. This
was about Thou Shalt Not Stand By And Let The Biggest
Object Of Thy Lust Be Usurped By Someone Else Without
Putting Up A Big Fat Hairy Fight.

We were having one of our rare songwriting get-togethers.
Lucy's schedule was so full (and her brain so empty) that we
were down to meeting once every two weeks to write now. Tops.

It became immediately apparent upon entering the building
that the room across the hall from ours was now being rented out
to another band. The walls shook with the force of drums, countless guitar amps, an egomaniacal bass player (his volume was
the loudest) and Satan at the vocal helm. Death rock. One of my
least favorites. The band groaned and grunted while Satan
growled lyrics like: "Running on bloody feet, / the apocalypse is
here. / The universe will swallow whole / all except your fear!"
Lucy and I stood outside their door in shock.

"Sounds like a bunch of Boy Scouts have moved in," Lucy
said.

"How are we gonna get any writing done? I already have a
headache," I moaned.

We went down to our room and closed the door. The floor
vibrated so much it was rattling Scott's snare drum. Lucy and
I stared at each other.

"This is ridiculous," she said. "Wait here. I'll be right back."
She headed out the door, fluffing up her hair. She came back a
second later, grabbed an empty beer bottle "for protection,"

and headed back out. I heard the music stop and a bunch of voices. Laughter, shouts, and a door closing. Five minutes later Lucy waltzed back in.

"Well? I was fully prepared to run out and call the cops," I said.

"They're definitely on the spooky side. They painted the walls black and put red bulbs in all the lights. But they were nice enough. They said they were almost done."

We stood in silence for a second and then moved our amps in front of the door. "From now on we should only come up if Scott's with us," I said, testing the waters.

"Yeah. He'd definitely agree with that," said Lucy, his best friend who knows everything about him already.

"Big sacrifice for us, huh? He's such an eyesore," I said, jumping in all the way.

"Oh my God! You want to scoop him up with a spoon, don't you? To get every last *drop*!" gushed Lucy.

"You'd better not be breaking any more of your rules, Lucy. Your report card is already in pretty sad shape. Henry still hasn't recovered."

"For your information, Miss High and Mighty, Henry told me he could handle it. I should have known he couldn't, but oh well. I'm not as big a monster as you're making me out to be, thank you very much."

"It's just that I've been working my ass off with this band, and I'll be way upset if you fuck this up too," I grated.

"Give me some credit!" she said, visibly insulted. "I'm not a complete ass. I never mix business and pleasure. Ever. That's for amateurs and weaklings."

I kind of believed her, and I wanted to feel better but I didn't. I still had Scott's crush on her to worry about. And if there were any chance of the tides turning and my big dumb crush on Scott being reciprocated . . . amateur? Weakling? Both could easily apply.

NOTE TO SELF:

Fall in love with Pete.

I am writing this from the depths of despair. Rodney's biological mother finally took him back for good. I kind of always knew this day would come. I knew he wasn't really mine, but I still want to burn her house down.

He had a major blowout destructo kegger the night after Bullet Hole. Word got out that Bullet Hole might be there, and people came from miles away. Lucy and I stopped by for about ten minutes to say hi but left for fear of bumping into someone we used to babysit for. He had so many people show up, a small fraction being those he knew, that he had to call the cops before the floor caved in. He couldn't get anyone to leave. It got totally out of control.

Luckily, the second the cops arrived people dispersed like cockroaches. They were experienced. He said the place was trashed and empty when they got there, and he was so drunk they could have thrown him in jail. He tried to pretend he'd gotten robbed. They told him to drink a lot of water and get the hell to bed.

He somehow managed to clean the place (he had to mop the ceiling) spotless by the time his mom got back. She applauded him for being so trustworthy, and he acted insulted that she'd even think otherwise.

September 10

Then about a week later his mother picked up some film at the drugstore, and they gave her a roll of Rodney's as well. People with mohawks sitting on her couch doing tequila shots. Drunk teenagers playing dress-up in her closet. Underaged girls lighting cigarettes off her stove. He swore I wasn't in any of those pictures, and I believe him because I'd be writing this from prison if I were.

He's not allowed to leave the house until he goes to college. Except to go to church, which he now attends every Sunday. Poor kid! And poor me.

How the hell am I ever going to make this fucking CD and get on with my life?!

I am so frustrated. And I have a bridal shower to throw in exactly three days.

I cast out the freak net once again for bass player number three and haven't received any calls. Rodney was so perfect! So sweet, a great player, and he gave us cred with the kids. I thought about scouting around for bass players at his high school, but I just couldn't. It would make me officially creepy. One step away from trolling around with candy bars. Moments away from a subscription to *Teen Beat* magazine.

Lucy, Scott, and I are practicing through this hugely annoying time. The better Scott knows the songs, the faster we can get into the studio and get onstage again. Which we really need to do before all our new fans forget about us. I'm annoyed to report that being locked in a room with just the two of them has confirmed my worst fears. Scott can't take his eyes off her, which makes Lucy become ten times more

Lucy with all the attention. Today we were treated to her fascinating story about the deafening noises from the other end
of the hall.

"Oh my gawd, you guys have to go check out their room. I
know they're trying to be all Satany and scary and stuff, but I
think it's kind of cute! Like they're playing haunted house or
something." She was such a liar! She'd come back from their
room looking like she'd just witnessed a lynching.

"Is that why you moved your amp in front of the door? So
they wouldn't come in and cuddle you to death?" I asked, calling her on her false bravado.

"Oh yeah, I guess I was kind of freaked, wasn't I?" she
laughed, completely unconcerned that I'd just busted her in a
lie. How the hell does she do that?

"What are they called?" asked Scott, chuckling at her irre-
sistibly darling little story.

"They're called Zildjian or something ridiculous like that," I
said. "I saw a sticker on the door to their practice space."

"Actually—," Scott said.

"—that's a brand name," Lucy cut in.

"Cymbals," Scott finished, holding up his Zildjian crash
cymbal.

"Oh. Never mind," I said, feeling even more left out. I decided the only way to get through it was to look at the bright side.
As long as Lucy didn't crumble and Scott's crush never dwin-
dled and my crush was never reciprocated, the band could live
happily ever after.

Now all I had to do was figure out how to look on the bright
side.

Today I had my big meeting with that manager guy from the Bullet Hole gig, Jeffrey Todd. I brought Lucy, the human magnet, with me to try and woo him. He took us to lunch at Spago. He paid! Katie told me Rosebud is a huge fucking big-deal management company, so Lucy and I were as cool as we could be. Katie also told me not to tell him that we had no bass player and that Lucy and I should definitely lie about our age. A lot.

"They want fresh, young talent. You could pass for twenty-four, maybe even twenty-three on a good day. Don't act too smart, and wear something skimpy. And for fuck's sake, keep those eyebrows waxed. No one's going to want to sign someone who looks like she lives in a fucking cave," Katie ever so helpfully offered.

NOTE TO SELF:

Find out what the hell a manager does and why we need one.

When Lucy and I showed up at the restaurant, we were led through a sea of plastic surgery to a table over in the corner. Spago is one of those many L.A. places that's so proud of itself, it always makes me a little uneasy. Like I'm missing something or like I'm invisible. And I know it's stupid, but I want to be part of it. Badly. Unlike Lucy, who snorted her way through the crowd and kept a loud tally of the number of nose jobs we passed on our way to our table. I was glad to have Lucy with me and glad that we were both black-eyelinered and furred and feathered and freaked for the occasion. For the first time, I actually felt like I was somebody.

ROCK AND ROLL TRUTH #5:

If you walk around looking like a rock star in a really expensive restaurant, everyone assumes you are one. If you walk around my neighborhood looking like a rock star, everyone assumes you're unemployed.

Our waitress and her breasts came up to take our drink order. Jeffrey was on the phone and waved at us to get whatever we wanted. Lucy wanted a martini and I decided I did too. Jeffrey made the waitress wait until he was done with his call before letting her leave. Finally he hung up.

"Pellegrino, no ice, please," he said, rubbing his hands together and looking at us. "Okay, guys, let's get down to business." His phone rang again before the sentence was out of his mouth. He picked it up.

"Yo. Yeah. Oh Jesus, not again." He rubbed his forehead and sighed. "I'm in a meeting, but I'll stop by on my way back to the office. Thanks, Shirley." He shook his head and looked up at us. "Lead singer in one of my bands got picked up for buying coke. Again. You guys don't do drugs, do you? I mean, not big ones. And not lots of them?"

"Not really. We're kind of nerds," I said, kicking Lucy under the table before she could launch into her most recent Ecstasy-riddled, sex-on-the-beach story.

"Great," Jeffrey said. He was talking really fast, but I could tell he was exhausted. Each of his eyeballs was dragging around some pretty heavy luggage.

"I'll tell you right now that you guys have something. Did you bring me a CD?"

"We're actually going into the studio in a few weeks," I said, acting like it was all so no big deal, all this laying down of tracks and hitting-the-road stuff.

"Good, good. I can't wait to hear it." His phone rang again. Our waitress showed up with our drinks. and Lucy and I were suddenly sitting behind a giant wall of glass and vodka. Luckily, as the lunch progressed and my glass emptied, Jeffrey got eight more phone calls, so I didn't have to do too much talking. I noticed that at most of the other tables, at least one person was on the phone at some point, if not at all people at all points.

BRILLIANT OBSERVATION #15:
Being rude is now an accepted part of our culture. Pathetic.

I was officially bombed by the time the check came. Apparently during the course of our lunch, Jeffrey had decided he was "this close" to signing us!

"I just need to see a few more shows and hear the CD," he said, handing our waitress his credit card without looking at the bill. "But that's just standard procedure. I know gold when I smell it."

"Excellent! We smell like gold!" Lucy screamed, holding up her empty martini glass and smiling around the room at our unimpressed, irritated fellow diners. Jeffrey gave me his card again and made us promise to let him know the dates of all of our shows and to alert him the second the CD came out.

"Really great talking to both of you," he said, shaking our hands as the valet drove up in his Lexus. My last image of Jeffrey was of him peeling out of the Spago parking lot, waving his cell phone at us, and screaming, "Call me!"

A drunken Lucy waved back frantically and looked at me

with raised eyebrows. "We're on our way, my friend. We could really do this!" she squealed.

Maybe it was the excitement of our lunch and eight gallons of vodka, but suddenly the revelation hit me too: we really could!

I'm horrified to say that I couldn't find a way to unload my bridal shower duties on someone else. I didn't have much time, really. John and Carla were so excited, they'd started planning the wedding months before they'd made their announcement. A surprise attack. The reality finally sank in that today I'd be sitting with a bunch of women who would be screaming at the top of their lungs over naughty undies and idiotic games.

I figured I had two choices:

1) THE DEVIL SAYS: Since Carla knows it's me who's throwing it, she deserves what she gets for not stopping it. A keg, a band, and some pigs in a blanket.

2) THE ANGEL SAYS: Remember, I really do love my sister, and this is really important to her, and for once in my selfish life I should put myself aside, act on the will to please, and find joy in the joy of others.

It took every ounce of strength I had, but I did it. I giggled on the phone with Carla's friend Shannon and decided that while all the girls hid over at her house, I'd pick Carla up and pretend to be taking her to my auto mechanic's to finally get her timing belt changed. We'd swing by Shannon's because she has a book I want to borrow (how I would know Shannon has a book I want to borrow considering the fact that I never speak with her is beside the point) and then . . . oh my God! Oh

September 13

my God! Oh my God! Tears and screaming and hugs all around. And more screaming. Carla is so surprised!

BRIDAL SHOWER TRADITIONS I BRAVED:
1) The Safety-Pin Game
   Every girl takes a safety pin when she walks through the door and pins it to her shirt. Every time she catches someone sitting down with her legs crossed, she gets all her pins. And screams. The girl with all the pins at the end gets a prize.
   Scream factor: 10
   Organizational-pain-in-the-ass factor: 2
   Irritation factor: 10
2) The Memory Lane Circle
   On all the shower invitations, I ask them to write a little story about some memorable event they had with Carla and bring it to the party. All the stories are put in a hat and pulled out randomly. Everyone gets a chance to read one, and the group has to guess who wrote it.
   Scream factor: 10
   Organizational-pain-in-the-ass factor: 5
   Irritation factor: 5
3) The Tray Game
   The same one I remember from grade-school birthday parties. I bring out a tray with a bunch of small items on it and slowly parade it around the room. Then I hide it and all the ladies write down as many items as they can remember. The one who remembers the most gets a prize.
   Scream factor: 10

Organizational-pain-in-the-ass factor: 8
Irritation factor: 10
4) The Gift Journal
Someone other than me sits next to Carla and writes down all the comments she makes while opening her gifts. They are then read back verbatim after all the gifts are opened.
Scream factor: off the scale
Organizational-pain-in-the-ass factor: 1
Irritation factor: 10

BRIDAL SHOWER TRADITIONS THAT I WAS PHYSICALLY UNABLE TO CARRY ON:

1) The Male Stripper
Among many, many other things, this tradition involves a Speedo or, even worse, its cousin, the G-string. I can't. I really just cannot.
2) The Pin-the-Penis-on-the-Man Game
The same as the second-grade birthday party game but stupider. And even more degrading to men than the stripper.

I made tons of food and took tons of pictures and smiled like a crazy person. I also got so that at some point I blow-dried my bangs straight up in the air and led the girls in a rousing round of "I Love Rock 'n' Roll."

I also burst into tears and told Carla I loved her six times.

But good old Carla was a trooper and nothing but thankful.

I swear, the tiny black hardened clump of coal that is my heart grew two sizes that day. For that afternoon I was in perfect harmony with all that is pink and ruffled. Even though it took about seven Bloody Marys to get me there.

And because the universe recognizes true acts of heroism, I returned home to the following message on my answering machine:

"Hey, Jenny. I saw your ad in the paper for a bass player. My name's Jake, and I'm actually looking for someone named Jenny whose demo I heard and loved and lost when my wife gave me the boot. If this is you, hopefully you're still looking. My pager's (213) 555-0141. If it's not, I guess don't call me back. I'm not ready to forfeit my quest just yet. Thanks. Peace. Later."

Once again, teetering on the brink of hopelessness, the back door swings open and smacks me on the ass. . . .

September 14

Lucy made the very good point that although we've lost our token teenager, we are now perhaps the best-looking band in the country. I can't argue with her when she's right. Jake's a babe, and he fits us like a tube top.

"That was high quality!" he said to Lucy after we'd finished our first practice together.

"Not bad for a bunch of sissies!" Lucy said, laughing and taking off her guitar. Jake grinned around the room at all of us, but his eyes kept hanging on Lucy.

Of course. Seeing people fall for Lucy is like seeing the sun in the sky. An obvious, everyday occurrence. At this point I swear, if someone met her and *didn't* drool, I'd probably take them aside and demand they 'fess up to their alien origins.

We decided to go with the more expensive analog studio. We liked the guy who runs it better, and if you're going to make a record, it should be as pleasant an experience as possible.

I've already blocked out time to go into the studio. Less than two weeks away! I can think of nothing else. Jake says that's all the time he needs to learn the songs.

"My old band broke up, and my employment status is of the nonexistent variety at the moment," he said, "so time abounds for me to practice." He's an electrician. He's a fast learner. And every single word out of his mouth cracks me up.

We've started selling T-shirts, stickers, posters, and baked goods at our gigs to raise money. All overseen by Tami, of course. She's like the town crier and an arts and crafts teacher mixed into one tiny promotional machine. How she has time to work at Kinko's, stay out all night seeing bands, and help us out is beyond me.

She's our band's Sucker.

We now have a dedicated group of girls from the Bullet Hole show who come to every gig their fake IDs can get them into. We call them the Bulletchicks. Devout, loud, unable to hold their liquor. The kind of fans every band dreams of. Two of them came up to me crying and said they'd started their own band because of us. Few things have made me feel better about myself. I autographed their butts.

Pete's starting to act squirrelly. I guess our biweekly booty call is too much commitment for him. Who am I kidding anyway? I'm always the one to fall, and of course I'm starting to fall for him. Which is good, because it keeps my raging lust for Scott in a cage, but ridiculous, because Pete's a hopeless cause. Aside from the fact that he's gorgeous, a rock star, and great in bed, he's totally fucked up and unavailable. Sample conversation:

ME: You want to do something tonight?

HIM: I don't know. Why don't you page me later?

ME: Well, it's like nine o'clock now. What do you mean by later? Like midnight?

HIM: Uh, okay.

The page is placed at midnight by the desperate loser. She receives no return call. She clings to the assumption that he couldn't raise the thirty-five cents for the pay phone. She goes to bed. She's woken at 2 A.M. by Pete knocking on her bedroom window.

HIM: Shorry. Did I wake you up?

ME: No. I was just lying here. I was awake. What's up?

HIM: Cool. You got any of that lashagna left?

She gets up and feeds him in the hopes that it will lead to sex. It does, but only after she's kept up until four listening to his latest guitar riff. She's late for work the next day and leaves her house with the unemployed Pete snoring happily in her bed. She can't help noticing how angelic he looks with his eyes closed.

IDIOTIC SEX TRUTH ABOUT ME #1

I suck at having cheap sex. My imagination provides my partners with brains, personalities, emotions, and vocabularies. All they have to do is show up.

The problem is that I start to believe it. My gut doesn't, but the rest of me does. My gut remains wearily unimpressed while the rest of me happily skips straight into the wood-chipper like the masochist I am.

Last night we had our final gig at the Opium Den before locking ourselves away in the studio next week. We played with this crazy power trio called Squinch. Very angry. Very bad. Very fun to watch. Jeffrey Todd's been calling ever since our lunch date, wondering when he can see us play again. I lied and told him we were focusing on the recording but would call the second we hit the stage again. I wanted to give Jake time to get up to speed and give Jeffrey time to forget what Rodney looked like.

September 17

Katie insisted on being there, even though I didn't want her to come until we were better. Or until she got a personality transplant. After Squinch's set, Lucy and I stood eyeing the bar, watching the poor bartender make Katie's margarita right this time. I'd been desperately trying to keep Lucy and Katie apart because (surprisingly) Lucy thinks Katie's a pain in the ass.

"That girl is a drag. I don't care how many connections she has—life's too damn short. What she needs is a good hard spanking," Lucy complained. "If I hear one more whine out of her, I'm going to do the honors myself."

"If you say anything, Lucy, I swear I'll kill you," I warned.

"I don't know how you can live with yourself," Lucy said.

Katie walked up, sipping her drink with a foul look on her face.

"Jesus Christ, how can that guy call himself a fucking bartender? This tastes like someone pissed in it."

"Maybe someone did," replied Lucy.

"Yeah, right?" Katie was completely oblivious. "I forgot how much I hated this fucking place," she said, just as Scott walked up.

"Katie? Fucking hate something?" he said. He'd had the pleasure of hanging out with her after our last gig and was as enamored of her as Lucy was.

"Maybe they just got a new bartender or something," I said, desperately trying to prevent a Katie-bashing.

"Maybe Katie's just—," Lucy started to say.

"Maybe we should get onstage," I cut in. "It looks like it's about that time." Scott winked at Lucy as I dragged them both away. I couldn't believe they were bonding over my humiliating Katie situation!

Normally I would have told them both to fuck off, but this was Scott. And there was his arm. And shut was my mouth.

Just to add to my pleasure, Dad's spaceship had an emergency landing in town, and he decided to come to the gig too. As luck would have it, I didn't notice him standing there until long after we'd started playing and I was about to break into my new song about S&M.

NOTE TO SELF:

Never extend an invitation to Dad secure in the knowledge that he won't be able to make it. Space, time, and mass as we know it do not apply in his world. He can materialize anywhere, at any time, in any form.

I got through it by focusing on the fact that he's a terrible listener when the subject matter has nothing to do with him. (I willfully avoided the thought that perhaps the subject of S&M did pertain to him. I'd rather have my eyes gouged out.) I had to summon up some major *cojones* to get the lyrics out without mumbling them.

NOTE TO SELF:

I am an artist.
Artists are not ashamed of their sick little thoughts.

Luckily, Dad was his usual clueless self. Lucy said she was watching him the whole time and he just looked confused. She said he wasn't even really paying that much attention because he was talking the door guy's ear off. Of course! Half of me was relieved and half of me wanted to kill him for showing up and ignoring me.

When we were done playing, I went up and asked him what he thought. By that time he was talking to Henry, who I hadn't seen come in either. Henry was thankfully back to wearing khakis and button-downs, but I noticed he'd kept the earring in as a souvenir. He was scoping the room for Lucy while pretending to listen to Dad, who clearly had no idea who he was, even though they'd met on several occasions.

"Hi, guys," I said, putting my arm around Henry's waist. "Nice to see you both could make it."

"You guys are getting really good," Henry said. "Your new drummer is great."

"I was just telling Harry here that he's likely to have back problems like I do when he gets up in years," Dad said. "You see, when the spinal cord of taller-framed people like us is supporting . . ."

"What did you think of my band, Dad?" I asked, cutting him off.

He stared at me for several seconds, unsure of how or why he'd suddenly stopped talking.

"What's that now, dear?" he said, confused.

"My band. Did you like my band?" I asked, more out of

amusement than from actually expecting him to have a real answer.

"Well, Jenny, of course I'm very proud of you, but it's not exactly my type of music. I'm more interested in classical and jazz from the forties. Now there's something to listen to, Harry . . . ," he said, expertly bringing the conversation back to Dad's Fascinating World of Dad.

"I haven't seen you in ages," I said to Henry, ignoring Dad completely now. Suddenly Lucy appeared out of nowhere.

"I haven't either," she said, forcing herself around him in a hug. Henry froze and stood there, arms pinned to his sides.

"My, Lucy, your hair certainly has grown quite a bit since I last saw you," offered Dad.

"Hi, Mr. Troanni," Lucy said.

"I'm leaving," said Henry, pulling away from Lucy. "It was stupid of me to come."

"You should be able to come see my band anytime you want to," I said.

"I'm sorry. I won't bother you again," said Lucy, genuinely hurt.

"My word. You're all grown up!" said Dad, still staring at Lucy's hair.

"Henry, come on. Let me buy you a beer," I said, trying to get him to stay.

"That's okay. I'm leaving," Lucy said, walking away. I saw her belly up to the bar with Scott, Jake, and Flowers, all of whom were overjoyed to see her. I was left stuck with my idiot father and a pouting Henry.

"I can't believe she can just act like nothing's wrong," Henry moaned.

I looked at him, patted him on the back, said, "That sucks, Henry. Goodnight, Dad," and walked away.

I am officially sick of every single person I know.

Today I began my career as a professional phony. The tutoring gigs I set up a few months ago with Rodney's friends finally kicked in, and I'm now stealing money from desperate parents in exchange for pretending to know more than their children do.

September 21

INSPIRATIONAL NOTE TO SELF:
Just because you're totally unqualified doesn't mean you can't pull it off.

I need the money so badly, I'd teach surgery at this point. Plus, I have to admit, it's kind of nice being around Rodney's friends. I miss him more than I thought I would and any contact with his world, regardless of how removed, is comforting.

My first victim, Caroline Block, eleventh grade, would rather take a bullet than speak in public. She has to give an oral report on *The Catcher in the Rye*. She has yet to get up in front of a classroom without suffering incapacitating stomach cramps and severe memory loss. My task is to help her write said oral report. Then I must perform miracle therapy sessions that will change her entire personality in one month so she can give her report without being rushed to the hospital.

She wanted to talk about my band way more than Holden Caulfield, and I figured it was an okay ice-breaker, especially since she hadn't even read the damn book yet. She was surprisingly funny and animated once she got going. Maybe there was hope. Maybe I wouldn't wind up in prison.

I asked her about Rodney. She said no one hung out with him anymore because his mother won't let him do anything. Thinking about that woman still gives me a rash. I sent Caroline off with a note to give him at school.

> *Hi Rodney! Just wanted to let you know we all still think of you. I hope you're doing great and practicing and working your ass off to get into a good college. Feel free to call me if you need any help or just want to chat. Please eat this note after you read it.*
>
> *Love, Jenny*

On my way out the door, fifty dollars richer and ten times guiltier, Mrs. Block asked me, "Well, what do you think?"

MULTIPLE CHOICE ANSWERS TO MRS. BLOCK'S QUESTION:

1) That mothers who hire tutors who are best known for luring young boys into rock bands get what they deserve.
2) That I will have to save every dime Mrs. Block gives me so I can pay my lawyer when she sues me for fraud.
3) That Caroline is loaded with personality. She just needs to get over whatever's holding her back.
4) All of the above.

I had a little album-naming brainstorming session disguised as a cocktail party. I invited the boys in the band plus Flowers and Henry and conveniently scheduled it on a night when I knew Lucy had Afreaka! because:

September 22

- I wanted Scott to myself.
- I wanted Henry to come.
- I wanted Flowers to myself.
- I wanted Jake to myself.
- I wanted to be the only girl.
- I am a small person.

Nobody had any good ideas except Flowers. Scott ran around with his camera the whole time while Jake played DJ and Henry acted like he was being held at gunpoint. Even without Lucy there. I'd forgotten how shy he is in groups and how, especially around my friends, he's about as much fun as a pantsload of wet sand. I wish he'd just be himself. But I guess for someone who can split the atom, watching Scott open a beer with his feet isn't all that fascinating. He must think we all have brain damage.

What shall we name the baby?

SIXTY-FOOT QUEENIE:
Roll Out the Barrel
Sixty-Foot Weenie
Kiss My Ring
Sixty-Foot Queenier Than Thou
Lovinyouiseasycuzyou'rebeautiful
Music to Rule By
The Freaks are All Right
Over Your Head

We gave up on the naming thing pretty early on and opted for just hanging out. Henry hovered around in the kitchen, poking his head into the living room every now and then (mostly "then") to add to the conversation. Jake manned the stereo in the corner while Flowers spread out on the only chair available, a gigantic, overstuffed yellow thing I inherited from my uncle that we called "the banana boat." Scott plopped down next to me on the couch, making it impossible for me to focus on anything other than the fact that Scott had just plopped down next to me on the couch. He'd just finished showing us his latest short film about two eighty-year-old men on the prowl for chicks. It was hilarious.

"So tell me, Scott," Flowers said from across the room. "What else are you filming these days?"

"Mostly commercials right now. But I want to start shooting music videos," the genius answered.

"Well, I'll tell you right now, you belong in front of the camera, baby, not behind it. I could watch that all day," Flowers said, winking at him.

"I bet you could, Flowers. That and the Puerto Rican Day Parade," Scott said. Flowers had a thing for Puerto Rican boys. And both the guys in my band. Scott thought it was funny. Jake did not.

"Ah, so true," said Flowers. "Jake, honey, why don't you tear yourself away from that stereo and come sit by me?"

"Because I find that a most unsavory concept, dude," Jake answered.

"I think I'm going to go," Henry announced, suddenly entering the room. I stood up and gave him a hug good-bye instead of trying to convince him to stay. I was actually relieved that I didn't have to watch him squirming around anymore.

"Can we finally get Lucy over here now that Frankenstein is gone?" Scott asked after Henry had left. "I still can't believe she went out with that guy."

"For a whole couple months," I said, opting to stick up for both of my friends.

"Maybe he's sporting the monster wood," Jake laughed.

"Can we talk about something else?" I asked, the idea making me completely uncomfortable. Scott turned to me and grinned.

"Yeah, let's talk about you and Pete," he said. "He hasn't slept at home all week."

"Really?" I asked, genuinely surprised. The room suddenly went silent.

The fact that Pete's infidelity was being broadcast through the perfect, full lips of Scott made it that much more humiliating. What he might as well have said: *Hi. I'm gorgeous and you're a giant loser.*

"I think," Scott said, failing at an attempted save.

I shrugged and in my best Cosmo Girl voice said, "It's just a sex thing with Pete. We can both do whatever we want."

The reality of the absurdity of my "relationship" with Pete came crashing down around me. It was hard to tell if at that moment I was more upset for being such an idiot or for looking like one in front of Scott.

NOTE TO SELF:

Wake the hell up.

THE SLEEP DEPRIVATION EXPERIMENT OTHER-
WISE KNOWN AS RECORDING A CD.
DAY NUMERO UNO:

I was up late last night making enough lasagna to feed eight bands (the better they're fed, the harder they'll rock) and attempted to ignore the hideous realization that I'm just like the woman who gave birth to me. I kind of overdid it, and by the time I got all the food in the car, there was barely enough room for our gear.

"It looks like we're playing an Italian wedding, for fuck's sake!" Lucy said when I went to pick her up.

We drove to the studio together and got there early so I could work out the money stuff with Eddie, the guy who owns it. Eddie's a big southern moose of a nice guy, who always looks like he just woke up from not enough sleep. He's cute in that scary, redneck kind of way: face full of hair, ponytail, could beat up anyone he wanted to without putting his plate of grits down. He's got a quirky, Spanish-style house way out in the middle of Topanga that's surrounded by bizarre plants, totem poles, dogs, cats, rabbits, and a horse who looks like he'd really rather die and get it over with.

When he greeted us at the door sporting major bed head and a clown nose, I knew we'd chosen the right man for the job. "Y'all ready to kick some butt?" he asked as he led us inside his messy kitchen. "Yes indeed," I said.

"Coffee's on the stove, help yourself to everything. Ask if you don't see it, don't ask if you do," he said. Lucy had wandered into the next room and was looking at all his crazy equipment. The room was filled with vintage amps, stacks of unidentifiable electronic equipment, and baskets full of noisy toys.

"Yeehaw! This is going to be fun, fun, fun!" Lucy called from the other room. "This place is like a rock-and-roll Disneyland."

"Allow me to give you the grand tour," Eddie said, handing me a cup of coffee the size of my head. He had to remove his clown nose so he could drink out of his cup, and he studied it before slipping it into his pocket. "I'm gonna need that later," he said.

I followed him into what had once been a dining room, where Lucy was standing. He handed her a cup of coffee and said, "This here's the playroom. Been collecting equipment since I learned how to pull money out of a wallet." The room, like the rest of the house, was low-ceilinged and dark but cozy. The walls were thick white stucco. He'd put sliding glass doors between this room and the one next to it, which he slid open and explained, "This here's the control room. Y'all will play behind the glass while I twiddle around in here." The control room was a large round room with a fireplace and two big ratty couches. His mixing board and other confusing-looking recording equipment lined the walls, and a weird lighting fixture made out of a giant textured green glass ball hung over it. A long window looked out onto the driveway. Another sliding glass door led outside to a brick patio with a grill, a picnic table, and a fountain with a little boy peeing into a jar. Scraggly grass grew up between the cracks in the brick, and the patio was surrounded by big leafy trees. It was like sitting in the middle of a jungle.

"Patio's out back. Very vital to the creative process," he said, leading us back out to the dining room and to the base of a tiny staircase. "Up these stairs and to the left is the crapper. To the right's my bedroom. And that, ladies, is all she wrote."

"I love it," said Lucy, jabbing me in the ribs.

"Glad to hear it," Eddie said, heading out toward the kitchen. "Now let's get all your gear inside. It can get hotterna half-fucked fox in a forest fire out there. Can't tell you how many tapes have liquified in my truck. Let me just find my motherfuckers." He wandered around until he found some flip-flops and slid them on his feet.

"So did you make all those totem poles that are out in your yard?" Lucy asked.

"No way. I converted those garages out back into studios. Got a couple of freaky artist types who come out and whittle stuff. Keep me company and help pay the rent. Ready, dar-lins?" he asked, holding the door open for us.

"Wow," whispered Lucy.

Uh-oh. I'd heard that wow before. It was the sound of The Man-Eater's stomach grumbling. I shook my finger and mouthed the words *business and pleasure* at her. She stared back at me and bit her fist.

The rest of the day was just amazing. Scott and Jake showed up about an hour after us, and we got right to work. My excitement plus the ten-gallon mug of coffee I'd drunk made my teeth chatter so much, Eddie had me walk around the house a few times "before you chew a hole through something expen-sive." We laid down all the drum tracks and most of the bass.

Scott played like a superhero except for this one spot on "Rib Eye" where he just kept fucking up. Then it became the part where he kept fucking up so every time he got to that part he'd freak out and fuck up. He got really moody and pissed off. You couldn't say anything to him.

Eddie took him out back and made him lie on the hammock while he rained cold water on him from the hose. He gave him a beer, told him to go smoke a cigarette, and then stuck him behind the drums again, and he played it perfectly.

ROCK-AND-ROLL TRUTH #6:

The drums are my favorite instrument. When played well they are the most breathtaking, all-consuming, sexy-assed thing on this earth. Which describes exactly how Scott plays them.

There was much cheering and toasting, and then Scott took his shirt off to dry in the sun. I will not comment on what a guy who plays drums like that looks like when he takes off his shirt, because I have a band to run here.

We finished all his drum stuff and got a good chunk of the bass done too. Jake played like an animal. Unbelievably huge. When he was done, everyone ran into the studio and piled on top of him.

We all got along great. Everyone's playing was great. Life is great.

Eddie has a huge orange cat with six toes on his front feet named Murray, who sat on my lap the entire time.

Scott got some hilarious footage of Eddie telling this story about a pride of wild, six-toed cats that rule a mountain somewhere in the Deep South. Hikers would go up there and never return. One man made it back but never spoke or ate again. Just lapped milk out of a bowl on the floor and slept curled up on the hood of his car.

I took tons of pictures. We played kickball when we took a

break. Me, Scott, and Jake versus Lucy, Eddie, and some trippy artist who lives in one of Eddie's buildings. They kicked our asses. The artist chick makes giant legs and feet out of clay. She read my palm and said my life was about to take off in a radically different direction. She did not say I needed to get my eyebrows waxed.

We ate about ten pounds of lasagna and worked for twelve glorious hours.

RECORDING, DAY TWO:

September 25

I'm sitting here waiting for coffee pot number three to finish dripping. We just had our first creative slap-fight. Me versus Jake. Jake wanted to put this major walking bass line in the down part of "Put That Thing Away." I told him it would junk it up. He disagreed.

"If the song's raging along at all times, you have nowhere to go. Nothing to build from," I said.

"It should rock nonstop. The bass is the heartbeat. Turn it off and kill the song," he said, staring straight at me like I was an idiot.

Scott, Lucy, and Eddie watched in silent discomfort.

"I'm not turning it off, I'm toning it down. And at the end of the day, Jake, I wrote the song, so if I want to fuck it up, then that's my decision," I said.

"Then you play it," he said, putting down his bass and storming out of the room. Scott ran after him.

"Jake! Chill out, man!" he said, putting his arm around Jake. Jake shrugged it off and shut himself in the bathroom.

"Time for a sanity stroll," Eddie said wearily, putting the

equipment on standby and getting up. He went upstairs to the bathroom door and knocked. "Jake, we're gonna have a walk. Get your hide out here."

"Negative," said Jake through the door.

Eddie came back down and said, "All righty then. He's staying. Let's go."

We set off down his driveway and walked along the street. Up in the Topanga hills, stuff grows all over the place like a rainforest, and hippies roam free like buffalo. When we got to the top of Eddie's hill, we could see the ocean and Eddie said, "Thar she blows!"

Lucy was jumping around and skipping all over the place. "I've got to get some blood pumping through these veins," she screamed, trying to get Eddie to chase her. Which, much to my surprise, he couldn't have been less interested in. Could it be that Lucy's perfect batting average was about to be taken down a notch by Eddie?

I, on the other hand, was tormented and couldn't stop stressing over my pushiness with Jake, even though I knew in my gut I was right. I stared out at the ocean and tried to center myself, and Scott came and stood next to me, close enough to touch shoulders. Suddenly torment number one was chased out of the room by torment number two.

"Good job holding your ground back there," he said, practically whispering in my ear. I turned to him, the sea air gently blowing through my hair. "Sometimes I feel like such a witch," I said, locking eyes with him.

He licked his lips and said with a mischievous smile, "You are far from a witch."

The music swelled. The waves crashed in the sea. A gull's

lovelorn cry tore through the air. "Put your meat-hooks down and step away from that man!" the gull's call suddenly seemed to scream. "Amateur! Weakling!"

"We should probably head back," I heard myself say.

"Sure," he said, completely unheartbroken that our climactic moment had come to an end. Had I just made that whole moment up? Was I just flying solo there on cloud nine? "Where did Lucy go?" he added, as if to answer my question. It was like a hard slap in the face. I already felt like a dope over the Pete thing and now Scott, the one I really wanted, was professing his love for Lucy.

"I don't know," I said, turning back toward the studio and my role as The Undesirable Bossy Bass-Line Nazi. I saw Eddie coming over the top of the hill.

"Where'd Lucy go?" he asked, just in case I'd forgotten that she was the one everyone was looking for.

"How the hell should I know?" said I, the fourth grader, as I stormed off back to the house. I could feel Eddie and Scott exchanging confused glances behind me.

BRILLIANT OBSERVATION #16:
I do not handle difficult situations with elegance and grace.

By the time I got back to the house, I was fully ready to turn my frustration on Jake. How dare that little twerp think he could push me around! I burst through the door fully prepared to out-temper-tantrum him (he had no idea he was dealing with The Master), but when I walked in, he was practicing the bass line I'd wanted him to play.

The bastard.

He saw me come in and put down his guitar. "Dude, I owe you many apologies. My life's most brutal at the moment. I fear I've taken it out on you," he said, looking so sad, it completely deflated my hot air balloon. "I promise to lighten up on the antics."

"That's okay, Jake. Forget about it," I said, giving him a hug and becoming teary-eyed. "I'm sorry for being such a control freak." I couldn't stop hugging him because I was in danger of sobbing. He had no idea how much better it felt to have some-one around who flipped out uncontrollably too!

I finally tore myself away, and when he saw my tears, he mistook them to be over our little altercation. "Jenny, there's no need! In this instance the bossiness was completely called for. Undoubtedly."

I nodded and thanked him and tried to pull it together. I managed to calm myself down and appreciate the fact that even though I'm an emotional infant, I do know how to arrange a song.

I did notice that he never said I wasn't a control freak, though.

When I got home there was a message from Jeffrey Todd, wondering how the recording was going. I'm terrified to talk to him because I'm afraid I'll say something so stupid he won't want to work with us, but I know I should keep in touch. I still have no fucking idea what a manager does! Every time I try to get Katie on the phone to have her pull my head out of my ass she's either too busy to talk or puts me on hold for a decade. I can't put off calling him much longer.

September 26

RECORDING, DAY THREE:

It took me most of the day yesterday to get all my parts down exactly the way I wanted them. Eddie and I experimented with every piece of equipment he had, hooking five different pedals up to an amp at a time and playing my guitar using an empty can of tuna for a slide. When we finally got the sounds down we took a break, and Eddie came back a little distracted and impatient. Which I took personally. Which made it impossible to play well. He told me later that his ex-wife had called and taken his "ear for a stroll down Crotchety Lane."

NOTE TO SELF:

I am not the center of the universe.

This morning was a whole different story. Lucy finished all her parts in about six seconds. She's a monster. She nailed everything in one take. Everyone was blown away. And as much as I'm having a hard time dealing with her these days, I couldn't help but be proud. I told the trippy artist chick she should build a statue of Lucy's foot.

BRILLIANT OBSERVATION #17:

People get jealous when they feel something they could have is being denied them. For this reason, I am not jealous of Lucy. Being jealous of Lucy's playing would be like watching the Olympics and being jealous of the women's figure skating gold medalist.

When Lucy was done and the cheering had subsided, Eddie started breaking down her gear. "You're a jaw-dropper, darlin'. A real natural," he said.

"You're not so bad yourself," she subtly shot back. But he didn't take the bait! He just nodded and wheeled her amp over to the wall. Lucy was dumbfounded. So she tried again.

"So how come you never bring your girlfriend around?" she asked.

"'Cause she don't exist," Eddie laughed. "Last I checked, all I got's an ex-wife who won't give me my truck back and a bed full of dogs. Cute dogs, anyway."

"Lucky dogs, anyway," Lucy said, laughing. Eddie just looked at her and shook his head, laughing.

"Like I said, you're a jaw-dropper," he said and went back into the control room. Lucy shot me a "what are you looking at?" look and went outside to the patio.

Welcome to the real world, Lucy.

I closed myself in the kitchen with the phone to check my messages. There was one from my mother telling me she'd gotten some darling pictures back from Carla's shower. "You might like to see them to remind yourself to go easy on the sauce," she kindly remarked. Like that lush should talk! Then there was one from Flowers wishing me luck in the studio and requesting a full report on what Jake and Scott were wearing. Which made me laugh out loud right when Scott walked in the room.

"Oh, sorry, you need to be alone?" he asked. I shook my head no and he closed the door behind him.

"You have to hear this message Flowers left me. It's hilarious," I said, holding the phone up to his ear. Instead of taking the phone from me, he put his hand over mine and pressed the phone against his head. I could feel his breath on my hand as I watched him laugh. When the message was over, he slid the phone off his ear but continued holding on to my hand.

"Jenny, I just have to say, I can't believe how great it's going. I'm totally blown away!"

"I know," I said, fully aware of what he was getting at. "Can you even believe Lucy can play like that?"

"Well, yeah, I mean, no, Lucy's an amazing player. That goes without saying. But you . . ." He took the phone out of my hand and put it on the counter. Then he took both my hands in his. "You're scary good. At all of it," he said, moving in closer.

"Wow. Thanks, Scott," I said, suddenly unable to access oxygen. Is he flirting with me? Is he just doing this so I'll let him go out with Lucy? Hello? Brain? Gut? Anyone? Help! "Well, I just wanted you to know that," he said, looking down and playing with the silver ring on my finger. I stared at my finger too, unable to speak but also unable to remove myself from such cozy proximity to him. Lucy's just amazing. I'm the scary one!

After a hundred thousand years, he cleared his throat and looked up. "Well, we should probably get out there. They'll be wondering what we're doing locked in here together," he said, chuckling and heading for the door. He held it open for me, and I walked out in a daze. I wasn't making it up this time, was I? That was flirting. Right?

When we came out of the kitchen, Eddie was setting up the vocal mics.

"We're just tearing through this shit like a box of candies," he said, grinning up at me until he got a good look at my face. "Shit, girl, you look like you got a fever," he said, putting his hand on my forehead. "You're red as a monkey's ass. You feel okay?"

"I'm fine," I said, pushing his hand away and laughing. Eddie looked at me funny, and then he eyed Scott, who shrugged. Eddie looked back and forth one more time and shook his head.

"Let's see if this is the right height for you, Jenny," was all he said, standing me in front of the mic.

We worked our asses off the rest of the day. Every time I went anywhere near Scott, I felt like the whole room could feel the tension, but no one seemed to notice. Did he? He seemed fine, but I swear he made a point of standing closer to me. I watched him with Lucy too, and even though he looked at her a lot, I noticed it was more because she cracked him up. He wasn't looking at her that way. He didn't look away the second she caught him staring, as if he were guilty or something.

That was how he was looking at me!

Now that I thought that there was a possibility I could have him, I had to do everything in my power not to find out for sure. Due to the fact that I was still eating meat and had to pay Flowers to beat me into practicing, I was less than confident of my willpower. I really, really (half) hoped he had some.

We miraculously finished all the vocals and Eddie said we could start mixing next weekend. He also said I should whip up another one of them there lasagnas before I come back.

For some reason, when I bring my lunch into work at The Great Outdoors and people see me eating it, I get embarrassed. I don't like people looking at my food. It seems very personal to me. Which seems potentially insane to me. I asked around, and nobody else seems to have this problem.

September 27

Which verifies my insanity suspicions. They promised to not look at my lunch, though, which is so not the point.

Now that the CD's almost done, I need to start setting up some more gigs. Scott's in charge of helping me contact local press and radio. *Muy importante* if we want to play to a sea of fans instead of a lonely, snoring bartender. He's also in charge of never touching me again. I wrote the words *Thou Shalt Not* on a sticky and stuck it on my bathroom mirror.

Lucy's in charge of showing up for practice and writing a song with me every once in a while.

Jake's in charge of finding himself a place to live and a job. He's been sleeping on his friend's couch and picking up odd jobs ever since his wife kicked him out. For a depressed guy, he's holding it together pretty well, but I know we're only getting the surface. He's the most private person I've ever met. I hope he doesn't take a nosedive.

Tami said she wants to be in charge of all the merchandising. She'll make sure we have T-shirts and stickers and posters. We all have personalized notepads already. She's going to get thrown in Kinko's Prison if she doesn't watch out.

September 30

Rodney and his biological mother came into the store to buy him a backpack. He was so surprised to see me. "I didn't know you worked here!" I almost crawled inside his shirt, I was so glad to see him.

He wanted to know all about the band, and I tried to downplay how well it was going. I said he could have as many CDs as he wanted when it was done. I also said we should go out for coffee one of these days. "That would be all right wouldn't it,

Mrs. Nitzer?" I'd just informed her that everything they bought would get the employee discount, so she couldn't say no.

I got home to another message on my machine from Jeffrey Todd.

"Jenny, Jeffrey Todd here. How's the CD coming? When's my favorite new band playing again? I've got everyone's panties in a twist over here about you guys. They don't believe me when I tell them what I've found. Play a gig! Prove me right! Drop me a line and let me know what's up. Thanks."

He left a message a few days ago too, but I didn't want to call him back until I talked to Katie. The problem: it was still impossible to get her on the phone. Shit, shit, shit. Was I blowing the biggest opportunity we'd ever have? I knew I had to do something before he got sick of me not returning his calls and left us in the dust!

Finally I decided it was time to take drastic measures. I got in the car and drove to Hollywood to the Capitol Records building. It's located right on Hollywood and Vine, one of the sleaziest, most piss-infested blocks of L.A., and is one of the most famous buildings in the city. It looks like something George Jetson designed, because it's weird and giant and round, and it could easily handle a few spaceships landing on its roof. I've always wanted to check it out, actually, and was highly annoyed when the security guard wouldn't let me upstairs.

"Katie Hebard's not picking up, ma'am. You'll have to wait for her down here."

"Can't her assistant buzz me up? Tell her it's Jenny Troanni. The one who calls freaking out all the time."

"I'm sorry. You'll have to wait."

I found a nice overstuffed chair with a stack of magazines next to it and watched hip person after hip person come and go from the building. It was about four o'clock, but I swear some of these people were coming back from lunch. They all had cool jobs and big expense accounts, unlike me, who had to drive around for a half an hour to find free parking.

At one point a group of people walked in with shaggy hair, tattoos, crazy clothes, and that thing. A band. No doubt about it. They were laughing and excited and were immediately let into the elevator. They had that certain air about them that only the truly free and the madly in love have. That should be me! I screamed in my head. They'd probably just come back from a photo shoot in some cool, stripped-down, industrial space with stylists and caterers and make-up artists rushing around all over the place. They were checking in with the label to see how their album artwork was coming along before boarding a plane to London to finish up the mix-down. They'd hang out in the airport bar: everyone who walked by would pretend not to stare. Then they'd get in their first-class seats and down free drinks paid for by their record company. They'd get to London, get set up in their five-star hotel, and hit the clubs, breezing through the velvet ropes and dancing the night away with all the other fabulous people.

The security guard cleared his throat. I was kicking the shit out of the leg of the chair I was sitting in without realizing it.

"Sorry," I said. Suddenly I felt like an idiot. I'd been sitting there like some sort of stalker for over an hour.

"I'm just giving her ten more minutes and then I swear I'll

be out of your face," I told him. "She's a good friend of mine, you know." He nodded as if to say, "That's nice, freak."

Then finally Katie came bursting through the door. She was on her phone and headed straight for the elevator without seeing me. The security guard flagged her down and pointed at me, poised to run defense if necessary. She looked completely surprised.

"Jesus, Karen, hold on a second," she said into her phone. "What the fuck are you doing here?"

"I really need to talk to you. Just for a second."

"I can't! I've got a roomful of people waiting for me in my office, and I'm already late," she said, grabbing my arm and talking into the phone again. "Karen, I gotta go. Just do what I said and if he doesn't like it, tell him he can blow me," she said, hanging up. "Okay, what the hell do you want?" The security guard was still standing by. He wanted to know what the hell I wanted too.

"Can't we go upstairs?" I asked, desperate to get away from him.

"I've got six extremely pissed-off people upstairs waiting to drill me a new asshole at this very second. Just tell me what it is," she said, pushing me toward the wall and out of the way of the elevators. I suddenly felt like an annoying little kid with an annoying little question. Even though I was a foot taller than her.

"Well, Jeffrey Todd from Rosebud Management keeps calling, and I don't want to call him back until I talk to you," I said.

"Jeffrey Todd left you a message and you haven't called him back? Are you fucking brain-dead?"

"Two messages, actually . . ."

"You *are* fucking brain-dead!"

"Well, I don't know what to say! What if he wants to sign us? I don't even know what the fuck a manager does or if we even want one," I said.

"Jesus Christ, sit down," she said, pushing me back into my chair, still warm from the hour I'd just spent in it. Katie sat on the arm and looked down at me like the insect I was.

"Managers are babysitters. Mommies. Dominatrixes. They get you on good tours and make sure the label is distributing, promoting, and advertising your record just like they promised. They'll get you equipment, lunch, and bail money. They'll throw your ass in rehab, or an STD clinic, or both if you need it. They have the worst fucking job on the planet. They get around fifteen percent of all the money you make."

"We don't have a label yet," I reminded her, "or any money."

"If Rosebud Management is interested in you, you will. Trust me. Why you'd want a label is fucking beyond me," she said, "but you definitely need a manager." Her cell phone rang and she answered it.

"What? Yeah, I'm in the lobby. I'll be right up."

"Thanks, Katie," I said, as she hung up and headed toward the elevator.

"Try and act cool. And don't sign a fucking thing without showing it to me first!" she said, getting on the elevator and disappearing into the spaceship. I turned around and headed for the door. The security guard's stare accompanied me out.

"That's right, get a good look. Get a good, hard look at this face," I said, walking to the door. I pushed instead of pulling, failing to open the door and nearly knocking my tooth out in the process. I smiled and backed up, pulling the door open dramatically and breezing out.

I called Jeffrey Todd on his cell the second I got home.

"Yo," he said, and I swear I heard an elephant scream in the background.

"It's Jenny Troanni," I said. I definitely heard an elephant scream.

"Hey! Great to hear from you. I thought you'd gone out and found another manager there for a second!" he said, sounding genuinely relieved.

"We've just been really busy," I said, realizing for the first time that stringing him along had actually made him want us more!

BRILLIANT OBSERVATION #18:
Sometimes being a complete idiot is a shrewd business tactic.

"When are you playing next? Did you finish the CD?" he asked.

"We're just starting to mix it down. Should be done in a couple days. Where are you?"

"Great. The Playboy Mansion. Band photo shoot. Can you get me a copy? A tape is fine."

"Sure."

"Killer. Got to run. Can't wait, Jenny!"

A real live manager whose bands have photo shoots with elephants at the Playboy Mansion wants to maybe sign us.

We are huge!

We just got back from Happyland and our first day of mixing down the record. Eddie's a great explainer of confusing things. Taking 24 tracks of music and mixing them into two is an awe-inspiring feat. We got three songs done today.

He said we could probably do all four tomorrow now that it's all set up. You can put effects on the instruments, pan stuff, and cover up stinky singing with layering and more effects. But Eddie says if the performance isn't there, there's nothing you can do. "You can't shine a turd, darlin'. Luckily, all this here needs is a little gussying up."

If Scott is anywhere within a ten-foot radius of me, I can't form a sentence properly. I managed to stay as far away from him as possible and to never be in a room alone with him. I have to stay focused. I have to not look at his arms.

NOTE TO SELF:
Change note in bathroom to wall-sized mural.

Jake showed up late with a black eye and a fat lip. I swear a black eye is the fastest way to silence a room. We were all hovered around Eddie at the controls when Jake walked in.

"Dudes," he said. We just stared.

"You're probably questioning the unsightly condition of my face," he said as only Jake could say it. We nodded. "Well, I was trying to concoct a sturdy lie on the way over here but, suffice it to say, I paid a failed reconciliatory visit to the ex-wife. When I showed up I found some dude there, so I left, went to Tequilaville, and returned to inform them of my displeasure."

"Shit, boy, you look uglier than a pig with its tail pinned up!"

Eddie said, in a failed attempt at levity. Jake looked miserable.

"Most weak, I know. Wearing the shiner of shame now," he said, sitting down. He pretended he was fine, but I felt bad for him. I passed him the tray of lasagna, which he polished off completely. It was like he'd been shipwrecked for weeks. He didn't even chew.

THE LAST DAY AT HAPPYLAND:

I was kind of sad for most of the day. I think I'm having separation anxiety. Or is it postpartum depression?

We spent the day mixing the last four songs, and all of a sudden the album was officially done! The Meek and a bunch of our other friends stopped by for our final celebratory barbecue. Everyone was out on the patio when Eddie suddenly burst out, blowing a kazoo.

"Shut your damn pie holes!" he screamed. "Please bow your heads in respect. And . . . behold!" He went back inside and blasted the final mix of our album over the patio speakers.

TOP THREE MOST EXCELLENT MOMENTS IN MY ENTIRE LIFE:

1) Seeing the Radio Shack Super Hi-Fi II stereo system, complete with stadium-sized speakers, under the Christmas tree with my name on it when I was fifteen.
2) When Josh Braun (college senior and Certified Most Gorgeous Guy Ever) informed me (Certified Giant Dork and College Freshman Loser) that my crush was mutual.
3) Right now.

October 3

Our album is the best thing I've ever made. Every song is perfect and huge and worth every pain-in-the-ass thing I ever had to do to create it.

"That's *us*!" I screamed after the last note faded away. Much cheering and hugging and pouring of beer on heads ensued.

And not that we care anymore, but Pete barely came near me all night until Eddie played our album and Pete heard how obese it was. A few minutes later he sneaked up behind me and whispered in my ear, "Can I shtop by tonight, rock shtar?"

I'd just heard concrete evidence that I was the greatest thing to ever hit the planet. Why the hell would I waste my time on a dope like Pete? Plus I'd completely forgotten about him ever since Scott said I was scary.

"Actually, Pete," I said, "I don't think you can stop by at all anymore."

He looked kind of shocked for a second, but rather than ask me what was going on, all he said was, "Bummer."

Bummer? I wore lipstick to bed every night for weeks in hopes that a guy who says "bummer" might stop by at 2 A.M.? What the hell is wrong with me?

I suddenly felt like I'd snapped out of a long, gluttonous ether binge and seen myself for the very first time.

GIRL THINKS SHE'S WORTHLESS LOSER. SLEEPS WITH NOTHING BUT IDIOTS AND SLEAZEBALLS. STORY AT ELEVEN.

The cries of my poor little gut had finally cut through my giant wall of denial, and I suddenly felt nothing for him other than pity. I stuck out my hand for him to shake.

"Friends?" I asked. He looked genuinely confused, but stuck his hand out anyway. "Great," I said and walked away.

The grand total for the recording came to $1,589, including tape. Eddie was incredibly generous when he added up the hours. I made him promise to still hang out with us, which he did. He made us promise to not forget him when we're famous. I hugged him until he asked me to please let go. He gave Lucy a friendly kiss on the cheek. He gave me his clown nose.

On the way home I dropped a tape of our masterpiece in the mail and sent it to Jeffrey Todd, Rosebud Management.

I tutored Billy Moorehead today. Twelfth-grade English. He canceled last week because he was sick. I arrived today to discover he has a ten-page story due tomorrow that he's had two weeks to write. When I walked in, he was surrounded by soda cans with a blank screen in front of him, looking like he was going to throw up. My kind of kid.

October 9

ME: What do you want to write about?

BILLY: Dunno.

ME: Let's see. What do you know about? Karate, right? What about writing about a guy who's really into karate?

BILLY: Nah.

ME: Video games?

BILLY: Tried. Sucked.

ME: A story about how sucky suburbia is?

BILLY: No!

I could tell he was getting annoyed with me. Lucky for him I'd sat in that very same chair and shot the very same attitude at my mother for eighteen years. Rather than inform him of the dark consequences of procrastination, à la Mommy Dearest, I made him write a sentence. About anything. He had three seconds and could use no swear words.

I wanna hurl this stupid computer through the window and hear it smash all over Mom's stupid vegetable garden.

When I left him an hour later, he was well into the narrative story of Benjamin Smith, a father of three, incarcerated for the accidental homicide of his gardener.

REASONS I LIKE TUTORING:

1) I'm surprisingly good at it.
2) It's not my ass that's on the line.
3) It reminds me I'm not in high school and never, ever will be again.
4) It pays great.
5) My inner geek is finally being accepted by high school kids. Not for being cool, but for saving them from certain detention.

October 10

Henry took me to his friend Rob's for a housewarming party. I hadn't hung out with Henry on his turf in a long time, mainly because his turf makes me as uncomfortable as mine makes him. Rob is one of the few, the proud, the barely-over-thirty who hit the dot-com jackpot. His place was colossal. The driveway alone was a weeklong road trip.

Since I use three quarters less of my brain than any of

Henry's friends, I played the only social trump card I had. I showed up in full rock-and-roll regalia. Go-go boots, a plastic skirt, and a devil-may-care attitude amongst a sea of khakis and friendly smiles. I stuck out like a circus tent. I felt like an ass.

HENRY: So what do you think of Rob's house?

ME: Henry. This isn't a house. It's a kingdom.

MY BANK
ACCOUNT: Mommy? When we get home can I have a cookie?

A bunch of guys step out of a Gap ad and walk up to us.

GAP GUY #1: Henry! So glad you could make it. And you must be Rock-and-Roll Lucy that I hear so much about.

HENRY: This is Jenny, actually.

ME: And you must be Rob. Nice to meet you.

HENRY: Did you get that e-mail I sent you about the Bernacki Technologies–Biggs Games merger?

GAP GUY #2: Oh my God! They're going to totally revolutionize 3-D pro-gramming.

MY BRAIN: Two plus two am seven!

Suddenly I was a teenager again at one of my parents' cocktail parties. People talked about stocks and computer codes while I smiled and nodded and wondered when they all last had sex. Everyone was duly impressed by my fringe lifestyle, but I still felt like they were taking time out from discussing their real, adult issues for some fun in the peanut gallery with me.

NOTE TO SELF:
Subscribe to the Wall Street Journal.

NOTE TO SELF ADDENDUM:
Figure out how to read Wall Street Journal *without falling asleep.*

At first Henry tried to involve me in every conversation, but I kept glazing over and decided I'd be much happier in front of the giant-screen TV in the pool room. I sat there for about an hour before Henry came and got me.

"Are you having a miserable time?" he asked.

"I'm okay. If you're still having fun we can stay," I said, dying to leave.

"Just give me, like, ten more minutes," he said. I could tell he felt guilty, but I could also tell he really wanted to stay.

"No problem," I said.

He came back about a half an hour later and we left.

BRILLIANT OBSERVATION #19:
Henry and I are from two different planets. We cannot survive for long in each other's atmospheres.

I called a little band meeting at Canter's, a diner near me, before practice. I wanted to make sure everyone was cool with our upcoming gigs, since there were a lot of them. I also really wanted a plate of potato pancakes. We sat in the middle of the restaurant in a booth, and I somehow wound up sitting next to you-know-who. He took up most of the seat, sitting with his legs spread wide and refusing to move all the way over to his end,

October 11

which meant our thighs were pressed together. Which meant I was too nervous to eat my potato pancakes. Lucy ordered a club sandwich that was bigger than her head, Scott had a burger, and Jake just ate the free pickles out of the bowl on the table.

"Jake, eat some of this sandwich. I'll never be able to finish it. It's like a yacht!" Lucy said, picking up a quarter of it and handing it to him. He grinned like a fool, greatly moved that the Goddess of Beauty wanted to nourish him. He didn't move.

"Check him out!" Scott said, elbowing me in the ribs.

"Jake?" Lucy said. Jake finally spoke.

"You're most kind. But I'm really not hungry," he said. But then he took the sandwich out of her hand and swallowed it in about two bites.

I swear he was looking worse and worse these days. The bruises on his face had finally faded away, but he still looked kind of yellow. And he was a lot skinnier than when I first met him. I knew something had to be up because he was superquiet and would disappear all the time, but I didn't know what it was. I did know it probably wasn't great.

"Whatcha got in the bag?" Scott said, leaning over and trying to peer into my knapsack, putting his hand on my thigh in the process. I took a deep breath and closed my eyes, reveling in his scent. I couldn't move.

At last I snapped out of it, grabbed my bag and pulled out my notebook. "Stuff for our band meeting. I'm sending the CD off to be manufactured, making stickers, posters, T-shirts, fliers, and in general, having no life. I need to make sure you guys know what's going on." I handed out copies of the notes I'd made beforehand and then went through it all, trying to ignore the way

Lucy was snickering. I knew collated handouts with bullet points and highlighted sections weren't very rock and roll, but I had to do it. I didn't want anyone pleading ignorance down the road.

Here's one of my best handouts:

STAGE TIPS TO REMEMBER:

- Practice how you play. Be it high heels, dark shades, big spleef, air splits—the stage is not the place to learn how to do it.
- Listen.
- Let's stick with the white theme. All white isn't necessary, but it should make up the majority of your outfit. We want to look like we're a posse. A posse of powdered donuts.
- *Lack of charisma can be fatal.*
- The crowd doesn't know the songs, so when you fuck up, do not advertise. Act like nothing happened and so will they.
- Make sure you have extra drumsticks, guitar picks, strings, pasties, whatever the hell might fly away, break, or get puked on.
- *Be nice to the sound guy.*
- Friends don't let friends get wasted and rock. Pregig two-drink maximum.
- Did everyone go pee-pee?

"Thanks, Mom," Scott said when I was done.

"Hey, Jenny, this stuff is most helpful," Jake said.

"Mama's boy," Lucy sniffed.

"Fuck you all," I mumbled, embarrassed. "Except you, Jake."

October 12

I went on my big date with Rodney this afternoon. I gave him a Bullet Hole T-shirt and took him to Jay's for a three-dollar chili cheeseburger. We sat at the outdoor counter as the traffic tore by behind us on Santa Monica Boulevard, adding that special bus-stop ambience found only at Jay's.

"So," I asked in a serious, motherly tone, "how's everything going?"

"It's boring. I can't wait to go to college and get out of Mom's house," he said, biting into his burger and smearing some ketchup on his chin. I wiped it off with my napkin.

"How's church?" I had to know.

He rolled his eyes and said, "It sucks, but I deserve it. Mom trusted me and I lied to her. I need to repent."

My look of horror was met with a solid stare, daring me to bad-mouth his mother. And his Jesus. That woman was brain-washing him! I was infuriated, but I let it go. He'd be going off to college soon, and I knew he'd snap himself out of it then.

"Well," I finally said, "you'd better stay in touch or I'll come find you and cut you up into tiny little pieces."

"I will. Hey Jenny?" he asked, all puppy-dog eyed. Whatever it was, the answer was yes.

"Yes?"

"Um, if there's like, any way or any reason you ever need me to play with you guys again, I just want you to know that I totally will. Once I'm out of the house, I mean."

"Well, you never know, Rodney. That could happen. I'd love that!"

I drove him back to his house with Jane's Addiction's *Nothing's Shocking* in the tape deck. He was blown away.

He'd never heard it. I'm a hundred and seven years old. I made him take the tape and told him it's one of the top three most important albums ever recorded.

I also told him he'd better get a band going in college or I'd burn his church down.

October 14

> *To whom it may concern:*
>
> *This day marks the transformation of Sixty-Foot Queenie from just another awesome band to an awesome band with a real live manager! I started this band on May 11, a mere five months ago, and I am standing here today as a proud new client of Rosebud Management, which just so happens to manage at least twenty bands you have heard of. So you can take all the nasty stares and condescending remarks you've ever shot my way and cram them up your wormhole.*

This was just a little note that I whipped up and filed away with the rest of the letters I've written but never sent to people. This one is not being sent to my mother. Or the security guard at Capitol Records.

Jeffrey Todd is now our manager! We have a manager. You'll have to call my manager. Did my manager send those papers over? I have to run, that's my manager on the other line.

Here's how it happened:

We'd been playing out about twice a week, which means three gigs so far, and Jeffrey Todd came to every single one of our last three gigs. "I think your CD is brilliant! You guys have got it in the bag. You're beyond," he said, at the first gig. At the next, he showed up with a group of hyperenthusiastic co-workers who bought us all drinks and pointed out all the other industry people in the audience. Then, finally, last night, he showed up at Spaceland and offered us a deal. He walked into the little backstage area as we were hauling our stuff off the stage and handed me a contract the size of the Bible.

"What the hell is this?" I asked.

"It's a marriage proposal," he said. "Take a look at it and let me know what you think. I highlighted the parts that matter. Most of it is just standard crap."

"Are there any pictures? Looks rather hefty," Jake asked.

"Jeffrey, does this mean we're in?" I asked.

"If you want in, yes," he said, smiling and holding his arms out for a hug.

I was no way on any sort of hugging basis with Jeffrey Todd at this point, but, as on-the-go as he was, he had this warm and fuzzy side to him, like a career mom. So I did it. I went in for the hug.

"We're the real deal!" Lucy screamed, running up and giving Jeffrey a hug and me a pat on the ass. Scott was watching the whole thing from behind a pile of drums, and he came around to the front and shook Jeffrey's hand. Then he came over to me and put his hands on my waist.

"Congratulations, superstar," he said, nearly dropping me to my knees. It had to be written all over my face! I swear my entire body changes color if he so much as sneezes in my direction, but nobody seemed to notice anything. Jake was hugging Lucy and Lucy was watching Scott and me, but all she did was shoot me a thumbs-up.

Could it be I was noticing something that wasn't even there? Could it be that only an idiot would care about this stuff on the very day she got signed to a huge management company?

October 15

I actually got a phone call from Katie "Hold Button" Hebard today. It's amazing what a legitimate contract with a legitimate management company can do to someone's phone manners. I wasn't put on hold once, and Katie was genuinely excited. Not positive, but excited.

"Jenny, are you even aware that you guys have a huge fucking buzz in the industry right now? All of a sudden you're the shit. It's unfuckingbelievable." I heard her assistant come in the room and Katie tell her to come back later.

"Really? What does that mean?" asked Jenny the Middle Schooler.

"It means people from every major label are going to show up at your shows and you're about to go up on the auction block. It means you're about to be shackled to the giant slave ship called the Recording Industry of America."

"That's awesome! Who's interested in us?"

"Only everyone," she said. "But you're just the flavor of the week. You need to jump on it fast before they start looking for someone else to stick it in. These motherfuckers are like a bunch of goddamn wind socks."

"Wow, I can't believe it. We're legit!" It was all so surreal! It was all happening so fast.

"Legit in a fucking hellhole of bottom-feeders and sleaze-balls, anyway," the ever-encouraging Katie said. But I didn't care how hostile she was. I knew she got off on it as much as I did.

BRILLIANT OBSERVATION #20:

No matter how sleazy something is, if it involves money and fame, everyone wants to be a part of it.

Take away her job and the word *fucking*, and Katie would spend her days quietly playing with her lip in the corner. I spent the rest of the day on the phone calling all my bandmates and every other single person I knew and alerting them to my impending stardom.

ACTUAL MESSAGE ON MY ACTUAL ANSWERING MACHINE:

"Dear Jenny,

How are you? I am fine. This is your father. I am wondering if you can please pick me up at the airport for Carla's wedding. I suppose I mean myself and Mrs. Paskow. We will be staying at the Sheraton with your Aunt Lauren, who has very kindly offered to drive us to the ceremony. What? What is that? Oh, and your cousin Diana will be there too. Yes. Anyway, I hope you are well.

Love,

Daddy"

The invention of the answering machine blew my father's mind so severely that only now—ten? twenty? years later—does he barely grasp the concept of leaving a message. He used to begin talking as if I were on the other end, and then he'd hang up and call back ten times.

Now he leaves messages like he's writing a letter.

I have yet to get a message without his girlfriend, Mrs.

Paskow, screaming something inane from the background. I have no idea what her first name is. None of us does. We often wonder if Dad does. Or if it really is "Mrs."

I was just thinking about him too, because I got this month's *Scientific American* in the mail. It's my little monthly reminder that my father has no idea who I am or what I'm into. He actually assumes that because he enjoys *Scientific American*, both of his children will too. Which is why Carla and I receive subscriptions every year for Christmas, even though neither of us could name more than three of the planets or give two shits about ions.

Asking Dad to stop goes as unnoticed as asking him anything else. The only upside is the endless fun the jokes about *Scientific American* have brought his two neglected, menaced-by-science children.

I made another goddamn lasagna and asked Katie over to tell us all what the hell is about to happen. I knew we'd have to suffer through a complain-a-thon about the industry, but we're so clueless, we need serious help.

I made Tami, Scott, Jake, and Flowers come because I was afraid I wouldn't understand it all. (Lucy had a photo shoot for Afreaka! They're going on tour as well. Could everything explode in my face at once, please?) Tami and Flowers took great notes, Scott filmed the whole thing, and Jake acted shy and weird for some unfathomable reason.

Katie stood in the front of my living room like she was at the head of a kindergarten class. Here is what she had to say: *ROCK-AND-ROLL HIGH SCHOOL.*

Or, as Katie says, *BEND OVER, YOUR SHIP IS PULLING IN.*

ROCK-AND-ROLL TRUTH #7:

Only two percent of artists signed to record labels make money.

This is a real statistic. You'll probably be offered a seven-album deal, and if you're lucky, it will be two firm. "Two firm" means you get the advance money for the first two albums no matter what, even if they drop you right after the first one.

They can drop you at any time.

You're fucking handcuffed to them until you give them seven albums.

Remember, you are huge, you are invincible, and you have to pay every cent of it back.

Nearly every penny the label spends on your album, your video, your tour, your dinner, your hairspray, your toilet paper, is recoupable. Which means you have to pay it back. You have to sell enough records to cover all those costs before you start seeing any profit.

MOST POPULAR WORDS IN THE RECORD INDUSTRY:

- Recoupable
- Buzz
- Creative control
- Youth
- Recoupable
- MTV
- Sold out
- Hit
- Recoupable

When you sign you will get a chunk of money called an advance. Probably a couple hundred thousand—if you go with a big label—with a couple hundred thousand strings attached. This money you will spend on making a record that you do not own. The label owns it. You will pay producers, engineers, and all other studio costs. This is also the money for you to live on while you make the record.

RECORD LABELS:

A&R people sign bands to labels and oversee their development. If you bomb, they get yelled at or fired. If you are huge, they buy new cowboy boots, leather jackets, and homes.

Product managers market your CD and tend to all aspects of the project. They're like switchboard operators, fielding info from the band, promotion, label heads, management, lawyers, the art department, your parents, your fans, your crazy ex-girlfriends, everyone. They are underpaid and underappreciated, and their lives suck.

Katie is a product manager.

The promotions department sucks up to the radio stations to get them to play your songs. In the old days they used to do this by sending them big bags of cash and blow and hookers and stuff, but they got in trouble.

Do not sign anything without running it by Katie.

Be wary of false promises.

Keep your day jobs.

When Katie left, we all sat in stunned silence.

"Man, who peed in her cornflakes this morning?" Scott asked.

"Is all that true?" Jake wanted to know, as depressed as the rest of us.

"She lives to complain, so I'd take it with a grain of salt," I said. But I wasn't sure. It was hard to tell if it was the truth or if Katie was just on her way to McDonald's with a machine gun. Or both.

Today we all went over to Rosebud Management to meet everyone at the company and sign some final papers. Jeffrey made us feel a billion times better about the giant Katie-bomb that was dropped on us yesterday.

"Yeah, the labels definitely have the upper hand, but come on, they're gonna put a truckload of money behind you. You guys'll have access to stuff you'd never get within ten feet of otherwise. Plus, think about it: if they were so evil, why would anyone ever sign?"

NOTE TO SELF:
Stop asking Katie for advice.

Jeffrey made us use his special Bugs Bunny good-luck pen to sign our contract and strapped party hats on our heads. I'm really starting to love this guy. I couldn't help but notice everyone in my band has awesome, important-looking signatures. Mine looks like something ripped out of a penmanship class homework assignment. It was the only one you could read. I felt like a Girl Scout.

NOTE TO SELF:
Come up with funky new illegible signature.

November 10

Jeffrey took us around to meet everyone at the company. Rosebud handles some gigantic-ass bands, some of which Jeffrey promised we'd be touring with, thank you very much. He handed us each a big pile of CDs, T-shirts, and special Rosebud air fresheners. Everyone we passed was blasting music and screaming into a phone.

This is what some people call going to work.

They threw us a little party, and I swear people were nervous to meet us! Some chick was bragging that she'd seen us at the Joint. Another guy said she never would have been there if he hadn't turned her on to us. I caught Lucy's eye and she made a crazy face.

Do these people have any idea that in middle school I was hung by my undies in the girls' locker room on a regular basis?

Everything I wished for is coming true. Nothing feels real.

When we left the building we were all skipping and happy and had that thing. We were a real band! Jake, who was uncharacteristically energetic today, stopped us in the parking lot and demanded we get in a huddle.

"Dudes, I just want to pause and note the fully colossal paths our lives are now strolling," he said, rosy-faced for the first time since I met him.

"I was just thinking the same thing. And it's going so fast!" I said, attempting to ignore the fact that Scott's face was practically pressed up against mine.

"They acted like we were famous. How weird was that?" Scott said.

"Of course they did," Lucy said. "And soon, so will the rest of the planet!"

We all stood in silence, holding hands as a unified, bulldozing rock machine. We were poised to conquer the world—regardless of taboo crushes, African dance troupes, stupid bass lines, and control issues.

We were on our way.

The CDs will be here in less than a month. A thousand little bundles of joy arriving almost exactly nine months after I changed my life. Coincidence? I think not.

Our CD release party is set for November 28th at Spaceland. We'll be playing with The Meek, Abiogenesis, and Squinch. We will sell enough CDs and T-shirts to make back the money for the CD. It will be infested with eager recording industry professionals fighting for our hand. We will be carried out on the shoulders of giants. We will be remembered fondly by this town as The Ones Who Made It.

November 11

Carla's wedding. Lah-de-dah.

Sometimes I think I was put on this earth to screw up seating arrangements at weddings.

My table contained four couples and me, and while they all merrily chatted away about vacation packages, I looked longingly at the kiddie table. One little girl was stuffing ham up her nose while her brother rolled around under the table, aiming his fork at people and making shooting noises. Not one of them was talking about what a lovely wedding it was or how pretty Carla looked. They were making sculptures out of butter balls. They were taking their pants off. They were the party table.

November 14

Carla did me a major service by not asking me to go out and buy a five-hundred-dollar doily-posing-as-a-dress and be in the ceremony. She either noticed that the shower nearly killed me or realized that it nearly killed her and thought it best for both of us this way. I thanked her. She said it was her pleasure.

The whole thing was held at the "house" of a high school friend of Carla's who's now a rich Beverly Hills trophy wife. Her husband is some big movie producer guy who's a hundred years old, and there were pictures of him everywhere with his arm around various movie stars. At the end of the night, I found Mom standing in front of one of these in the living room, swaying back and forth to the music of the band, her half-full wineglass leading the way. It was a picture of Mr. Big Rich Geezer with Bette Midler, Mom's idol. "Bette is a great, great lady. What pizzazz!" she'd always say. "I'd push you in front of a bullet meant for her, if it ever came to that. My own child. That's how much I love her."

NOTE TO SELF:
Don't go to the ghetto with Mom and Bette Midler.

"So are you gonna steal it or what?" I asked, sneaking up behind her

She jumped, causing a splash of wine to come flying out of her glass.

"Oh, now look what you've done!" she cried, licking the wine off her arm.

"Jeez, Mom," I said, looking around the room for a cocktail napkin to wipe it up with.

I didn't see one. Instead I saw something even more disgusting than my mother licking booze off her arm. I saw my father sucking face with Mrs. Paskow behind the grand piano across the room. He was bent way over, due to the fact that he's a good foot taller than she is, and I was treated to an unobstructed view of her pudgy hand gripping and releasing his left butt cheek. I froze and somehow stifled a scream.

"Close your mouth, Jenny. You look like an imbecile," said my freshly groomed mother. Then she followed my terrified gaze over to the barnyard scene in the corner.

It took a second to register but then Mom, unlike me, was unable to control her emotions. "Oh! *Oh!*" she wailed, putting her hand over her heart and nearly collapsing onto an eighteenth-century French loveseat. She steadied herself and marched up to the happy couple, now no longer smooching, thanks to the bucket of cold water her scream had tossed on them, and stood there with her arms folded across her chest.

POINTS OF NOTE:
- Theirs was not an amicable divorce. Mom kicked him out and swore that if she ever saw him again, she'd see to it that he paid dearly for wasting the best fifteen years of her life.
- Mom and Dad haven't seen each other since Carla's college graduation. And even then we managed to skillfully keep the two camps separate.
- Up until this moment, Mom had no idea that Mrs. Paskow even existed.

- Mom is still mad at Dad.
- Dad is still scared of Mom.
- Everyone involved is drunk.

"Marie! Why, look at you! You look exactly the same," my father said, cowering behind Mrs. Paskow.

"How dare you come here and embarrass me like this!" my mother shrieked, ensuring that anyone nearby who might have missed the show was now informed it was starting.

"Okay, Mom, why don't you give me your wineglass," I said, imagining my father with the stem sticking out of his forehead. I somehow managed to pry it out of her hand and put it safely on the table behind me.

"You! Acting like a teenage boy with this—" She turned to Mrs. Paskow and searched her horrified face for an adjective. "—this—this beanbag!"

"I am not a beanbag!" Mrs. Paskow screamed.

"She is not a beanbag, Marie," my father agreed.

"It's a disgrace!" Mom said, turning to her audience. "Acting like animals in this house, where Bette Midler herself has been!"

I held Mom by the arm, partly to calm her down and partly to prevent her from throwing a punch. I smiled at the crowd and said, "It's fine. Everything's fine."

"No, Jenny, everything is not fine!" said my mother, on the verge of tears.

"Dad, could you please leave now? And take Mrs. Paskow with you?" I said, now holding both of Mom's arms.

For the first time in his life, Dad actually heard what I said and started pushing Mrs. Paskow toward the door.

"Oh no. Not until she apologizes. I am no beanbag!" Mrs. Paskow said, holding her ground. Great. There was going to be bloodshed over an insult that didn't even make any sense. Dad was now looming over the tiny Mrs. Paskow the same way I was hovering over Mom, holding them back like we were at a cockfight waiting for the whistle to blow.

"Hah!" said Mom, thrilled by her success. None of the ten or so audience members offered to help, and I was moments away from just dragging Mom out by her hair, when The Life of the Party suddenly came crashing into the room. He's the drunk guy at every wedding who makes long, not-funny toasts and inevitably ends up onstage, taking over the lead vocals for the band. He was about twenty-five, and I recognized him from the wedding party as one of John's friends. He came screaming into the living room followed by a throng of follow-ers with his tuxedo shirt unbuttoned and his bow tie wrapped around his forehead.

"I'll be taking requests and tips," he announced, taking a seat at the piano as people filed into the room. Nobody seemed to notice there was about to be a rumble, and before I knew it, a large crowd had come between the two contenders.

"I'd like to begin with an old favorite my mother taught me back in the day. Gather round and don't be afraid to sing!" He started playing the old classic, "You Do Something to Me," which, shockingly, was Mom and Dad's "song." I couldn't fucking believe it! I imagined a loud, dramatic howl spilling forth from my drunken mother as she tore herself out of my kung-fu grip and lunged for my father's windpipe.

But much to my surprise she started singing, and when I let

go of her arms, she walked over to the piano and snuggled up next to Mr. Entertainment on the bench. Moments later Dad was by her side, his hand resting on her shoulder out of old habit. And she didn't even take a bite out of it! In fact, they started singing together, causing Mrs. Paskow to storm out of the room in a huff.

Carla must have heard the song begin because she burst into the room in a panic, only to stare drop-jawed at the bizarre thing happening on the piano bench. She made her way over to me and gripped my arm.

"What the hell is this?" she whispered.

"I don't know, but I don't trust it. Be prepared to run defense when the song's over," I said. But it was truly a miracle. The song ended and my parents were so caught up in the moment, they actually hugged! Carla's nails dug into my arm as we watched The Impossible Embrace. Both of them stepped back, suddenly embarrassed.

"Very nice to see you, Marie," Dad said, scared again. But Mom looked completely confused and somehow tinier than ever. All the fight had drained out of her.

"Jenny, I'm ready to go now," she calmly said, and headed through the crowd and out of the room.

I think in the normal world this is what they call closure. She spent the entire car ride home chatty and happy! It was like she'd been body-snatched. All she said about the incident was, "I can't believe it. *That's* who I've been getting terrible stomach gas over for all these years. Incredible." I had no idea she still thought about him that much. I wonder if this means Mom will finally spend some time doing something other than being pissed off.

Aside from this slight slip into an alternate universe, Carla's wedding turned out to be like every other wedding. The bride sobbed her whole way down the aisle, drunk married men made passes at me, and the band played a terrifying version of KC and the Sunshine Band's already terrifying hit, "Celebrate!"

WEDDING TRUTH #1:

A wedding is a wedding. No matter how much cash the couple puts into decorating, getting a great band, serving interesting food . . . you always feel like you're just at another wedding. Save it for the damn honeymoon.

WEDDING TRUTH AMENDMENT #1:

The only wedding that felt like a party was my high school friend Cassie's. She got knocked up at eighteen and sent out invitations with two crossed rifles on the front. The caption read, "There's gonna be a weddin'!" We all went up to her lake house and hung out for the weekend. They got a bluegrass band and a slew of kegs. We played capture the flag and went hiking. Cassie was so big, she couldn't do much but referee.

I wonder what ever happened to her.

5 SIGNS THAT YOUR BASS PLAYER IS LIVING IN YOUR PRACTICE SPACE:

1) He's always the first one there and the last to leave.
2) He has fragments of the carpeting in his hair.
3) His car resembles a closet.
4) His playing improves exponentially every week.
5) The room smells like his car.

November 16

Clearly, I had to have a big fat talk with Jake. Our landlord was renting us that room for way cheap, and he would not be happy knowing someone was living there. I stopped by unannounced on my way back from work, after picking up the fliers for our CD release party and before driving all over town to hang them up.

A mother's work is never done.

The building was eerily quiet when I walked in. As terrifying as I find the death rock band across the hall to be, it's almost more upsetting when they're not jamming and I'm alone. At least when they're making noise, you know where they all are. If it's silent, I feel like they could be lurking around every corner. Or hanging by their feet from the ceiling of their practice space, sleeping with their wings wrapped tightly around their bodies.

So when I saw the light peeking out from under the door of our room, I was relieved even though it confirmed my suspicions about Jake. I knocked on the door.

"Who is it?" I heard Jake's voice ask from the other side.

"It's Jenny."

"Oh, just a second." I heard rustling around, and it took him a good couple of minutes to open the door. When he finally did, he was standing there in a ripped flannel shirt, jeans, and no shoes. He was having trouble looking me in the eye, and I swear he was fucked up on something.

"Hey, just getting in some extra practicing," he said, ushering me in through the door. I walked in and closed the door behind me. Then I stared at him until he had to stop fidgeting and look me in the eye. He was so glassy-eyed, I could almost see myself in the reflection.

"We could all lose this practice space if the landlord finds out you're living in it, Jake," I said.

He sighed, then sat down on the floor and rubbed his head. "Understood. Most weak of me. I apologize. I don't know what to say—I've got nowhere to go," he said, his eyes darting all over the room.

"You could have told us instead of sneaking around." I was starting to resent constantly having to be a bitch.

"Sneakiness. The worst. A thousand apologies. Really. Sorry for the turmoil. I'll be out today."

"Where will you go?"

"No worries. There are plenty of couches in this town I haven't surfed yet. I can also crash in my car," he said. "Are you guys, like, gonna cut me loose?"

"I wasn't planning on it," I said,

"Awesome. Thanks, dude. I really appreciate it. This band is all I've got." I could tell he was really uncomfortable and wanted me to leave. He must have been totally humiliated.

"Okay, Jake. And if you get stuck, let me know. There's always my couch."

"Thanks, Jenny."

I really wanted to ask him why his eyes looked like a pair of marbles, but it was all so upsetting already, I didn't have the heart.

I can't stop thinking about Scott. He's my first thought when I wake up and my last before falling asleep. He's filled the time slot I usually reserve for freaking out about money.

"What am I going to do?" I whined to Flowers, the only human being alive allowed to know about my little obsession.

I heard him sigh on the other end of the phone. "Nothing," he finally said. "Absolutely nothing. Over time it'll fade and

November 19

before you know it, you'll be losing it over some new guy who can't say his *s*'s."

"I don't think so. And to make it worse, I keep catching him staring at me. I'm not kidding, Flowers. It's really bad."

"I wish I had your problems."

"Flowers!"

"Well, what do you want me to tell you? Go ahead and fuck him and break up the band. Or kick him out and fuck him. Or send him over here and let me fuck him! Now there's an idea."

He was absolutely no help. What I wanted him to tell me was that I could do exactly what I wanted with no repercussions. I needed incentive.

"Make a bet with me," I said.

"What kind of bet?"

"If I sleep with Scott, I have to . . . do your laundry for a year."

"Too easy."

"Give you two hundred bucks?"

"Not humiliating enough."

"Well, what then?"

He was silent for a moment. I could hear his evil little wheels spinning. Suddenly he shrieked with delight. "Oh, I do believe I'm a genius! Okay, here it is: If you sleep with Scott, you have to bring me Mrs. Nitzer's motorcycle lighter!"

It was pretty damn brilliant. Enter the dragon's lair, befriend the beast, and capture the Holy Grail. Luckily, the mere thought of that woman was enough to dry up my sex drive completely. It was perfect. Especially since Flowers would absolutely hold me to it. No matter how hard I begged.

The deal was sealed.

I spoke to Mom today. I figured I had to invite her to our CD release party and just pray she wouldn't come. I now realize I was mad at her before we even opened our mouths. I had the whole thing played out in my brain before she even picked up. My irritated defensiveness. Her stubborn disappointment. Here's what I imagined I'd hear:

THE CROAK: Well, I don't know. It sounds like making a CD and then throwing a party to celebrate costs a pretty penny for someone who just got a ten-cent raise up from minimum wage.

ME: Twelve-cent. And if you have a better way for me to get my music out there and land a record deal, I'm all ears.

THE CROAK: I have a better way, but it doesn't include music or record deals.

Like sitting back on a comfortable old couch and watching reruns of your favorite boxing match. But it didn't go that way at all. I mean, I was still mad, of course, but not because she rained her usual monsoon of insults on me. I was mad because she didn't! She was too distracted! Mom actually had the audacity to be consumed by something other than my mountain of faults, and I swear I've never been so insulted in my life. Here's how it really went:

ME: So that's it. It's all recorded and ready to go. The party's next week.

MY ALLEGED
MOTHER: Well that certainly sounds like quite a bit of work. . . . Oh hell.

ME: What?

MY ALLEGED
MOTHER: I just dropped my damn flea market folder and now everything's out of order.

ME: What flea market?

MY ALLEGED
MOTHER: Didn't I tell you? I thought I told you. I'm organizing a flea market in the high school parking lot. All the vendors are giving ten percent of their earnings to the community garden. Isn't that wonderful?

ME: Yeah. Maybe they can pass some on to me. I'm beyond broke.

MY ALLEGED
MOTHER: Oh, that's my other line. I have to take it. Talk to you soon!

In thirty short seconds everything had changed. She suddenly had better things to do than give me shit. And the weirdest part was, I was hurt! I felt like someone had died. How ridiculous is that?

I think I'm insane.

I think I'm being forced to grow up.

I think I hate it.

NOTE TO SELF:
People have lives. Just because they decide to live them doesn't mean you suck.

November 26

Our CD release party is only two days away. I told Katie to drag as many company people along as she could; then I put up posters, sent out e-mails, fliers, and death threats. My new manager said he was doing much the same. "Jenny, this is my job now. You just focus on being a rock star," he said.

How bizarre. I suddenly felt naked and weird about handing it all over to someone else. Like giving your baby to a wet nurse.

"Did you put an ad in the weekly?" I asked. I could hear the wind whipping through his cell phone. Perhaps he was on a yacht in the Caribbean shooting a video?

"Yes, ma'am. I've also made sure that everyone who's anyone will be there."

"Great," I said.

"Jenny, you get final say over the stuff I do, so don't worry," he said, noticing my lack of enthusiasm.

NOTE TO SELF:
Trust Jeffrey, you butthole. He's a professional.

While I was killing myself with all this, Lucy was frantically getting ready for her Afreaka! performances. She graced us with her presence at practice today for the first time in ten days. Our CD release party is only one of the biggest gigs we'll ever have. Who needs to practice?

"Afreaka! is warming up for Erykah Badu at the Hollywood Bowl tomorrow night! Can you believe it?" she said, taking her guitar off and leaning it against the wall. "Check out this dance sequence I'm going to do. It's crazy!" she said, launching into a bent-over, squatting run, windmilling her arms and tearing around the room like a drunken chicken.

"Whoa!" said Jake, fully impressed. Scott watched her intently before looking over at me for a reaction.

I shook my head and turned my back on her. I couldn't

believe the one time she showed up for practice, she was trying to piss away our precious time! I hit the first few notes to "Put That Thing Away" and Scott joined in. Jake eventually started playing too. Lucy stopped dancing and stuck her tongue out at me, then picked up her guitar with an attitude and started playing. When the song was over she stood rigid and stared at me.

"What next, boss?" she asked, sarcastically.

"How about 'Rib Eye'?" Jake said.

"That okay with you, boss?" Lucy said, still totally in my face.

"Gee, what a bossy bitch I am, getting upset that the one night you actually show up, you spend it waddling around the room," I said.

"A whole three minutes of your time," Lucy shot back. "You need to lighten the hell up."

"You need to grow the hell up!" I said.

"Guys? Let's not waste any more time," Scott bravely cut in.

"Shut up!" Lucy and I shouted, at the same time, shutting him up and making Jake laugh.

"Did it ever occur to you that maybe I want to show you, my best friend, what I'm doing? Since you never ask or, God forbid, come to any of my shows?" said a calmer, gentler Lucy.

Why the hell would I want to go see Afreaka! the Other Woman? Did it ever occur to her that Afreaka! is the bane of my existence? I pleaded with my inner babysitter to give me strength. The sitter reminded me that happy children eat all their peas. Unhappy children throw them across the room. If Lucy felt I was more involved in her projects, maybe she'd be more involved in mine.

"You never asked," I said, trying not to vomit.

"Well, shit! Come tomorrow night! I can get you in for free—I can get all of you in for free. Let's get Flowers to come too!" she said, and it was decided. We were all going to revel in the glory of the enemy.

NOTE TO SELF:

Keep your eye on the pea.

As if the evening ahead weren't irritating enough, I had to spend the day at work kissing Brad's ass so he'd let me off early. He's already given me tons of time off for gigs and hangovers, so today's request was really pushing it. Luckily, his crush on me was still healthily intact, but I really resented having to humiliate myself just to go see Lucy's stupid ethnic hoedown.

"I swear I'll make it up to you, Brad. I'll polish all the canoes. I'll sell more poop shovels than anyone ever has in the history of The Great Outdoors!" I said, making sure to stand close to him.

He shook his head. I'd cornered him in the supply room where we kept all the shoeboxes, and I was backing him up against a wall of men's size 9. He tapped me on the head with the clipboard he was using to take inventory.

"I'm sorry, rock star, but I just can't. I already got yelled at for giving you special treatment," he said.

"Screw those guys. You're their boss. You can do whatever you want," I said, trying to stroke his ego.

"It wasn't the staff, Jenny. I got yelled at by *my* boss," he said, pushing me back with his clipboard. He wasn't going to risk losing his job for me. I had to pull out the big guns.

November 27

"I'll let you take me out for dinner," I said, tugging on the top of his clipboard. He looked at me sideways.

"Isn't this sexual harassment?" he asked through squinted eyes.

"I think it would have to be the other way around, since you have all the power," I said. "I'm just the lowly employee with a crush on her big bad boss." I am revolting! I am going to burn in hell!

"Well, since you put it that way," he said, lowering his clipboard and moving closer. "What night's good for you?"

And it was all downhill from there. Next, Flowers called from the hospital with a broken leg.

"I got flattened by the UPS truck while I was crossing the street! When am I going to learn the art of getting hit by someone rich?" he moaned. "He didn't even have any packages for me."

"Were you jaywalking?" I asked.

"Of course I was! How come everyone asks me that? As if I'm the only renegade who doesn't cross between the white lines."

"Well, I'll stop by and see you later," I said. "I have to run to Lucy's thing."

"Tell Miss Lucy I'm devastated I'm missing her big show! I'd hop there if my nurse didn't scare the hell out of me."

Then, as if that weren't bad enough, Scott came to pick me up. Alone.

"Where's Jake?" I asked.

"Haven't been able to find him all night," he said, checking me out. "Have you heard from him?" He was wearing a black skullcap and a blue zip-up uniform jacket with "Ted" embroidered above the right pocket. Every time I see him I'm a little surprised that he really is as gorgeous as my imagination makes him out to be.

"No. You think he's okay?" I asked, as worried for myself as I was for Jake. The Hollywood Bowl is Romance Land, an outdoor amphitheater where people bring picnic dinners and wine and snuggle beneath the stars.

"I hope so. Hey, got a blanket we can bring? It can get kind of chilly out there," he said, moving in closer. "You look great," he added, as if the idea of curling up under a blanket with him weren't enough to make me claw at myself already.

I'm going down, I thought as Scott led me and my blanket out the door. I'm so going down.

We had pretty good seats, off to the right and not too far from the stage. Scott brought a bottle of wine and a bag of potato chips, and since Jake and Flowers weren't there, we had four seats in a row to ourselves. Did I mention it was a full moon and a perfectly clear sky? Did I also mention that the second we got into our seats, Scott put his arm around me? I sat as rigid as a shovel, fully aware that if I softened up even the slightest bit, it was all over. In this case, with this guy, I was either a rock or a melted puddle of butter. He popped the cork out of the wine and handed me the bottle.

"Madame," he said. I put the bottle to my lips and tipped it up, glaring at the moon and wondering how I figured wine would aid me in my quest for chastity. Scott's eyes never left my face, and when I handed the bottle back, his gaze remained steady while he took a swig. He licked his lips and smiled, his perfect face two inches from mine.

"Oh boy," I said, turning my face toward the stage and

away from danger. I slid down in my seat and Scott's arm was around me again, his hand slowly working my head down onto his shoulder.

"Finally. You're relaxing a little," he whispered in my ear.

"I have about a million reasons why I should get up and run instead," I said, attempting to not fall through the cracking ice.

"I have a million reasons why you shouldn't," he said, rubbing my neck.

Thankfully, Lucy's stupid performance finally started. The stage exploded in yellow light as a long line of dancers filed on in brightly colored, flowing clothing. They were accompanied by one drum at first, but more and more kept joining in until it sounded like millions. Then there were other instruments, twangy, clicky things I'd never heard before, and wailing voices rising and falling in offbeat harmonies. The dancers broke out in a chaotically choreographed explosion that seemed totally unorganized one second before coming tightly together the next. I was utterly blown away. It was brilliant.

The Other Woman was a babe!

"Can you see Lucy?" Scott asked. I pulled out my binoculars and handed them over without looking at him. I decided if I didn't look, I had a screaming chance in hell. Out of sight, out of mind.

"There she is!" he laughed. "She's in purple," he added, handing them back to me. I took the binoculars and looked at the stage. I finally spotted her, twirling, leaping, and bounding like the giant Afreaka! freak she was. I suddenly felt like an idiot. Of course she was missing stupid band practices! These guys were already at the Hollywood Bowl and talking about a world tour. This was a real thing! I felt incredibly rinky-dink in the face of this big-budget extravaganza.

Somehow, Scott picked up on it. "Hey, what's the matter?" he asked, pulling me in closer to him.

"Nothing," I moped.

He sat up and put his hands on either side of my head, forcing my face toward him. "Bullshit. What's wrong?"

I was looking right at him now, and as miserable as I was, having his hands on me like that was a total turn-on. I rolled my eyes.

"Just having doubts, that's all," I said.

"We'll be playing at bigger places than the Hollywood Bowl," Scott said, reading my mind. "There's no doubt about that." How the hell did he know what I was talking about? How come I never noticed how perfect his ears were?

"Doesn't it all seem kind of childish to you sometimes?" I asked.

He thought about it for a while. He's a guy who thinks about things for a while. "Everything's childish, really, until it hits big. Think about it. Before you saw Afreaka! you thought it was a bunch of hyper ethno-enthusiasts jumping around to a drum."

"That's true. I guess you're right," I said.

"I know I am. And I know our band will really make it. So shut up and let me kiss you before I go insane."

Oh boy.

Needless to say, we pretty much made out for the rest of the show. I don't know if it was the excruciating weeks of tension or if Scott was schooled by the finest masters in the world, but I've never been with anyone who could kiss like that. I decided that just for this one night I was going to go with it and worry about the consequences later.

We floated down to the backstage door to find Lucy after the show. I was now in such a removed state of bliss, I had no trouble telling her how blown away I was, even though I hated her for it.

"Thanks! You guys really liked it?" she said, exuberant. She was still dressed as The Purple Afreakan, with her fellow tribemates milling about in costume as well, making the whole night feel even more surreal than it already was. She was so high from her performance, she didn't notice that I was barely able to form a sentence.

"You guys are incredible, Lucy. Unbelievable drumming," Scott said. Lucy hugged him. And me. For the fifth time.

"I'm so glad you came," she said to me. "I really am." I couldn't bring myself to return the sentiment, so I just smiled like an idiot instead.

We stayed for Erykah Badu because I didn't want the night to end since, as far as I was concerned, it couldn't continue outside the safe confines of the Hollywood Bowl. That would be the kiss of death. So Scott and I returned to our blanket and spent another two hours grossing out the people in the row behind us. I left having completely raw lips and absolutely no clue what a single note of Erykah Badu's music sounds like.

When the concert was over, we walked out holding hands and joining the solid mass of people trying to squeeze through the same doors. We were just about to the final exit, where the crowd was its thickest, and Scott was behind me kissing my neck, when all of a sudden I was face to face with Henry! He just popped out of nowhere like the Saint of Ill Conduct. Had he seen Scott kissing my neck? Hadn't he noticed how crowded it was and that countless guys had practically kissed my neck on my way out the door? He must have realized that. He must know there was no way to know for sure.

"Henry! Fancy meeting you here," I said, trying to be as casual as possible.

"Hey, Jenny. Hi, Scott," he said. I suddenly realized he was embarrassed, that he was busted too. He was just there to be near Lucy. He'd probably been to every damn performance, in fact.

"Pretty awesome show," I said. "Who knew she had it in her?"

"Yeah," said Henry, visibly upset. "Could you guys do me a favor and not tell her you saw me here? It's kind of embarrassing."

"Scout's honor," said Scott.

"No problem," I said.

"Thanks," said Henry, eyeing the two of us. "So how are you guys?"

"Good," I said, trying to back into someone else to show how anyone, anyone at all in this crowd, could come close to kissing my neck. There was a very uncomfortable pause.

"So did you have good seats?" I finally asked.

"Yeah," Henry said, smiling. "About four rows behind you."

"We're so busted!" Scott yelled, laughing. I didn't think it was funny. I trusted Henry not to say anything, but I was still planning on growing a backbone while I slept tonight and ending the whole stupid thing in the morning. Somehow, having Henry know gave it more life than I wanted it to have.

When we got back to my house, I somehow managed to make Scott go home.

"We'll just sleep! I swear! I just want to be with you tonight," he said.

"Believe me, Scott, so do I, but we can't! We'd have to hide your car in the bushes, for one thing. Lucy only lives a street away—what if she drove by and saw it?"

"There are plenty of bushes!" he said.

I broke down. "Please help me," I begged, falling to the floor and grabbing his ankles. "This is such a very bad idea and I am such a very giant weakling. Go home, please."

He laughed, helped me to my feet, and planted another long, deadly kiss on me. "To be continued," he said, slipping out the door.

Oh my God, I'm never going to get to sleep. I couldn't call Flowers because he'd just revel in the glory of Mrs. Nitzer's soon-to-be-his lighter. I couldn't call Henry because I refused to sympathize with him on the Lucy thing anymore. No way was he going to hold my hand through this even stupider mistake I was making. I sure as hell couldn't call Lucy, and Carla was definitely asleep, so I opted for crawling into bed with my headphones on and blasting thoughts of Scott out of my head until I finally fell asleep.

Tonight is our rilly big shew. Luckily, I've had so much to do, I haven't had time to see Scott. Not that I haven't been thinking of him at all times. In fact, I was an hour late for work this morning because I misplaced my keys (in the refrigerator), backed my car over my neighbor's mailbox (I forgot I was in reverse), and put cat food instead of litter in the litter box.

BRILLIANT OBSERVATION #21:
There should be live-in nurses for the romantically preoccupied.

I've been sitting on this whole Scott thing for a while, stuffing it down like a snake in a can, and now that I've let it pop out, I know I won't be able to get it back in again. Who am I kidding? I wish I could talk to Lucy about it, but I've broken the cardinal rule of all bands. Plus I've been riding her ass so hard that now I'm not just a weakling and an amateur, I'm a hypocrite too.

So far he's called me three times, just to make sure everything's fine.

"Define 'fine'," I said to him.

"That we're cool. That what happened the other night was good."

"Yeah, it was great, Scott. But it can't go on," said I, the queen of high drama and bullshit.

"I can't stop thinking about you," he said.

"Stop anyway. Good-bye," I said. I moved to my refrigerator and straightened the picture of Mrs. Nitzer that Flowers had sent me in the mail.

And as if my day weren't already complicated enough, Jake

finally reappeared as I was on my way out the door. He was on foot and looked like he'd spent the night underneath someone's porch.

"Jake! Are you all right? What the hell happened to you?" I said, ushering him inside and praying that he didn't sit down on any of my furniture before I could stick a towel under him.

"Long story. My apologies for last night, but I got booted off the couch and spent the night trying to regain possession of my stuff," he said, looking like he could fall asleep at any second. I had no idea what he was talking about, but I led him to the bathroom and handed him a towel.

"Take a shower and then get some sleep on my couch. I'll be back from work around five, and then everyone's coming over to get ready for the gig. We'll figure out where you're going to stay later," I said.

"Most kind of you Jenny," he said, sheepishly. "I think I can crash at Lucy's place, so I'll be out of your hair tonight."

Crash at Lucy's! He wouldn't be in her door for two seconds before she was all over him like a starving cannibal. No way in hell.

"I think you should stay with me," I said.

"Wow, Jenny, really? That's righteous," he said.

Jake wasn't around when I got home, which meant I was home alone when Scott showed up. The bastard was wearing The Perfectly Fitting Pair of Jeans and carrying a bouquet of flowers. He walked right in the door without saying a word and started kissing me before I could even pretend to push him away.

When we finally came up for air, he handed me the flowers and said, "Don't tell me how I shouldn't have and we shouldn't have or any of that shit, okay? It takes all the fun out of it."

"Well, I don't think potentially fucking up the band is fun!" I said, somehow removing myself from him and walking into the kitchen to get a vase. He followed close behind me, rubbing his hands over my back. I could have easily locked the door, turned out the lights, blown off the gig, and spent the entire evening with him.

"I missed you," he said, rubbing my neck.

Suddenly I heard the front door fly open. *"Buenas noches!"* Lucy screamed. I threw Scott's arms off me and ran into the living room.

"Lucy! What's up?" I asked, trying to act normal. She couldn't have seen anything that was going on in the kitchen, but I needed to make sure. She was oblivious and looked exhausted.

"I'm about as tired as I could be, that's what's up," she said, putting her stuff down. "I've been gigging like crazy, working my ass off, and damn Jake woke me up in the middle of the night looking for a place to sleep."

Uh-oh. Had she already done the deed with him?

Before I could broach the subject, Scott walked into the room. Her face lit up.

"Hey, you," he said, giving her a hug.

"Hey, Scotty," she said. Scotty? Since when the hell did she call him Scotty?

"Is Jake with you?" he asked.

"Jake?" she said, shaking her head. "Jake's on another planet."

"He's pretty far gone, isn't he?" Scott asked.

So I wasn't crazy—he was doing something! "Yeah, I noticed that too, you guys! I think he's doing some pretty serious drugs," I said.

"You think?" said Scott, sarcastically.

"Jenny, the guy's a full-blown junkie. Wake up," Lucy said, marveling at my ignorance.

A junkie! I mean, I've done my share of dabbling with drugs, but heroin just seems so big and scary to me. Something that people who steal from their mothers and live in skanky motels do. Not Jake!

"I know that," I lied. "I just wasn't sure how bad it was."

"Well, I'm sure as hell not letting him stay with me," Lucy said. "I've been down that road before and it ain't pretty." I suddenly felt like a giant boob for letting him stay with me. But someone had to take care of him!

"Well, do you think we should talk to him?" I said, worried as much for my band as I was for him.

So far we had:
1) A lead guitarist who was only half in the band,
2) A moronic lead singer who couldn't help molesting the drummer,
3) A drummer with no conscience or common sense what-soever, and
4) A homeless, drug-addicted bass player.

How the hell was I going to keep it all together long enough to get famous?

"Like talking ever does anything," Scott huffed.

How come everyone was a heroin expert all of a sudden? Where the hell was I while these guys were hanging with the homies at the crack den?

There was a knock at the door and Tami walked in, wearing

a dress made out of glued-together photographs of the band. That broke up the solemnity.

"Our little sandwich board!" Lucy screamed.

"I made a banner to stick behind the stage too," Tami reported, "and a thousand Sixty-Foot Queenie pins, magnets, posters, and bumper stickers."

Jake showed up a few minutes after her, looking pretty well-rested for a junkie. Everybody acted like everything was just fine. He was all ready to go, and I realized that even though he might have been swirling down a scary tunnel, all this time he hadn't been fucking up his band responsibilities. I decided to worry about it after the gig. After all, we had a record deal to snag.

I'm writing this from bed after having a pepperoni pizza delivered for breakfast. My new roommate is snoring away like a lawn mower on the couch, and as much as I fear I've made a great mistake by letting him stay, it may just be the chastity belt I needed. No can bring Scott home with Jake sleeping on the couch. I'm praying desperately that Jake + Mrs. Nitzer's lighter = will of steel.

I'm too hung over to do the evening justice (the mere movement of my pen is threatening to make me puke) but, among many other things, Jeffrey said three whole labels are interested in signing us! He said there'll be a bidding war and it's only a matter of time before we're signed. He also said we should put any plans for a tour on hold. He told me to stop thinking about it. Which is the same as telling someone to stop slamming their hand in a car door. I swear, the thought of not having to figure out what fucking bar in Utah we should send our CD to is equally as exciting as the thought of three whole labels being interested in us.

At this moment, however, nothing is more exciting than this pepperoni pizza.

THE CD RELEASE PARTY HIGHLIGHTS:

- We raked in $1,276 at the door.
- The bubble machine short-circuited, and burning soap fumes nearly killed us all.
- Squinch played naked with "Sixty-Foot Queenie" written across their bodies.
- The Meek dressed up as us.
- Lucy puked in the parking lot but still took some guy home.
- Some chick named Dana Burgy flirted with Scott, and I nearly lost my mind.
- Tami sold nearly everything she brought and had to jump some guy who tried to steal a sticker.
- Two drunken fights broke out and three toilets overflowed.
- Steve from Abiogenesis fell off the stage and broke his arm.
- We raffled off the ugly-ass pink bridesmaid's dress I wore in a wedding three years ago and made $64. Some guy named Aaron Singer won it and wore it proudly all night.
- Every single person in the crowd loved us.
- Scott and I made out in the men's bathroom.
- Flowers came onstage and did a handstand, leg cast and all, for the duration of our last song.
- I was the center of attention.
- It was the funnest night of my entire life.

At the end of the night, some guy named Rex from Elektra Records took us to the legendary rock-and-roll bar, the Whiskey. The place was crawling with rock stars, including Courtney Love, whom I went up to and said, "I love you." She responded by telling me my fly was open. Courtney Love told me my fly was open! How cool is that? I gushed a thousand drunken thank-yous and stumbled back to my seat. The Elektra guy paid for everything and gave us all Elektra Records T-shirts, baseball hats, and tickets to see Stereolab. He said he loved us and was dying to work with us.

ROCK-AND-ROLL TRUTH #8:
Being in a band is the only situation where a "job interview" takes place while you're wasted, wearing something ridiculous, and screaming lewd things into a microphone.

I've finally found my perfect job.

Scott called this morning and told me, among other things, that The Meek broke up right after our gig. It turns out the entire band was sleeping with the lead singer, and the whole thing finally blew up. Aside from the satisfying reconfirmation that Pete is a complete moron, it really sucks. They were one of my favorite bands.

November 30

NOTE TO SELF:
Warnings are all around you, stupid!

"Is Pete upset?" I asked him.
"I can't tell. I haven't really seen him in a while," Scott said.

"Still out prowling the town?" I asked.

"I don't know. He doesn't live here anymore."

"Really? When did that happen?"

"About a week ago. I kicked him out because he never pays his rent. And because it makes me nervous having him around."

"Why?"

"Because of you. It makes me uncomfortable knowing you guys had a thing. I wouldn't want him around if you came over."

"Pete and I had a stupid thing, Scott," I said, "and you and I have no thing, so calm down." Wasn't he getting a little territorial a little fast?

"Yeah, we have no thing," he said, laughing. "You're right. You never even think about me, right?"

"I'm hanging up," I said.

"Here you go again with the hanging up," he said.

"Good-bye," I said.

"Sweet dreams," he said.

Red flag number two: possible jealous freak. As if red flag number one (definite drummer in my band) weren't enough, this new unsightly development should push me even further away from him. But was it even true? Would I feel weird if I lived with someone Scott used to sleep with? I wasn't sure.

NOTE TO SELF:

Keep an eye on the green-eyed monster.

ANSWERING MACHINE MESSAGE
FROM JEFFREY:

"Jenny, Jeffrey. You guys are *the shit*! I've never seen any-thing blow up like this. Mastiff, Columbia, and Matador are inter-ested now too. We've got to strike while the iron's hot. I've tacked you on to a showcase gig at the Knitting Factory on the fifth with a bunch of my other bands. After that it'll only be a mat-ter of choosing which label you want. Get ready to be a star!"

It's really happening. *It's really happening*. I called in sick and took myself shopping. I spent $473 on clothes, $83 on hair prod-ucts, $112 on makeup, $239 on shoes, and $64 on a fur hat for Scott. I put it all on my credit card and didn't even think twice.

Making the transformation from The Great Rock-and-Roll Dream to The Great Outdoors is killing me. It's torture drag-ging myself into work at all, and with all that's going on, get-ting excited about the new fleece sleeping bag liners is well beyond my capacity. Plus most days I'm running on about two hours of sleep and a frozen burrito. I've been late almost every day and completely blew off work yesterday. If Brad didn't have such a thing for me, I definitely would have been fired by now.

Speaking of which, I went into work today having totally forgotten about my heinous promise of having dinner with him, as well as my heinous promise of having a crush on him. I remembered just as I was about to walk in the door.

"Oh shit oh shit oh shit *oh shit*!" I said, apparently more out loud than I thought, due to customer response. I wasn't even

December 2

December 3

inside the building before he was standing next to me, leaving me no time to:

a) Flee.

b) Make up a plausible lie.

c) Play dead.

"Hey, tiger," he said, making my flesh crawl clear off my body.

"Hi, Brad," I said, wincing in pain. What the fuck was I going to do?

I couldn't have dinner with him. Any more encouragement on my part would be cruel and unusual punishment. And as much as I hated the thought of hurting the guy, I had to be realistic. I was too busy to waste my time pampering the crushes of vegan managers. Anyway, I was about to sign a big fat record deal and wouldn't be needing this stupid job anymore. What if the head of Warner Brothers came in and saw me bent over tying the laces on someone's new hiking boots? I was about to be a real rock star. Time to start acting like one. He'd get over it.

"I was thinking about where to take you for dinner, but then I thought, what the heck? I'll just have her over to my place. I'm a great cook. Among other things," he said. My God! He was farther gone than I'd thought.

"Brad, I'm sorry, I lied. I can't have dinner with you. I'm beyond busy," I said, handing him my nametag.

"But you promised," he said, looking hurt and confused. "Why are you giving me your nametag?"

"Because I quit," I said. I was quitting? What was I doing?

"You can't quit. We just got an entire shipment of ski bindings in. I need you to put them away," he said. He was such a nice guy. I felt awful. I took my nametag back and pinned it to my shirt.

NOTE TO SELF:

I'm a rock-and-roll wuss.

"You're right. I'm sorry," I said, "but I am giving you my notice. I'll work till the end of the week, but then I've got to get out of here. And I really can't have dinner with you. I'm sorry," I said again.

"Why not? You made a deal," he said.

"I have a boyfriend," I said, thinking of Scott.

"What, did you just get him last night?" Brad demanded.

"Actually, kind of," I said. "We met the night I needed to leave early."

"Damn!" Brad said. "Well, I hope he treats you well."

He really is such a nice guy. I am such a boob.

When I got home, Jake was still asleep on the couch. Something about my invigorating break from work made it infinitely annoying that he was lying there like a lump. I swear he's even outslept the cats. They look at him wide-eyed and treat him with the reverence reserved for the God of Slumber. When I came home today, they were all spooning.

I shoved him with my foot to wake him up. It took him a long, long time to come to.

"Rise and shine, Jake," I said. He sat up and rubbed his eyes. His two furry disciples curled back up after shooting me irritated looks.

"Hey. What time is it?"

"Time to get a life." I was quickly becoming unsympathetic to his cause. It's sort of hard to find a job if you sleep until two o'clock every day.

I went into the kitchen and made a sandwich. Jake went

into the bathroom and eventually joined me at the table, pretending not to stare hungrily at my food.

BRILLIANT OBSERVATION #22:

It's physically impossible to eat in front of a starving person, no matter how many times he leaves wet towels in a heap on your bathroom floor.

I handed him half of my sandwich.

"Jake, we need to talk. We all know you're doing heroin, shooting up, or whatever the hell you call it," I said, hoping I didn't sound as dumb as my mother had when she'd accused me of being on pot.

"It's an unfortunate truth," he said simply, getting up and helping himself to some orange juice.

Wasn't he supposed to deny it? Wasn't he supposed to freak out, slam shit around, steal something, storm out of the house?

"Well, um, do you have any plans for rehab or something? I mean, you can't just continue to slouch around, sleeping on people's couches, drinking people's juice," I said, stopping him midgulp.

"I'll sleep elsewhere. No problem," he said, putting the juice back in the fridge.

"Jake, I just want you to get better," I said.

"Me too, Jenny. I am attempting. I really am."

"How?" I asked.

"I'm cutting down massively on my intake. I hardly use at all," he said, sounding proud of himself.

What could I say? I'd never met a real junkie. I couldn't even tell when he was high. But the solution seemed so obvious to me.

"Well, great, but why not just stop altogether, then?" I asked.

He laughed and shook his head. "No can do."

"Yes. Just stop. Right now."

"So who's going to play bass while I'm having the heaves?" he asked, daring me to know what the hell he was talking about.

"Oh right, the heaves. I forgot about those," I said, nodding like an idiot.

NOTE TO SELF:

Get the junkie lowdown from those in the know.

We somehow managed to play the Knitting Factory gig without wetting our pants. The place was packed with The Industry as well as a ton of Rosebud people. It was a very un–Sixty-Foot Queenie crowd. Usually it's a bunch of hygienically challenged, thrift-store bohemian hipsters nursing their cheap beers. Everyone tonight looked like they sent their jeans to the dry cleaners.

December 5

OUR NORMAL CROWD	THE INDUSTRY CROWD
Drunk	Working
Bloodshot eyes	Designer glasses
Dance and shriek	Nod and smile
Looking for someone to connect with	Looking for someone to sign
Invite you to a barbecue	Invite you to the Playboy Mansion
Buy you a shot	Tell you their corporate card's at the bar. Get whatever you want.
Give you their own band's CD	Give you tickets to Beck

After the gig some guy named Chad from Mastiff Records herded us all into a limo and took us to the Sky Bar, yet another too-cool-for-school L.A. hangout. We were instantly ushered in through the velvet ropes that separate The Shit from The Who Gives a Shit. I've never been The Shit before. We were all giggling like idiots.

Chad was a big hefty guy, about thirty-five, with a goatee and a halo of curly black hair. He dressed in all black and laughed with his mouth closed. He was with this other guy named Tony who we learned is a big famous producer.

"Tony would make a *monster* of a record with you guys," Chad said as he ushered us all around a table. Tony smiled and mouthed the word *monster*. There was something funny to me about seeing Tony next to Chad. Tony sort of looked like he was a piece of Chad that had fallen off, gotten flattened by a steamroller, and been propped back up again. He was the skinnier, smaller, straight-haired version who laughed with his mouth open.

"This guy's magic, and with what I've heard you guys do . . . ," Chad licked his lips, "it could be sick!"

"We've already got a producer," Lucy said. "This guy Eddie. Did you hear our CD?"

"Yeah," Chad said, "it was a great demo. A great demo. But I'm talking about the real deal. Taking it beyond hanging out with your buddies in a home studio. You guys could go all the way," he said, pumping his fist for emphasis. "And just wait until you have the Tony Experience—you're gonna cream when you hear what he can do!"

As much as that last expression makes me sick to my stomach, there was something about the two of them that I liked.

They were genuinely excited about my band, and I could tell Jeffrey really liked them, so I figured they couldn't be all that bad.

Jeffrey started talking business with them, and we started swilling champagne. The place was crawling with the fabulous and the famous, and Scott and I held hands under the table the whole time. We had a blast.

We ended up at Tony's swank-ass hotel suite at the W. There was some sort of party going on with very plastic-surgeoned people and tons of free food. Everybody was gushing over our show. I had about a million boozy conversations with about a million people that I don't remember. It was surreal. It was my second taste of fame.

Scott and I snuck out of the room and headed outside to the pool. There was a bar and a bunch of little private tentlike things with cushy chairs and TVs around the pool. We slid into one and he closed the curtain.

"Alone at last!" Scott said, pushing me back on the chair and kneeling down in front of me. We started making out. A lot. Then he suddenly pulled back and got very serious.

The following is a description of my willpower taking its final swan dive:

SCOTT:	I want to spend the night with you.
ME:	We're fucking up so big time.
MY BRAIN:	I will lose. I know I will lose. I don't even know why I showed up.
MY LIBIDO:	So leave! No one invited you, anyway. I need this. I won't survive if I don't get this. I'll never see anything this stunning again.

SCOTT: What do you mean? We haven't even done anything!

ME: Yet.

MY LIBIDO: Exactly.

SCOTT: Exactly!

He kisses me again. I push him away with the little strength I have left.

ME: This band is going to make it, Scott. It's all I've ever wanted! I just hate that I'm even entertaining the thought of fucking everything up because I haven't been able to stop thinking about you.

SCOTT: You can't stop thinking about me either? Excellent!

He kisses me again. Longer. I feel myself slipping. I realize I'm actually falling in love with this idiot.

MY BRAIN: So, like, I'll see you guys later?

He pulls back and holds my hands in his.

SCOTT: It doesn't have to fuck everything up, Jenny. We can make it work.

ME: Oh, come on. No one in the history of rock and roll has ever been able to stay together.

SCOTT: Thurston and Kim.

ME: Stevie and Lindsey.

SCOTT: Bruce and Patty.

ME: Gwen and Tony.

MY LIBIDO: He's a great kisser and an amazing drummer with a cool job, and he's crazy about you! You're holding out for . . . Brad in a Speedo?

ME: It's a well-known rule.

SCOTT: And you, my dear, can break a rule like nobody's business. That's what I love about you.

And he stared at me with those huge, dark, heart-vacuums of his—eyes that could suck the chrome off a tailpipe.

My brain was never heard from again.

As luck would have it, Jake hooked up with some boob-jobbed woman last night, which meant Scott and I had free run of my house. It was, of course, the best sex I've ever had in my entire life, hands down, period, holy fucking shit! And of course I'm totally freaking out and will hate myself forever if I've sabotaged the most important thing in my entire world. And of course I'd do it again in a second.

Here's the thing, though. Even though I have a pathetic relationship with my father—the root cause of all catastrophic female love lives—I swear I think this time it could be good. I asked my gut, and she's not completely against it, which is a very rare and encouraging sign. My brain has recovered from the humiliating events of last night and was available for comment as well (BTW, none of my erogenous zones were invited to join this discussion. They're a bunch of wild banshees. My heart was left behind too, on account of the fact that she's dumber than a sack of hammers).

December 6

TOP FIVE REASONS SCOTT'S NOT THE NEXT IN A LONG LINE OF FATHER-INDUCED FAILURES:

1) He listens to me and responds in full sentences.
2) He's got a phone, an address, and he puts the toilet seat down.
3) He has a job that's good, that he loves, that's legal.
4) He knows what feelings are and trusts that they won't

rise up and knife him in his sleep if he talks about them.

5) He knows how to use an answering machine.

Now we just have to figure out how to keep it a secret.

I also have to figure out what the hell I'm going to do about my bet with Flowers!

Jeffrey took us all out for a last-minute dinner meeting at El Chavo down the street. He was freaking out because things were happening "at an exponential rate."

"Every time I turn around, someone else is trying to kiss my ass! We need to make some decisions," he had said on the phone.

Lucy came and picked me up after a long, luxurious, unemployed day spent cleaning my house and scrubbing Jake residue out of the bathtub. I got in her car and immediately put on my seat belt. Lucy's the worst driver in the world. She drives way too fast and looks at you when she's talking, not the road. For this reason, I usually blast the radio or immediately fake sleep, but I really needed to talk to her about Jake. To make matters worse, she was holding a soda can and trying to steer and shift with the same hand.

"Want me to hold that for you?" I asked, grabbing at the can. She pulled it away and shot me a look.

"I'm fine," she said, insulted. She's caught onto the fact that I think she drives like the blind. I think it's due to the fact that almost every time she drives me somewhere, I shriek and brace myself against the dashboard at least once, usually twice, during the trip.

"What are the heaves?" I asked, wondering if they were an actual thing or just another one of the many Jake-isms.

"The whats?" she asked.

"Jake said if he stops doing heroin, he'll get the heaves," I said.

"Oh. Withdrawal. Sweating, shaking, jonesing, puking. It can go on for days or even weeks, depending how hooked you are," she said, taking a swig after her long soliloquy, adding an extra three seconds to her vacation from watching the road. I grabbed the wheel and saved the basket on some woman's bike from getting ripped off by Lucy's front grill.

"I wasn't gonna hit her," she said, grabbing the wheel. "You are uuuptight," she said, as she flew through a red light.

I was silent. I was too terrified to keep the conversation going, so I turned up the radio. She turned it down.

"Is Jake having the heaves or something?" she asked.

"He's not heaving yet, but I'm worried about him. Aren't you?"

"Of course. Totally," she said, shaking her head. "But what can we do?"

We screeched into the parking lot of El Chavo, and I said a silent prayer of thanks that I was still alive.

"I think I'm going to tell Jeffrey," I said as I took my seat belt off.

Lucy thought about it for a second. "Good idea," she said.

I found out yesterday that Jake's officially surfing the couch and the tasty waves of the boob-jobbed one he met at the party. I felt even more helpless not having him around, but it's not like there was anything I could do for him. I was sure Jeffrey would have a much better handle on these types of situations, and since I'd gotten the green light from Lucy, I decided to tell him right away.

"I'll see what I can do," Jeffrey said when I cornered him by the bathrooms and poured out my woes. "This is very upsetting news, Jenny. These types of things can cause huge problems."

"I'm sure they can," I said, "but Jake's an excellent guy!"

"They always are," a suddenly exhausted Jeffrey said. We headed over to the table and sat down. Scott wasn't there yet, and I was proud to say I'd successfully sobered up from the sublime evening he'd spent at my house the night before. I was doing just fine until he walked in, looking so stunning that I knocked my full, freezing-cold glass of water all over poor Jeffrey's lap. He jumped up and screamed.

"Oh my God! I'm so sorry!" I said, attempting to mop his crotch up with a napkin and then attempting to pretend I didn't just attempt to do that.

He grabbed the napkin from my hand.

"It's totally fine, don't worry about it," he said. The waiter came running and gave him a towel.

"Dude, you're in for some major shrinkage," Jake laughed.

"Jake, that's not really helpful," I said.

"I've got some pants in my car. Want me to go get them?" Scott asked.

"I'm fine, thanks, Scott," Jeffrey said, sitting down. "Everyone sit down. I'm fine."

"Why do you have pants in your car?" Lucy asked. "In case you forget them when you leave the house?"

"That sounds more like you, Lucy," he said.

"Can I wear your pants?" Lucy asked.

"Can I watch you change into them?" Jake asked.

"Okay, now, settle down, class," Jeffrey said. "We have a ton to talk about here."

Our table was as far from the mariachi band as possible so

we could talk, which really didn't make that much of a difference since El Chavo is about the size of a broom closet. They've got a shrine to Dolly Parton in one corner and neon sombreros hanging from the ceiling. This is where I now have business meetings. This is the way life should be.

Jeffrey was even more hyper than his usual incredibly hyper self. Even after his nice cold bath. When we all sat down, he took a moment to look at each and every one of us with a big silly grin on his face. I swear I wouldn't have been surprised to see a tear fall from his proud eye.

"You guys have no idea," he started. "I can't tell you the response we're getting!" We were like a bunch of giddy kids waiting for our ice cream to be brought to the table.

"Really? Do tell," I said.

"Well, we have offers from five, count 'em, five different labels at the moment. Which is . . . astounding," he said reverently. "There'll be a bidding war, but I want you guys to be familiar with the terms and the labels so you can make your decision. You've got to pick one with the same creative vision as you. I've made up little packets for each of you to look at," he said, handing out different colored folders to each of us.

"My God, Jenny. He's more anal than you are!" Lucy said, flipping through her folder.

I've decided I really, truly like him. And not just because he's more anal than I am. It's because he really does give a shit. Even if I want to force-feed him his cell phone half the time.

"There are some other things I need to make clear as well," he went on. "First, things are going to get really hectic really quickly, but you can't quit your jobs just yet."

"Too late," I said

"Too early," said Jake.

"Second, you need to start writing new songs. As many as you can. They're going to want to go into the studio immediately, and you should have material ready."

I looked at Lucy. "Do you have time?" I asked her. "Or will you be too busy exploring your African roots?"

"I'll have time," she shot back.

"Make sure, because it's important," said Jeffrey. "And lastly, I just found out this morning that Bullet Hole's filming a live broadcast from the El Rey next week, and they want you to play with them! It'll be on VH1, and they're going to use some of the stuff for their live album. Which you, no doubt, will be pulled onstage to play on."

"Far fucking out!" Scott said.

"And it'll make the bidding war that much more insane," said a smug little Jeffrey. "We're looking at December tenth. Mark your calendars. I've got a ton of other gigs lined up as well."

Jake punched me in the arm in excitement. "Awesome!" he said.

"That hurt!" I said, smacking him back and rubbing my arm. He gave me a noogie and Scott threw an ice cube at us. The only one who didn't join in the reindeer games was Lucy. She just sat there, stirring her drink and looking kind of green.

"Mama Africa? Penny for your thoughts?" I said.

"Afreaka!'s performing at the Getty that night. Peter Gabriel's playing with us. It's a huge deal," she said, staring into her drink.

We all glared at her. She looked like she was going to throw up. Nobody said anything, but it was perfectly clear to the rest of us which gig was more important. For a while, there was complete silence. Finally Jeffrey spoke up.

"You have until tomorrow night to make up your mind, Lucy."

I will fucking kill her if she doesn't pick us!

Scott didn't have a job to shoot today, so we spent the entire day in bed. Regardless of the fact that it was one of the most luxuriously decadent twenty-four hours of my entire life, irritating little pangs of stress still managed to slip their way in between the sheets.

December 8

BRILLIANT OBSERVATION #23:

Anyone capable of being anything but delirious with that lying naked in bed next to her is definitely my mother's daughter.

We were joined in bed by:

- My old buddy money: I'd figured I could quit my job and live off the advance money from the record, but Jeffrey's little speech last night had stuck a big fat hole in that cream puff. I knew I could get more tutoring gigs, but I wanted to be a rock star already! Rock stars don't spend their afternoons dissecting thesis statements and figuring out hypotenuses!

- My old buddy guilt: I was in bed with my drummer. I was also lying to Flowers by not telling him I was in bed with my drummer. I was secretly hoping he'd forget about our bet, but I knew it would never happen. How the hell was I going to get Mrs. Nitzer's lighter? I had to do it, though. There's no Flowers like an angry Flowers.

- And finally, my old buddy Lucy: I couldn't say a damn thing about her little scheduling snafu because I was sleeping with Scott, but I still knew I'd kill her if she quit.

BRILLIANT OBSERVATION #24:

It's impossible to lay an effective guilt trip on someone when you're guilty yourself.

I asked Scott what he thought she'd do while we were lying in bed.

"She'll quit Afreaka!" he said.

"What makes you so sure?" I asked, surprised by his unflinching certainty.

"I know Lucy."

"Oh my God," I said, "I've known her since I was in a training bra, and you act like you're better friends with her than I am!"

He was silent. And I realized he was kind of right. He *is* better friends with her these days.

I suddenly felt really sad.

Well, sing hallelujah and praise sweet scrawny Jesus—we are the chosen ones! Lucy decided to turn in her tribal gear and strap on her guitar for good. She called last night to tell me the good news, and I was so excited that I ran, instead of drove, all the way to her house.

December 9

BRILLIANT OBSERVATION #25:

If you sprint for a solid three minutes after not having run in five years, you walk like you have a rake up your ass the next day.

When I got there, Lucy, Jake, and Tami were all out sitting on her porch drinking beer. The second I walked in I noticed Jake had a hickey on his neck the size of the Titanic. Lucy stood up and gave me a long-overdue hug.

"You've made me the happiest woman in the world," I said, still panting and nearly dying from my run. She pulled away and took a sip of her beer.

"Well, as much as that decision sucked, at least it's over," she said.

"I was so worried! I thought I was going to be homeless," Tami chirped from her seat on the porch. "This band is like my home."

"Then you live like a pig, dude," Jake said.

"Where's Scott?" I asked, just to see if anyone knew he was in my bed, waiting a little while to show up after me.

"I left him a message," Lucy said. "Want a beer?"

"Sure," I said, following her into the kitchen, undetected and relieved. "You know, I'm so glad you stayed for a million reasons, one of which is that I feel like our friendship has been sucking the fat one for a while now."

"I hear ya," she said, handing me a beer. "And it's mostly due to me fucking up right and left. But everything I do from now on will be in the interest of making us the biggest band to ever walk the earth!"

We tapped cans and drank.

"That was a brutal decision, Jenny. I'll be devastated if I made the wrong choice."

"You didn't," I said, as I heard Scott greeting everyone on the porch. What could go wrong? I'm only sleeping with the drummer!

The Bullet Hole show was insane! It was completely sold out, and the security guards had to keep the crowd from climbing onstage while we played. Bullet Hole's crowd completely loved us! And I must say, with all the pressure of the TV cameras everywhere and our impending bidding war, we managed to play like seasoned pros. Jake and Lucy danced all over the place while I attempted my first-ever Jump and Twirl with Ground-Split Finale and didn't trip over my guitar cord or rip any tendons! I was even able to get myself off the floor without putting my guitar down (a true-blue miracle since the aforementioned rake was still up the aforementioned ass from the aforementioned sprint). The cheering was deafening when we were done, and Scott came out from behind the drums and we all took a bow.

It was the biggest, most appreciative audience I've ever played to.

I've never, ever felt anything that great before in my life! I swear I felt like any second I could wake up on Mom's couch, covered in cat hair with a plate of cold mashed potatoes by my head.

Bullet Hole was amazing. They played each song like their lives depended on it. Then, when they got to the encore, another miracle happened. The lead singer came on and said, "This is a cover we swiped from Sixty-Foot Queenie! Where are they?"

They pulled us all onstage and started playing "Rib Eye." A song that I wrote all by myself! Broadcast live on VH1! I almost died! Lucy and I sang backup and Scott and Jake stood around looking dumb until someone threw a couple of tambourines at them. When it was over, the entire band hugged us and waved to the crowd as we all walked offstage together. Kevin, the lead singer, took my hand and dragged me back out with him for one more bow. It was completely surreal. When we got backstage, he was all over me.

"Jenny, that song kicks my ass so fucking hard. I just can't get enough of it," he said, practically looking like he was going to kiss me.

"Thanks! You guys kick *my* ass so fucking hard!" I said, still unable to grasp that this was happening. Scott was suddenly right next to me, sticking his hand out for a shake.

"Thanks so much for letting us join your party, man," he said to Kevin, moving in so close to me he stepped on my foot.

"Scott! Watch it!" I said, pushing him back.

"I'm so sorry!" he said, grabbing my arm. I could tell he was. I could also tell he was jealous. I removed him from my arm and stepped back.

"It's fine. We should probably head out and find our friends," I said, saying good-bye to Kevin and heading toward the door to the concert hall and attempting to act cool.

Scott followed me like a hawk.

"Are you all right?" he asked. Anyone paying even the slightest attention could tell we were having a lovers' spat.

"Scott," I said, faking a casual smile, "I'm totally fine!" Then I laughed and smacked him on the shoulder in case anyone was watching. He looked at me like I was insane.

"Okay," he said, and wandered out the door ahead of me.

When we got out onto the floor, we were mobbed by fans. Everyone was shoving CDs in my face for me to sign, and a bunch of girls were freaking out over Scott. Lucy was screaming with laughter the whole time, and Jake was attempting to have sincere conversations with his cutest fans. Lucy clawed her way through the crowd to me.

"I'm getting mauled!" she screamed, laughing her ass off.

"This is unreal!" I said.

"It's fabulous! And your song is going to be on Bullet Hole's live CD!" she said, grabbing my face and kissing me.

At some point Jeffrey, always hard at work, put his arm around me and introduced me to a guy with huge muttonchops and a big toothy grin. "Jenny, this is Josh from Columbia Records," he said.

I shook his hand and Josh said, "Pleasure. You guys want to go to a party?"

"Of course," I said.

"He signed Bullet Hole," Jeffrey whispered in my ear. "Did you get a chance to read about them in your folder?"

I shot him an "are you insane" look, and he nodded and said, "Sorry, you're right, sorry."

Jeffrey and I went off to find the rest of the crew. I insisted that Tami and Flowers come with us, and once everyone was wrangled up, we piled into our cars. Henry was at the gig as well, but this was a big moment for me. I mean, I love the guy, but ever since the Lucy thing he's been Mopey Moperson, and I didn't feel like lugging the dead weight of that responsibility around. Luckily, neither he nor Katie was anywhere to be found when we left.

We were whisked off to an ultraexclusive private party at Le Deux. Everyone was milling around on the candlelit outdoor patio. I felt way too cool for school being in there since the line to get in was a mile long and everyone was getting turned away. Even some supermodels. Josh slapped his card down on the bar and told us to get whatever we wanted. Jake immediately glommed on to the nearest pair of gigantic, unabashedly fake party tits, while Tami wandered around and attempted to stick our sticker to every available surface. I saw Jeffrey go up to her and put his arm around her. He loves her. Ever since he watched her in action at our CD release party, he's referred to her as The Mini Merch Machine and has made sure she never pays for a drink.

Everyone was wasted and seemed like they knew each other, including me. Very strange, since the place was crawling with famous people and last time I checked I didn't know any.

FAME FACT #1:

There's an unspoken camaraderie amongst those who are "where the action is."

I managed to get next to Scott in a really crowded part of the bar and squeeze his hand. He was still moping a little over the whole lead-singer incident, but I wouldn't let go until he smiled. Which he finally did.

Our first spat!

We somehow wrestled our way to the front of the bar, and within moments Flowers was behind us with his arms draped around both our necks. His drink was dangling obnoxiously in my face.

"Fabulous party, kids!" he slurred, removing his arm and downing the last of his drink before slamming it on the counter. He was covered in glitter and was wearing a white-and-gold pantsuit.

"Having fun?" I asked.

"Too much. And you?" he said, eyeing Scott. "Enjoying the fruits of success?"

"You know it," Scott said, turning to the bartender to try and get her attention. Flowers glared at me and raised an eyebrow.

"Perhaps there's something you'd like to tell me. Hmmmm?" he said, tilting his head and drumming his fingers on his chin.

"Like what?" I asked, my stomach crashing through the floor.

"Do not insult me. I could sense it the second I saw you onstage together. Tsk, tsk, tsk," he said.

I sighed as a black cloud in the shape of a Harley lighter descended on my perfect evening. The jig was up. I was on my way to Mrs. Nitzer Land.

December 16

First I couldn't get Lucy to show up for practice, and now I can't get rid of her. Ever since she ditched Afreaka! all she wants to do is get together and write songs, which is great, but all the time? Doesn't she realize I'm having a top-secret illicit affair with our drummer and need to spend a large majority of my time lying around in bed with him? We've managed to crank out about six new songs, but the other day I had such a close call, I realized we're going to have to seriously tighten up security. Lucy does live just one small block away.

Scott and I were lying around in bed, as usual, on one of his days off from work, when all of a sudden there was a pounding at my door.

"Get lost!" Scott screamed. I covered his mouth, horrified. I knew it was Lucy.

"Jenny?" I heard her say uncertainly. She knocked again, a little less aggressively this time.

"Just a second!" I called. "Scott, shit, you have to hide." We both jumped out of bed and threw on some clothes. I closed the bedroom door and went out to let Lucy in. She was standing there with her guitar, deep in thought.

"Hey, Lucy. How come you're not at work?" I asked, zipping up my fly, which I'd just noticed was still open. She looked at me funny.

"They let us go early today. Do you have a guy in here?" she asked.

"Not that I know of," I said, letting her in the house.

"I swear I heard a guy's voice say 'get lost,'" she said, looking around suspiciously.

"Could have. Maybe it was a neighbor," I said, oh so casually. She didn't move.

"And isn't that Scott's truck out there?" she said, pointing out my door. I walked outside and pretended to look around.

"Where?" I asked.

"Across the street," she said.

"Oh. Yeah, huh, it sure looks like it, doesn't it?" I said. She would fucking kill me if she found out she'd just dumped Afreaka! for my little charade! But she knew. She totally knew. She still hadn't put her stuff down.

"What have you been doing all day?" she wanted to know.

"Stuff. Surfing the 'Net, trying to buy stupid Christmas presents for everyone," I said, coming back inside and looking over at the computer on my desk with a pile of dirty clothes on its keyboard.

NOTE TO SELF:

Do laundry.

"Uh-huh," she said moving toward the bedroom. She quietly put her hand on the knob while she stared at my face.

"And what have you been surfing for in here?" she asked, swinging open the door.

I froze, then burst out laughing with relief when I saw what was inside.

Scott had not only made the bed, but he'd thrown a bunch of magazines around on it like I'd been lying around flipping through them all day. He'd even found a notebook with a partially written song in it and put that on the bed in full-frontal view. With a pen next to it. He was a genius.

"Okay, freak, want to take fingerprints while you're at it?" I asked as she dropped her hand to her side.

"Sorry. I think I'm losing my mind," she said. The bedroom window was open a crack, so I knew Scott had run out. I went into my closet and swung open the door, just to erase all doubt from her mind.

"I need a sweater. It's a bit nippy in here," I said, pulling one off the top shelf and putting it on. About a minute later some little blond guy got into Scott's truck and drove away. The front door was still wide open, so Lucy and I saw the whole thing. (I later learned Scott paid the guy five bucks to do it. Brilliant.)

"Wow. I was sure I'd busted you with Scott!" she said, laughing and shaking her head. "That was so weird!"

"I should be so lucky," I said, laughing.

"No shit! It's a good thing we're all in a band, or I'd gladly kill you to get to him," she said, finally putting her things down. "He's a babe, and he so obviously has the hots for you." I had no idea what to say. I didn't want to lie by pretending I hadn't noticed, but I didn't want to say the feeling was mutual, either.

"Well, can you blame him?" I asked and then changed the subject. "Ready to write our next biggest hit?"

NOTE TO SELF:
Make Scott help you get Mrs. Nitzer's lighter, regardless of the humiliating confession involved. He's a natural.

I couldn't believe Lucy and I were finally becoming good friends again and I was keeping this secret from her. I felt like a heel.

Last night was the 856th gig we've played this week. As usual, the place was packed, and people were fighting for our attention afterward like girls at a sample sale. I'm not even tired and I swear I've seen the sun rise every damn day.

ROCK-AND-ROLL TRUTH #9:
The fewer hours of sunlight you see, the bigger a rock star you are.

Some guy from Ten-Ton Records gave me tickets to see Johnny Cash. He said they were for my mother. Now they're kissing up to my mother! In any case, I'm selling them. She wouldn't know what the hell to do at a concert and besides, she hasn't exactly been supportive during all this. I'm already reconsidering my promise to buy her a house in Palm Beach.

Chad from Mastiff invited us to a party at the loft of some superimportant artist who I'd never heard of. Some freak from Warner Brothers Records gave me six passes to Disneyland and invited us to a party that night at the Playboy Mansion. Shockingly, Jake was beyond excited about

December 19

the Playboy thing, and Lucy and Tami decided to join him.

"I don't think I could go to that place without getting into a fist-fight," I said to Lucy as we were all standing around in the parking lot.

"Are you kidding? I'm dying to see it. It's like the Jerusalem of sleazery," she said. "I'll tell you all about it."

"Keep an eye on Jake," Scott said, "or we may never see him again."

Chad came out the back door of the club with that producer guy Tony and clapped his hands.

"You kids ready to roll?" he said, whistling to his limo driver.

"We're going to depart," Jake said, putting his hand on Scott's shoulder. "Dude, you certain about bailing? It'll be a sight to behold."

"Yeah. It doesn't really do it for me," Scott said. I couldn't tell if he was trying to be the Quality Male who pretends to hate strip clubs and porn when he's around his girlfriend but secretly partakes all the time when she's absent.

"Scott, you sure?" I said. Better to find out now, I figured.

"For the last time, yes," he said, getting annoyed. Jake shrugged and followed Lucy and Tami over to Lucy's car. Scott, Chad, Tony, and I were waiting around for Jeffrey when I decided maybe I should see if Henry wanted to come along. Lucy wasn't with us, and I was feeling kind of bad about blow-ing him off so much lately.

"I'll be back in a second," I said, heading back into the club to find him. As luck would have it, he was trapped at the bar by Katie. Her back was to me, and from the look on Henry's face, I could tell she was complaining about something. Her poor boyfriend, Chris, stood silently holding her hand. He looked exhausted, as usual. As I walked up, Henry saw me coming, and his expression turned to horror.

" . . . and now that she's on her way it's like I don't even fucking exist anymore. I haven't had a fucking conversation with her in weeks! I'll tell you right now, one in eight fucking billion bands makes it. She could be out on her fucking ass tomorrow, so she should watch who she fucks with," Katie said.

"Hey, guys," I said loudly, pretending I hadn't heard any of it. "Want to come to this party downtown? It's at some famous artist guy's place. There's a rumor that Belle and Sebastian are gonna play."

Katie turned around slowly. Chris lit up. "I love Belle and Sebastian!" he said.

"Sure," said Henry. Katie was silent. I decided to try and defuse her.

"Please come," I said to her. "I feel like I've been so busy, I haven't had any time to see my friends."

"You can fucking say that again," she huffed. Chris pleaded with her, and she finally, grouchily, agreed.

I can't believe I'm begging Katie to hang out with me. It's like begging someone to hit you with a baseball bat.

I brought them all outside, where the rest of the crew were waiting in Chad's limo. I introduced everyone and squeezed in next to Scott, whose face fell when he saw who I was with. I could feel his body tense up against mine, and when we got to the loft he was as cold as a dead cat.

"This place is amazing!" Henry said when we walked in. It was on the top floor of an old warehouse building that had been converted into lofts. Half of the ceiling was a giant skylight, and two huge doors led out to a rooftop balcony that was three times the size of my apartment. They had a kick-ass DJ, and all the walls were covered in art made out of old car parts. The part of the ceiling that wasn't glass had giant, morphing, kaleidoscope-type images projected onto it. Everyone there was superfunky, and the second we walked in the door, a bunch of guys were all over Tony.

"Tony Fanucci, in the flesh. What an honor," one of them said, shaking Tony's hand. He turned to his friends. "This guy's responsible for the three best albums that came out last year. He's a genius."

"I wouldn't go that far," Tony said humbly. I could see a couple of other people pointing at Tony and talking across the room. I guess he was a bigger deal than I thought.

"Every record he produces turns to gold," Chad butted in, making sure Scott, Jeffrey, and I heard it. Tony's posse agreed.

"I'm going to hit the bar. You want anything?" Scott asked me.

"I'll go with you. I could use a fucking drink," Katie said, making Scott cringe.

"Let me get it for you, Katie. What do you want?" I said quickly, running defense.

"Oh, all right. I'll take a vodka tonic. And tell them to put a lot of lime in it."

"I'll take a Bud," Chris said.

"Henry?" I asked. He looked terrified to be alone with these people.

"Can I come with you?" he asked, breaking my heart.

"Of course," I said, holding out my arm for him to hold. I put my other arm around Scott's unwelcoming waist and headed toward the bar.

"I've never seen anything like this place," Henry marveled.

"I'd love to know how they got their fractals to project on the ceiling like that!"

"You okay?" I whispered in Scott's ear.

He nodded an unconvincing nod. "You sure?" I pressed.

"Yes," he said flatly.

"You know, they make a software that lets you manipulate fractals on your computer," Henry went on. "It's amazing what you can do with them."

"What the hell are you talking about?" I asked him.

"He's having a dork overdose," Scott mumbled.

"Sorry," Henry said, "I just get a little excited. So Scott, how's all your film stuff doing?"

"Great. I'm gonna take a look around, you guys," he said, removing himself.

"I don't think he likes me," Henry said as Scott walked away.

"He's just kind of shy," I said, wondering what gigantic bug had crawled up Scott's ass.

For the first half of the night, Henry clung to me like a baby monkey—until he had about five drinks. Then he was totally out of control. I think this was the first time he'd ever been around famous people. It wasn't pretty. He was running around telling stupid jokes and shaking hands. At one point I saw him across the room talking to three bored supermodels about the Nasdaq. Humiliating. Everyone was nice about it, but I could tell they thought he was someone's strange nephew.

NOTE TO SELF:

Leave Henry at home.

Then there was Katie. Scott and I had finally gotten a few minutes alone, when Katie slid up to my side like a snake. She sipped her drink and pointed to an old beat-up truck fender hanging on the wall.

"What is this shit? I work my ass to the bone every day to live in a shoebox, and this asshole nails a fender to the wall and has a palace? That is fucked up."

"Shoebox?" I asked. Suddenly her Hollywood Hills home complete with guest rooms and pool was a shoebox?

"At least he's got cool fractals," Scott said bluntly.

"No shit," she said, pretending to know what he was talking about. "And what the fuck is up with the light show on the ceiling? It's making me nauseous."

"Those are fractals, Einstein," Scott said.

"Oh, really?" she said, embarrassed. "Well, whatever they are, they're sick."

"Are we leaving soon?" Scott said.

I was exhausted from being the damn friend referee all night. "Yeah," I said, grabbing his hand and not caring who saw. "Let's go find Jeffrey."

BRILLIANT OBSERVATION #26:
Trying to make sure everyone around you is having a good time is the best way to ensure you don't.

The limo ride home was a nightmare. Henry was so drunk and excited, the only time he shut up was to puke out the window. Chris moped in the corner because Belle and Sebastian never showed.

"Big fucking surprise. People lie about that shit all the time," Katie said.

"They suck, anyway," said Scott.

"As if!" said Chris, ready to fight for the honor of Belle and Sebastian.

"What did you think about that art?" asked Jeffrey, taking over my job as ref.

"I loved it!" Tony said, giggling. "I lost the gas cap to my old Beamer months ago and have had a bitch of a time replacing it. Now, thanks to Mr. Artist . . ." He pulled a gas cap out of his pocket.

"You stole that?" I asked, shocked.

"Why not? The guy makes over two million a year for nailing junk to the wall! At least I'm going to put it to use," Tony said. I had to admit I thought it was kind of funny. In fact, Chad and Tony ended up being the saving grace of the whole ride home. They put on a puppet show using Chad's socks and taught me how to flip my eyelids inside out. Little did they know that having a good sense of humor is worth more to me than a thousand front row tickets to a Bjork concert.

Scott and I got dropped off back at the club so we could get our cars. We drove halfway to my house, parked his truck on the street, and he rode with me the rest of the way. Never again would we be foolish enough to park it in front of my place.

"That's a good spot to know about. You can leave your car there as long as you want without getting a ticket. We should use it from now on whenever you stay at my place," I said. Scott was silent.

"What is the matter with you tonight?" I asked. "You've been driving me nuts!"

"*I've* been driving *you* nuts! Your fucking friends have been driving *me* nuts! I can't believe I passed up a chance to see the Playboy Mansion to stand around and listen to those idiots all night," he said.

"I knew it! I knew you wanted to go!" I said, infuriated. "Why the hell didn't you? You thought it would be more fun to stick around and make my life hell all night?"

"Who made whose night hell all night?" he shot back.

"Whose night was more hell than whose night?" I said, completely pissed off and making no sense. As angry as we were, we both had to laugh.

"It's not that I wanted to go to the stupid mansion, I just wanted to spend a fun night alone with you," he said. "That's all."

"I guess I should have warned you I was bringing them," I said.

We both apologized, and by the time we got to my house we were all over each other. There was a little pinprick in the very back of my head that wouldn't go away, though. It was a sharp little reminder that jealousy leads to disaster. Always has, always will. If Scott can't handle the fact that I have friends and that occasionally I'll have to have conversations with other men, we are in deep doo-doo.

Then I decided to worry about it later. I was too busy falling in love.

December 21

In the midst of all this chaos, I can smugly say that I've managed to stick like glue to my practicing schedule. Flowers put the fear of God into me and does everything short of smacking me with a ruler when I fuck up. Losing a hand would be the only way to get off the hook for not having done my homework. That or introducing him to Madonna.

TOP FIVE BEST NEW THINGS ABOUT ME:

1) I can now play guitar behind my back.
2) Nineteen people have asked me for my autograph.
3) I'm in love.
4) Bullet Hole is covering "Rib Eye" nearly every show they play.
5) I am in.

"How's our bet coming along, loser?" Flowers wanted to know at my last lesson. I'd been living in denial about the whole thing ever since I'd lost.

"Um, I'm still trying to think of a plan. One that won't get me arrested," I said.

"Well, I can't wait forever. I'll give you until the end of next month."

"Next month! How the hell am I supposed to do it that fast? I'm so busy these days!"

"Oh, please. You expect me to feel sorry for you?" he said, eyeing me while he filed his nails.

"I don't think I can do it," I said.

"Well, you should have thought of that before you went dipping your hand in the honey pot!" he said in a terrifyingly reprimanding tone. I swear, there's no one scarier than Flowers when he's unamused.

"Fine, you'll have it by the end of next month," I said, pouting.

"Hee hee! I just can't wait to see this!" Flowers said, joyfully clapping his hands.

NOTE TO SELF:

I do not have the Bet Winning Gene. Quit making them.

I will admit right here and now that as uncool and selly-outy as it may be to want a big record deal, I want one. Bad. It's like admitting I love Wal-Mart. I can't help it, even though it lumps me in with the unprincipled, bovine general population that I so enjoy being above. I'd rather be on MTV than the dive-bar circuit. And three tank tops for twelve bucks is a deal I'm just not gonna pass up.

Jeffrey really got on our cases about choosing a label after our last gig. "You can go cold as quickly as you got hot. We need to jump on this pronto," he said. So I gathered the troops at my house for an evening of spaghetti and told everyone to bring their colored folders.

Jake couldn't find his, and Lucy had spilled red wine all over hers, so they looked on with me.

NOTE TO SELF:
If band fails, teach nursery school.

Scott not only brought his but had read it in full and was the only one with intelligent things to say.

"Indie labels are cool, but they just don't have the resources to take it all the way. I mean, why be a front-porch light when you can be a star!" I said, taking my empty plate off my lap and putting it on the floor. I was on the couch between Lucy and Jake with Scott directly in front of me in the big yellow chair.

BRILLIANT OBSERVATION #27:
Sitting near Scott and not touching him is as torturous as sitting near a pizza and not having any.

"You have less control over your music at the big labels," Scott argued, "plus they may throw a ton of money at you, but you have to pay it all back in the end anyway, so who cares? Might as well go with an indie and make an album you love."

"But we could make a killer album with some money behind us. Actually spend some time on it and use the best equipment possible. That would be so cool! Besides, that guy Chad from Mastiff said we'd have total creative control," I said.

"Chad's a cheeseball," Lucy said.

"The more dough, the bigger the cheeseballs," Jake said.

"I know he is, but who have we met yet that isn't?" I asked. The class was silent. I continued. "At least Chad was the biggest on letting us call the shots. Plus I really feel like he gets our music. And he makes me laugh."

"Well, they do have a ton of awesome bands signed to them," Lucy said.

"Does this mean I won't have to find employment?" Jake asked hopefully.

"Maybe you're right," Scott said.

We went back and forth all night, but we eventually decided on Mastiff.

I called Jeffrey the next day with our decision. He was enthusiastic.

"They didn't offer you the most in the bidding war, but I like Mastiff. It's one of the smaller big labels. They put out some great stuff. I think you guys'll do great there," he said. "I'll start tying the knot! Merry Christmas!"

This is, hands down, the greatest Christmas present I've ever gotten in my entire life.

Ever since I was born, I have been well aware that Jesus's birthday, like Carla's, is far more important to my mother than mine is. This fact, along with the many other irritations that show up singing on your doorstep on the 25th of December, is why I always break out. I swear to God, every year I wind up with the same giant red sugarplum zit on the end of my nose, adding the nickname "Rudolph" to my long list of reasons to be annoyed.

My acne isn't helped by the fact that my mother is one of Santa's head cheerleaders. Her house is the one that people in the neighborhood tell their friends they *have* to see. The manger with the life-sized Mary and Jesus, the one that always scared the shit out of me, is set up in the front yard. Santa and his reindeer take their place on the roof, a job my tiny mother did all by herself until she landed in the hedge with a broken arm. Now Carla's poor husband has to do it. She's got all the lights and the fake snow and the idiotic carols blasting through outdoor speakers too. Mom's not religious. She just loves to shop for sparkly things.

CHRISTMAS FACT #1:
Italian-Americans single-handedly support at least one half of the Christmas decorating industry.

But this year was going to be different. This year I wasn't going to spend the whole day lying facedown on her couch.

I'd shown up with my own ammo in the form of a record contract, and I was going to wag it under her nose like smelling salts for her soul. Jesus and Carla never had one of these!

I was sitting around the table with the usual cast of uncles, aunts, and cousins, digging into a roast beef the size of an elf. Uncle Vic had just finished describing in detail what it felt like to pass his kidney stone, miraculously quieting the unquietable table for the first time in Troanni history. Everyone was in a deep, disturbed silence. My cousin Theresa even stopped eating for a second. I saw it as my only opportunity.

"I got a record deal," I shouted, making sure to speak loudly since half the table was hard of hearing and the other half was thinking of a way to top the kidney-stone story.

"You *did*?" Carla shrieked.

"A real one?" John asked. Carla hit him. "I mean, on a label I've heard of?"

"Mastiff," I said.

"Mastiff?" Carla asked. "I've heard of them. They're kind of a huge deal, aren't they?"

"I swallowed my tooth once. Had to pass that too. Oh, I looked for it every day!" my eighty-four-year-old great-aunt Alberta chimed in.

"Are you guys gonna be on MTV?" my cousin Theresa asked. She's a year younger than I am, but she's already on her second husband and her third child.

"Yes," I said.

"I can't believe it, I really can't," said Carla. "My big sister is going to be famous."

I looked at Mom. She was staring at me, but I couldn't tell if she was going to launch into a story about how giving birth to me was more painful than passing a kidney stone or if she was actually going to acknowledge my success.

Then she said, in a funny, quiet voice, "Well, I'll be. My little girl, famous. Wait until the girls at the office hear about this."

At last! I'd finally blasted through the impenetrable wall of familial expectation! Marriage, babies, furniture sets, mutual funds—they're all eclipsed by the almighty fame. Mom wouldn't let anyone even try and talk about anything else for the rest of dinner. She also didn't try to take any credit for it! I swear, ever since Carla's wedding she's been a different person. She hasn't said the words *disappointment* and *Jenny* in the same sentence since. Carla noticed it too.

"I think she's just finally over Dad," she said.

I think Carla's right. Lucky Mom. I can't imagine how restful that must be.

December 27

I finally got up the nerve to tell Scott about my bet with Flowers. I told him everything—how Mrs. Nitzer had stolen the lighter from some scary guy in a bar and how Flowers had ingeniously come up with the bet to help me keep my hands to myself. For days I tried to think of ways to get her damn lighter on my own, but everything I came up with was too ridiculous. I knew she kept it in her purse, but she was so tightly wound, you'd need to break her fingers to get it out of her hands. I swear I had no idea how to do it without going to jail or seriously injuring at least one of us. I needed some serious help.

FIVE WAYS TO GET MRS. NITZER'S MOTORCYCLE LIGHTER THAT ARE SO DUMB I CAN'T BELEIVE I THOUGHT OF THEM:

1) Wear a disguise. Sit outside her house until she gets in her car. Follow her to her destination. Get out of car and walk along beside her. Trip her. When purse goes flying, pick it up and remove lighter. Give it back as I help her up.

2) Wear a disguise. Sit outside her house until she gets in her car. Follow her to her destination. Get out of car and ask her for a light. Grab lighter and run away. (Make sure to practice running first.)

3) Find a passage in the Bible that could somehow imply that smoking is a sin. Write it down and mail it to her twice a day. Pick through her garbage until I find lighter.

4) Ask Rodney to steal it for me. Risk him getting caught and thrown in Catholic school. Spend rest of life disgusted with self for making sweet Rodney cover for my pathetic lack of self-control and professionalism.

5) Start going to her church. Win her over with my new-found piety and tasteful style of dress. Tell her I'm volunteering at a children's hospital and one of the little girls collects lighters.

I told Scott my ideas to push home the reality of how badly I needed his help. I figured this kind of thing was right up his alley. I was shocked to discover that not only was he not interested, but he found my suffering hilarious.

"I personally would love to see number five. You snuggling up to Mrs. Nitzer in church would be quality entertainment," he said. "Hell, I'd even get dressed up and join you just to watch."

"Scott, this isn't funny. Flowers is being a total prick about it. Why won't you help me?" I whined.

"You made the bet," he said, laughing.

"Yeah, but you helped me lose it," I said.

"So what? I have no problem with what we're doing."

I couldn't believe he was being such a weenie! I tried another angle.

"Don't you think it would be kind of fun to come up with a great idea and pull it off?" I asked.

"Actually, I think it would be cheating on your part."

He was useless. I was annoyed. I made him leave.

NOTE TO SELF:

No more blow jobs for Scott.

I called Rodney's house three times, hanging up on Mrs. Nitzer the first two until I finally got Rodney.

"Hey, Jenny," he said, sounding worried.

"Is your mom in the room? Is this a bad time?" I asked.

"No, she's not home," he said.

"Great. Listen, Rodney, I hate to ask you this, I really do, but I need a big favor." There was silence on the other end of the phone. "Rodney? You there?"

"Yeah," he said weakly.

"Rodney, are you all right? You sick or something?" I asked.

"No, I'm fine. It's just that Flowers called yesterday and

told me that you might be calling. He said to tell you that, um, 'Thou shalt not rely upon the children of the world to do thy dirty work, weasel.' He made me memorize it."

I was stunned.

"Well, I have no idea what he's talking about," I said, trying to save face, "but what I wanted to ask you is if you have Caroline Block's phone number. I have to tutor her next week and I lost it."

"Oh. Sure!" he said, sounding hugely relieved. "I'll go get it!"

I was so screwed. I looked over my options again and ruled out the first two. A six-foot-tall woman in a lame disguise doing something moronic could only be me. Even Mrs. Nitzer was hip enough to know that. Since Flowers had squashed my hopes for Rodney's help and the Bible idea was the dumbest on my list, I found myself with nowhere else to turn but the House of the Lord.

BRILLIANT OBSERVATION #28:
Humiliation is not one of those things that gets easier the more you're exposed to it.

I AM A MASTIFF RECORDS RECORDING ARTIST!

We signed with Mastiff this morning! I'm on Mastiff. Sixty-Foot Queenie, the debut album, out now on Mastiff Records. Jenny Troanni appears courtesy of Mastiff Records.

It rolls off the tongue like a marble.

The label threw us a party in this huge, swanky conference room, complete with stadium-sized TV screens and enough food to sink even my mother's ship. We met all the big mucky-mucks, and

December 30

I swear they were starstruck. Rich, powerful, adult people kissing my minimum-wage butt. They may be rich, but I'm cool, and soon I'll be both. Which means I win.

The whole contract thing is annoying, though. Who the hell came up with all that legal lingo, anyway? Is it so only people who went to law school can understand it? Because they'll never be cool and this is their payback? Luckily, Jeffrey's a great teacher and explained everything using colored pencils and little pictures.

We got the seven-record thingy but not the twofer-Tuesday or whatever that thing is Katie was talking about. As far as I understand it, it means if we get booted, we don't get paid for a second record.

Which will never happen because we are huge.

Chad also decided he doesn't want "Put That Thing Away" on the first album. That bummed me out, even though he says he wants to save it for our second album because it's "such a strong follow-up." Whatever.

I decided I should call Katie to tell her the good news. I knew she'd be her usual barrel of piss, but I felt she had a right to know since she was kind of involved. Plus I was feeling guilty about never wanting to see her.

"Well, you still need to watch your fucking backs. It's not whether or not you're gonna get fucked, it's just how hard," she reminded me over the phone. She was ridiculous. I swear, if someone handed her a pot of gold, she'd complain that it was too heavy.

"If you hate the industry so much, why don't you quit?" I asked her.

"And pay my mortgage with what? My fucking charm?"

"Get another job somewhere else. One that you like," I said.

"I'm too fucking busy to look for another job, fool."

"Why can't you admit that you like it, Katie? That you love the glamor and the swanky lunches on your corporate card?" I asked. I was determined to make her see it, even though I knew getting Katie to admit she liked anything was like getting a fish to whistle.

"It's the least they can fucking do," said poor, put-upon Katie.

"Well, I'm excited," I said, "and you should be too."

"About what?" she huffed.

"That you eat at the best restaurants in L.A. on a regular basis and never have to pay for music. For starters."

"It's easy for you to be all happy, now that you have a record deal."

"I thought I was going to get fucked by my record deal," I said.

"Oh my God, you so are!" she said. She was hopeless! I suddenly had no idea why the hell I even bothered talking to her. I decided we needed to break up. Right now.

"Katie, you know what? I don't need you calling and pissing all over my parade anymore," I said.

"Hello? You called me, asshole!" she said.

"Well, I'm not going to anymore."

"Fine with me! Like I enjoy this?" she said, slamming down the phone. And it was silent. And it was good.

I suddenly felt a hundred pounds lighter.

THE BIG OOO

We played our big New Year's gig on a boat in Marina del Rey. It was on some sort of old cargo ship that they'd turned into a floating club called the Raft. The crowd was a mixture of our usual bohemian following, industry people, and a bunch of tripping twenty-year-olds. Considering the world was supposed to blow up, everyone seemed to be in a pretty great mood. All I cared about was that we headlined, which meant I was onstage when the big odometer flipped. Which meant that if the apocalypse did happen, I was going to go down rocking. Or what would have been rocking, if I hadn't done shots with every single person from my new record company. Every time I turned around, someone was handing me another shot, and if Jeffrey hadn't magically appeared with a ham sandwich and a bottle of water, I doubt I would have made it. He really is the best.

Strangely enough, I don't remember much that happened when we finally got onstage. I do remember Lucy helping me flip my dress around because I'd put it on backward. And I remember letting loose a ripper of a burp right into the mic, which secured us instant success.

At midnight the lights went low, and everyone braced themselves for the world to end. The band sang the countdown. Four, three, two, one . . . and then it happened.

Scott and I made out in front of everyone.

A lot.

That was last night, and due to the fact that I'm a gigantic coward, I've refused to answer the phone all morning. I figured I'd be in trouble from the following people for the following reasons:

1) Lucy, for mixing business with pleasure.
2) Scott, for breaking up with him. (I was convinced that since we'd let the cat out of the bag, we had to end it. I was also very, very drunk.)
3) My whole band, for being too drunk to play well at our very first gig as Mastiff recording artists.
4) Jeffrey, for forcing him into babysitting overdrive.
5) Lucy, for throwing up my ham sandwich on her leg as she helped me into her car to drive me home.
6) Scott, for calling him at four in the morning sobbing and begging forgiveness. (He forgave me but was unamused at being woken up.)
7) Myself, for being such an irresponsible loser.

I spent the day in bed, cursing McDonald's for not delivering. Every time I tried to call Scott, either he wasn't home or the line was busy. I felt awful about my drunken hissy fit and wanted to make sure everything was okay, I finally got up around four and made some eggs and sausage while I listened to the messages on my machine:

1) *Scott:* "Hey baby, where are you? I'm having everyone over for a morning-after recovery feast. Just so you know, I think we survived the gig undetected. I told everyone you were so wasted you went after six other guys when you were done with me. Get your buns over here. I have bacon. It's sometime around noon. Bye."
2) *Lucy:* "Drunk whore! I'm heading over to Scott's, one of the many guys you nearly raped last night, remember

him? I'm going to have to keep my eye on you two. Anyway, he's having a party and said there'll be free food. Let me know if you want me to come get you."

3) *Carla:* "Hi, sis. Just wanted to wish you a Happy New Year and find out how your gig went. John and I went to an awful party at some paranoid guy's house. Some accountant with two kids, a minivan, and a secret desire to be Mr. Millennium. He had a generator, gas masks, rifles, five hundred cans of food, and he hid under the table when the clock struck midnight. He was a total weirdo and was a little disappointed the world didn't blow up. We all got drunk and pigged out on his canned peaches, so I guess the night wasn't a total loss. Anyway, I have a feeling your evening was a lot more fun. Bye."

4) *Henry:* "Sorry I missed your show last night, but you know how obnoxious I think New Year's is. And Lucy. Anyway, hope yours was happy. Hope the hangover isn't too bad. Hope I get to see you soon."

5) *Scott:* "Jenny, where the hell are you? Did you choke on your own puke last night or what?"

I called Scott back and finally got him on the phone. I found out the party was over.

"How come you didn't answer the phone?" I asked, upset that I'd missed everything. Especially the bacon.

"The music must have been too loud. That sucks. I really wanted to see you, especially after all that went down last night."

"Me too. I'll come over now," I said.

"I have to help Pete with something."

"Well, you want me to come by afterward?" I asked, feeling suddenly lonely.

"Yeah, but I have to get up really early for a shoot and I'm fried. Maybe tomorrow night, okay?"

"All right." I'd blown it. I'd wasted the whole day sick in bed feeling like an idiot when I could have been hanging out with my friends and the best guy I've ever dated.

"I'll talk to you tomorrow. I love you," he said, nearly knocking me over.

"You what?" I asked.

"Wow, I said it, didn't I?" Scott said, amused. "It came out pretty naturally. I guess it must be true."

I didn't know what to say. If I said it back, it would seem like I was only saying it because he did, but if I didn't, it would probably make him feel stupid. In the end, all I said was, "Wow."

He laughed. "Go back to sleep. I'll see you tomorrow."

—A normal, gorgeous, employed, thoughtful, smart, kick-ass drummer with no police record loves me. —

NOTE TO SELF:

Anything is possible.

We had our first real meeting with Chad at Mastiff today. We walked through the lobby of the building, past the security guard, and into the elevator as a band! Finally it was me who had that thing. Everyone in the lobby, including the damn security guard, stared at us and knew we were someone.

January 4

BRILLIANT OBSERVATION #29:

We have arrived!

The Mastiff building's in Santa Monica. It's surrounded by big, leafy, banana-type trees, palms, and huge bamboo stalks, creating an island of jungle around the gigantic, dark wooden building. It reminds me of an overgrown tropical hut, a place where you drink rum cocktails and duck low-flying toucans rather than do business.

We—the whole band plus Jeffrey—were sitting in Chad's swanky office, staring out a picture window overlooking the jungle and a large fountain that spouted water every six minutes. Chad was in his usual all-black ensemble and had a tiny rubber band tied around his little beard, creating a ponytail on his chin. Was he serious? He kept twisting it around his finger while he talked, and Lucy kicked me every time he did it.

He's really pushing for us to do our record with Tony instead of Eddie. He reiterated that our demo is good, but that it sounds like a demo.

"Tony'll take you to the next level. The guy's produced three gold records, for fuck's sake!" Chad informed us, after sending his assistant down the hall to get us all sodas.

"Eddie's much more our style, though," Scott said. "Tony's kind of overproduced. Plus all he works with are pop bands."

"No offense," Chad said, "but as great as you guys are, you're still nobodies. It would be more than wise to hook up with a somebody. If you want to actually get somewhere, that is."

He had a point. I loved working with Eddie, but I wanted to sound professional. I wanted to have a number one hit!

"Let's listen to some more of Tony's stuff," I said.

"Now you're talkin'," Chad said, putting on one of Tony's latest and greatest and cranking it at top volume.

It was some light rock/pop band that sounded like a million other boring bands that had made it big this year. It wasn't necessarily bad. It just wasn't good.

"Five hundred thousand in sales and counting!" Chad screamed over the music. He was rocking out, nodding his head and drumming his hands on the desk. Jake stuck his finger down his throat and Scott stared at me blankly. Chad turned the music down.

"Well, is that the shit or what?" he asked.

"Did someone say shit?" Jake asked.

"It was a little scary, but he did get some great guitar tones," I said.

"Exactly!" screamed Chad, thrilled to have even the tiniest thing to cling to.

"Can't we just use a different producer with just as big a name who's not quite so . . . gloss oriented?" Lucy asked.

"Yeah!" I said. "You guys are one of the biggest labels out there. Hook us up, Chad."

Chad looked pained. He let loose a heavy sigh and clasped his hands together.

"Listen. Yes, we do have access to just about every producer on the planet, but from the second I heard you guys, I knew Tony was it. You have to just trust me on this one. I've been in the business for fifteen years and I know what I'm doing," he said quietly. "I understand your reservations, but it's only because Tony hasn't worked with a band as raw as you guys yet. The combo of his slickness with your rawness will make a record unlike anything the world has heard yet. I promise you."

We all looked at each other, uncertain. We looked at Jeffrey.

"He could have a point, you guys," he said.

"I do. And like I said, you guys will have total creative control!" Chad said, exasperated.

"If we get last say over everything he does, then he can't ruin it, right?" I asked, looking at Lucy. She shrugged.

"Absolutely. That's what this is all about," Chad gushed. I stared at my band. They looked back at me blankly.

"That way, we'd get his big fat clout, his knowledge of all the new equipment, and have the power to keep his cheesiness in check," I said to everyone. They all looked dubious.

"That could work," Jeffrey said.

"Of course it could work. It could work like fucking magic," Chad exploded.

We decided to at least meet with Tony. Jeffrey said we should have him come to band practice.

"Just see who he is, what ideas he has. If you hate him, then you don't have to work with him," Jeffrey said, looking at Chad.

Chad nodded hopefully. "Sound good?" We all agreed.

By the end, the fact that we were sitting around discussing whether or not one of the biggest producers in the country (cheese or no cheese) was good enough for us had sunk in. We were all giddy.

Scott and I went down to Mom's to help her with some manual labor. Apparently she's been redecorating. She was a nightmare. She came at me with paint chip samples and fabric swatches for lawn furniture as if I could give her some decorating advice. I still have sheets nailed to my walls for curtains. What is she missing here?

She called this morning in a panic because Carla and John were nowhere to be found, and she wanted to rid her home of all the furniture she'd bought with my father back in the day.

"I need to be a free woman," she said over the phone. "Time to sweep him out of my life for good." Not that I felt I owed her anything, but she was so not completely obnoxious anymore, I figured it wouldn't hurt to try and forge a new relationship with her. She had to haul several large pieces of furniture to the dump, so I decided to ask Scott if we could use his truck. He was invited as a Moving Guy, not as a Boyfriend-Meeting-the-Parents Guy.

"I'm more than happy to just tell her you're my neighbor, so you don't get the Boyfriend Third Degree," I told him as we drove down to her house in his truck.

"I'm more than happy to be your boyfriend," he said. "I love you, remember?"

"I love you, too," I said, finally.

"No, you don't," he said.

"Yes, I do!" I said. "What the hell is that supposed to mean?"

"Well, it's pretty hard to tell! I'm always thinking about you, and you're so distracted with the band and writing songs and your friends," he said.

"I am, Scott, but that doesn't mean I don't love you," I said, amazed. "One has nothing to do with the other." I couldn't believe he was serious, but judging from the look on his face, he was.

NOTE TO SELF:

Pay more attention to Scott.

When we pulled up to Mom's, she was outside sweeping the driveway. Scott pulled onto a part she'd already swept, and got out of the car. Whenever I pull that maneuver, I'm welcomed with, "I just cleaned that, dammit!"

Not Scott. The second Mom laid eyes on him she transformed into someone I've never met before. She twittered away like a little bird in springtime, and I swear I even detected a slight southern accent. She swooned on and on about the piano lessons she'd taken as a small child while we moved her sofa out to the truck.

"But the piano was nothing compared to the almost, well, psychic connection I've felt with the drums. They speak to me in a way most people could never understand, Scott."

I nearly dropped the couch on my foot.

"Really, Mrs. Troanni," Scott said, amused. "I think I know what you mean."

"I'm certain you do," she twittered, patting her forehead with the sleeve of her blouse. When we went back inside, I cornered her in the pantry.

ME:	Have you been drinking?
SCARLETT O'HARA:	Heavens, no! Why on earth do you say that?

ME: Because all of a sudden you're from a plantation in
             Georgia. And since when the hell do you give a crap about
             drums? Last I heard, that noise was going to permanently
             wreck my hearing.

SCARLETT: I like the drums! You don't know everything about me.

ME: No kidding! I guess I'm just going to have to tell Scott
             you've finally started having senior moments.

SCARLETT: I beg your pardon! I'm not allowed to enjoy myself?
             Besides, I think Scott likes me. We had an instant connec-
             tion.

ME: Mom! Admit it. You have a crush on my boyfriend.

SCARLETT: Oh, stop it. You just can't stand to see people having a
             good time that's not focused on you. You never could.

ME: Mom. This is not about me and my raging ego. You're act-
             ing like an ass. Knock it off.

SCARLETT: I have no idea what you're talking about.

But her southern accent was mysteriously gone when we returned. She was still nervous, but at least she seemed distantly related to my mother. Scott thought she was sweet. He was flattered that she wanted to impress him. He said I should be too. I told him that if he wanted to wake up with his head still attached to his neck, he'd be wise not to get involved in my relationship with my mother.

As unappetizing as the whole situation was, deep down I was screaming with victory in the Mom department. I had something she wanted—even if he was a moron. We drove out to the beach, and Scott treated me to the most romantic dinner I've ever had, making it impossible to stay mad at him for long.

I could no longer ignore the fact that I had to make good on my bet with Flowers, so I did the impossible. I went to Mrs. Nitzer's church.

I couldn't believe I was actually going through with it. I kept looking over my shoulder, paranoid that Scott was following me with his video camera. I was wearing the smart blue business suit my mother gave me the day I sold my soul to the corporate devil. Putting it on again was like putting on a cold, wet bathing suit, and the smell of it brought back all these horrible memories of being trapped in a life I hated. By the time I got in the car, the idea of sitting quietly in church, meditating on all those candles and pretty stained-glass windows, actually sounded kind of good.

NOTE TO SELF:

Kill Flowers.

I drove to the Immaculate Heart of Mary church, conveniently located way the hell out in Pasadena. When I finally found a parking place, I followed the other parishioners, all nice, white, middle-class people, into the church and started looking around for Rodney and that woman. I almost turned back a couple of times, too humiliated to go through with it, but then I saw Rodney, dressed up like a little angel, holding his mother's purse while she fixed her hat in the fifth row back from the altar.

He was holding the purse with the Holy Grail!

I made a dash for it, narrowly beating out an old lady to the fifth row pew, and crammed my way in next to Rodney. The old lady shot me a horrified look, and I signaled to her that Rodney was saving my spot. I've only been to church about three times in my life (my parents were terrible Catholics), but I definitely got the vibe from Old Sourpuss that it wasn't a dibs kind of place.

Rodney looked at me with shock too, like he'd just been hit in the back of the head with a snowball.

"Jenny?" he blurted out.

The second Mrs. Nitzer saw me, she instinctively grabbed her purse out of Rodney's hands. Goddamn her! She eyed me suspiciously.

"What in heaven's name are you doing here?" she asked.

"Well, sometimes I just feel like going to church, you know? And Rodney spoke so highly of this one that I thought I'd give it a shot." Just then the organ music kicked in, and the priest came out to his podium. I decided to hit Mrs. Nitzer with my cause. "I'm working with children. . . ."

"Shhhh!" said half the congregation, Mrs. Nitzer included.

I was then forced to kneel, stand, sit, pray, sing, and listen to a very hostile sermon for two whole hours! I learned that, without a doubt, I was going straight to hell. The priest then proceeded to inform me just exactly what hell looked like, leaving nothing to the imagination.

The hell part was the only section of the six-hundred-hour sermon that held my interest. I could barely stay awake, and standing still for that long nearly made me go crazy. How the fuck did Rodney do it? Every time I looked over at him for help, he was glazed over, his lips slightly moving and his fingers wiggling. He looked like he'd had a stroke. Finally I realized that he was practicing his bass.

When at last people started to file out of the pews, I was so exhausted, I wanted to weep. Is that how they do it? They bore people into states of utter submission? If they'd told me at that moment to give all my money to the Church, I would have done it gladly just to get the hell out of there.

But it wasn't over.

The navy blue suit and I spent another hour meeting and greeting the eight million good suburban Christians that Mrs. Nitzer flagged down outside the church.

"And who's this?" some perky-looking, middle-aged goody-two-shoes asked as she stuck her pudgy hand out for me to shake.

"That's . . ." Mrs. Nitzer made a face, trying to explain what this . . . thing was.

"I'm Rodney's social studies tutor," I said, shaking her hand. If Mrs. Nitzer was relieved that I'd come up with a respectable title, she certainly didn't show it.

"Oh! How nice. I didn't realize Rodney was having trouble in school," she said, kicking sand in the face of my great save.

"To be perfectly honest, he's probably taught me more than I've taught him!" I said, still struggling. I looked at Rodney, who was still glazed over, practicing his bass.

"Well, Jean, how are you faring these days?" the woman asked Mrs. Nitzer. "I hear you're looking for a job."

Mrs. Nitzer's lips grew tighter and whiter. "On and off," she said. "How'd you know?"

"I actually didn't know, but Sally told me your alimony dried up several months ago, so I just figured . . . ," she said smugly.

Church is a shark tank! This bitch was out for blood! I suddenly felt incredibly protective of Mrs. Nitzer. I wanted to tell the woman to go fuck herself. Instead I just stood there and looked pious, knowing that anything I said would certainly be used against me.

"Well, you figured correctly," was all Mrs. Nitzer said. She looked at Rodney and me and said, "Time to go."

She scowled all the way to the car, clearly mortified that I knew about her new impoverished status. "Where did you park?" she asked me.

"A few blocks that way," I said, pointing in the direction of my car. It was time for us to part, which meant it was time for me to state my plea.

Mrs. Nitzer stared at me in silence. My nerves were already shot from finding out all about hell, and I now found myself terrified that she was going to peck my eyes out.

"Why don't you tell me what you're doing here?" she said.

"Well, I've got this gig working with sick children . . . ," I started.

"You do not," she said, taking the motorcycle lighter out of her bag and firing up a cig. And then she actually laughed! It was such a shocking and unnatural gesture for her, I swear she could have ripped her clothes off and I would have been equally as stunned. Rodney, now fully out of his bass-playing daze, watched us with huge eyes.

"Try again," she said, blowing smoke in my face. "You want something. Is it the boy?" She nodded at Rodney without taking her eyes off my face.

What could I do? My one measly lie not only didn't work but got laughed at! I had no backup plan and no brain to come up with one, so my only option left was to tell the truth.

"I want that," I said, pointing to her lighter.

"This?" she said, surprised, holding it up. "Oh come on, you can do better than that."

"No, really, I sat through two hours of fire and brimstone because I want that lighter," I said, suddenly getting my strength back.

She looked at Rodney and then back at me. Her eyes narrowed, and her claws tightened around it. "Why?" she asked.

"For Flowers," I said.

Her face lit up, and suddenly I heard a choir of angels singing. I'd forgotten how much she liked him!

"Is that why he called the other day?" Rodney chimed in, adding some much-needed validity to my story.

"Probably," I said.

"What in heaven's name does Flowers want my lighter for?" she asked, suddenly very interested.

"Well . . . he . . . always admired it," I babbled, "and I thought, he's done so much for me lately that—"

"Bzzzt. Stop. Close, but no cigar," Mrs. Nitzer said.

"Don't even bother," Rodney said glumly. "She's impossible to lie to. Trust me."

I looked at her expressionless face and felt all hope leave my body. I had been so close—and then I'd utterly blown it. I couldn't tell her the sordid truth. We were in a church parking lot! Plus the woman had no soul. She wasn't going to give me a damn thing.

"Never mind," I said, turning my back to her. I gave Rodney a hug. "I'll see you around," I said, walking away.

I had clearly put on the wrong stupid disguise. I was going to have to trade in the blue business suit for a fake beard and try plan number one.

Well, it looks like Tony's producing the record. It just kind of happened. He started showing up at practice and brainstorming on the songs, and here we are in the studio. I feel like I blacked out or something. At one point Lucy and I went up to Chad's office to talk to him about other options, but he looked at us like we had antlers.

January 15

"Don't worry so much. I know what this guy is capable of. It'll be a killer record. And the label will be much more into it and give you tons more support. I promise. You watch," he said, twiddling his chin ponytail.

"So . . . what? They'll just send us straight to the bargain bin if we use Eddie or someone else?" Lucy asked.

"Honestly? No. But if you use Eddie, you'll go straight to the 'never heard of 'em' bin," he said. Lucy and I didn't laugh. Chad tried harder. "How about this? How about we have Tony produce it and bring Eddie in for the mix? Huh? That way everybody's happy! I'd say that reeks of magic!" He clapped his hands, overjoyed with his own brilliance. He handed us each tickets to see Moby as a bonus incentive.

Lucy looked at me. "What do you think?" she asked.

"I think it sounds okay. What about you?"

She shrugged and nodded. We stood up and shook Chad's hand. "We'll see you later," I said to him.

"Don't forget the photo shoot next week," he said as we walked out. "We got you guys the most amazing photographer!"

That was a couple days ago, and as I write this we already have all the drum parts down for the first six songs. We're recording at the Sound Factory, one of L.A.'s proudest and most famed recording studios. The place is so swank and set up, it makes Eddie's studio look like a repair shop.

We were all hanging out, listening to Scott be a genius behind the drum set and freaking out over what a cool place we were in.

"Those speakers sound massive!" Jake said when Tony played back Scott's part.

"Just you wait, my friend, just you wait," Tony said. It was so far so good with the Head Cheese (our nickname for Tony. He was clueless about its double meaning). He worked incredibly fast and was so excited it was infectious.

"How many serious rock stars' asses have sat on this very cushion, I wonder," Lucy said, bending down like she was about to sniff her seat.

"None as disgusting as you," I said.

By the end of the day, Tony had gotten almost all of Scott's drum parts down and we were all no longer upset with our decision. Tony had his shit together and, judging from how well he'd recorded Scott's drums, everything was going to be excellent.

We all went home high on the high life.

Scott edited all the footage he's shot of the band so far and had a screening at his house. It was great!

BRILLIANT OBSERVATION #30:
Scott is as big a genius as he is a babe.

Jake showed up with his latest representative from Implantville. I swear, the bigger we get, the bigger *they* get. Jake was looking pretty gnarly. I didn't know if Jeffrey had talked to him yet, but if he had, it sure wasn't working.

Lucy came with some weird friends of hers from work. One of the chicks was hitting on Scott so hard, it was painful to watch.

"My God, I thought *I* was a cannibal," Lucy said to me as we watched her talk to Scott on the other side of the room. She had one of her hands on his chest while she coyly twirled her hair with the other. Scott was being nice, but I could tell he was uncomfortable. He removed her hand and pretended to look at her ring, dropping it back by her side when he was done.

"Smooth, Scott, smooth," I said, making Lucy crack up. But at the same time, I could see her watching my face for a reaction. She was more than a little suspicious of Scott and me, and is a far better detective than I am a liar.

Luckily, Scott's little situation didn't bother me at all (I trusted that it would go nowhere). Having Lucy study me was making me a nervous wreck, though.

"Let's go find Jake and see if his new girlfriend will let us touch her fake boobs," I said, trying to change the subject to something I knew Lucy would cling to.

"Great idea!" Lucy said.

I have to admit I got some kind of sick satisfaction out of watching Scott squirm back there. I knew that if the tables were turned and it was me with some guy, Scott would get pouty. I felt like if I was going to get in trouble every time I stood next to another guy, at least Scott had to suffer a tiny bit too. But my fun didn't last long. As the night went on, I got more and more frustrated that I couldn't just be with him in public. And I was so paranoid that Lucy was going to see through me that I could barely be near him at all. It sucks being in love with someone and never being allowed to show it.

"Welcome to the world of a fag," Flowers said, when I complained to him in the kitchen.

"I hate it!" I said, just as Scott walked in the room.

He came up and put his arms around both of us.

"What do you hate?" he asked, smirking. "That you still haven't gotten him his lighter?" I'd lost my sense of humor about the whole lighter thing ever since my run-in with Mrs. Nitzer. It was so humiliating, not in a funny way, and I felt completely at a loss.

"So the forbidden fruit knows about the bet!" Flowers said, laughing. "You don't have much time left, my pretty," he went on, jabbing me. I smacked his hand away. I was pissed.

"Ooh, Flowers, this is serious," Scott said, laughing. They both stared at me expectantly.

"I know you think it's hilarious, but I humiliated myself so majorly the other day, and I still didn't get it," I said.

"What do you mean, humiliated yourself? Oh, Jenny—you didn't!" Scott said. I said nothing.

"You did!" he said. I said nothing.

"What, what?" Flowers screamed.

"She went to church with Mrs. Nitzer," Scott said in disbelief.

I said nothing. They both burst out laughing, and I stormed out of the room.

When Scott and I were going to sleep that night, he brought it up again. And again, I didn't think it was funny.

"Man, you are so sensitive," he said.

"*I* am?" I said. The bastard had no idea what I'd gone through! Plus he was a much bigger baby than I was. "Well at least I don't pitch a fit every time you talk to another girl."

"That chick at the party, you mean?"

"Why? Are there more?" I asked.

"So you *are* jealous!" he said happily.

"No. I don't get jealous, Scott. I was just teasing you. Jealousy's idiotic," I said.

"We'll see about that," he said.

"I mean it. You need to stop. It's deadly."

"I need to stop! What about you?"

"I'm so not jealous!" I said, exasperated.

"I'll prove to you that you are!" he said.

All I'd wanted to do was discuss this problem, and I'd somehow turned it into a contest! I couldn't believe it. And no matter how hard I tried to talk to him about it, he wouldn't let it go.

I think I've created a monster.

We're on our fourth long day in the studio, and we're all still blown away by how having a real budget and a real studio makes all the difference. We can take our time, get any sound we want, and someone else pays for lunch!

January 20

ROCK-AND-ROLL TRUTH #10:

It's physically impossible not to have fun in a recording studio.

Tony seems okay so far. I had to wrestle him a few times over some guitar parts, but he let me have my way in the end. About those, anyway. He didn't let me have my way about restructuring all the songs, but when Jeffrey stopped by to see how everything was going, he assured me that that's a producer's job and that it's totally normal.

"How do you like everything else?" he asked, looking over my shoulder at Jake.

"Okay, I guess," I said.

Jeffrey patted me on my back. "Good," he said, walking over to Jake.

Jake rolled his eyes as he saw Jeffrey approach. Jeffrey dragged him over to the corner, and a heated discussion ensued. A few minutes into it, Jeffrey's cell rang and Jake took the opportunity to leave the room. Jeffrey finished up his call and went out after him.

I looked at Lucy and she shrugged. I figured the Drug Talks had begun after all but that they weren't going so well. I was glad it was Jeffrey dealing with it and not me.

Tony brought some freak in to play piano on my road song, "Drivin'." He was about 193 years old, with a severe case of the shakes. But he could play the shit out of that thing. Tony told us he used to play with the Stones. Earl Molins. Never heard of him. I doubt Mick has either.

People from the label kept stopping by and offering their opinions.

RACHEL, PRODUCT MANAGER:	Wow, you guys! This sounds awesome!
ERIC, CHAD'S ASSISTANT:	Holy shit. Holy shit! Holy motherfucking shit!
CHAD:	Does this make you cream in your pants or what?
SUE, ART DIRECTOR:	You guys are so totally fucking hot, I want to cook an egg on your ass.

"Holy accolade overload," Jake said when the swarm had left.

"Get used to it. It's only going to get more insane once I'm done with it," Tony said. We all looked at each other in amazement.

"Does it really sound that good? Does anything sound that good?" I asked.

Everyone shrugged.

"Fuck it. We're that good. Why not?" Lucy said.

Out of everyone, Sue, our art director, hung around the longest. She's an old fan; she was at the show where Rodney broke his toe when he discovered he didn't have the Throw Your Bass in the Air and Catch It Gene. She has a high tiny voice and jet black dyed hair. She took a bunch of pictures, and we talked about album cover ideas. She got us all excited about the photo shoot we're going to do tomorrow.

TOP FIVE MOST EXCELLENT THINGS ABOUT PHOTO SHOOTS:

1) They do your hair and makeup and put you in all these crazy clothes. You feel like Rock Band Barbie.
2) Everyone passing by stares at you.

January 21

3) They're catered.

4) They sometimes make Scott take his shirt off.

5) When you're the lead singer, you're the center of every shot.

We took a break from the studio and spent the whole day on location at a Ralph's supermarket. Sue and her stylee staff pulled up in a Winnebago full of makeup and clothes. The photographer was this guy named Brendan Von Somethingpretentious and his pants were so tight, I swear his nuts were bulging out in shock.

"Should we tell him?" Lucy whispered hysterically. We were posing for a shot while Captain Testicle focused his camera. I was sitting in a shopping cart that the rest of the band were pushing.

"What the hell are you going to say?" I asked.

"Got any franks to go with them beans?" Jake said, making us all lose it.

"I bet he does it on purpose," Scott said. "We should ask to look at his portfolio. I'll bet everyone in it is smiling. Hard."

He shot us in the frozen food section, in the checkout aisle, and standing up in the convertible of some guy who he gave fifty bucks to in the parking lot.

"Everyone having a good time?" Von Nuts asked.

"A ball!" Lucy said, killing us all again.

He had us get out of the car and spread out in the parking lot. "Okay, now I need all of you to back way up," he said, holding my arm to keep me close to him. "Not you. You're up front."

He proceeded to take close-up shots of me with the rest of

the band about a mile off in the distance. Finally he just got rid of them altogether. "Susan, please, more eyeliner on Jenny here," he said, leading me over to a palm tree. "I want these to be trés glamorous!"

Sue and the makeup girl came over and worked on my face while the rest of the band sat around. Brendan shot me for about an hour before Jake finally asked if he could leave.

"Yes, all of you, go, go!" he said, waving his hand at them. They all made fun of me as they left, primping and acting like prima donnas, but I felt like some of it wasn't a joke. They were probably a little pissed. I would have been.

But I didn't have to be.

BRILLIANT OBSERVATION #31:
I love being the center of attention.

What a difference a day makes.

The honeymoon with Tony is officially over. We came in today to discover that on our day off he'd completely rewritten "Drivin'" and pretty much turned the rest of our songs into a heaping plate of poo! He was playing back some stuff for us, all excited at how "rawly perfect" it was.

January 22

"Isn't it amazing what a little sprucing up can do?" he said, infinitely impressed with his own terrible taste.

"Tony! What the hell? You can't just take our shit and do whatever you want to it," I said, horrified.

"I do it all the time! Sometimes I have to rewrite songs from start to finish, they're so awful," he said. "That's how this works."

"So you can make them even more awful?" Lucy asked.

"Ever occur to you to ask us first?" I asked.

"It stinks in here," Jake said, pushing his chair violently against the wall. He'd spent most of the day looking like he was going to fall asleep. But now he was livid.

"Hey everyone, calm down! This is still a work in progress. We're all working together here," Tony said, treating us like a bunch of whining crybabies. "Nothing goes on the album that we're not all happy with, okay?" he said, a big cheesy smile lighting up his liar's face.

STUDIO BATTLES I WON:

Don't make the drums so busy on "Left You Alone."

Keep the bass line constant all the way through "Bomb."

Order lunch from the sandwich place instead of the pizza place.

STUDIO BATTLES TONY WON:

Put cheesy, synthesized drum effects on 75 percent of the songs.

Rearrange the structure of 75 percent of songs to make them more pop.

Pare down giant, booming wall of guitars. Make it more like a silly little fence.

Put perky hand claps in 75 percent of songs.

I soon discovered, with the arrival of Chad and a panicked phone call to Jeffrey, that we were officially screwed.

"You said if we didn't like it, we could work with someone else," I screamed at Chad.

"I did. And now the company's already spent a week on studio time for you guys. If you didn't like him, you should have said something sooner. Besides," he said, condescendingly, "you're getting upset over nothing. It's not even mixed down yet. It's going to be godhead! You'll see."

"We're having Eddie mix it, right? Or was I dumb enough to believe you on that one too?" I said. Chad rolled his eyes at me.

"If you insist," he said.

That was a relief, even though I was mortified to let Eddie hear it. I mean, Tony even brought in children to sing in the background of "Drivin'," one of our most rocking songs! He said he wanted to make it sound like a family road trip. The guy's a pinhead. It sounds like a milk ad.

Luckily Scott filmed it all, so when this turd rolls out of the studio there'll be proof we had nothing to do with it. It's small consolation, though. I worked my ass off to get here. It made my heart sink to the bottom of the earth.

BRILLIANT OBSERVATION #32:
Nobody gives two shits about your creative vision. All they care about is making money.

We've been duped.

In an effort to lift our spirits, Jeffrey suggested we take a chunk of our advance money and go shopping.

"You guys have been stressing way too hard. Go spend some damn money. Get some clothes to make yourselves feel like the rock stars you really are," he said, calling me from his cell in his car.

January 25

"Don't we have to pay it all back?" I asked.

"Stop worrying so much! Jenny, the album is going to be great. You're just on overload! Relax, have some fun. This is your dream, remember?"

Jeffrey actually made me feel better. The album sounded scary, but I had to remember that it wasn't over yet.

NOTE TO SELF:
Premature freakouts are a waste of time.

I rounded up the troops, who were all very excited by the idea, and we hit Melrose for a day of unbridled spending. First I swung by Flowers's place to see if he'd join us. We needed a stylist.

Lucy and I jumped out of the car and banged on his door. He opened it wearing workout clothes and a layer of sweat. He was bright red and panting.

"It's you!" he said when he saw me, looking at me like I'd just wrecked his life. He quickly glanced over at Lucy. "Hi, Lucy," he said.

"Good to see you too," I said.

He grinned and shook his head. "You are a piece of work. Hah! I must say I'm impressed, though. You sure had me fooled," he said.

"What's he talking about?" Lucy asked me.

"I have no fucking idea," I said, staring at Flowers. He winked at me, still shaking his head and grinning. I really had no idea.

"Well, what do you want from me now?" he asked.

"We're all going shopping. We need a stylist. Wanna come?

I'll buy you whatever you want, up to two hundred bucks," I said.

"I'll be right out," he said, heading inside to change.

"What was that all about?" Lucy asked as we walked back to the car.

"Fuck if I know," I said.

When we finally found a parking spot on Melrose, we weren't out of the car for five minutes before two girls came up and wanted their picture taken with us.

"We saw you play with Bullet Hole," one said, handing her camera to Flowers to do the honors. The other one made a beeline for Scott and put her arm around him. She was grinning like an idiot and too nervous to speak.

"Everybody say, 'squeeze me!'" Flowers said, taking the picture. He handed the camera back and the girls giggled off down the street. After that I noticed that everyone in the band, including yours truly, started walking with a certain cocky strut we hadn't possessed before.

It was one of those perfect L.A. days where the sun was shining, as usual, and the air was actually breathable for a change. It was crisp and clear and had that sweet smell of whatever it is I smell all the time here. . . .

"Jasmine?" I asked as we headed into our first store.

"Success!" Lucy said.

"Indeed," said Jake, eyeing a pair of black leather pants in the window of a store we were passing. "And those will soon be mine!"

We went in, and Jake immediately headed for the dressing room with the pants. Scott and Lucy went off to look at shoes while I showed Flowers a purple velvet cape I wanted to get for Tami.

"For our marketing magician," I said. "What do you think?"

"I think Jake's been in that dressing room far too long. Hey, Jake," Flowers called out, "need some help?"

"Fuck off, Flowers," he answered.

"How do they look?" I asked through the dressing room door.

"Most excellent, actually," he said, opening the door and stepping out into the room. They fit him like a sausage casing. Lucy and Scott clapped from across the room, and Flowers held up his lighter.

His motorcycle lighter!

"Oh my God!" I said, grabbing it out of his hands. I had no idea how he'd gotten it, but I suddenly realized that the cryptic conversation we had when I went to pick him up was about this. I had to act cool. He had to think I made it happen.

"So, want to tell me how it went down?" I said.

He glared at me and shook his head. Again.

"I want to hate you, but it was really just so brilliant I can't. I guess you deserve all the gory details," he said. "Well, let's see, the doorbell rang at about seven o'clock last night. I was working on a sculpture and baking some blueberry tarts, excited about spending a productive evening alone. When I opened the door, there she was, dressed to kill, with the lighter sticking out of her cleavage," he said, raising his eyebrow.

Did he mean Mrs. Nitzer? Was it possible?

"Excellent," I said. "Tell me more."

"She said, and I quote, 'I hear I have something you want,' as she slithered past me into my house," he said flatly.

Mrs. Nitzer! It was too good to be true!

"Go on," I said, grinning.

"That's all you get, you evil thing. Suffice it to say I spent the rest of the evening fending off rape by flinging every piece of gay paraphernalia I had at her. I did everything short of beating her to death with my dildo," he said. He stuck out his hand to shake.

"Nice job, creep," he said. We shook.

"So, does she hate you now that she knows you're a dirty homo sinner?" I asked.

"I should be so lucky! She thinks all I need is a good woman to show me the ways of the Lord! I'm terrified I won't be able to get rid of her."

Why did it make me so happy that Mrs. Nitzer had the hots for Flowers?

I was dying to tell Scott, but it was too risky with everyone around. Lucy already wanted to know what Flowers and I were giggling about over in the corner. Plus Scott was so busy flirting with every woman in every store that he was starting to piss me off. But I couldn't say a damn thing, because that would mean I was jealous, not that he was acting like an idiot.

"Dude, you writing a new phone book with all those numbers?" Jake asked him as we were crossing the street, much to my satisfaction. Scott was busy gloating over a receipt that some salesgirl had written her number on.

"I'll be too busy to write, my friend," he said smugly, putting it in his pocket.

"What the hell did you eat for breakfast, Scotty?" Lucy wanted to know. "Viagra?"

"You're not the only one around here who needs to get laid, Lucy," Scott said.

"Too bad you can't just jump Jenny. You so obviously want to," Lucy said, making my right knee suddenly give out so that I gripped Flowers's shoulder.

Scott, ever the pro, kicked the ball right back in her face. "And too bad you can't jump *me*. You so obviously want to," he said, grinning at her.

Lucy let loose a howl and spanked him.

"Well, that is for sure, baby!" she said, laughing. "Ain't life cruel?"

Okay, I was jealous. Flirting with strangers was one thing, but flirting with The Man-Eater was mean. He had no idea he'd just hit me in the jugular.

"I wouldn't touch either of you with a ten-foot pole," I said flippantly, praying my participation would confirm my lack of concern.

"You can borrow mine, then," Flowers said. "It goes up to eleven."

Luckily, everyone got distracted by a shoe sale, and I wasn't required to keep up my charade any longer.

But that was a close one.

NOTE TO SELF:

Find a boyfriend for Lucy.

At around six o'clock we went to some place for Indian food and everyone showed off their purchases. I awarded blue ribbons to items in the following categories:

FLASHIEST:	Flowers's Lycra hot pants with battery-powered siren and flashing light attached to crotch.
UGLIEST:	Lucy's woven poncho.
MOST EXPENSIVE:	Jake's leather pants.
MOST RIDICULOUS:	Lucy's hair bikini made out of wigs and twine.
MOST LIKELY TO GET YOU LAID:	Scott's supertight see-through black shirt with a snake stripe running down his treasure trail.
MOST CONFUSING:	Jake's tank top made out of Barbie doll heads.
BEST ALL-AROUND ITEM:	My new sequined bra with tiny disco balls dangling from the nipples.

All in all, we spent over five thousand dollars on flashy clothes. That's more than I paid for my car.

I love being a rock star.

Today marks the first day of our mix-down with Eddie. No more Tony. No more cheese. No more tears. I put a Band-Aid in my shrine for good luck. We needed to do some major plastic surgery on our very ugly baby, and we were going to need all the help we could get.

I got up early and drove Scott to his truck, like I did most mornings of Operation Undercover Relationship. We still hadn't discussed his infantile quest to make me jealous, but I wasn't about to bring it up if he wasn't. I could tell he thought he'd failed, and I feared discussing it would just make him try harder.

January 29

It was excellent to see Eddie again, but kind of weird too. I realized I'd never seen him outside his studio, and he seemed a little smaller. Naked.

"Hi darlin'," he said, giving me a big hug when I walked in.

I was the first one there, other than Chad.

"I take it you two have met?" I said.

"Oh, yeah. I was just walking Eddie here through the tapes Tony left behind and telling him how jazzed we are about the project," Chad gushed.

"Have you heard any of it yet?" I asked Eddie.

"Nope," he said.

"That explains why you're still sitting there, then," I joked.

Chad gave an uneasy laugh. "Jenny thinks Tony could have done better. I think she'll be kissing his ass when she's rolling in dough," he said. He was soon proven to be alone in his sentiment, however. After the rest of the band had showed up, we listened to poor old "Drivin'," and when the children's chorus kicked in, Eddie shrieked like a wet cat. He grabbed my hand.

"We can take that indecency out," he said. He went on to say that very same sentence about a hundred more times as he listened to the rest of the tapes.

He started mixing down the first song, and it was painful to watch. Like seeing someone perform surgery on a patient who had very little chance of making it. I've never seen Eddie so somber.

"Is it hopeless?" Lucy asked, cozying up next to him at the mixing board. She was just as smitten with him as before.

"No, darlin', not exactly," he said. He concentrated harder than I'd ever seen him, adding effects, dumping tracks, and shaving off cheese. We sat in silence and watched. When he was finally done with the first song, he stood up, stretched and turned to peer into our depressed little faces. He rubbed his hands together.

"What we are doing here, ladies and gentlemen," he said dramatically, "is shining a turd."

And an album title was born.

Sixty-Foot Queenie: Can't Shine a Turd, the debut album out now on Mastiff Records.

We couldn't stop laughing. He's a true genius.

BRILLIANT OBSERVATION #33:
If you work with great people, it will be a great experience. Even if you're shoveling shit.

January 30

Eddie's a miracle worker. He loves working in a fancy-schmancy studio. He snuck old Murray in, even though the studio doesn't allow animals.

"Never go a day without an animal, darlin'. Never go a day," he said, scratching the cat on the head.

By the end of the day, I was actually excited about the album again. It still kind of sounded like poop, but it was getting better.

"Eddie's awesome," I said to Scott on the way back to my house. "He's making me feel a lot better about the album."

Scott grunted. He was brooding. He'd been kind of brooding all day, actually, but I was having too good a time to deal with his temper tantrum.

"Is there something wrong?" I asked him.

"No," he said, unconvincingly.

"Scott, come on, tell me," I said.

"I'm fine! I'm just tired, that's all," he snapped. When we got home, he collapsed on my couch and immediately turned on the TV. I went into my room and read.

About an hour later there was a knock on the door. Scott came flying into the bedroom and cracked the window in case he needed to escape. I left the room, closed the door, hid all traces of Scott, and went out to see who it was.

BRILLIANT OBSERVATION #34:
We've gone pro.

It was Henry!

"Hey! What's up?" I said, pulling him inside and giving him a hug. I hadn't seen him in ages. He never comes to our shows anymore since it makes him so miserable to see Lucy, and I've been spending most of my free time with Scott. He'd called a couple of times, but I hadn't been able to talk.

"It's just Henry," I yelled to Scott, who came shuffling out of the bedroom.

"Hey," he said to Henry, resuming his place on the couch in front of the TV.

"Hi, Scott," Henry said, clearly uncomfortable.

I stuck Henry in the big yellow chair across from the couch and dragged another chair in from the kitchen for myself.

"You want anything to drink?" I asked him.

"No, thanks. I'm fine," he said. I sat down.

"I'll take a beer," Scott said from the couch.

OPTION #1:

Tell Scott to get off his lazy, passive-aggressive ass and go get it himself. Remind him that he practically lives at my house, eats all my food, and, last I checked, is able to walk.

PROBLEMS WITH OPTION #1:

This could majorly aggravate an already gigantic moping session. It will make him feel justified in accusing me of treating my friends better than I treat him, as well as embarrassing him in front of Henry. Moping session will turn into full-blown ice storm.

OPTION #2:

Get Scott his fucking beer.

PROBLEMS WITH OPTION #2:

Scott will feel smug that he's punished me, as I so richly deserve, for allowing boring old Henry to visit. I'll be degraded in front of Henry, who already has a less-than-glowing opinion of Scott, and I'll be pissed at Scott for manipulating me.

I went for option number two, finessing it by getting myself a beer while I was at it. I asked Henry again if he wanted one.

"You sure? I'm gonna have one," I said, going into the kitchen.

"All right," he said, giving me the victory. I walked over to the couch to give Scott his and stood above him until he took his eyes off the TV set. Then I handed it to him.

"Thanks," he said, grouchily.

"Kiss for the servant?" I asked, bending over to get a kiss. I figured he couldn't honestly be that upset—I knew he didn't adore Henry, but this was ridiculous.

I got a weak little peck and an irritated look for getting in his face. I guess I was wrong. Handing Henry his beer, I sat down again.

"So what's new?" I asked. "I don't think I've seen you since you puked all over the side of Chad's limo."

"Oh, right," Henry said. "Thanks for reminding me."

"No problem," I said.

"How's the rise to stardom?"

"Awesome! The album's a little spooky, but we've been doing photo shoots and shopping and having meetings and signing autographs. It's so great!"

"Wow. I just can't believe it," he said, grinning at me. He paused for a second and made a pained face. "How's Lucy doing? She seeing anyone?"

"Not really. She's got the hots for our producer, though."

"She's not the only one," Scott suddenly said from the couch.

I almost fell over. Was that the reason he was being such a baby all day? I couldn't believe it.

"He's just kidding," I said to Henry.

"No, he's not," Scott said.

"Scott, come on! I can't like another guy without wanting to fuck him?"

He was silent and very pissed off.

"Henry, maybe you should go," I said.

Henry just sat there sipping his beer. "I see you for five

minutes in how many weeks and you're already kicking me out?" he said.

"Yeah, well, it's not exactly a good time," I said.

Henry shook his head and got up. "It's never a good time anymore, Jenny," he said, looking at Scott.

Scott glared at the TV screen, and Henry finally walked out the door.

I sat next to Scott on the couch and turned off the TV. Scott switched his glare to me.

"Scott! Come on! How can you think I have a thing for Eddie?"

"Maybe because all you do is gush about him twenty-four hours a day," he said, "and scream with laughter every time the guy opens his fucking mouth."

"That doesn't mean I want to fuck him, Scott. Yeah, I like the guy. But I love you. Two very different things," I said.

"And then I have to come home and watch you with Henry?"

He was jealous of Henry too?

"I've known Henry since I was sixteen. He's like my brother, you idiot."

"I bet Lucy used to say the same thing," he said, smugly.

"Okay, this is exactly what I'm talking about, Scott. You're jealous over nothing, and it's driving me crazy!"

We managed to argue for a good three hours. Scott accused me of ignoring him and being a flirt. I accused him of stifling me and being a baby. Finally we both just got too tired to fight anymore.

"Let's just say we'll try and be more aware of each other's needs, okay?" I begged, dying to put it to rest.

"Okay," he said, taking my hand and leading me into the bedroom. Then we had the best sex I've ever had in my entire life.

We've been in the studio, looking over photos, meeting with the label, meeting with our manager, and basically just getting primped, tucked, and primed to be the next big thing.

I wake up every single day and still can't believe it's happening.

We took a lunch break from the studio to meet with Jeffrey and our art director, Sue, to look over the photos and talk about a bunch of stuff. We took Eddie with us, and Lucy nearly knocked the waiter over making sure she got to sit in the booth next to him. I slid in next to Scott, with a very disheveled-looking Jake on my other side.

"We got some really great stuff from the other day," Sue said, getting immediately down to business. She whipped out a bunch of prints from the photo shoot with Brendan Von Testicles. They were fabulous, and I was more the center of every shot than I'd thought. Hee hee.

"Well, look at y'all, dressed up and de-stanked for the camera. Looks like Jenny's the belle of the ball," Eddie said, winking at me. I grabbed Scott's hand under the table and squeezed it.

"I was thinking about using this as the album cover," Sue said, sliding the picture of us in the shopping cart onto the table. My face was front and center.

"Great shot," Scott said.

"Our little cover girl," Lucy said. I couldn't tell whether she was actually being pissy or just giving me shit.

"We've got a few more shoots coming up," Sue said. "We need stuff for posters and promos and a million other things."

"We've also got to get started on the video the second the recording is done," Jeffrey said. "And you should all be thrilled to know we got Max Della Flora to shoot it!"

Scott nearly tore the fingers off my hand. "Max Della Flora!" he screamed. "That guy's the shit!"

"In a word, yes," Jeffrey said, smugly.

I'd never heard of Della Flora, but I quickly learned he was the biggest deal in the world.

"The guy's a genius," Scott raved, "easily the most important video director out there. He's doing stuff nobody's even come close to."

"Cool," Lucy said.

"I've also got the majority of your tour planned out," Jeffrey said. "We'll print up a quickie promo CD and send you guys out on a radio tour to get a buzz going so that when the album hits, the world will be ready. You hit the road April first."

"How'd you do all that so damn fast?" I asked Jeffrey.

"Evil never sleeps," said Jake darkly.

Well, that was a real conversation stopper. Everyone was silent for a moment, and I jabbed Jake in the ribs to lighten up. Then Jeffrey went on as though no one had spoken. "So the tour's in about a month. I'll get you all the details the second I have everything ironed out."

The waiter came and took our order. I got a twenty-dollar piece of fish and a twelve-dollar glass of wine. Scott rubbed my leg under the table as I raised my glass for a toast.

"To being huge," I said, looking around the table at every single excellent person I work with. Every situation has its problems, but I'd have to say, ours are pretty damn minimal compared to the pluses. As Eddie would say, I'm as happy as a pig in shit.

Today's the last day of shining the old turd. I dragged Lucy into the bathroom with me to find out what was up with her and Eddie. If the two of them were together, maybe Scott would quit torturing me by flirting with her.

February 7

"Believe me, I've tried everything. He finally told me that I'm too wild for him. He said to give him a call when I'm ready to settle down," she said, leaning against the sink.

"Well, tell him you're ready to settle down," I said.

"I tried that! He didn't believe me."

"Well, are you?" I asked.

"Fuck no! I'm in a band, I'm going to see the world! I don't want to worry about some guy back home holed up in a studio somewhere," she said.

My fears were confirmed. She was just as big an animal as ever.

Toward the end of the day, Chad, Tony, and Jeffrey showed up to hear the final product. I also invited Flowers and Tami to come by the studio for some honest opinions. Not that it really mattered. The album was finished. There was nothing we could do about it now. We just needed a reality check, since everyone at the label continued to gush over it like they had guns held to their heads.

THE COMMENTS:

FLOWERS: Well, let's just say I wouldn't want to wake up naked next to it or anything. I might take it home if I was drunk enough, though. You know, you guys sound kind of like Hootie and the Blowfish.

LUCY: It's too . . . clean and indecisive. It sounds like us after we went to charm school or something.

SCOTT: You can barely tell there's a real drummer behind all those effects. The whole album sounds like it was squirted out of a can.

JAKE: Moderate to fully weak. A yawn of an album.

TAMI: You guys rock.

JEFFREY: Not bad. Not great. Not what I imagined, but let's see how far it takes us.

CHAD: Can you say "next big thing"?

TONY: Some key elements have been taken out, but I still think this could change the direction of rock completely.

EDDIE: "Left you Alone," "Sucker Punch," and "Bomb" are passable. The rest I wouldn't feed to my pigs.

ME: We sound like every other band out there who's been over-produced and stripped of their originality. Here's hoping the entire record-buying public has terrible taste.

The album, in a word, sucked. But I'd come too far to just give up.

"You guys, we still have our live shows," I reminded the band after we'd gotten rid of Chad and Tony. "We can just go out there and get as big a following as possible and make sure our next album is actually good."

"If we don't get laughed out of the running before then," Lucy said.

"I'm gonna sell the demo album at every show," Tami said.

"We're chumps," Jake said.

"I wouldn't even have this record in my house," Scott said.

"Oh, would you please!" Flowers suddenly shouted. He glared around the room at all of us. "Every artistic venture sprouts a few warts. Why should yours be any different? Quit moaning and just go out there and be fabulous. You are all talented enough to blast through far bigger roadblocks than this. Isn't that what rock and roll is all about anyway? Defiance?

"Show these idiots that they can't stop you!" he went on, getting carried away and standing on his chair, shouting. "Look at where you're sitting! Look at all the money behind you! I've never seen such a bunch of whining sissies."

Flowers was standing on his chair with his fist high in the air like the Statue of Liberty. Suddenly everyone started applauding. He took a bow.

But ridiculous as he looked, he'd given us hope. He'd given us a spanking. And so we had a plan: the world was to bend over, and we were to kick its ass with our big, stinky foot.

February 15

We had a gig last night for the first time in weeks. We'd been in the studio so long, I'd forgotten how much I loved the rush of being onstage.

It was an all-ages show at the Palace with Truth or Dare and the Nippleheads, two bands way bigger than us, but I swear at least half the crowd was there to see us. Our glossy new posters (a shot of me standing by a palm tree with the rest of the band dispersed in the background, thank you very much) were up everywhere, and there was a crowd in front of our T-shirt table, which, of course, was manned by Tami. I waved at her as I walked by, but when I saw who she was talking to, I nearly fell over. Rodney!

"I'm so glad you came!" I said, running over and giving him a hug. "Did Tami give you a free T-shirt?"

"Of course I did," Tami said, insulted.

"It's about time you guys played an all-ages show. I'm so sick of having to come with my mother," he said, laughing and looking at Tami as he rolled his eyes. She giggled.

"Well, but it's cool that she came with you all those times so you could play with these guys. You're an awesome bass player," Tami said, very seriously.

"Thanks, Tami," he said, staring down at his feet. Did he blush? Did she?

Oh my God. They were flirting! They had a thing for each other!

I wanted to know how long this had been going on! I wanted to demand they tell me just exactly what they thought they were doing. But I didn't. Instead, I cleared my throat and picked up my things. This was clearly no place for me.

"Well, I guess I should go set up. I'll see you two later."

I went onstage and started setting my gear up with Jake and Scott. Lucy was up to her old tricks, hanging out at the bar and flirting with five people at once.

"Is she planning on setting up anytime soon?" I asked Jake.

"I know not. I'm getting a beer," he said, leaving Scott and me alone onstage. Scott kept poking me in the ass with his drumstick.

"Quit it," I said, smacking him. He looked great—he was wearing his new see-through black shirt and jeans. Seeing him onstage behind the drums was a very welcome, very sexy turn of events.

"Let's go do it in the bathroom," he said.

"Are you nuts? We can't!" I said, laughing.

"Oh come on! Live a little. It'll just be a quickie."

"It's way too risky."

"That's what's so hot about it!" he said, getting up and begging me to follow him, which I finally did. When we got to the bathrooms they were too packed, so we went outside and got in his truck.

"Everyone walking by can see us," I said.

"Who's walking by? We're in the back of a parking lot," he said, taking off my shirt. He was right.

A FEW THINGS TO KEEP IN MIND WHEN HAVING SEX IN THE FRONT SEAT OF A TRUCK:

1) Stick shifts. Not as sexy as everyone wants to think they are.
2) Cold steering wheels will always find a way to press against a naked ass.
3) The horn.
4) If you're both over six feet, it's nearly impossible, making the successful completion of the act all the more satisfying.

By the time we got back inside, me first with him following behind a couple of minutes later, Lucy was onstage setting up.

"Where the hell did you guys go?" she said. "I've been looking all over the place for you."

"I was in the bathroom," I lied. "I wonder where Jake and Scott are. We're probably going on soon."

Lucy was staring at me with a weird look on her face. "What were you doing in there? You look like you just got laid," she said.

NOTE TO SELF:

Hiding sexual activity from Lucy Hanover is like hiding raw meat from a dog.

"I did get laid," I said. "Didn't you see the line out the bathroom door?"

Scott walked up and I prayed to God—yes, the same God that was sending me straight to hell—that she didn't notice any sexual smoke rising off him.

"All right, you hot mamas—you ready to rock?" he screamed, sitting behind the drums and beating the shit out of them.

Lucy put on her guitar and stared at Scott. I couldn't tell what she was thinking, but I was thankful he was playing so loudly she couldn't say. Suddenly Jeffrey appeared at the front of the stage.

"Where the hell is Jake?" he asked.

"He said he was going to get a beer about twenty minutes ago," I said.

We took off our instruments and went backstage to wait for Jake. Another ten minutes went by and Jeffrey came running back.

"Has he shown up yet?" he asked.

"No," I said, starting to worry too. "Want us to take a look around?"

"No, you guys just stay put," he said, running off. When he came back, he was even more freaked out than before.

"We need to go on! We're so late!" he said, taking his glasses off and rubbing his eyes. He stared at us.

"I don't know what to do," he said flatly.

"I hope he's okay," Lucy said.

"What the hell could have happened to him? Should we call the police?" I asked.

"I'll take care of it. I think we're going to have to cancel, guys. This is really bad. I promoted the shit out of this show," Jeffrey said.

Then I got a brilliant idea, if I do say so myself.

"You know, Jeffrey, Rodney's here. Jake's equipment is all set up—maybe Rodney could play! We'd have to stick to our old songs, but the kid's amazing, and I know he'd love to do it. I mean, if everyone's up for it with Jake missing and all."

We all thought about it for a second. I was worried about Jake, for sure, but I really wanted to play.

"Yeah, I want to play," Scott said. "Without a doubt."

"Me too," said Lucy.

"Excellent!" I said. We all ran out onstage and put our instruments on. The crowd cheered their asses off. I turned on the mic and spoke to the mass of heads below.

"Jake Novicoff, our fabulous bass player, was unexpectedly called away. So tonight, if he'd do us the great honor, I'd like to welcome Rodney Nitzer to the stage."

It took Rodney all of three seconds to climb up, since he was standing in the front row at my feet.

Everybody cheered, and Rodney was so excited, he asked me three times if I really meant it.

It was one of the best gigs we ever played. Maybe it was because we hadn't gigged in so long, or maybe it was because I had my little boy back, or maybe it was the fact that I'd just fucked Scott in the parking lot, but something about it was magical. Rodney played flawlessly and everyone was crazy for us. When the set ended, we were all covered in sweat and grinning like idiots. Rodney came backstage with us and couldn't shut up.

"That was so amazing! I can't believe how good everyone's gotten! Did you hear that crowd? I was so nervous! I can't believe I remembered all those songs! Jake's bass is awesome! Where is he, by the way?" Rodney asked.

I'd kind of forgotten about Jake. Suddenly it all came back to me, though.

"Where the hell is Jeffrey?" I asked. I turned to go find him, nearly knocking him over as he flew through the door.

"Did you find Jake?" Scott asked him.

"No," Jeffrey said, "but I called the police. Hopefully he'll turn up soon."

We all stood in silence. Then Jeffrey exploded.

"Awesome fucking gig, guys!" He stuck his hand out to Rodney. "I don't think we've met, but I'm Jeffrey Todd. Thank you for saving our asses. You're a really fantastic player. How old are you?"

"Seventeen. I'll be eighteen next week," Rodney said, shaking his hand.

"Really incredible. You were playing the first time I saw these guys, right?"

"Yup," Rodney said, proudly.

"Thanks again, Rodney," Jeffrey said, patting him on the back. "You guys were amazing!"

By the time we left the Palace, Jake still hadn't shown up.

"If anyone hears anything, please call me. No matter what time it is," Jeffrey said as we were all getting ready to leave. We'd been invited to a huge party, but no one felt like going. Scott and I decided to sleep at our own houses, since we didn't know who Jake would call.

At 4 A.M. my phone finally rang. It was Scott.

"Jake just called me from jail," he said.

"Is he okay? What the hell happened?" I asked.

"He got busted buying dope, I guess," Scott said. "I called Jeffrey, and he's on his way down there right now." Poor Jake. Poor Jeffrey!

"Does this mean he's going to be in jail for a while?" I asked, suddenly remembering we had a tour to go on in six weeks.

"I don't know. But I doubt he'll be able to go on tour even if he's not. They probably won't let him go out of state."

"So we'll have to wait until they will?" I asked.

"Or find someone else for the tour," Scott said.

"I wonder if we could get Rodney," I said. Immediately I felt guilty for being disloyal to Jake. But at the same time, I was already trying to come up with a scheme to woo Mrs. Nitzer into making it happen.

"We don't even know what the deal is with Jake yet," Scott said. "Relax."

But I couldn't. I just had a feeling Jake was history.

I didn't even know if the record company would let us tour with someone else, since Jake was on the album, but I spent the whole night trying to figure out ways to get Rodney. And then feeling guilty about Jake. And then trying to figure out how to get Rodney again.

It was only a two-week tour. Missing two weeks of the last half of your senior year of high school is no big deal.

Getting Mrs. Nitzer to see it that way was the problem.

Henry made another unannounced drop-by tonight while Scott and I were hanging out watching a movie. It's Henry's new thing. He stops in every once in a while to make sure I know how fucked up my relationship is.

Scott did his usual brooding routine, and I did everything in my power to get Henry to leave. He knows Scott's going to freak out. Why does he insist on making my life a living hell?

"Henry, I think you should leave," I said, five minutes into his visit. Henry didn't budge.

"I'm your friend. Friends hang out. Remember?" he said.

"How about calling first?" I said, annoyed.

"We never call first!"

"Well, things have changed," I said.

"That's for sure," Henry said.

"Could you guys have your little lovers' spat in the other room? I'm trying to watch a movie," Scott said.

Henry finally stood up. "I'm not coming by anymore, Jenny," he said.

"Break my heart," Scott mumbled.

February 20

"You do nothing to try and include me in your life," Henry said, "and every time I try and include myself, you ask me to leave."

"It's not that simple, Henry," I said, feeling sick. I was cutting him out of my life because Scott didn't want him in it, and he knew it. Everything was fine with Scott and me as long as we stayed in our little cocoon. Which meant that as long as the cocoon wasn't disrupted, I could pretend to be in a happy relationship.

BRILLIANT OBSERVATION #35:

Being in denial is a lot harder when someone else has witnessed the truth.

"If you want me, you know where to find me," Henry said, storming out the door.

"He's a barrel of fun," Scott said.

"Look who's talking," I said. Part of me wanted to run out the door after Henry. But I knew that would lead to a fight I was too damn tired to have.

I ended up just going into my room and reading. Scott stayed in the living room until the movie was done and then came and got into bed with me. He acted like nothing was wrong, and since I wanted to get some sleep, so did I.

NOTE TO SELF:

I have hit a new low.

February 25

We had a meeting at Mastiff today to go over a bunch of stuff. Jeffrey called and said he'd get Jake and told the rest of us to meet him there early because we needed to talk.

REASONS WE ARE HUGE FOR REAL INSTEAD OF JUST HUGE IN MY HEAD:

1) Our posters were up everywhere at Mastiff. They have a ton of bands, and I swear we were on more walls than any of them.
2) Our music was blaring out of three, count 'em, three offices.
3) Everyone knew who we were. Everyone was too nervous to talk to us.
4) Someone screamed "Fuck yeah!" at us as we were leaving the building.

I drove out with Scott and Lucy, and when we walked into the third floor conference room, Jeffrey was yakking away on his cell phone next to a very tired-looking Jake. Jake looked up at us, clearly embarrassed.

"Dudes," he said, waving his hand.

"Hey, Jake," I said, sitting down next to him. Scott sat next to me, and Lucy sat next to Jeffrey.

"How was the slammer?" Scott said, punching him in the arm.

Jake wasn't amused.

"I'm getting axed from the tour. I can't leave the state," he said, very pissed off.

I knew it. I knew it!

"What did they get you for?" Scott asked.

"Possession. Third time. Most weak," he said.

He'd gotten busted twice before? Jake's life suddenly seemed like one of those cop shows.

"So what does this mean?" I asked.

"It means he's going into rehab while you guys go on tour," Jeffrey said, off the phone at last. Jake looked mortified.

"Well, it's only a little two-week tour," Lucy said. "I'm sure you'll be cleared when the real traveling kicks in."

"I was hoping we could snag that Rodney kid for this job," Jeffrey said, looking at me. "Do you think it's possible?"

"I'll see what I can do," I said. I felt weird talking about it in front of Jake.

"Excellent," Jeffrey said, immediately getting down to business. He handed us each a sheet with a bunch of bullet points and a pencil so we could make our own notes.

NOTE TO SELF:

Jeffrey is a nerd.

JEFFREY'S NOTES:

- Two-week radio tour begins April 1. CD single is being printed up and shipped to stations. You will schmooze DJs and play live on stations all over the country. If they love you, they will play your album. If they play your album, you will be hugely famous.
- The label is going with "Drivin'" for the single. This song will be used for the video.
- The video shoot starts March 9. Get plenty of rest the night before. It will be serviced to MTV and VH1 upon its completion.
- Label hates the album title, but I convinced them to let us have it.

- Full album is set to be in record stores sometime in May. Major touring will happen before and after album's release. You will most likely go on the road opening for a much bigger band.
- Features and reviews in *Spin*, *Rolling Stone*, *Magnet*, and other magazines are in the works. Jenny will appear on the cover of *Bust* and *Seventeen*.
- TV appearances on Letterman and *Saturday Night Live* are being negotiated.

"Any questions?" Jeffrey asked, looking around the room.

I couldn't believe that the stuff on that page had to do with me!

He gave us a million details and we all scribbled away like there was going to be a quiz the next day. Then we set off down the hall to meet with Sue and go over the final ideas for the album cover.

"You guys rocked my ass at the Palace the other night!" Sue said while we looked at her ideas, all of which were awesome.

Her office had things tacked to every available surface. She had a bird hanging from a string on her ceiling that whizzed around in circles above our heads.

"It was fun, wasn't it?" Lucy said.

"And I heard you guys are shooting a video with Max Della Flora! Is that true?" Sue asked.

"Unbelievable, right?" Scott said.

"Totally. I hear he's a slave driver, but he's the best out there. Congratulations," she said.

"Too bad the song blows chunks," Jake said.

"It doesn't blow chunks. It just doesn't do you guys jus-tice," Sue said. "You died for Chad's sins."

"What do you mean?" I asked.

She looked over her shoulder to make sure her door was closed. "Well, you didn't hear this from me, but Chad's got a pretty serious gambling problem. Rumor has it that Tony's dad, who's some big mafia dude, loaned him a chunk of money that he can't pay back. Tony, Mr. El Stinko Pop Producer, wants to start mak-ing rock records, but no rock bands will work with him. So in exchange for not getting his knees nailed to the floor, Chad had to find Tony a rock band to produce. Enter Sixty-Foot Queenie."

I almost threw up.

"I don't believe it," I said.

"I know, I know, it sounds really HBO-movie-special, but it could totally be true," Sue said, shaking her head. "I mean, I love my job, but sometimes it's hard to get out of bed in the morning."

EXCELLENT QUOTE FROM SUE #1:

Working at a big label is kind of like eating meat. You just can't think about it too much or it'll make you puke.

"But you guys'll pull through," she went on. "I have no doubt about that. Just keep playing live and you'll be stars."

"I'm gonna nail Chad's fucking knees to the floor," Jake said.

"I can't believe that shitbag!" Scott said.

"Is that legal?" I asked.

"Probably not. But you guys, don't you dare say anything," she said, "or my ass is so grass."

I thought about Flowers's grand speech and tried to remind myself that this is what rock and roll is all about. Sex, drugs, and overcoming the motherfuckers.

It didn't really help.

On my way home I stopped by his house for a much-needed pep talk. He was in the middle of giving a lesson, so I gave him a teary summary of everything I'd just learned while we stood at his front door.

"Well, doesn't that take the cake?" he sighed. "Wait here." He disappeared into his house. He came back with a folded-up piece of paper and two homemade oatmeal cookies. He patted me on the head and shooed me out the door.

I opened the piece of paper on my way to my car. It read:

The music business is a cruel and shallow money trench, a long plastic hallway where thieves and pimps run free, and good men die like dogs. There's also a negative side.
—Hunter S. Thompson

Beneath that, Flowers had scribbled:

. . . and most people never even get close to the trenches. Congratulations!

I invited Lucy and Scott over for breakfast this morning to have a little band meeting. Which meant, since Scott spent the night last night, we had to get up early, go get his truck from our secret parking place, and park it in front of my house.

March 3

BRILLIANT OBSERVATION #36:

Being covert is exhausting.

Lucy showed up while Scott and I were drinking coffee in my living room. She opened the door and slammed the L.A. *Times* down on the table.

"Will you just grab a big fucking eyeball at that!" she said. I picked up the paper. A picture of President Clinton joining the members of Afreaka! onstage was on the front page.

"It says they're playing in every single country on the damn globe to promote world peace," she said, shaking her head. "Every single country!"

"Big deal," Scott said. "We're going to Oklahoma next week."

"Fuck you, Scotty," she said. She sounded only half playful.

"Well I guess you're stuck here, being a boring old rock star," I said.

"We'll see about that. I'm starting to think I'd be better off with Afreaka! Things are so shaky around here with Jake and Tony and who knows what else," she said, looking at us suspiciously. My old pal guilt surged up and threatened to swallow me.

ROCK-AND-ROLL TRUTH #11:

I am officially a pimping, thieving, lying member of the music business.

"Who wants eggs?" I said, changing the subject. I went into the kitchen and started cooking.

I made everyone scrambled eggs with Swiss cheese and

avocado, rye toast, and breakfast sausage. I brought the plates out into the living room.

"Okay," I said, "here's the deal. Rodney's actually eighteen now, but he's too much of a mama's boy to do anything Mrs. Nitzer disapproves of. Which means we will have to kiss Mrs. Nitzer's very bony ass if we want him on tour with us." I paused and crammed some toast in my mouth. "But I just so happen to know that she's hurting for money, and she'd probably love Rodney to make a little. And since he's already sent all his college applications out, the rest of high school is pretty much a waste of time. So . . ."

"But she hates us. Especially you," Lucy said. "Why the hell would she let you take him away from her?"

"Money," I repeated patiently.

"It would take a ton of money to convince her to let her young, God-fearing son hit the road with a rock band, especially a rock band led by someone she detests, don't you think?" Lucy said.

"Well, let's have Flowers call her then. She loves him!" Scott said.

"Great idea!" I said. "Except he'd never do it. He's already trying to shake her off his leg."

We all sat and thought a while.

"Jeffrey can talk her into it. He'll talk money, maybe even throw a little fame in there too, and casually mention that Flowers thinks it's a good idea. I'll bet she'll go for it, especially if she's hard up for money and Rodney's starting college," Scott said.

It was the best we could come up with. I called Jeffrey and

told him the plan. He said he'd get right on it. I called Flowers to make sure we could drop his name.

"Just because she loves you so much. Do you mind?" I asked.

"No. But if you could come up with a way to get that woman to hate me in the process, I'd appreciate it," Flowers said. "Did I tell you she sent me an almost-naked picture of herself?"

BRILLIANT OBSERVATION #37:
There is pain and suffering in this world, the degrees of which we can't even conceive .

"Flowers, I'm so sorry," was all I could think of to say.

"I thought of gouging my eyes out, but . . ." He didn't have to finish. I knew what he meant. An image like that would be burned on your brain instantly and permanently.

Today we started shooting the music video with Max Della Flora. He's a huge guy with wild red hair, a big puffy mustache, and a voice like a bullhorn. He has hair growing out of his ears, on his knuckles, and he needs eyebrow wax far more than I do. He's scary, like a pirate, and with all the talk about what a gigantic deal he is, I was a nervous wreck before he even said hello. I was so nervous, I asked him how he was three times and dropped my water bottle twice.

NOTE TO SELF:
Shut up.

We met him at 5 A.M. at the beach. He wanted to get the light of the sunrise.

BIG DIRECTOR TRUTH #1:

The earlier you can force your crew to show up on set, the more important a director you are.

When we got there, an entire crew and three Winnebagos were waiting. Max ushered us in to have our hair and makeup done immediately.

"We've got seven locations to shoot in three days. What does this mean? I'll tell you what it means. No dillydallying!"

I didn't know people still said things like "dillydallying," especially people like Max.

Scott was starstruck, and I could tell he was dying to talk to Max but was afraid he was going to get his head chewed off.

"I'm gonna wait until we've hung a little," Scott said while we sat in the Winnie getting our hair done together. Scott wanted to show Max all the band footage he'd shot. He thought he could use it in the video.

"What's the hold-up?" Max's voice suddenly boomed in the room. "Where's the star? We need her out here pronto."

The girl doing my hair pushed me out the door and into the sand. Huge speakers were set up on the beach and "Drivin'" was suddenly blaring at top volume. It was still dark out, but Max wanted me to practice. I had to lip-synch while I ran into the water, all in a skintight, mermaid-shaped, rubber skirt thing. It was basically like running with your ankles tied together and was incredibly difficult, especially for someone who stubs her toe in her own kitchen every morning.

"I'm not the most coordinated person," I explained after falling down three times. "There's a pretty good chance I'll end up in the hospital if we don't widen this skirt a little. If you could—"

"Practicing, not pontificating, makes perfect!" Max shouted, focusing the camera and cramming a bagel into his mouth.

We did shots of me all day. I felt bad for the other guys. They pretty much just sat around; there was no need for them to have gotten up at the crack of dawn. But at least it looked like they were having fun. Watching Max was like watching a cartoon.

"We need to get the star shots done first. The rest of the galaxy follows later!" Max said, as he held my face at the perfect angle. He was trying to get me against the backdrop of a cloud that looked just like an octopus.

"Do you see that?" Max screamed hysterically. "Magnificent! The sky provides what we below could never in a million years imagine!" As scary as he was, he was so into what he was doing that it was hard not to like him, and by the end of the day I could actually talk to him without shaking. I even made him laugh once, so hard that he put his arm around me and nearly dislocated my shoulder in the process.

"This one is extra spicy," he said, laughing for another second, then pushing me away. "Okay, no dillydallying, let's get the next shot set up."

We shot in three different spots down the beach, and aside from the fact that I have sand in every orifice (from wiping out a total of six times), the day was a full-on blast.

ROCK-AND-ROLL TRUTH #12:

When your day begins with a crew of four doing your hair and makeup, chances are it will be a goody.

I went home afterward to change, and then went over to spend the night at Scott's. I had had no time to talk to him all day because Max was all over me every second, but I couldn't wait to hear what he had to say about working with his hero.

Little did I know what I was in for.

FADE IN—EXTERIOR, THE HOUSE OF MOODS—NIGHT

An unsuspecting JENNY walks up to the front door and turns the handle. It creaks open. A loud thunderclap tears through the silent night. Bats dart out of hiding. A woman screams.

INTERIOR, THE HOUSE OF MOODS—SIX SECONDS LATER

SCOTT, The Prince of Darkness, is sitting in the filthy kitchen reading a car magazine. He looks up and grunts.

JENNY: Hi, sexy.

THE PRINCE

OF DARKNESS: Hey.

He focuses on lighting his cigarette. It is the most important union of tobacco and fire in the history of mankind. Scott knows this. He is calm, focused, the right man for the job.

JENNY: Are you okay?

A heavy sigh escapes him. What kind of imbecile stops by for idle chatter when the most important cigarette moment in history is about to commence? Folly aside, Scott continues with miraculous strength and tenacity. Then . . . success! It's lit at last!

THE PRINCE

OF DARKNESS: Yeah. Are you?

He gets up and walks into the other room.

JENNY: Okay, well, I'm really glad I stopped by. I
        think I'll go hang myself now.

THE PRINCE

OF DARKNESS: What's your problem? You just caught me in
            the middle of some pretty heavy thoughts.

JENNY: Scott. You were reading a car magazine.

THE PRINCE

OF DARKNESS: Did you come by for a reason?

JENNY: Excellent question!

Jenny walks out the door and slams it behind her. A thunderclap. A cat screams.

FADE TO BLACK.

When I got home, there were three messages from him.

#1: "Call me when you get home."

#2: "You home?"

#3: *"Click."*

I called him and he was at least able to talk, but he was still steamed. "So you and Max sure hit it off. Every time I turned around the guy had his arm around you."

This was getting really old. I was so tired.

"Scott, I don't suppose there's any chance that if I told you I loved you, you'd just be happy and secure and believe me, would you?" I said.

"If you acted that way, yeah, I would," he said.

I just couldn't fight with him anymore. No matter what I

did, he was always going to be freaking out on me. If I could have broken up with him, I would have, but even aside from the fact that that would have totally tanked the video and the tour, I really did love the asshole.

At the moment, the best thing I could hope for was getting to sleep at a normal hour for once.

"Scott, I'm sorry. I don't know what to say. I shouldn't have let him touch me," I said, cringing.

"That's for sure," he said. I could hear him moping on the other end. He wasn't going to let it go until he felt coddled.

"Can I come back over now?" I asked, dying to just get into my own bed and pass out.

"Yeah," he said, "that would be nice."

I hung up the phone and drove back to his house.

Sometimes I think I'm crazier than he is.

Today we shot out in Joshua Tree. The desert! Jeffrey rented a van and drove us all out there so we could get some extra sleep on the way. It's about a two-hour drive, so we had to leave at the crack of dawn again, which meant I had to get up around four to get back to my house undetected. Which meant I got about two hours of sleep, which made my eyes look like two pissholes in a snowbank, as Eddie would say.

March 10

We arrived at the shoot around six-thirty and found ourselves on some dirt road way out in the middle of nowhere. The weird, twisty, spiky Joshua trees cast crazy shadows on the cactus-speckled hills. Adding the Winnies and the lights and the camera to all this made it even more surreal.

"Whoa, this place is twisted!" Jake said, stumbling out of

the van. Lucy was still asleep and had asked us not to wake her up until it was absolutely necessary.

Max came storming over to the van, took one look at my eyes and yelled, "Someone put some hemorrhoid lotion on those saddlebags!"

The makeup girl came running over and dragged me off to the Winnie. Moments later, Lucy stumbled in, with Scott and Jake right behind her.

"Sleep when you're dead," Max called behind them.

We were all dressed in flowing, robelike clothes that matched the colors of the desert around us. Max had this whole landscape montage vision that he wanted to do. He had Lucy and Jake play their guitars on top of some rocks and set up Scott's drums between two giant cacti. I ran around singing to my bandmates and the trees, while a giant fan blew my dress and my hair in nine different directions at once. It was ridiculous, but so fun!

"Close up on the star!" Max shrieked. He ran over and tousled my hair. He rubbed a little dirt on my face. I was terrified to let him touch me, since the amount of attention I got from Max would be inversely proportional to the amount of sleep I would get tonight. In fact, I was now afraid to let anyone touch me. I shot a quick look back at Scott but he seemed okay.

ROCK AND ROLL TRUTH #13:

Making a video is equally as much fun as being in the studio. I can't imagine how much fun it must be if you're actually capable of having fun.

It was all going fine until Max decided to get artsy. He wanted to do a shot where you couldn't tell if you were looking at mountains or boobs.

"The landscape of the body versus the landscape of the earth. Which is the breast and which is the mountain? A humbling reminder to the viewer how similar we are to our Mother Earth!" he said, running around, making a square with his thumbs and forefingers to frame the scenery.

"Right here! See those hills? Set the camera up here," he said, excitedly. He swept off a rock that I guess I was supposed to lie on and dragged me over to it.

"You need to take your shirt off. We'll shoot the hills behind the breas—" He stopped in the middle of his sentence as he noticed my less-than-ample chest.

NOTE TO SELF:
My breasts silenced the unsilenceable Max Della Flora.

"Which is the fried egg and which is the mountain?" one of the production assistants said, making every single person on the set crack up. I was mortified.

"Sorry, star, but we need a body double. Where's that catering girl? Is she here today? She has a great set," Max said, looking around.

Who the hell did he think he was? I didn't care how famous he was. He was a pig like the rest of them.

"I think it's a shitty idea," I said, right in his hairy face, "but if you just have to do it, you have to use me. It's our video about our band, and our lead singer doesn't have any tits."

Max looked surprised, then laughed.

"It's an artistic statement, not a literal representation of the band!" he said, waving me off and scanning for Ms. Juggs.

"Have you even listened to the lyrics? It's a song about driving! What the hell does 'are they tits or are they mountains' have to do with driving?" I screamed.

Suddenly Jeffrey was holding my arm.

"Just do what he says, Jenny. He's the director, not you. Please," he said, gently pulling me away.

Max barely noticed my little outburst. "There she is! Lovely, now just lie up there on that rock. . . ." How humiliating. I went back and sat with the rest of my band.

"He's an ass," Lucy said.

"You don't want your naked tits on TV anyway," Scott said.

You mean *you* don't want my naked tits on TV, I wanted to say but couldn't.

"This is bogus," Jake said, standing up to get a better view of the catering girl's rack.

I swear I heard the PAs laughing at me.

March 13

We didn't have to show up to the set until ten o'clock today. We were shooting downtown at some big weird hotel, and Mastiff rented one of the suites upstairs for us to get ready in. It was superswanky and crawling with our crew. Our crew for our video in our swanky hotel room. I still couldn't get over it.

My earlier irritation with Max was replaced by sadness that this was the last day.

"That is, until you get back from your tour. I'll have to look at what we've done so far, but I may need some live footage. So no one go out and get fat on me," Max said. He'd come up from setting up the shot downstairs to yell at everyone to hurry up.

I nudged Scott. We were sitting on the bed while a couple of chicks put eyeliner on us, and I nearly made the one working on him poke his eye out.

"Ow!" he screamed, smacking me.

"Sorry! But did you hear what Max said?" I said.

"Hey, Max," Scott said, "I've got a ton of footage of the band. Been shooting pretty much since we started."

Max wasn't listening. "We need to hustle, people! This ship has a lot of sailing to do today!" he said, heading for the door.

"Max!" Lucy, Jake, and I all screamed.

He stopped and turned around. "What?"

"I have tons of live footage," Scott said again.

"Really?" Max said, intrigued.

"He's an amazing videographer," I said.

"Well, why didn't you say so? Send it to my office. Absolutely. Now, I want everybody downstairs in five!" he screamed, storming out the door. I squeezed Scott's hand. Lucy saw.

NOTE TO SELF:
Squeeze Lucy's hand later to show that friends squeeze friends' hands all the time.

We all marched down to the lobby. Max had set us up playing our instruments in the cargo elevator. Tony's version of "Drivin'" was, as usual, blasting away at top volume, and the fact that we were in an elevator with terrible acoustics made it even more torturous to listen to than it usually was.

"If I have to listen to this shitass song for another second, I may perish," Lucy said dramatically when we stopped so Max could chew out one of the lighting guys.

"No shit," Scott said.

"Most appropriate that we're listening to it in an elevator, wouldn't you say?" Jake said.

Jake has a knack for pointing out the depressing truth. Our once-huge rock anthem now hit with all the ferocity of elevator music. I'd heard it so many times in the past few days, I thought I was just numb to it. I now realized it was just numbingly boring.

The next shot was in the hotel restaurant. Max had the band pretend to be eating while I was wheeled up on the dessert tray. They had to close down the entire restaurant, so the staff just hung out and watched. At some point I realized that it wasn't just the staff, though. A bunch of our fans had somehow found out we were shooting and they showed up too, gawking and giggling out in the lobby. It was awesome.

"Step back before I saw your heads off!" Max screamed at the crowd. He was following me across the room on my tray with his camera, barking out orders. He stopped in mid-shot.

"Okay, we need to push this thing much faster," he said, pointing to my dessert tray. "It should look like she's flying. And star, could you fluff it up more? Your attitude is definitely not dessert. I don't see cream puff. I see meatball."

"You try holding on to this thing for dear life and see how cream puff you look, Max!" I yelled at him. He laughed at me.

"This one's the spicy one, right?" he said. "A spicy meatball. Just fluff it up," he barked. "Let's go."

I was wheeled back and forth a million more times until I was convinced my body was going to have permanent scars from that damn tray.

The end of the day was spent on just me. He wanted to shoot me singing the song through a giant fish tank in the lobby. Then he got another brilliant idea.

"Hang her by her ankles and lower her down into the tank. Upside down and underwater! What a way to view the world!" Max said, off again on one of his creative visions. "You can all go," he said to the rest of my band. "We're done with you."

"Oh no, we wouldn't miss this for the world," Scott said, cozying up between Jake and Lucy at a table. Max had two huge guys climb up on ladders on either side of the tank. He had a third guy hoist me up in the air on a huge dinner tray (I'd gone from being a cream puff to being the salmon special) so the two guys could grab my ankles.

"Stick your legs in the air," Max screamed at me. "Give them something to hold on to!"

I stuck my legs up, kicking one guy in the face and getting nowhere near the other.

"Slide to your left. That's it!" Max screamed. I felt hands grabbing me on each ankle. Suddenly "Drivin'" started up again, and I was lowered into the tank. I tilted my head back and saw a thick layer of pond scum on top of the water. Were we sure there weren't any piranhas in there? But it was too late to ask.

"Sing, star, sing!" Max screamed. I started lip-synching the song, and my head was lowered into the slimy tank. The last thing I saw before going under was Scott, Lucy, and Jake, all grinning like idiots. The last thing I heard was the hideous caricature of my once-excellent song being blasted through the lobby.

If those guys slipped, I could break my neck and die.

This was not how I wanted to go out.

I took a shower in our room afterward while everyone waited for me at the bar. When I came downstairs, Max was on his way out.

"Good-bye, star!" he said, giving me a bone-crushing hug. "Good luck on tour. And send that footage over pronto," he said to Scott. He stormed out of the building.

I was gonna miss him.

I sat at the bar next to Lucy, and Jeffrey handed me a margarita.

"Congratulations, everyone. Very well done!"

We all clinked glasses. I tried to gauge how pissed Scott was about me being lowered into fish tanks, wheeled around on trays, and violently hugged by various men throughout the day. He seemed okay, but it was hard to tell. The monster could just be sleeping.

"Now, I have a few items of business to tend to before we get too carried away," Jeffrey said, pulling out his notebook. "First, the tour. I have all the locations you'll be playing, with maps and dates for each. I hired Tami to go along as your road manager. And here's the best news: I just got word this morning that Rodney can go!"

I wanted to cheer, but Jake's glum face stopped me.

"Sorry," Jeffrey said, patting Jake on the knee. "But I need to get this squared away."

"No problem," Jake said sadly. My heart almost broke! It sucks when something that's really great for you makes someone you like really sad.

"It won't be the same without you, Jake," I said.

"Absolutely not," Scott said.

"Dude," Lucy said, putting her arm around him.

"Be mighty," Jake said, holding up his glass.

"If you need help with anything to get yourselves ready to leave, just call me," Jeffrey resumed. "Tami and I will take care of everything. We'll have a meeting at my office tomorrow to iron out any details. That's all. I need to take off," he said as his cell rang. "You guys were great!"

Jeffrey left, and the four of us hung out at the bar for a few more hours and basked in our glory.

The aforementioned glory came to a screeching halt, however, later that night at Scott's.

"Max is going to have a field day with all that footage of his favorite star, or should I say, his favorite spicy meatball," Scott said, finally crawling into bed next to me and waking me up. He'd stayed up much later than I had, and even though everything had been fine all day, I had a feeling a storm was brewing. I hunkered down for another sleepless night.

"Scott, the guy's a freak. Can we just go to sleep?" I begged.

"Carting you around on a tray like a piece of meat! It was disgusting," Scott said. He didn't let it go. Anything I said either went unheard or fueled the fire, so I just got silent. Every time I fell asleep, he'd wake me up and accuse me of not caring about him.

I can't live like this anymore. But I don't want to fuck up the band by breaking up with him. And I'm still in love with him.

I am spineless and irresponsible. I knew the guy was trouble the second I laid eyes on him, and I did it anyway. I saw all this coming eight hundred miles away.

If this band fails, I have no one to blame but myself.

NOTE TO SELF:
Don't sleep with your drummer. Dumb-ass.

We started out our radio promo tour by playing at KCRY in L.A. last night. It was our first official gig with the new lineup, and I'm proud to say that Rodney had a firm grasp on all the new songs. Jeffrey and Chad gave us strict instructions to be nothing but overjoyed about the album.

BRILLIANT OBSERVATION #38:
We're door-to-door salesmen selling poop on a stick.

The radio guys loved us, had heard all about us, said our album was, and I quote, "mother-hung."

"That was weird," Lucy said as we headed out to our cars in the parking lot, "I can't believe they were serious."

"Do they owe Tony's dad money too?" I asked.

"If not, they definitely had some kind of other incentive," Scott said.

"Why couldn't it be that they just really liked it?" Rodney asked.

"Do you?" I asked Rodney.

He made a face. "Not really."

"That's why," I said.

"A lot of people have stinky taste, though," Rodney said. "I bet a lot of kids at my school will like the album."

I dropped Rodney at home and headed over to Scott's place. We had decided to throw Jake a surprise rehab send-off party.

"He may not exactly feel like celebrating," I'd pointed out when Scott came up with the idea.

"It's more so he knows that when we go on tour we're thinking of him. It's not really about rehab," Scott said.

I still thought Jake would be kind of freaked. He's starting rehab tomorrow, and he's a pretty private person. But what the hell do I know?

Scott, Lucy, and I sat there waiting with a bunch of food and some dopey presents, but Jake was late. Really late. He ended up stumbling through the door at midnight, just as Lucy and I were getting ready to leave.

#1 MOST FUCKED UP PERSON I'VE EVER SEEN:
Jake Novicoff, midnight, March 26, 2000.

He slurred his way into the room and collapsed on the couch. I thought he was going to pass out, but all of a sudden he jerked to attention. "Sorry about the tardiness. Last night of freedom, you know."

I wanted to take him to the hospital. Scott wanted to kill him. Lucy handed him a huge glass of water and some aspirin.

"He's fine, leave him alone," she said, propping him up on the couch and helping him swallow the aspirin.

"What did you do tonight, Jake?" Scott asked.

"Many things too sordid to mention," Jake said, laughing to himself. He drank the glass of water and slammed it on the table. We were all standing over him, looking down. Jake finally noticed that there were presents and food on the table.

"What's all this?" he asked.

"We were just having a little going-away party. For you. And us," I said.

"Really?" he asked, and then he burst into tears.

Jake crying was more than I could handle. Lucy and I sat next to him on the couch.

"Dudes, just know that I feel most saddened by this turn of events," Jake said. He sniffed and wiped his nose on his sleeve.

"So do we," I said.

"Just get it together, Jake," Scott said, "we'll pick up where we left off when we get back."

I felt a twisting feeling in my stomach. If I didn't fuck it all up before then.

THE TOUR OF FOOLS!

Tami pulled up around nine o'clock this morning in a shiny white minivan with a small storage trailer attached to the rear bumper. She leapt out in a funky knitted dress with a colorful silk scarf tied around her shaved head. She looked fabulous.

After all, she was going on tour with Rodney, her man.

"All aboard," she yelled, strutting into my house and starting to load my stuff. Lucy hopped out of the van and stretched.

"Well, here we go! On a real live tour!" Lucy said, jumping around my front yard with excitement. I couldn't believe it either. Jeffrey said the label was promoting our shows like crazy and to expect more than a warm reception.

"They've got really high hopes for this record. Chad says the label is behind it one hundred percent," he said.

I bet. Chad doesn't want to wind up in the bottom of the ocean in cement shoes one hundred percent.

After we packed up the van, I said a tearful farewell to my cats. Well, not so tearful. They've been acting up because they figured out in their mysterious cat way that (A) I'm taking a trip, and (B) they're not invited. For the last two weeks I haven't been able to stand still for more than two seconds without Schmoo trying to mount me. He weighs twenty pounds. I'm amazed I'm not in a wheelchair.

Neil ripped up the back of my sofa and pooped in my new plant. He's one piece of upholstery away from being reintro-duced into the wild.

Anyway, all good-byes said, we finally headed off to Hollywood to pick up Scott. His stuff was in a pile outside his front door, and he was leaning against his house smoking a cigarette, looking extraordinarily sexy. The bastard.

His face dropped when he saw the minivan pull up.

"A minivan! How uncool is a fucking minivan?" he said. Tami was devastated.

"They were out of regular vans," she said, "I tried to get one, but this was all they had."

"Who cares, Scotty? It's really comfy," Lucy said, loading his stuff in.

"We look like we're on our way to pick up the kids from soccer practice," he moped. I got out of the van and stared at him. I was wearing a short summer dress that I knew he loved, in eager hopes of starting everything out on a good note.

"Aren't you at all excited?" I asked.

He took in my outfit and his frown lightened. "Totally," he said, sheepishly.

"I'll say he is," Lucy said, throwing his duffel bag in the back of the van.

"Do we have everything?" Tami asked Scott, whipping out a clipboard.

"Yeah," he said, sitting down next to me in the backseat.

BRILLIANT OBSERVATION #39:
As much as I hate Scott, he can still make all the hair on my arms stand up just by sitting next to me.

Then it was on to the Nitzers'. I still didn't believe the old hag was actually letting Rodney come with us, and I didn't feel like I could completely relax until he was in the van and we were on our way. When we pulled up to the house, Rodney was outside, surrounded by his equipment and about four suitcases.

"Jesus Christ, what the hell is the kid bringing with him?" Scott asked. "All his stuffed animals?"

"He's not a kid anymore, Scott," Tami said, adjusting her 'do rag. "He's eighteen."

Scott raised his eyebrows at me as she leapt out of the car and gave Rodney a hug. We all climbed out to help him get his stuff in.

"What is all this stuff?" I asked, picking up a suitcase and reaching down for another, which happened to be Mrs. Nitzer's purse.

It was then that the realization smacked me on the head with a witch's broom.

Mrs. Nitzer thought she was coming with us.

At that moment I heard the front door slam, and there she was, her sweater over her arm and two brown-bag lunches in her hand. She handed one to Rodney.

"We were out of pickles so I put salami in the tuna fish. Just a warning," she said. Scott, Lucy, and Tami all stared at me.

Why do I always have to run defense?

"Mrs. Nitzer," I said, "um, do you think you're coming with us or something?"

"What kind of idiotic question is that? Of course I am," she said.

We all stared at her in horror.

"No way in hell," Scott said, laughing, "I'm afraid you're not invited." He took the purse out of my hands and handed it to her.

She snatched it from him and dusted it off. "For your information, young man, I don't need your invitation as badly as you need my son right now," she said.

"And he doesn't need your permission anymore, because he's eighteen," Scott shot back. "For your information."

Mrs. Nitzer glared at Rodney. He looked at his feet.

"I told her she could come," he whispered.

"Well, tell her she can't," Scott said, "and let's get moving."

Rodney looked up at me, his big sad eyes filling up with tears.

"She doesn't have anyone else," he said.

Scott sighed and threw his arms up. Lucy shrugged and Tami froze. I put my hand on Rodney's shoulder.

"She'll be just fine on her own, Rodney. It's only two weeks," I said.

Mrs. Nitzer scowled.

"It'll be good practice for when you go off to college," Lucy said.

"Which bags are yours?" Scott asked Mrs. Nitzer. She pointed to three of the largest suitcases. Scott moved them aside and started loading Rodney's stuff in the van.

Mrs. Nitzer marched over to me and put her wrinkled face right in mine. I could smell cigarettes on her breath.

"If anything happens to that boy, so help me, God," she said, stopping to cross herself, "I'll have your hide!"

"I'll take very good care of him," I said. Rodney came over and gave her a long hug.

"Bye, Mom. I love you," he said.

She pulled away from him and pinched his cheek. "God loves you, son."

We all piled in the van and drove off. Mrs. Nitzer stood in the driveway, surrounded by her suitcases, smoking a cigarette. Rodney waved frantically to her out the back window. Nobody said a word about it, out of respect for Rodney, but I knew they were all dying to.

Rodney sat in the back by himself for the first couple of hours, but after a while he lightened up and switched places with Lucy so he could sit next to Tami.

Puppy love ensued.

Our first gig was in Phoenix. We got there around six o'clock and checked into the Ramada Inn. Tami and her clipboard took care of everything.

"She makes Jeffrey look like a scatterbrain," Lucy said as Tami led us down the hall to our rooms. We'd gotten adjoining rooms, each with two queen-size beds. A cot was set up in the corner of one.

"This is the girls' room. I'm on the cot," Tami announced.

Scott and I exchanged glances. Clearly, there would be no sneaking into bed with each other on this tour. I wasn't sure if that would make things better or worse between us.

At seven-thirty we headed down to play at KCMU. As it turned out, the DJ was this bald guy named Frank who was a huge fan of ours.

"I used to live in L.A.," he explained over the air, "and I've seen these guys play a million times. They're awesome."

"Thanks, man," Scott said.

"They'll be playing in Albuquerque tomorrow night at the Launchpad—"

"With Bullet Hole!" Rodney yelled.

"—with Bullet Hole," Frank went on. "So if any of you out there have friends in New Mexico, send them out. It'll be well worth their time. They rock, and Jenny and Lucy are babes!" He winked at me. In fact, he'd been staring at me the entire time. I smiled and looked at my feet, afraid to see Scott's reaction.

NOTE TO SELF:

Hide in the girls' bedroom and you'll be safe.

Frank picked up our CD and looked at it.

"The CD's interesting. It sounds a lot different than your live shows. What's up with that?" he asked. We all froze and smiled.

"We're really excited about the record," I said mechanically, knife sticking out of my back.

It's like eating worms.

"Well, let's put her on and see what the public thinks. This is 'Drivin',' the first single off Sixty-Foot Queenie's debut album, *Can't Shine a Turd,*" Frank said, and we were once again treated to the disturbing sounds of our future hit song.

When we got back to the hotel, I went straight to bed and hid under the covers like a scared rabbit. Luckily, we were all exhausted and had a huge day tomorrow, so nobody really felt like staying up.

I woke up three times that night, terrified that Scott was standing over my bed. But he wasn't.

Then I was bummed.

NOTE TO SELF:

Seek professional help.

April 2

We got up early and headed east on I-10 to Albuquerque. Everyone was in a great mood. Even Scott seemed happy. He was chatting away with Lucy like he hadn't seen her in years. I knew he was doing it to make me jealous, but I didn't care. It's kind of hard for me to worry about anything while I'm driving through the desert.

NEW FACTS I NEVER KNEW ABOUT:
TAMI: terrified of moths
LUCY: double-jointed
SCOTT: allergic to mold
RODNEY: doesn't know what hummus is
ME: likes to ride backward

I was sitting with my back against the last seat, facing backward and looking out the rear window. Lucy and Scott where whooping it up in the middle seat while the high school prom took place up front. I was watching the red earth of the desert roll by, marveling over the fact that I'd quit my job just thirteen months ago, and here I was on tour with a signed band whose record was coming out in May. It was a beautiful day, and I felt the sun warm my face as I looked out over the endless expanse of sky in front of me. My eyes danced merrily over the road . . . until they caught sight of a dark blue Olds Cutlass with California plates.

"It couldn't be," I said out loud. I sat up and pressed myself against the window to get a better view.

The Cutlass was four cars behind us. Billows of smoke poured out the driver's side window. It had to be her.

Mrs. Nitzer was following us.

TOP THREE OPTIONS WHEN BEING TRAILED BY THE WICKED WITCH:
1) Say nothing and pray that a flying house lands on her.
2) Alert the van and upset Rodney.
3) Demand to drive and try to lose her.

I asked Tami to pull over at the next rest stop. When I got out of the van, I looked behind us and sure enough, parked way down at the other end of the parking lot was the Cutlass. I had a pretty good view of Mrs. Nitzer; I could see her tiny, pointed head through her window. She bent over for a second and came back up with binoculars pressed to her face. She was staring right at me!

"Shit," I said. She was on to me.

"Hey Tami, mind if I drive for a while?" I asked.

"Not at all," she said, handing me the keys and going in to pee. Everyone went in except Scott and me.

"Having fun?" he asked, leaning up against the van next to me. He was in a T-shirt and jeans and looked as cute as fuck. Why am I so shallow? I swear I fell in love with him all over again just because he was having a good hair day.

He looked over at the bathrooms to make sure no one was coming, then leaned over and planted a huge kiss on me. It didn't help matters that he was a great kisser. He pulled away and stared at me.

"I love you," he said.

"I love you too, Scott," I said, horrified all over again to realize that I actually meant it. He was insane and I knew I had to break up with him eventually, but I loved him anyway.

He went to kiss me again, but I suddenly remembered that Mrs. Nitzer was watching. I panicked and pushed him away.

"They're all inside!" he said. "I can see from here."

I wanted to tell him about our stalker, but I was worried he'd get upset with Rodney. "It just makes me uncomfortable, okay?" I said, jumping into the van.

Everyone started coming out of the bathrooms and climbing aboard.

"Let's go!" I said, starting up the engine and pulling out.

The Cutlass followed behind, far off in the distance, and I gunned it. I knew I couldn't outrun her, but I wanted as much distance as I could get.

When we finally got to Las Cruces, I pulled off at the first exit that actually showed signs of life, tore into a Motel 6 parking lot, and hid behind the building.

"What the hell are you doing?" Lucy asked, clinging to the side of her seat for dear life. I was sure I'd gotten off the exit before Mrs. Nitzer had time to see where we'd gone. I'd lost her!

"I know this is going to sound paranoid, but there was some freak following us. I was watching him for hours out the back," I said.

"That blue Cutlass with California plates!" Tami said. "I saw that too! I thought I was just being crazy!"

I looked in the rearview mirror and saw Rodney's horrified face.

"Was it a dark blue Cutlass, Jenny?" he asked. We both knew I knew exactly what his mother's car looked like. I had had to wash it on several occasions.

"I couldn't really tell," I said, unconvincingly.

"Um, what the fuck is going on?" Scott asked.

"Jenny just ditched my mom!" Rodney cried. "I can't believe you did that, Jenny! She's terrified of driving long distances alone."

"Rodney, she'll be fine," I promised. But he was so mad, he wouldn't even look at me. It was like a dagger in my heart.

"That freak is following us?" Scott asked.

"Shut up, Scott," Rodney said.

"Did you at least lose her?" he asked, laughing.

Rodney opened the door and ran out of the van. He ran all the way to the on ramp for the highway.

"Rodney, I'm sorry. I'm so sorry!" I said, chasing after him.

BRILLIANT OBSERVATION #40:
Eighteen-year-old boys can run twice as fast as twenty-nine-year-old women.

"I'm waiting here for her. I can't believe you'd do that to a person," he said.

"Rodney, she'll be fine. She's not as helpless as you think," I said, exhausted and feeling the muscles in my legs starting to seize in shock. I bent over and gasped for air.

"I'm not leaving until she gets here," he said.

"We have to play a radio show and a gig in Albuquerque tonight," I reminded him. "We can't sit here all day."

"How far away is Albuquerque?" he asked.

"About three or four hours," I said.

He still wouldn't look at me! He finally turned and started back toward the van.

"I guess she can make that trip okay alone," he said, leaving me bent over in pain.

"What do you mean? How will she know we're in Albuquerque?" I asked.

"She has our whole itinerary. I gave it to her before we left," he said as I hobbled along behind him.

Great. I just pissed off Rodney for nothing.

When I got back, everyone was standing around waiting outside.

"Everything okay?" Lucy asked. Rodney was already inside the van.

"She has our itinerary," I whispered to Lucy.

Tami came up and tapped me on the shoulder.

"I'm so sorry," she said timidly, "I didn't know."

"Whatever. It's not your fault," I said.

We all got back in the van, and Scott drove. Lucy sat up front with him while Rodney and Tami talked quietly in the back. I looked out the window and worried.

We got into Albuquerque at around six, checked into the Sheraton, and immediately headed over to KUNM for our radio show. Lucy and Scott did most of the talking while Rodney and I moped on opposite ends of the room. Once again, the DJ marveled at the difference between the CD and the live performance. Apples and oranges. Joy and pain. Suck and Not Suck.

Can't anybody hear us screaming behind these smiles?

Then we headed to the club. The Launchpad was in down-town Albuquerque, right in the middle of the party strip, and there was actually a line out the door. There was also a dark blue Cutlass parked out front.

We walked inside and she was the first thing I saw, perched on a bar stool like a vulture, sucking on a cigarette. Rodney ran into her arms and gave her a hug. She glared at me over his shoulder.

"So you found us after all," I said, trying to make light of our situation. Rodney pulled away and glared at me with his mother, and for the first time I noticed that they had the same eyebrows.

"I'm lucky to be alive," she hissed.

"I'm sorry about that little ditching thing back there," I said. "It was a very bad judgment call on my part."

"It looks like you've made a few," she said, nodding at Scott.

Crap. If she told on us, I was dead. I had to kiss her ass twice as hard now.

"Can I buy you a drink?" I asked.

"No," she said, "but you can tell me where we're staying tonight so I can go freshen up." She was playing hardball, but I had no choice. I gave her the room keys.

I started lugging our stuff to the stage. The Launchpad was an industrial-type space with a bar in the front and a stage in the back. Near the stage was a door to a back parking lot. Kevin, Bullet Hole's lead singer held it open while I wheeled in my amp.

"Thanks," I said.

"My pleasure," he said. "I'm so psyched we get to play together again."

"Me too." Scott was going to have a conniption if he saw me talking to Kevin, so I wiggled away as quickly as I could. As I dragged my amp over to the stage, I saw Scott staring at Kevin with narrowed eyes.

By the time we hit the stage the place was packed. Rodney still refused to look at me, but I could tell he was having trouble staying mad because he kept grinning. Lucy came over and licked my cheek, making the crowd cheer. I finally looked back at Scott, who was expressionless and stared right into my eyes as he counted off the first song.

We played with the energy of four people who'd been cooped up in a minivan for two days. The second the music kicked in, it didn't matter who was jealous of who or who had ditched whose mother at a Motel 6. We went into auto-rock.

ROCK-AND-ROLL TRUTH #14:
Being in a band is just like being married. The children are the songs and the sex is playing live onstage.

When we were done, Scott came out from behind the drums and we all took a bow. Mrs. Nitzer clapped from her spot way in the back and Kevin blew me a kiss from the side of the stage.

"You were awesome," I whispered in Scott's ear.

He either didn't hear me or pretended not to. We started breaking our stuff down, and Lucy ran over to me with a shot of tequila.

"To fun!" she said. We clinked glasses and did the shot. She was happier than I'd seen her in a long time. I could tell she loved being on the road.

We stayed to watch Bullet Hole play, but though I kept looking around for Scott, he'd vanished. When it was time to go, Tami rounded everybody up.

"Where's Scott?" she asked.

"I haven't seen him all night," I said.

"He left about an hour ago with some redheaded chick," Lucy chirped, sending my heart through the floor.

Shit. Shit, shit, shit.

Then, when we got back to the room, Mrs. Nitzer was asleep in my bed.

"I'm sleeping with you," I said to Lucy.

"No way," she said. "You wiggle too much. Go sleep in Scott's bed. He's not using it tonight."

"Right. What if Mrs. Nitzer wakes up and finds me sleeping in the same room as her son? She'll totally freak!" I said.

"I'll sleep with her," Tami said. "You can have the cot."

"Never mind, I'll sleep with her," I said, crawling in next to The Lizard. I couldn't get to sleep. I kept worrying that I'd make a move on Mrs. Nitzer in my sleep, thinking she was Scott. Or worse, that she'd make a move on me, thinking I was Flowers.

I was also tortured by Scott's little maneuver this evening, and realized I could no longer ignore the elephant in the room.

Scott and I suck. It must end. Now. The band will go on without us being together.

I just have to figure out how to make it all work out and nurse a broken heart at the same time.

NOTE TO SELF:

You can sit around and have a broken heart any old time. Rock stardom happens only once in a lifetime.

NOTE FROM FRANK ZAPPA:

Broken hearts are for assholes.

NOTE FROM KISS:

I wanna rock and roll all night. And party every day.

NOTE FROM LUCY:

Look what's happening to little old us!

NOTE FROM THE ARMY:

Be all that you can be.

NOTE FROM BOB MARLEY:

Lively up yourself.

I was woken up twice last night by Mrs. Nitzer's razor-sharp toenail ripping into my shin. This was followed by an ice-cold foot rubbing up against my leg and a round of snoring. I finally got up, grabbed a blanket, and attempted to sleep in a chair out on the porch. In the morning, while it was still dark out, I was woken again by Mrs. Nitzer, but this time she was screaming.

April 3

"What the hell is going on?" I heard Lucy say as someone flicked on a light.

I flew into the room to find Scott standing over Mrs. Nitzer in bed. She was covering her face in horror.

"That monster stuck his tongue in my mouth!" she said.

Scott looked totally confused and more than a little green, while Tami and Rodney cowered in the corner. When Scott saw me come in off the porch he turned white.

Mrs. Nitzer reached for her cigarettes and lit up. I noticed that Flowers had given her the motorcycle lighter back. For some reason, I knew this was a bad omen.

She took a deep drag and looked around the room.

"I know a little too much about the sick goings-on around here, and I want no part of them," she said. "For me or for Rodney."

I felt my whole world getting sucked up into a giant black hole. Lucy sat down on the edge of her bed and made herself comfortable. She glared at me, then nodded at Mrs. Nitzer.

"Do tell," she said.

I looked at Scott and he shrugged. He was still drunk from the night before and was wiping his lips, trying to get all traces of Mrs. Nitzer off of them. He had a giant hickey on his neck, and his fly was unzipped.

I threw it all away for that?

Tami and Rodney sat down on Tami's cot. It was story time with Satan.

"I don't know what kind of crash course to hell you're on, mister," Mrs. Nitzer said to Scott, "but I see you kissing this one one day"—she motioned to me—"then sleeping in a strange woman's bed the next night, then coming in here and trying to have your way with me in the morning!"

"I didn't sleep with her," Scott said to me.

"Scott!" Rodney screamed.

"Not your mother, stupid!" Scott said.

Nobody had the heart to laugh at the idea of Scott having his way with Mrs. Nitzer. Lucy shot me a stare that blew my head off. Tami was scarlet-faced, and Rodney stared at his feet.

"And you and your demented friend Flowers!" she huffed at

me. "Making frivolous bets over the sacred practices of chastity and fidelity!"

Crap! Flowers had spilled the beans!

I didn't even bother railing at Mrs. Nitzer for being a sex-monger hypocrite. I was more concerned about my once-best friend, Lucy, who was staring at me, waiting for me to explain. And about Rodney and Tami, whose shocked expressions made them both look about eleven years old.

And about my band, which was hideously disintegrating before my eyes.

I owed it to them all to be honest, at the very least. So I told them everything, from my bet with Flowers to the Afreaka! performance to that day Lucy thought she'd caught me in bed with Scott.

"I'm so sorry," I said, knowing how lame that just sounded. But there was really nothing else for me to say.

"All of you, get out," Mrs. Nitzer said, "I need to get dressed. And then Rodney and I are going home."

Rodney nodded in agreement with his mother and glared at me.

I couldn't move. Two days into it, the tour was officially over.

Everyone retreated into the other room while I sat there, frozen. Mrs. Nitzer ignored me and took her clothes off.

She was clearly sent here to punish me for my sins.

I stumbled through the door into the other room feeling like I'd just had battery acid sprayed in my eyes. Everyone was just sitting around looking stunned. Tami and Rodney were sitting on the edge of Rodney's bed and Scott was lying on top of his, still neatly made and unslept in. Lucy was staring out the window.

I sat on the edge of Scott's bed.

"What do we do now, Jenny?" Tami asked.

"I guess we go home," I said.

"Does this mean it's all over? Is there no more band? Can't we just piece it back together and go back on the road?" she asked. "You guys just made an album, and I know you could be huge! And—and—and I've been working my ass off!" She burst into tears.

"I know," I said sadly. I looked at Lucy, who just shook her head, staring hard out the window.

"Are you guys really in love?" Rodney asked.

I wanted to carve tiny holes all over Scott's body at that very moment, but I was still in love with him.

"Yes," I heard Scott say behind me.

"Yeah, but that's over too," I said.

"I didn't sleep with her!" Scott said from behind me.

"Doesn't matter. It's over," I said, turning to stare at him. Do not look at me with those eyes. I turned back around.

"How come?" Rodney asked.

"Because we suck at making each other happy," I said.

"It's sort of hard to make other people happy when all you care about is yourself," Lucy finally said from her post at the window.

"I know, Lucy," I said.

The phone rang in the silence. I reached for it.

Little did I know the knockout punch was on the other end.

THE FOLLOWING IS A DRAMATIC REENACTMENT OF ACTUAL LIVES TAKING ACTUAL SWAN DIVES OFF AN ACTUAL CLIFF:

The clock read 10:32 A.M. New Mexico time. The small hotel room reeked of mal humor and Mrs. Nitzer's perfume.

Suddenly, the phone rang. Jenny was on it in an instant. The room stared at her expectantly as her face slowly sagged through the floor.

It was Jeffrey.

Radio stations hate the record. Not one station wants to play the single. They all think it sucks big monkey turds. The label is totally freaked and is dropping the whole project.

What exactly does dropping the whole project mean?

Dropping the band. It's over. Termino. You have one more night as Mastiff recording artists but after that you are on your own. I'm so sorry, guys.

Do we owe them money?

No, I don't think so, but I haven't had time to figure that out yet.

Any thoughts I'd had in the back of my mind of summoning all the king's horses and all the king's men and putting my band back together again were suddenly splattered all over the sidewalk.

THE BIG FAT SUCKING END

UNEMPLOYED OBSERVATION #3

Pouring milk into an iced coffee always makes a different and exciting pattern.

June 11

I'm writing this from Flowers's vegetable garden. I'm sitting on a lawn chair made out of a giant papier-mâché elephant, watering his plants while he gives someone a guitar lesson inside. According to the back of the package of tomatoes, I'm supposed to water thoroughly and keep in direct sunlight. I read things and follow instructions. I'm dropped in chairs where I stay until I'm retrieved. I am moments away from a car seat and a drool bib.

I'm fully incapacitated. Crippled by sorrow. Neither beach nor desert nor mountain nor Flowers's stunning cousin Gordon can puncture the suffocating bubble of bleakness that surrounds me.

I look back through this journal and am alarmed to find a number of tearful entries. I know that each insists that it is the saddest and most tragic. Its pain could never be understood! But I swear this one is It. The Olympic gold medalist in the Women's Despair category. Because before, no matter how low I was dragging or how cruel he was being, I always had a goal. I always had my Thing. Right now I have no clue what to do or who I am or where my flip-flops are. I don't have the strength to put another band together, and even if I did, I don't even want to. I'm too disgusted with myself.

My Thing isn't mine anymore. I don't deserve it.

I have no idea what the hell I'm doing with my life. Everything I'm qualified to do sickens me, and my only other options involve wearing uniforms. And I'm mere months away from turning thirty.

I'm visiting Henry now, my other surrogate mother, lying on his floor, eating his cereal. Henry lovingly reevaluated our friendship when he heard my biggest dream come true had suddenly transformed into fertilizer. He decided to let bygones be bygones and rose to the occasion.

In a quick recap, I'll describe the last glimpses of Sixty-Foot Queenie as it swirled its way down the toilet bowl and out of sight forever:

Mrs. Nitzer finally put some clothes on and blasted out of town in her dark blue Cutlass with her motorcycle lighter and little Rodney. Lucy hitchhiked, unable to spend another moment with any of us, and Tami, Scott, and I drove back to L.A. in a silent minivan. Until Scott started screaming. It turns out he had an allergic reaction to the massage oil his red-headed fling had poured all over him the night before. It was so bad we had to stop at an emergency room in Tucson and get him some anti-itching medication before he tore himself to shreds.

I will not comment on the supreme karma of that situation, because I'm trying to not speak badly about people.

We had a sad meeting with Jeffrey, who gave us each a stack of our own crap-ass CDs and had us sign a bunch of papers. He said he felt terrible and wished there was some-thing he could do. We told him the band was pretty much kablooey anyway. Rodney was going off to college. The sec-ond he could leave the state, Jake was going to Vancouver to clean up and help his buddy build a house. Lucy was going around the world with Afreaka! I was going to lose my mind. Scott was going to hell.

"And just FYI," Jeffrey said with a pained look on his face, "Mastiff still owns all the songs on the album, even though they're not doing anything with them anymore. So if you start another band or something and want to rerecord them, you can't. Just thought you should know."

The universe was making sure I didn't try this again.

For a while I was so motherfucking pissed off at Mastiff, I could have flipped over a Buick. Fucking Chad! I swore if I ever saw him again, I'd chew a hole through his neck. How dare he take all my hard work and use it for his gain! I guess Katie was right about this business after all.

But deep down, I was even more pissed off at myself. I was just as disgusting and self-serving as he was. I wanted what I wanted, regardless of how it affected everyone around me. It made me scared of what I was capable of doing just to get what I wanted.

It made me never want to play music again.

Tami got hired by Rosebud as a tour manager. She was more devastated about the breakup than anyone. Actually, that's not true. She just didn't have to suffer as much of the stress, so she could be sad right away. It took me about twenty-four hours.

When I got home, I fell apart. I spent the next week cleaning, sobbing, and getting rid of stuff. I gave my amp and guitar to Flowers. I sold most of my furniture. I painted the whole place white. I didn't know what to do with myself, and everything in my house reminded me of Scott. As much as I hated him, I was still in love with him.

The fact that we were really over had finally, officially kicked in. I felt like I was tripping all the time. When you spend so much time with another person and then he's gone, you feel like a part of you has been cut off. Part of your consciousness.

The worst part was, I knew myself and knew I was dumb enough to try and get back with him even though he was a Certified Pig-Fucker Fathead. I had no job, no band, no money, and plenty of time to obsess over his good qualities and ignore the bad. So I finally removed myself. I went to Mom's. I resumed my post in front of the TV in my cat hair-covered stretchy pants and sweatshirt. Only this time I traded in eating for sobbing.

DEPRESSION TRUTH #1:
There are levels of falling apart. When I'm depressed, I can eat something new and large every ten minutes. When I'm devastated, I can only eat through an I.V.

Three days into it, Mom informed me she was having a big bash to welcome her new beau, Ronald Przyborowski, into her lair. She'd been dating him for two months, and suddenly the guy was a permanent fixture at her house, eating her food and parading around as an alarming reminder that my mother had a sex life. How dare she throw that obscenity at me in my fragile state! And how dare she throw a party in my rehab clinic! She said I could hide upstairs, but that was just too weird. The freaky daughter is locked in the attic. I hear she plays that devil music. I hear she's a spinster!

I didn't want to talk to anyone, but I didn't want to be alone, either. I dragged myself back to my empty house and got into bed. I had no idea who I was. If I got a dopey job, it had no point because I had no band. I'd be just another dope with a dopey job. And I couldn't go for a real job because that required ambition, not to mention the will to write a résumé, neither of which I possessed. I was an empty pod.

That was April and May.

June 27

I'm just sitting here. Looking around. My house is empty because I purged. I purge the way most people evacuate. I have nothing left. The cats have nothing to tear up.

I can't move. I have no money left. I have negative money left.

The ceiling in my living room has seventeen cracks. Five of them intersect.

Maybe we'll have an earthquake.

I wish I knew what to do.

Sometimes I feel like a page without a chapter.

July 7

I just can't believe that I could work so hard, get so far, and end up here. Flowers keeps leaving me messages. Everyone keeps leaving me messages, but I'm too depressed to call any of them back. When you're depressed, the last thing you want to do is chat. I swear, all I can do is stare at the damn wall. And think about credit card fraud.

Last night I was feeling so crap-ass shitty that I pulled the giant, loser, waffler move and called Scott.

He was perfectly nice, the way he is to his landlord or the MCI operator or something. But when I asked him to come over, he politely told me that that would be inappropriate.

I swear I don't even know what that means. Just like that? No torturous back-and-forths? Hasn't he read the breakup manual? No taboo rendezvous? It's the best part of any relationship! I don't believe it.

I asked him if he missed me at all and he said, Sometimes, but there's no point in talking about that. Just when I think he's the biggest baby in the world, he turns around and gives me a big fat spanking.

TOP 3 MOST HUMILIATING
MOMENTS OF MY LIFE:

1) The clogging of the toilet at the piano recital incident.
2) High school.
3) That phone conversation.

UNEMPLOYED OBSERVATION #4:
Iceberg lettuce dipped in ketchup tastes like shrimp cocktail.

July 12

I finally called Mom and asked her to talk to her friend about that job at the bank. An executive decision made because I was down to one box of crackers, three squirts of toothpaste, and no tampons. Plus I had to call her before my phone got cut off.

But a funny thing happened with Mom. Just when I expected her to rub it in and declare victory, she joined the other side, whooping it up with the enemy.

"Really, Jenny? But you worked so hard and got so far! You're going to just give up now?" she said.

Who are you and what have you done with my mother?

"It's not that simple, Mom. I'm moments away from cutting up my sheets to use as toilet paper. I need money."

"I understand, but it's such a shame. Ever since you were a little girl you've wanted to play music. And you were doing so well!"

"Well, I screwed it up, okay? And now could you please give me your friend's number before I have to deep-fry my cats?"

She finally handed over the number. How ironic is that? I would have killed to hear her say those words a few months ago, and now they just made me feel worse.

Good old Mom.

She's still got it.

THE FIRST DAY OF THE WORST PART OF MY LIFE

I hadn't spoken to another person in days. Cats, plenty, but people, none. It makes you weird. I think you have to practice

July 16

socializing or you lose it. Your own voice makes you jump with surprise and you're not quite sure how to make the *r* sound.

Today I put on pantyhose and sat in a room with a bunch of other trainees to learn about the wonderful world of bank telling. I went into soldier mode. Closed my eyes and charged headfirst into the enemy. I needed money bad, and I had no other ideas on how to get it.

I raised my hand and asked questions.

I joked about being on the local when the elevator stopped at every floor.

I wore pearl earrings.

I dyed my hair back to its natural color.

I freaked out over how many cups of coffee I drank with my new peers.

I took my customer-service workbook home and gave myself exams.

I ironed my clothes the night before and sat in traffic with the rest of the commuters while I drank my coffee and listened to NPR.

I learned about counterfeit money, surveillance cameras, and overdrawn checks.

In short, I changed identities. This was me in an alternate universe. My alternate universe persona was bringing money back to my real persona, who was about to die of scurvy in her empty apartment.

BANK TELLER TRUTH #1:

I see twelve full hours of sunlight a day. I am as far from being a rock star as a person can be.

I hate my life. I look like a real estate agent and say golly a lot. I never even think about sex anymore. Even though William Absher in accounting has a crush on me. He wants to take me out to hear some rock-and-roll music because he heard I used to be in a band.

I am thirty years old.

Last night I shot out of bed like a rocket because a gong exploded in my closet. I woke to find my poor, dust-covered acoustic guitar had busted a string in despair. Had literally just snapped. I hadn't touched it in months. How poetic.

August 9

Tami called to tell me that the demo album we cut with Eddie is getting tons of play on the college stations. In her message she informed me that she was still promoting it and that we were still her favorite band. She also said she'd string herself up naked by her thumbs from the telephone pole of my choice if I'd only start up the band again. It was like getting a message from a stranger. I felt nothing. I felt like she was talking about somebody else.

August 11

Just a quick note to say hello. I do nothing but go to work, complain about my job, and come home to watch TV. Mr. Nelson came in today with another crazy joke. What do potatoes wear to bed? Their yammies! I laughed until I started sobbing.

August 14

TO WHOM IT MAY CONCERN:

When this book is found lying next to my corpse, let it be known that performing the sick and unnatural act of customer service day in and day out is what did it.

I'm writing today because something actually happened to me. It's the first time anything's happened in weeks. I was at my shitass job and who should I see but Katie Hebard! She was shrieking into her cell phone and trying to cut in front of people in line. I nearly capsized. I was helping some guy deposit three hundred and eighty-seven dollars in quarters and I slowed to a halt. Katie was moving in on some little old Chinese man's spot, and if I held off long enough, she'd wind up at a different teller's window. But the little bastard held his ground.

"'Scuse me, miss, I think I was in front of you," he said.

She ignored him and continued her phone call. They were both tiny, and he was about forty years her senior, but they were equally determined. He shuffled quietly in front of her again and stood with his arms crossed over his chest.

"Hello? What the fuck do you think you're doing?" she said, holding her hand over the mouthpiece of her cell. "I'll have to call you back," she said into the phone.

Then the rest happened in slow motion. She folded up her cell and looked down to put it in her purse. Just as her head bent, the green light blinked, signaling for the first person in line to go to the next available teller. The little old Chinese man saw it and darted over at the speed of light. By the time Katie looked up he was gone, standing at the window to the left of mine opening up a new checking account.

BANK TELLER TRUTH #2:

Opening a new account is a process that takes much longer than counting out seven remaining dollars in quarters.

There was no way Katie, the next person in line, wouldn't wind up with me, the soon to be next available teller. I was screwed.

I handed my customer his crisp new bills and awaited my fate, staring straight ahead in numb acceptance. The light turned green, signaling Katie to hit the gas and run me down.

She came up to my window and didn't even look at me for the first few seconds. I felt a glimmer of hope. Katie treated everyone in the service industry like giant, faceless blobs—at least, until they fucked up her drink order. It was entirely possible she wouldn't look at me or even speak to me if I worked quickly and carefully enough.

"I need to deposit this," she said, sliding a check for ten thousand dollars under the glass with her perfectly manicured nails. I grabbed it and started typing on the computer trying to pretend that Katie was not about to deposit ten thousand dollars into her account! Suddenly Sheila, the new teller who was working at the window to my left, tapped me on the shoulder.

"Jenny, this gentleman wants to open a new checking account and I've never done that before. Would you mind walking me through the process?" she asked.

Katie's head snapped to attention.

"No way. That little fucker cut in front of me once already today. Tell him . . . oh my fucking God," she said, jaw dropping as she met my eyes.

"Jenny Troanni?" she said in shock.

I decided my only hope was to adopt a British accent to throw her off.

"I dunno who you thank I em, lass. Must've switched me

wiff sumone else, aye?" I said, sounding more like I'd suffered a serious head injury than anyone remotely English.

BRILLIANT OBSERVATION #41:
I do not have the Fake Accent Gene.

"I don't fucking believe it," she said, ignoring my lame attempt.

"Jenny, if this is a bad time, I can find someone else," Sheila said.

"No! No, I can help you," I said in desperation.

"Over my dead body!" Katie yelled, sending Sheila off and running. "So this is where you wound up, you fuck! I don't fucking believe it."

"Yep," I said. "Will that be checking or savings?"

"Checking. I heard all about Mastiff reaming you guys. Unfuckingbelievable," she said.

"Oh well," I said.

"Not that I give a shit, since you're such a fucker, but your band rocked. It was too bad. You guys got so screwed."

"Well, it was partly them screwing us and partly me screwing Scott," I said.

"Scott, schmott. That would have blown over. If Mastiff hadn't fucked you and you'd kept going, you could have made it."

"Oh well," I said again. I so did not want to continue this conversation. "I guess I got what was coming to me."

"Oh, please. Like every fucking band I work with doesn't have some sort of high drama going at all times. It's like a goddamn soap opera. I'm fucking exhausted. In fact, these motherfuckers are making me fly all the way to Havana tomorrow to make sure one of my artists is actually writing songs instead of lying around, snorting his advance money up his nose. Like I have nothing better to do? I need two thousand of that back in cash," she said, sticking out her hand.

"I'd kill to get paid to go to Havana! Why you waste your time complaining about everything is beyond me," I said.

"Well, I'd kill to have half your talent! Why you waste your time working in a fucking bank is beyond me. You have no idea how lucky you are," she said as my minimum-wage ass counted out twenty hundred-dollar bills into her hand.

I had no idea how lucky I was?

I had no idea how lucky I was?

I wanted to slam my teller window shut on her hand. That fucking ingrate was getting paid to fly first class to Cuba, while I was trapped behind the bars of my teller window for the rest of my fucking life. I'd gone and destroyed the one thing I cared about more than anything in the world and fucked over my best friend in the process, and I was lucky?

Then it struck me.

I had turned into Katie.

I felt like everything sucked so badly, including myself, that I was powerless to change it. All I did these days was complain and sit around feeling miserable. How could this have happened to me?

I really did have no idea how lucky I was. I had a demo tape that was a hit, a great manager, a ton of fans, and the ability to redeem myself.

All I had to do was choose not to be Katie Hebard.

All I had to do was choose to be happy.

August 24

Today I began putting it all back together again. Piece by piece. I had to move slowly for fear of sending my system into shock. I had to move carefully for fear of making the same mistakes twice.

I went over to Flowers' for the first time in a century and asked for his wise guidance. And some black-bean casserole that he'd just made. He was painting his kitchen cabinets silver and had me masking-tape the edges while we talked. I told him that Tami said our demo album was doing great and that I was thinking of putting a band together again.

"I think that's a fabulous idea," he said. "I'm so glad you're over your frumpy mourning period. You were starting to scare me. I'd decided that if you started going to male strip bars with the girls after work for happy hour, I was going to have to step in."

"I was moments away," I said.

"Do you have anybody lined up for the new band?"

"Nope. Since I've pretty much fucked over everyone I've ever played with at this point, I'm going to have to start all over."

"Oh, please, you're so dramatic. Like Lucy's never talking to you again," he said.

"I doubt she will! I doubt Rodney will, either."

"You wish you were that evil! Lucy does whatever she wants whenever she wants all the damn time. She has to forgive you. And Rodney's about to discover sex, which means Mommy's going to freak out, which means that whole love affair will come to a screeching halt and you, my dear, will once again be the apple of his huge brown eye."

I'd never thought of it that way. Maybe there was hope!

"Not that either of them would be caught dead playing in a band with you again, but at least they won't hate you," he added.

"That's a start," I said.

Flowers stopped painting for a second and stared at me.

"What? My hair? I know, it's got to go," I said.

"Yes, that too. But I was thinking. Watching you all up there onstage made me miss playing out. . . ."

"You want to be in my band?"

"Only if you promise never to fuck me."

"I promise! I promise!" I couldn't believe it! All of a sudden, I felt like anything was possible again. I left his house—with a new cut and dye job, of course—and got immediately to work.

I restrung my poor little baby and wrote a new song.

I sent Lucy a love letter.

I shaved my legs.

I set up a meeting with Jeffrey.

I burned all my pictures of Scott.

I had a realization that split my head right down the middle:

**NOBODY CAN TAKE AWAY YOUR THING
WITHOUT YOUR PERMISSION.**

September 2.

I talked to Dad today, and I swear it was the best conversation we've ever had. I stopped pouting my way through it and treated him the way I would any other person. Or space alien.

ME:	Life's too short. I don't care how reamed I got last time, I have to try it again.
ZIGGY STARDUST:	Yes. You know, when I was a little boy I . . .
ME:	Hey, Dad. What did I just say?
ZIGGY STARDUST:	To who?
ME:	To you, Dad.
ZIGGY STARDUST:	Well, let's see. I'm not quite sure.
ME:	Because you never listen to anything I say. Don't you think that's rude?
ZIGGY STARDUST:	What do you mean?
ME:	Just what I said. What did I just say?
ZIGGY STARDUST:	Well, let's see. I'm not quite sure.
ME:	That you never listen to anything I say and I think it's rude.

Wash. Rinse. Repeat seven more times. Finally, a long pause. Time heaves and twists, sunspots explode, particles disperse and reconnect in a new plane. Dad is sucked through the vortex and appears on earth for the first time ever. He looks at his own hands in wonder. What are these? They're magnificent! Where am I?

ZIGGY STARDUST:	I'm sorry, Jenny. I am listening.

And then we had a conversation. I'd say something, he would respond. Mrs. Paskow's invaluable input was screamed in the background, but at least I felt like he was holding the phone up to his ear, not his ass. I'm not going to pretend that he was all that affected by what I was saying, but at least he was listening.

Next phone call I will address the *Scientific American* catastrophe and free us all at last.

I've been sending Lucy an apology/love letter a day. I doubt she's even in the country, but I had to get it all off my chest. I don't expect her to work with me again—I just don't want her to hate me. And if she does, I want to know I tried everything in my power to get her to forgive me.

When I went in for my meeting with Jeffrey, I wound up having a surprise meeting with Tami as well.

"'Put That Thing Away' is getting so much airplay on the college and independent stations," she said, practically peeing in her pants. "And the demo CD is selling out everywhere I take it. And it's in the top forty downloads on mp3.com!"

"If you get a band together, you'll already have an instant following," Jeffrey said.

I couldn't believe it! All this was happening while I was gossiping about the chief loan officer around the coffee machine?

I felt like I'd just woken out of a coma to find my stocks going through the roof.

"I'm so glad you came back!" Tami said, jumping up and hugging me. I'd told them all about Flowers and they were overjoyed.

"Just FYI, Jake's doing really well. He's back with his wife, I guess, and really happy," Jeffrey said. "You should give him a call."

September 5

September 8

I got a postcard from Lucy today. It was postmarked from Egypt and said the following:

> *Afreaka! is a dream! Thank you for setting me free. We never should have married! Should have just stayed friends. Got your notes. I hate you for getting to fuck Scott. Other than that, I love you too.*
>
> *FYI, I fucked Pete. Just so you don't feel like the only heel.*
>
> *Up your nose with a rubber hose!*
> *Love,*
> *Lucy*

September 10

TO DO LIST:

Buy new couch.

Deflea cats.

Change oil.

Call tutoring students.

Practice.

Buy new journal.

Find new drummer. An ugly female one.

Like this is the only one...

Floating
Robin Troy

The Perks of Being a Wallflower
Stephen Chbosky

The Fuck-up
Arthur Nersesian

Dreamworld
Jane Goldman

Fake Liar Cheat
Tod Goldberg

Pieces
edited by Stephen Chbosky

Dogrun
Arthur Nersesian

Brave New Girl
Louisa Luna

The Foreigner
Meg Castaldo

Tunnel Vision
Keith Lowe

Number Six Fumbles
Rachel Solar-Tuttle

Crooked
Louisa Luna

More from the young, the hip,
and the up-and-coming.
Brought to you by MTV Books.

POCKET
BOOKS

More on the way...

The Alphabetical Hookup List

An all-new series

A–J
K-Q
R-Z

Three sizzling new titles
Coming soon from
PHOEBE McPHEE
and MTV Books